TALES OF THE CROWN

A TREMONTANE COMPANION

MELISSA MCSHANE

Night Harbor Publishing

For Erin,
whose beautiful work on the North sign and shield graces this cover

NORTHERN WASTES

⚜ RANSTJAD

THE EIDESTAL

RUSKALD

WASTELAND

SNOW RIVER

DAXTRY

MARANDIS

HIGHTON

STEEPRIDGE

AVORY

TREMONTANE

⚜ AURILIEN

OLONTON

SILVERFIELD

KEPA RIVER

CULLINAN

VERIBOLD

HARRODEN

WAXWOLD

KINGSPORT

⚜ HAIZEA

RAVENSHOLM

HUDDERSFIELD

ESKANDEL

UMBERAN

TREMONTANE AND ENVIRONS

CONTENTS

INTRODUCTION

This collection contains an alarming amount of writing connected to the Tremontane novels. For one, it has four short stories and almost every bonus scene I've written relating to The Crown of Tremontane series and the Saga of Willow North. It contains what is almost a full novel that runs parallel to *Rider of the Crown*, told from King Jeffrey's point of view. Additionally, it contains the full text of the novella/story collection *Exile of the Crown* and two previously published short stories, "Long Live the Queen" (originally in *Servant of the Crown*) and "Night Be My Guardian" (originally in *Agent of the Crown*).

When I put it all together in one place, I couldn't believe how much material I had. I've been writing about Tremontane for many years, and it was the bedtime story I told myself for decades before that. Many of the bonus scenes were written to help me understand the characters and events from a different point of view, usually that of the hero. Some of them represent different directions I tried to take the story in (and failed). But all of them are a window on the process behind creating one of my most beloved series.

Though *Exile of the Crown* is available as an e-book, it's too short for me to publish it in print. It appears here both so readers can appreciate it in chronological order, and so I can get it in a bound edition.

This entire book is organized chronologically, with headers indicating which novel a given section appears in as well as year and sometimes season in which the scene occurs.

Why only "almost" every scene? There is one rather lengthy excerpt from *Guardian of the Crown* in which I took the novel in the wrong direction for about 8,000 words. While it's interesting for its content, in practice it's very dull writing, and it bored me. So I chose not to inflict it on my readers. There are also a couple of alternate scenes I remember writing that I couldn't find in my files. But most of it is here.

The appendix is a collection of information about the world of Tremontane. It's available on my website, but I thought it fit here as well. Additionally, here is the chronology of the series, for reference if anyone wants to alternate reading the books with reading this bonus material:

699 Year of the Binding (Y.B.): The Willow North Saga

(*Pretender to the Crown, Guardian of the Crown, Champion of the Crown*)

903 Y.B. *Servant of the Crown*

928 Y.B. *Rider of the Crown*

952 Y.B. *Agent of the Crown*

963 Y.B. *Voyager of the Crown*

I hope readers will find these scenes and stories interesting and enjoyable.

—Melissa McShane

KERISH

(*Guardian of the Crown*, Summer 699 Y.B.)

I often write versions of certain scenes in my books from someone else's point of view, usually the hero's. This one struck me as an important one to see from Kerish's point of view, mainly because his perspective and understanding of his own actions are much different from Willow's. This story from his POV also helped me revise some earlier scenes in Guardian of the Crown, *making him a stronger romantic hero to fit Willow's own strength.*

THE MOONLIGHT STREAKED THE CEILING OVERHEAD, FILTERING THROUGH the gauzy drapes surrounding the bed. The room was in shades of charcoal and black, all color leached from the furnishings as if it had drained away. Distantly, Kerish could hear the sounds of two birds cooing to each other, as good as an alarm for keeping him awake: *tu-hoo, tu-hoo,* and then the second would chime in with *tu-whit, tu-whit.* He wished he could find the birds and strangle them.

They weren't what was keeping him awake.

For so many months, all the time they'd been together, it had

1

been his greatest fear: that she'd go out one night and just never return. That she'd disappear and he'd never find out what happened to her. And now it had come true.

Nearby, Felix snuffled in his sleep and rolled over. Thank heaven he'd finally fallen asleep. It had broken Kerish's heart to watch the boy struggle so hard not to cry when Kerish had come to put him to bed instead of Willow. He'd told Felix a comforting story, but it hadn't been very convincing; why under heaven would Willow spend the night in the Tremontanan enclave without sending word? Felix knew Kerish's fear as well as he did himself, and when Kerish suggested offhandedly that he spend the night in Felix's room, "just like old times," he'd accepted the offer so eagerly it had made Kerish furious with Willow for doing that to the boy.

He wasn't going to get any sleep that night. Kerish sighed and got up, went to the window and looked out over the grounds. Surely she would return soon. She wouldn't abandon Felix. Unless she didn't have a choice.

Kerish found his dressing gown and shrugged it on over his bare shoulders, then quietly left Felix sleeping and went down the stairs, past the bodyguards and through the corridors to the front door. More guards stood there; they ignored him as he went out into the grounds. It was cool now, a wonderful contrast to the heat of the day, and the air smelled of night flowers. Kerish walked to the front gate, ignoring the guards who became more alert at his approach. They'd better be alert, after two attempts on Felix's life, though granted they'd only been at fault in one of those. Even so, it was pointless keeping guards who didn't do their duty.

The pavement in front of the Residence was still warm, and it felt good, if rough, against his bare feet. He took several steps along the road before coming to his senses. Umberan was enormous; there was no way he could find her, even if he'd been as good a thief—

He closed his eyes. She was a good thief, she'd never been caught, but that was only true so long as her luck didn't run out. She'd nearly been caught the night they'd met, would have been caught if Kerish hadn't thought quickly. He'd never forgotten that moment, their bodies pressed together, her warm lips on his, and he'd fallen in love with her even before he knew her name.

He turned around and went back to the Residence. Damn her for caring more about midnighting than she had about him. They'd be married now if not for her stubborn insistence on being independent. There was nothing wrong with him serving an Ascendant, it was what his magic was for. If it weren't for Felix's sake, he wouldn't give a damn about where she was right now, since she was doing what she cared so much about.

He went into the grounds again, barely noticing the cool tickle of grass against his feet. Whatever Willow did was nothing to him. That was all in the past. She could be a thief if she wanted, and he didn't care what happened—

He came to a flowering azalea, its buds half-closed in the darkness, its rich scent filling the air, and stopped. They'd been at the scholia one day, he and Willow and Felix, looking at Gianesh's animals, and Felix had broken off a flower from one of the azalea bushes and given it to Willow. She'd worn it in her hair all the rest of the day, carrying the scent with her, her bright eyes and merry smile making his heart ache with joy.

Kerish sat down beside the bush and hugged his knees, swallowing hard against the lump in his throat. It was all a lie. His heart still belonged to her, even after everything they'd said to each other. He loved Willow, and not knowing where she was terrified him with his imaginings. He loved her.

He sat, staring at the dark leaves and lighter blooms, until his back and bottom hurt. Then he got slowly to his feet and found his way back to Felix's room in the darkness, lay down on the spare bed, and tried desperately to think of something other than Willow being beaten, losing her hand, trapped in a cell with the worst criminals Umberan had... It took him hours to fall asleep.

He woke an hour after sunrise with a headache and a stiffness in all his joints, like an old man after a day's hard labor. Felix was gone, but the smell of breakfast hung in the air, rousing his appetite if not his spirits. He went down to the kitchen hoping someone would feed him. Willow had always—he swallowed again. If she'd returned, someone would have told him.

The kitchen still smelled of hot flatbread and sweet jams and pungent soft cheeses, mixed with the tang of undiluted pomegranate juice that made him salivate. Derona, the chief cook, smiled at him when he appeared. "Come scrounging again, you young imp?"

"Nobody brought me breakfast," Kerish said, trying to sound wheedling instead of whining.

"You know where the cheese is. Don't come trying to get around me, I've work to do." Derona pretended to scowl at him, but he only grinned at her sourness; she'd been cook and then chief cook for the Serjians longer than he'd been alive. He helped himself to a wax-coated round and a couple of hot flatbreads, then dragged a tall stool over to one of the counters and began assembling his breakfast. This and a cup of *khaveh* would do nicely.

Someone knocked on the outer door, and a glance from Derona sent one of the under-servants scuttling to answer it. Kerish watched, idly kicking one leg of the stool, then sat up in surprise, because the man who followed the servant into the kitchen wore the green tunic of one of Umberan's city guards. His dark hair was greased and parted in the center, and he looked about himself curiously, as if he'd never seen a kitchen before.

His eyes passed over Kerish, who was dressed as plainly as any of the servants, and lighted on Derona, who was the oldest and therefore presumably the senior of the staff present. "I've news for the Serjian *vojenta*," he said.

Derona looked at Kerish, who slid off his stool. "What news?" *Not Willow, please don't let it be about Willow.*

"It's for her ladyship to hear first." The man sneered at Kerish, who thought about punching him in his smug face, but controlled the urge. Instead, he gestured for the guard to follow him.

He wasn't sure where his mother would be at this hour, though he doubted she was still abed, so he took the guard first to the harem's meeting chamber. Catrela was there, still in her dressing gown; she was a late riser. Kerish was a little surprised to find her there, already writing notes of invitation to other harems. She looked up at their entrance and asked a question with her thin, expressive eyebrows. "This...man...has news for Mother," Kerish said, and was satisfied at the jolt of surprise and, then, fear that went through the guard. It overrode his dread for a few seconds.

Catrela went to the bell-rope and gave it a good tug. "Janida is preparing to pay visits," she said to the guard. "I hope for your sake the news is good."

The guard paled, and Kerish's stomach sank further. It had to be about Willow. He realized his fist was opening and closing without his control and made himself stop, turned away and sat on one of the sofas. She'd been caught stealing and had been arrested. She'd been caught stealing and killed trying to escape. She'd been caught stealing and the person involved blamed Serjian. So many possibilities, and how the hell was he going to explain it to Felix?

He looked up at the sound of footsteps in time to see Mother enter the chamber, settling her gold cuffs on her wrists the way she did when she was annoyed. "Yes?" she said, focusing immediately on the guard. Behind her, Alondra appeared, fully dressed as if ready to accompany Janida.

The guard cleared his throat nervously. "*Sovi* Janida," he said, "I come with bad news. News of the death of...of Serjian Amberesh."

Catrela gasped. Then she collapsed, folded in on herself to kneel on the floor. Alondra rushed to her side, supporting her, but she made no other noise, just stared at the guard wide-eyed. Janida said, "You have proof? A body?"

"Yes, *sovi*, we took care to be certain of his identity before notifying you. We have the murderer in custody."

"Amberesh was banished, but we will demand private justice," Janida said. "The killer will be released to us."

"Who did this?" Catrela exclaimed. "Who killed my son?"

"A stranger to Umberan. A Tremontanan woman. We don't know why she did it, but she knew who he was. Kept saying something about the Serjian Principality when she was captured."

Cold horror crept over Kerish, and a dread certainty. "A blonde woman? Short blonde hair, about so tall?"

"Yes. How did you—"

Kerish grabbed the man and slung him up against the wall, his arm across the guard's throat. "When did this happen?"

"Yesterday, around noon," the guard choked out. Kerish barely noticed his struggles. Red haze filled his vision.

"Did she ask you to send word to us?"

"I don't—"

"*Did she?*"

"I don't know!" The man's face was turning red, and he scrabbled at Kerish's arm, clearly afraid to strike a son of a principality. "She was guilty. She still had the knife on her. She—she's in the cells awaiting the verdict."

"It took you *all day* to send to us? She's been in that cell for nearly twenty-four hours—"

"Let him go, Kerish," Mother said, her voice a sharp warning. Kerish cursed and released the guard. All night in a prison cell—he'd already imagined it, but knowing it was true made it so much worse. And killing Amberesh. It had to be self-defense; there was no reason for her to go out of her way to kill anyone, let alone Amberesh.

"I have to go to her, Mother," he said. "You know this was a mistake."

"A mistake!" Catrela shrieked. "Willow North killed my son and you call it a mistake?"

"*Enough*," Mother roared. "Kerish, go with him to the cells and have her released and returned here. I will arrange for Amberesh's body to be brought to the Residence. Catrela—" She closed her eyes and let out a long breath. "You will have to tell Salveri. Alondra, go with her. Tell him what we know. The time for grieving is later. Now we must defend this principality."

Alondra helped Catrela stand, then embraced her tightly. Kerish took the guard by the shoulder and spun him around. "Outside," he said.

It took all his self-control not to beat the man senseless. The guard moved slowly, hesitantly, as if he was afraid Kerish might attack him again, which seemed a likely possibility. Kerish took him to the court-yard and arranged for a carriage to take them to the cells. The man sat on the very edge of the satin-padded seat, keeping as little of himself in contact with the seat as possible. Kerish gripped the seat and felt the pearls dig into the flesh of his palm. It felt good, real, something he could control. "If you've hurt her, I will make every one of you suffer," he said.

"She's just in the cells," the guard said. "It's not my fault."

"I don't care whose fault it is. She'd better be unharmed."

"Yes, sir."

"Shut up."

"Yes, sir."

The ride to the cells took far too long, and Kerish's nerves were keyed up to the point that, when they finally arrived, he almost ran to the stairs descending to the cells ahead of the guard. The dark, windowless room stank of sweat and burning torches. To either side, manacled prisoners sat on benches and stared at the floor, overseen by guards with long knives. Against the far wall stood a tall bench that was battered with time and use. Another guard sat there, writing something in a ledger. "Where's the woman who killed Serjian Amberesh?" Kerish shouted.

The man at the desk looked up. "Don't shout at me, boy," he growled. "Who the hell are you?"

Kerish crossed the room until he stood facing the man. Even sitting on his tall stool, he was shorter than Kerish. "My name is Serjian Kerish," he said, "and I demand the release of that woman to our private justice. And if she's harmed at all, I'm going to take it out of your hide."

"How dare you threaten me?"

Kerish leaned closer. "Did I just hear you challenge me?"

"I—" The man blinked at Kerish. "She's a prisoner. Sir."

"Who killed Serjian Amberesh in self-defense. Which in no way makes her a criminal."

"You don't know that." But the guard's expression of certainty wavered.

"I do know that. Amberesh was my *fuoreno* and a total bastard. If Willow killed him, it was in self-defense. And I think you know that."

"She confessed to the killing. She's lucky she wasn't just executed—"

"No, *you're* lucky she wasn't just executed, because if she had been, I'd have seen every one of your lives forfeit. Now, bring her here. And pray she's uninjured."

The man slid off his stool and motioned at one of the guards standing near an interior door, who disappeared through it. "She was injured in the fight," he said. "That's not our fault."

Kerish had another moment of red-tinged rage. "Injured, and you still blamed her for his murder?"

The man had the good sense to say nothing.

Kerish paced a tight circle in front of the desk. If they hadn't taken so damn long to send word—injured, the man had said, but how badly injured? Wounded, and confined in those cells; he'd never seen them, but they couldn't be pleasant. He caught himself opening and closing his fist and made himself stop again. It would be all right. She was safe now, and everything else could be dealt with as it came.

The door opened, and Kerish looked up quickly. The guard pushed the door open, and gave his companion a little shove. Kerish caught his breath. *Willow.*

Sweet heaven, she looked terrible. Her blonde hair was dark and matted with sweat, her shirt was bloody and filthy and missing a sleeve, and she was limping heavily. Her hands were manacled in front of her—iron, it had to be killing her to be so close to so much iron. "Those aren't necessary," he said, and was surprised at how furious his voice sounded. He wanted nothing more than to take her in his arms and carry her away to where they couldn't hurt her anymore.

The guard who'd brought her out of the cells unlocked the manacles, and Willow rubbed her wrists gingerly, as if they burned. She looked around, her eyes lighting on him, and his heart broke to see the dullness there, as if she'd spent the night wakeful and exhausted. He wasn't totally sure she recognized him. "Willow," he said. "Let's go."

"My things," she said, her voice raspy. "They took my bag, my... everything I had."

"Bring her her possessions," Kerish told the chief guard.

The man shrugged. "Prisoners have no possessions."

Kerish grabbed the man and slung him hard against the wall, making him cry out in pain. "Who do you think you're dealing with?" he shouted. "This woman is under Serjian protection! You've locked her in a cell with untreated injuries sustained while fighting for her life and *you're going to try for petty theft?* Get her things. Now. Or I'll cut you open and see how far Serjian privilege will take me."

The man was purple, gasping for breath. "Her things—" he managed, and one of the guards left the room at a near-run. Kerish released the man with an oath and turned away, catching Willow's eye as he did so. She looked so confused, so at a loss, it made his heart hurt more.

Finally the guard returned with a couple of familiar pouches and Willow's knives. "Is that everything?" Kerish said. Willow nodded. She held the little pile as if she wasn't sure what to do with it. Kerish held the door for her, then steered her up the steps to the street where the carriage waited. Willow's limping gait slowed them both, and when they reached the carriage, Kerish had to take her things so she could step into the carriage, using both hands to steady herself. He dropped everything on the floor and gave the driver directions.

"Are we going to the Residence?" she said, her voice as dull as her eyes.

"We're going to the scholia for healing," he said.

Willow nodded and fell silent. Kerish couldn't bear to look at her. He wanted so badly to comfort her, to hold her close and reassure himself that she was still alive, but she looked to be in pain still from whatever wound had soaked her shirt with blood. And she didn't want his comfort, anyway. She'd made that clear five years before.

He had to help her down from the carriage when they reached

the scholia, then hovered at her elbow as she made her halting way inside the building where the healers worked. A man and a woman looked up when they entered. "This woman has been wounded and needs healing," Kerish said. "We can pay whatever's required."

The woman said, "Is she Tremontanan? We don't speak her language."

"You don't have to speak her language to heal her, do you?"

"It's just easier if we can communicate with the patient. But it doesn't matter." The man came forward and took Willow's elbow, guiding her through a door.

Kerish took a seat on one of the many low, brightly-colored sofas and waited, elbows on knees, head bowed. He felt as if he'd passed a milestone. Willow freed, and now healed, and then...at some point they'd have to face the fact that she'd killed Amberesh. In a sense, it didn't matter that she'd killed him in self-defense; she was still a guest of the Serjian Principality and had killed one of its own, even if he'd been banished at the time. How under heaven had they even encountered one another? And why would Amberesh have attacked Willow at all? Things for Mother to ask her, when they returned home.

He heard someone enter the room. The male healer said, with some amusement, "She had no trouble communicating the fact that I wasn't acceptable. Tremontanans and their weird modesty taboos."

"I'll take care of her," the woman said, and the room was silent again. Kerish found he was smiling. That was Willow, all right. The day she'd gone to the Review—the sight of her in traditional garb—It wasn't as revealing as all that, but she'd made it look exotic, as if she really were just a breath away from revealing her nakedness. He remembered touching her, how her skin felt like satin, and made himself focus instead on how she'd looked when she left the cells. He wanted nothing more than to protect her from all of that, and it was irrational, but he felt guilty for not having done so.

"You're the responsible party?" the man said.

"Yes, I—" He felt inside his belt pouch and realized he hadn't brought any money. Well, it wasn't as if he'd needed it at the cells. "Wait a minute."

He went to the carriage and found Willow's belt pouch. He'd have to pay her back later. The man accepted the many, many coins and went back to his seat behind the desk. Kerish sat down again and prepared to wait.

He fell into a reverie alternating between rage at Amberesh for putting her in that position and pain at seeing her suffer, and didn't know how long he waited there, but eventually he heard movement, and looked up to see Willow there. She was wearing a yellow healer's smock and black cotton trousers, and looked so much better it was all he could do to keep from sweeping her into his arms. Her hair was still matted with sweat, and there was a trace of blood he didn't think was hers across her jawline, but she moved more easily, and that was all that mattered.

In the carriage, sitting across from her again, Kerish said, "I had to use your money to pay. I didn't bring enough."

"It's my healing. I think that's fair," Willow said.

Her voice still sounded distant, as if they weren't within arm's reach of each other. Kerish's jaw tightened. There was so much he wanted to say to her that time and anger had made impossible. He wanted to ask her what had happened that she'd killed Amberesh, but that was his mother's responsibility, not his. He looked off into the distance at the receding prison, squat and ugly as no Eskandelic buildings ever were. She was free, she was healed, but with Amberesh dead, the ordeal wasn't over yet.

He heard Willow shift on the satin-covered seat. "I'm sorry," she said, still in that empty, colorless voice.

He focused on her, startled. "Sorry for what?"

"For everything. For killing Amberesh." Willow drew in a ragged breath. "I swear I didn't mean to, Kerish, but he would have killed—I know you're angry with me—"

"What? Willow, I'm not angry with you."

"You certainly look like you are."

Kerish took in her anguished expression, the tears welling up in her eyes, the tremor in her voice, and felt as if he'd been punched. Without another thought, he sat beside her and took her in his arms. She buried her face in his chest, shaking. She thought he was angry with her. Once more, longing and sorrow surged within him. He stroked her hair, willing her to feel his love for her in his touch.

"I'm sorry," he said. "I didn't mean to hurt you."

"You looked so angry," she murmured into his shirt.

He remembered how close he'd come to attacking the guards. It hadn't occurred to him to think how that must have looked to her. "Of course I was angry. I was furious. It took them the whole damn day to bother sending word to us that you'd been arrested. Amberesh dead, you gone missing, and when we found out you'd actually told them to tell someone—"

He thought, again, of her spending a terrible night in the awful cells, and his arms tightened around her. "The guard didn't come until just after breakfast. He's lucky Mother was there, because I'm sure he was just a poor grunt who didn't deserve what I intended to do to him. His boss wasn't so lucky."

Willow shifted, but didn't move away from his embrace. "Thank you for coming for me."

For a moment, it was as if those years disappeared, and they were two people in love again. All his caution and fear vanished. "As if anything could have stopped me," he blurted out. "Oh, Willow. *Khaladesi*. Forgive my slowness. I came the instant I knew where you were."

"It's not your fault," Willow murmured. "I killed Amberesh. You should hate me."

"Never." Her eyes, those beautiful blue eyes, still glimmered with a trace of tears, and he couldn't help himself—he kissed her forehead, lightly, and a shudder of desire ran through him. "Whatever you did was in self-defense, I'm sure of it," he told her. "I know he was my *fuoreno*, and that ought to mean something, but he was a total bastard. If I had to choose between you, I would pick you every time. Willow, if he'd killed you..." The thought of Amberesh standing over

Willow's body made him shudder again, this time with suppressed fear and fury.

"He almost did," Willow said. "I was lucky."

Kerish's arms tightened around her. She was looking in his direction, but her eyes were unfocused, as if she were seeing something he couldn't. Then, to his surprise, she put her arms around his waist and rested her head on his shoulder. She'd been wounded, she'd been through an experience he could only imagine, and maybe all this was was a natural desire for comfort. Maybe it meant nothing. But his heart wouldn't believe it.

He stroked her hair again, so gently, and decided to risk everything. "After last night—after this morning—I realized you still hold my heart in your hands. I love you. I have never stopped loving you. Just...let me hold you, please, if only for a little while."

She shifted her position. "I love you," she whispered. "Kerish, I love you."

He drew in a quick, startled breath. It was so much what he wanted to hear that he thought at first he'd imagined it. His fingers stroked her hair again, twining themselves in her short locks, and she let out a sigh he remembered so well he knew this was no dream.

Gently, he kissed the top of her head. "I hoped," he said. "Sometimes, the way you looked at me...it was as if all those years had never happened. But then we would argue, or say the wrong thing, and I was sure we had no chance."

"I felt the same. But I wanted so badly...I never stopped loving you, either. I tried to forget—did forget, for a long time—but there was always a part of me that knew the truth." She raised her head to look at him. "I don't know how I was able to lie to myself so well."

He'd lied to himself, too. "There hasn't been a single day since we parted that I haven't thought of you. I was angry with you for so long, and then I was angry with myself, but I couldn't have felt that way if I didn't love you more than my own life." His hand trailed down to caress her neck. Her skin still felt like satin, warm and smooth.

Willow's lips trembled as if she were once again suppressing tears.

"I'm sorry I wasn't willing to change. I was afraid—I didn't know what I wanted—"

Kerish laid a finger over her mouth, stilling her speech. "I don't care about any of that now. I just don't want to be without you any longer. Even if it's only until the end of Conclave or until the end of this drive, I'm yours." Saying the words made his heart beat faster. She might still change her mind. She might still think this was impossible. But the way she looked... Hope once again rose up within him.

Willow's lips parted in surprise. "Even if nothing's changed?"

He couldn't help it; he smiled at her astonishment. "Don't you think it has? We chose our own paths once, and I've been miserable without you for five years. I think it's time for a different choice." He drew back to look at her more fully. "I know I can't go back to being a dowser, so maybe it means nothing when I say I'd give it up for you, but the truth is I would give up *Devisery* to have you. And I wouldn't regret it for one moment."

Her blue eyes went wide. "Kerish," she said. Then she threw her arms around his neck and kissed him.

He pulled her close and returned her kiss, feeling the years fall away until he was once more in that cold bedroom, his lips on hers for the first time, losing his heart to her all over again. She still smelled faintly of what he guessed was the prison, but he didn't care because he was kissing the woman he loved and he wanted it to go on forever.

Reluctantly, she drew back from him. "I must smell terrible," she said with an awkward laugh.

He kissed her forehead. "I can't tell."

"You can so. You're just being polite."

That made him smile and run his thumb over her cheek, wiping away tears. "If you think I only kissed you out of politeness," he said, drawing her close again, "it's been far too long since you've been kissed."

"Five years," she said. "There's never been anyone else."

That made him want to kiss her again. "No one ever came close to holding my heart the way you do, either," he said. "I suppose I've always been more attracted to midnighters than noblewomen."

Her smile disappeared. "I'm giving it up," she said. "No more midnighting, I swear it. I couldn't stop thinking of you while I was in there, that it was your worst nightmare—"

"My worst nightmare was last night, when you didn't come home," Kerish said grimly. "It was what I always feared, that you'd disappear and I'd never find out what happened to you. Seeing you come out of the jail looking like that was maybe third or fourth on the list."

"It doesn't matter. You were right. I don't have to be a thief to survive. I should never have put what mattered to you second. And I wish to heaven I'd realized that five years ago."

Kerish drew her close once more. "I think, five years ago, you weren't the sort of person who could realize it, any more than I could see beyond the needs of my magic. You're sure you're not going to end up resenting me for it?"

"No. Never. I love you too much."

"I love hearing you say those words," Kerish said, and kissed her again.

WILLOW: ALTERNATE ENDING TO THE WILLOW NORTH SAGA

(Champion of the Crown, Winter 699 Y.B.)

*T**his scene is the reason I don't write out of order. I wrote this ending on a day I was balked on* Guardian of the Crown, *and I liked the emotional weight of it. But the further I wrote into the series, the less relevant this became. I was able to salvage a few lines from it, but otherwise, it's now completely irrelevant.*

In this version, I'd planned for Willow and Kerish not to reconcile until the end of the third book. Hah. I have never had two characters more determined to be together than they were. Just another way in which this version was irrelevant.

THE HEAVY GOLD SATIN OF THE GOWN DRAGGED AT THE HEM. HER MAIDS assured her that was the way it was supposed to fit, though they looked uncomfortable when she asked if it was also supposed to be loose in the bodice. She felt a little guilty about that now, since she'd only said it to needle them, and it wasn't their fault they'd been presented with a Queen who knew nothing about court fashion but what she'd observed through people's windows. It was one thing having Caira fuss over her clothing and quite another having *four* women whose only purpose in life seemed to be carrying gowns back and forth from the dressing room for her approval. Four maids. A dressing room. None of this felt like her.

She stood at the window, hairbrush in hand—she'd finally banished the maids as politely as she could—and looked out across her city. People were setting off fireworks that burst silver and blue and green over the Hill and Lower Town alike. But then, this *was* a celebration, wasn't it? Tremontane had a Queen, and the Counts and Barons had peace, and everyone was happy and content and life was perfect.

Even Felix had what he wanted—hell, he was probably the happiest person in Tremontane *and* Eskandel tonight. Her heart ached, missing him already, but only a little, because she couldn't stop seeing the look on his face when she'd told him he didn't have to be King, how joyful it was. She'd managed not to show her own despair while he was still standing there before her, had kept it under control for that long first meeting with her new councilors, but now....

She realized she'd been holding the brush stationary at about shoulder height for long enough that her arm was starting to cramp and lowered it, then turned to go back into the dressing room to put it away. She should probably light a lamp or something, but the darkness calmed her. She remembered so many nights spent crossing the roofs of Aurilien, crouching low to the ground as she crossed gardens or courtyards, jigging a window open...well, that was all in the past now. Willow the midnighter was as dead as Felix Valant; Queen Willow North had to keep her feet on the ground. She'd chosen the path, and it was unworthy of her to pine after what she'd given up.

The dressing table was in perfect order, but she spent a few minutes tidying it anyway. She'd told the maids to take away the silver brush set and find her a wooden one, and they'd done it without argument. Was that what it meant to be royalty? You could make absurd demands and have them unquestioningly obeyed?

Willow shuddered. She was *never* going to turn into someone like that, no matter what else she had to give up.

The dressing room looked empty compared to the others she'd seen in her career, but then it was going to take time for them to assemble a proper wardrobe for the new Queen. She opened a few drawers and was relieved to see sensible trousers, hose, shirts, and some of those tunics that were becoming fashionable for men and women. She wondered when she'd be allowed to wear them, caught herself, and thought *damn it, I'm the Queen, I'm allowed to do whatever the hell I want.* Except it wasn't true, was it? She'd always thought the ruler of Tremontane was the freest person in the kingdom. She'd learned today that was so far from the truth it was almost a lie.

She shut the drawer a little too forcefully and set about getting out of the dress. It took only a few seconds for her to realize that would be impossible on her own. She cursed. She didn't want to call the maids back and endure their constant "yes, your Majesty" and "as you wish, your Majesty" just yet.

She wandered back into her bedchamber and sat on the bed, adjusted the bodice, and stared at her hands, clasped in her lap. She'd met with the Council, spoken to the housekeeping staff, taken a quick tour of the parts of the palace that were currently in use— that had taken a while—eaten her supper, and now there was only one thing left to do. And she would give anything not to have to do it.

Kerish was right: she'd been unfair to him. She'd demanded he change to suit her desires and scoffed at him when he protested. And now, just as she was prepared to return with him to Eskandel...when had she turned into the sort of person who could sacrifice her own needs for the sake of a country she hadn't even cared about a few months before?

She tasted salt, and realized she was crying, and quickly wiped away the tears before they could stain the satin. He was a Deviser; he belonged in Eskandel, where he could develop those skills, and it was wrong of her to ask him to give that up for her. Again. She wiped away more tears. She wasn't going to burden him with her misery. She'd see him tomorrow, and thank him for his help, and say goodbye, and then go on to the next item on her task list. She had a Chamberlain of the Hall now, someone to keep track of her appointments, and the daunting thing about that wasn't having yet another servant, it was that she would have so many appointments she'd need someone else to keep track of them all.

Something scraped along the wall outside the window, the smallest sound that nevertheless sent Willow to her feet. She flexed her wrist and cursed again when she remembered the blade was gone. Another scrape, and a tap, then movement along the side of the window. Willow scanned the room with physical and magical senses, hoping for something she could use as a weapon—nothing.

She crept as quietly as she could in the stupid gown to the window next to the one her visitor was attempting to open. He or she bore little metal, just a belt knife too short to be anything but utilitarian and the usual sprinkling of brass buttons, no money or jewelry except a couple of rings in a belt pouch. Willow carefully opened the window a crack so she could see out more clearly. Male, dangling awkwardly from a rope, fumbling with a wire he was trying to insert into the crack in the other window to raise the latch. He bent his head further, and Willow recognized him.

"*Kerish*," she said, then gasped as his grip on the rope slipped and the wire fell from his hand.

She swiftly unlatched his window and took hold of his shirt to pull him toward her. "What in the *hell* are you doing?" she said as he grabbed the window frame, hooked his legs over the sill, and landed a little gracelessly in front of her.

"Well, you came in through my window once," he said, breathlessly, "and I thought it was my turn. Sweet heaven, you made that look so easy."

"This window is five stories up! You could have been killed!"

"I realize that *now*."

"Why didn't you just come in the normal way?"

Kerish took a deep breath and let it out slowly. "I couldn't convince anyone that you'd want to see me, let alone that I should be allowed near your bedchamber. You have very diligent servants, your Majesty."

"Don't call me that. Ever."

"All right. It was meant to be a joke."

"I guess I don't have much of a sense of humor left after today."

"That's too bad. I've always loved your laugh." Kerish walked past her into the room. "Is there some reason all the lights are out?"

"I...was watching the fireworks." She turned back to the window as if that would make her lie into truth. What was he thinking, coming here like this? Her momentary fear for his safety was gone now, replaced by that terrible aching sorrow at losing him yet again. She wanted him gone; she wanted to be alone with her pain.

"You look extraordinary," Kerish said. "It's strange...you look so different in that gown, and yet you look exactly like yourself."

"I wonder how long that will take to change," she said. She closed the window and twitched the latch shut out of habit. "How long it will be before Willow North the midnighter vanishes entirely?"

"I don't think it works that way."

His assured, amused voice enraged her, and she turned on him and said, "Really? Then how does it work, Kerish? I've already given up midnighting and I've given up Felix and I've given up every friend I ever had in Lower Town, and I did it because it was the right thing to do, but that's no comfort when I look in the mirror and all I can see is the Queen! I don't even know if I like her! So spare me your reassurances, because I don't need platitudes."

She couldn't see him very clearly in the darkness, but she could sense his metal moving toward her a few paces, then stopping before he was close enough to touch her. "I'm sorry," he said. "I didn't mean to sound flippant. All I meant was that you are the strongest woman I know, and it's true you've changed and you'll probably go on changing, but who you are, at the core of you, isn't going to disappear no matter what happens. I'm certain of it."

"I hope you're right," Willow said. She suddenly felt very tired and wished she could just tell Kerish to go away. But she loved him, and she didn't want to hurt his feelings, so she said, "Are you leaving in the morning? Is that why you came? I was going to come to the hostel to say goodbye."

Kerish was silent, only his quiet breathing and the metal scattered about his person telling her he was still there. "If that's what you want," he said finally.

Fury gripped her again. "*Why* do you always say that?" she shouted. "I don't even know what it means! It's like you're putting the burden of what's going to happen on me and you never, *never* say what *you* want! I can't—" She turned away from him and walked back to the window, leaned her face against the glass, and closed her eyes against the hot tears that filled them.

She felt him approach, again stopping just out of her reach. "Willow," he said. "I didn't think—I only mean that I want you to have what makes you happy, even if it's not what I want. I've only ever wanted to make you happy."

"And you think your leaving is going to do that? That I could possibly be happy with you gone?" The words spilled out of her before she could stop them, and she closed her fist against the glass. Too late to let him go with a polite lie. "I never should have made you choose between me and your magic. I was selfish and stupid and proud and I lost you because of it, and I lied to myself for five years that I didn't love you anymore, that it didn't tear me apart inside to be without you. And then—this was all going to be so damned *easy*, Kerish, but you need to be in Eskandel and I just can't be with you. And my happiness doesn't matter." She laughed, a short, bitter sound. "Just one more part of Willow North chopped off and fed to the fire of queenly responsibilities."

He was once again silent, motionless, and Willow swiped at her eyes and wiped her wet hand on her gown, no longer caring if it stained. The maids would probably come up with a dozen others to take its place. Then he came forward and put a gentle hand on her shoulder. "How long have you been carrying that around?" he said.

"What difference does it make?"

"You sounded like someone who's been under a great burden for far too long. Will you look at me, please?" He tugged at her shoulder, and she turned in response, feeling the skirt twist around her legs. His dark eyes were intent on her face, and she remembered a cold midnight, so many years ago, and the pain of memory was like a knife through the heart.

Kerish sighed. "Come here," he said, and put his arms around her, drawing her close. She automatically put her arms around his waist and hugged him, feeling tension drain out of her with the comfort of his embrace. *Life should always be this simple*, she thought, and tried desperately to find a reason for this to go on indefinitely, just the two of them holding each other silently in the light from the stars and the glittering fireworks.

He began stroking her back, making her tingle with pleasure. "I was right," he said, "your skin is like satin."

Willow laughed quietly. "It's been a long time. I can't believe you remember that."

"I've never forgotten anything about you." His hands moved upward to touch the skin at the base of her neck. "How you'll never climb stairs if you can climb a wall instead. How you only drink red wine even if white's all that's available. How everything you feel, your whole heart, is in your kiss."

The ache was growing stronger. "Kerish, why—" she began.

He put his finger to her lips. "You're still the only woman I've ever loved," he said, "and I'm not stupid enough to let you go again. I'm not going back to Eskandel. I'm staying here. With you, I hope."

"Kerish, *no*. I don't want you to give up your magic. I swore I wouldn't ask that of you."

"You haven't. This is my choice. And I'm not giving anything up. There's no reason I have to stay in Eskandel to be a Deviser, Willow." He brushed her hair gently back from her face. "If anything, I'll be more successful if I stay here. So much source, and no one insisting that my inventions have artistic unity."

Willow gaped at him. "Oh," she said. "I didn't think of that."

"Well, you've been overwhelmed, so I'm not surprised you didn't think it through." He ran his fingers through her hair again, and she shivered. "You were really going to let me return to Eskandel without you? How much did you think you should sacrifice for your country?"

"I don't know," Willow said. "Up until forty-eight hours ago I didn't realize I cared so much about it. And I thought...I don't know what I thought. That I didn't want to make the same mistake twice."

"We're not the same people we were five years ago. I think we're guaranteed to make entirely new mistakes."

"I think I almost made a really terrible one. You wouldn't have gone just because I told you to, right?"

"I'm not your subject, Willow. I would have kept climbing through your window until you gave in or I fell to my death."

"Promise me you won't do that again."

"I can't believe I did it once." He ran his hands down her back again to rest just above her hips. "Tell me something. Am I allowed to propose marriage to you, or is that the Queen's prerogative?"

She laid her head against his shoulder and smiled into the darkness. "I think the Queen could allow it, just this once."

"I hope it won't take more than once. Will you marry me?"

"Yes. Soon?"

"I'd marry you right now if I could. I even came prepared."

She drew back a little. "What do you mean?"

He let go of her to reach into his belt pouch and rummage around. "This thing is too cluttered...here, hold this."

He held out a ring toward her, and she gasped. Gold inlaid with stars of silver gleamed in the starlight. "You kept it."

"Of course I kept it. I'm never without it." To her senses, it burned, like a star giving off bursts of fizzing light. She folded it into her skirt, closed her hand around it and watched him search. "This wasn't supposed to be so awkward," he said, and came up with a bright silvery spot. He hesitated, then said, "I thought wood might be too plain, and stone couldn't alter if it was the wrong size, so I hope I guessed correctly."

Willow reached out to take the ring in wonder. Solid steel, the only metal she could easily handle, but slimmer than his, and set with a dark faceted stone that might be any color. Sleek, unadorned, something that might fit easily under a glove.

"Sapphire," Kerish said. "I hoped...I know it will take a lot of caring for, but you do like it, yes?"

"I love it." She slid it onto the middle finger of her right hand. "It's only a little loose." `

"Well, it's not as if you have any other rings I could borrow for a better fit." He took both her hands in his and kissed them, one at a time, his lips lingering on her knuckles. "I love you."

She put her arms around his neck. "Show me," she said.

WILLOW: ALTERNATE ENDING 2— SAYING GOODBYE TO FELIX

Originally I intended Willow to seriously consider Alric Quinn's demand that she divorce Kerish, and to say goodbye to Felix on her own. My husband convinced me this was idiotic and completely out of character. He was right. Here's the original version.

THE NIGHT WAS CLEAR AND DARK, WITH NO MOON TO SHOW THE WAY, but it was a path she'd trodden before. She pulled the cloak close about her body, wrapping its folds around her gloved hands. Breathing in the cold, sharp air that felt like knives in her chest, she hurried along the road. It was nearly midnight, but the palace would still be lit by a thousand torches as the nobles danced Wintersmeet away. Her absence would be noticed, but she didn't give a damn about that. Let them wonder where she'd gone. Quinn would take up the space she would have occupied.

Her boots crunched through the snowdrifts, their surfaces melted by the sun and frozen again with nightfall. It was a pleasant sound that distracted her from her thoughts, for moments at a time. She stumbled over a hidden branch, caught herself on the tree nearest her, and stood hugging it as tears slid down her face. Her heart was already breaking, and she hadn't even seen Felix yet.

Finally she pushed away from the tree and proceeded down the road. She shouldn't have sent him so far away, but it was the only safe place she knew outside Aurilien. And at the time, she'd thought she would be going with him.

She'd sworn to protect Felix from all harm, and until now, she'd managed to keep that promise. What would he say when he learned the truth? How devastated would he be, despite everything she'd done to ease the blow? Or would he think she'd chosen power and the honors of men over him? As if any of that mattered to her. As if she hadn't been forced to this point. He was an eight-year-old boy; everything he knew about responsibility he'd been taught by someone else.

She felt a twinge in her chest, something sharper than the cold, and knew the solstice was upon them. More tears spilled down her cheeks. All her dreams shattered at once. No more Felix. No more Kerish, if she gave in to Quinn's demands. No family of her own except the empty one Richard Quinn would give her. Queen Willow North, giving up everything she was for the sake of a country she hadn't even cared about six months ago. She hated that woman.

The forest drew in more closely around her. She was the only one on the road that night, and it was easy to imagine being the only person in the world. How much easier life would be if that were true. Willow tugged the hood of her cloak lower over her forehead. It was as cold a night as the one when she'd met Kerish for the first time. You could say that was the night all of this had started, seven years ago, because he never would have brought Felix to her if they hadn't met, hadn't fallen in love. If she'd known how much pain would come from that meeting, she'd have let the guards catch her. Losing a hand, or dying, couldn't possibly be worse than this.

She counted the paths that branched off from the road until she found the one she wanted. It was easier to follow than it had been when she and Felix had left Aurilien in the summer, with most of the leaves gone and the undergrowth shriveled away in the cold. She stumped along, hoping and fearing to see firelight. What she didn't need right now was someone finding Felix and Gianesh and asking the right questions.

Half an hour's walking brought her to a clearing gilded with firelight. The old house was as dilapidated as ever, with snow clogging its roof and chimney and turning its steps into irregular humps. But the fire was in the open, a small fire in a cleared area, with an Eskandelic tent erected nearby. A dark figure crouched over the fire, but stood when Willow approached. "Did you have trouble getting away?" Gianesh said.

"A little. They're all busy with the Wintersmeet Ball. How is he?"

"Sleeping. He is still tired from his ordeal. Shall I wake him?"

"Not yet. Gianesh, things have changed."

"I see Kerish is not with you." There was a question in his voice. Willow didn't want to talk about Kerish at all. She just shook her head.

"That's part of it. Gianesh...I have to ask you the biggest favor anyone's ever asked of anyone."

Gianesh raised an eyebrow, but said nothing. Willow's words deserted her. She moved to the fire and warmed her hands. "I can't take Felix south."

"And you want me to. That is not such an imposition."

"That's not it. The reason I can't take Felix is...I'm going to be Queen of Tremontane."

Stark astonishment crossed Gianesh's features. "You?"

"It was a compromise. The only way we could avoid civil war. But it means..."

The tent flap stirred. "*Willow!*" Felix shrieked, and flung himself at her legs. Willow staggered, then crouched to put her arms around the boy. "Willow, I feel so much better," Felix said. "Gianesh told me we're going back to Eskandel. That you will be my mama for real!"

Willow clutched him tight. Her eyes burned with hot tears. "I know what Gianesh told you," she said. Then, "Sweet heaven, Felix, you're barefoot! Back into the tent, back into bed before you freeze."

"Come with me," Felix said, tugging on her hand. She followed him and helped him into the camp bed laden with blankets and a fur cape and a sleeping Ernest. Felix kept tight hold of her hand. "Where's Kerish?"

"Kerish...Felix, something's happened, and I need you to be brave."

His eyes and mouth went round with fear. "Is Kerish dead?"

"No. He's fine. It's just...Gianesh told you you didn't have to be King, yes?"

Felix smiled. "I know!"

"Well, someone still has to rule Tremontane. And I was going to choose someone. But the Counts and Barons...they want it to be me. They want me to be Queen of Tremontane."

"You can't be Queen!"

"I can if they all agree to it." She refused to think of Quinn and his horrible knowing smile. "And if I don't, there will be war."

"But...if you're Queen, you can still be my mama."

"No, Felix. They think you're dead. If they knew you were alive, you'd have to be King. And I don't want that for you. I want you to be free to grow up without that burden."

"But..." Tears filled Felix's eyes. "But who will take care of me?"

Willow stuck her head out the tent door. "Gianesh, would you come here, please?"

With Gianesh in the tent, it was crowded and a bit warmer. "Gianesh, I need you to take care—" Willow stopped, swallowed, and went on, "I need you to take care of my boy. Will you do that for me? I told you it was—"

"I will care for him as if he were my own," Gianesh said, putting his hand on Willow's shoulder.

"But..." Felix began sobbing. "But—*mama!*"

Willow gathered him into her arms and held him while he cried, unable to stop her own tears. "Felix," she murmured, "I will always be your mama, however far away you go. I will think of you every day. And someday I will see you again. I don't know how, but I promise you I will see you again."

She rocked him gently until his sobs turned into shuddering

breaths, aware that Gianesh had stepped outside to give them some privacy. Ernest whimpered and put his paws on her arm, so she patted him, then picked him up and gave him to Felix. "You'll have to be very brave," she said. "Ernest needs you to look after him. And Gianesh will teach you about animals—"

"But I want—"

"So do I. But we both have a duty. And this is the only way you get to have a normal life. Do you remember I once told you that parents want things for their children that sometimes the children don't like? Well, this is different. You're never going to be happy as King, and I want happiness for you. Unless you want me to go back and tell all those people we only pretended you were dead as a test for them?"

Felix recoiled. "I don't want to be King. Why can't Lord Quinn be King? Or Lady Heath?"

"Lady Heath doesn't want it either. And Lord Quinn would be a terrible choice. That's why they chose me—so Lord Quinn can't be King." Again Kerish's face flashed before her eyes, and she closed them against the memory.

"You shouldn't have to do things you don't want to." Felix wiped his eyes and his streaming nose. "It's not fair."

"This isn't about what's fair, it's about what's right." Willow hugged him again, careful of Ernest between them. "And...I have to go."

Felix clutched her. "Don't go!"

She would have given anything at that moment to stay where she was. "I can't be gone for too long, because they pay attention to me now. I'll tell you what—I'll stay until you fall asleep, and when you wake up, it will be morning, and you and Gianesh can go back to Umberan."

Felix shook his head, buried in her shoulder.

"Felix—"

"I know. I just don't like it."

"What would Hilarion say about doing things you don't like?"

"He says to drink the bitter spoonful now to prevent a stomachache later. But I don't think that fits right now."

"Close enough." Willow eased him back into the bed. "Do you want me to sing to you?"

"I thought you didn't know how to sing."

"That was me pretending to be bad so you wouldn't think about being afraid. I know a song my mother used to sing to me."

"All right." Felix petted Ernest's silvery gray head as the dog settled in next to him.

Willow wiped her eyes and cleared her throat.

Now the day is over,
The sun, it dips into the sea.
It burns a path along the waves
That brings you back to me.

THE STARS WILL BE YOUR BLANKET,
The moon will paint the grasses blue,
The night will be your guardian
'Til I come home to you.

THEN REST YOU ON YOUR PILLOW
Within your cradle, slumber deep.
I'll watch o'er you 'til morning comes
As peacefully you sleep.

She was crying again before the end of the song, but Felix was asleep, and only Ernest heard the last words. Willow bent and kissed the boy's forehead, then carefully rose and went outside, where Gianesh again crouched by the fire. "Thank you," she said.

"I love him too," Gianesh said, rising to face Willow. "And you have made the right decision."

"I fear I'm robbing him of his heritage. But then I remember…oh, a million little details that tell me he's better off not wearing the Crown. It's not as if I wanted any of this."

"Your country is lucky to have such a woman at its head." Gianesh put a gentle hand on her shoulder. "I honor you for your choice."

You wouldn't say that if you knew what I have to tell Kerish. "Thank you," she said again. "Will you...correspond with me? If you can find a safe way to do it?"

"I think we are friends enough that no one will think it odd that I write to you with news of the zoological collection and my newest assistant."

"That eases my heart. Goodbye, Gianesh."

THE WEIGHT OF THE CROWN

I wrote this after Exile of the Crown, *in which Zara refers to the first man she loved. It was my husband's idea for me to write about that part of Zara's life. It was never meant to be read because it was more or less a quick exercise, but I think it turned out well.*

Takes place in 897 Y.B.

ZARA HAD LOST TRACK OF TIME, HERE IN THE EAST WING DRAWING ROOM that had no clocks because her mother disliked the ticking. It was after midnight, judging by how dark it was outside the windows, but beyond that she couldn't guess. She felt caught in a timeless space, waiting for the news she'd been expecting for days. Her father had banished her and Anthony from his apartment, saying he didn't want them to see his struggle, but Zara had seen the look in her mother's eye and wished she dared disobey. It was probably his last request, and last requests should be honored, yes?

Anthony dozed in one of the chairs the color of iced lemon, his mouth hanging slackly open so he looked five years younger and more innocent than he did when he was awake. She felt ashamed of how she'd expected him to find an excuse not to sit this vigil with her;

he was so frivolous, so prone to stupidity, but when it came down to the final hours, he hadn't complained or said anything selfish. True, he was asleep, but she envied that rather than resenting him for it.

A door opened down the hallway. Anthony woke, sat up and wiped his mouth. "Is it—"

"Hush," Zara said.

Dr. Trevellian came toward them, his steps slow. "It's over," he said to Zara, paused, and added, "Your Majesty."

It didn't matter that she'd been expecting this, that it had always been at the end of this ordeal. It still felt like a blow to the chest, making her heart beat painfully hard like an animal fighting its cage. "There was no pain?" she said.

"No. I'm afraid that's all I could do for him." Dr. Trevellian said. "Rowenna would like you to join her now."

Anthony immediately ran down the hall and through the open door. Zara had to remind herself to move, one leg at a time, allowing the doctor to precede her so she'd have something to focus on.

Her parents' apartment looked so much like the drawing room, all those couches over-stuffed and upholstered in pastel colors, the fire trying vainly to heat the room—or maybe the cold was coming from her, radiating from her lungs and out her mouth like icy wind. She thought about asking the doctor to feel her breath, but realized that was lunacy. And she no longer had permission to indulge lunatic thoughts.

Her mother was kneeling beside Father's deathbed, holding his hand. Her eyes were dry when she looked up at Anthony, who'd come to stand just behind her and couldn't stop staring at the body of the King. Zara was certain he had no idea he was crying. She approached the bed and put her hand on Mother's shoulder. "I should have been with you," she said.

Mother shook her head. "My dear, it wouldn't have helped," she said. "But he wanted you to know how he loved you. Both of you."

Zara nodded. She'd had her last conversation with Father two days before, just after Dr. Trevellian had said there was nothing more to be done. "I'm not ready," she'd told him.

"Neither was I," Father had said. "I think on some level we never are. At least you have advance warning. My mother just died in her sleep one night."

"Don't be flippant," Zara had said, crushing his hand in hers.

"I can only face this with a sense of humor, little robin," he'd said. "I know how it is, grieving while the world expects you to be strong. I can't imagine anyone better suited to it than you. Anthony—" He coughed, and Zara supported his head until he could breathe again. "Watch out for him," he continued. "He still has a lot of growing to do."

"He's seventeen, Father. An adult. He should be able to make his own decisions."

"Nevertheless. Now. I've left you my notes, and you've spent enough time in Council meetings in the last five years that I feel confident leaving it to you. Keep an eye on Lestrange, he'll walk all over you if you let him."

"They're none of them going to take me seriously. I still look like a child and I haven't spoken out much."

"You will make them take you seriously, Zara. I have confidence in you. Remember in three months you'll need to replace the chief of Transportation. I suggest you keep my secretary; he knows everything I've forgotten and training a replacement at this time—" He'd coughed again, and Zara had shushed him.

"I know, Father. Don't worry about me. Worry about Mother."

"She has a great burden to bear. Take care of her, will you?"

Now, looking at her mother's white, drawn face, she felt selfishly that the greater burden was hers. The kingdom. Her wastrel little brother. Her gentle mother. All those people depending on her, and only one man she could depend on without question. She'd see him tomorrow afternoon; there wouldn't be time before that, but she wished more than anything she'd asked him to marry her a month ago, so she could take comfort in his arms tonight.

So many details. Finding a room for Mother to sleep in. Arranging for watchers to sit with the body all night, until it could be removed to the casket in preparation for the viewing. Arranging to be roused early so she could handle all the other details. She fell asleep almost against her will, her mind fighting her body for control and her exhausted body winning the battle, and woke feeling rested, and guilty about feeling rested. Her father was dead; she should have had a sleepless, agonized night.

All morning she had to remind herself that "your Majesty" meant her. She clung to her responsibilities like a tether connecting her to the world, welcoming the barrage of demands that gave her something to think about that wasn't cold grief. She didn't see Anthony or her mother, didn't really want to; it was hard enough to maintain her composure without their presence as well. She wondered how she looked to the men and women around her, whether they judged her tearless, somber expression an appropriate expression of grief. Well, let them judge. She'd cry for her father later. Or never. Tears hurt, which was why she never cried. She'd never understood why people felt you couldn't really grieve without tears. Her heart was cracked and frozen; wasn't that enough?

Finally, her awkward dinner with her silent family over, she left the east wing and took a familiar path through the palace halls until she came to the Long Gallery, hung with portraits of the Kings and Queens of Tremontane. Many of them hadn't been painted from life, particularly Kraathen of Ehuren, who'd established the kingdom some nine hundred years earlier, and all of them reflected changing artistic styles over the centuries.

She came to her father's portrait and stood with her hand on the frame. It had been painted the year she was born, when her father was in his early thirties, and he'd been right; she'd rather remember him as the hearty, laughing man he'd been than as the wasted, hollow skeleton he'd become at the end.

She looked at the empty space on the wall next to the portrait. How soon would they insist she sit for her own portrait? The idea felt macabre, as if she would be posing for her own memorial. And she looked young for twenty, young enough that people who didn't know them (as if there were many of those) mistook her for Anthony's younger sister. The whole thing was distasteful.

"Contemplating your own mortality?" an amused voice said. Zara turned and threw herself at the speaker.

"Jonathan," she said, and finally the tears came.

Jonathan held her close while she wept, saying nothing, just rubbing her back gently to comfort her. "It's been a long day for you, hasn't it, your Majesty?" he said.

"Don't call me that. Not you."

"I'm teasing, Zara. Are you all right? As all right as you can be, given the circumstances, I mean."

"I'll survive. I suppose I have to." Zara wiped her eyes and stepped out of his embrace. "Thank you for coming."

"I always do. Shall we walk?" He took her hand and drew her along back past the rows of portraits.

"I don't have long. There's a funeral to plan. Not much planning left, thank heaven, but there are still so many things only the Queen can decide."

"It's so strange, you being the Queen. I'd never thought how odd it would feel."

"My father was ill for a long time. I'd think you'd have gotten used to the idea."

"Knowing it will happen isn't the same as the reality, apparently."

They stopped by Kraathen's portrait and Zara turned to face him. "There's something I've been meaning to talk to you about," she said. "I've been putting it off because Father...anyway, this isn't the best time, but I don't want to wait any longer."

Jonathan put his other hand over their joined ones. "I know. Zara, we should have had this conversation a long time ago. I should have been the one to bring it up."

She smiled at him. "I think, legally, it's my responsibility."

He didn't smile back. "Zara—"

"Jonathan, you know how I feel about you. Will you marry me? Be my Consort?"

He was silent for a long, long moment. Zara's smile faded. "Jonathan?"

He shook his head. "Zara, you know I care about you, but the truth is—"

"Is what?"

"I'm sorry."

"Sorry about *what*?"

"Are you going to make me say it?"

"Yes, because I don't understand. If you love me...."

He looked away from her, toward Kraathen's grizzled face, and Zara's frozen heart cracked a little more. "You don't love me," she said.

"Zara, it's not about love—"

She snatched her hand away from his. "Explain," she said in a cold, cutting voice that made her sound a stranger even to herself.

"I do care about you. You're the most amazing woman I've ever met. You're strong and independent and you're going to be a wonderful Queen. I just...want someone who needs me. Someone I can take care of. You aren't that."

"I do need you."

"When it's convenient for you. It took your father's death to make you come to me for comfort. Everything you need, you provide for yourself. There's not a damn thing in this world I could ever give you that you don't already have. That's not the life I want for myself, Zara."

Her chest hurt so badly she was afraid her heart had stopped entirely. "I think," she said in the same cold voice, "you should call me 'your Majesty.'"

He took a step back from her. "I'm sorry I had to tell you this today of all days. I swear I didn't want to make your pain worse."

"I'm grateful for your consideration. You seem to have given it a great deal of thought. How unfortunate you didn't have the nerve to bring it up before."

"Zara—"

"Enough. Just go. I don't think we have anything left to say to each other." She stared him down until he ducked his head and walked away. Then she stood, staring at Kraathen's picture. His eyes were dark and as cold as she felt. How much power must it have taken to bind those three warring tribes together? What battles must he have fought? *I understand,* she thought, and hoped he could hear her from wherever in heaven he was. *You did this alone. So can I.*

She walked slowly back to her offices—*her* offices, what a horrible thought—and spent an hour organizing her desk, sorting through what had been her father's final papers. The funeral would be in two days. Her coronation would be the day after that. Then everything would return to normal for everyone except her.

She came across a little carving of a panther Jonathan had given her as a private joke, how she was like the creature on the North family sign and shield. She picked it up and fingered the smooth black wood. Then she hurled it to smash against the door, where it cracked and fell in three pieces on the floor. There was no point in crying over him; it wouldn't change anything, wouldn't do anything except make her eyes and head ache. She got up and picked up the pieces of the little cat and threw them into the fire, where they smoked and smoldered and didn't burn. No more tears. Not ever.

LONG LIVE THE QUEEN

I wrote this short story to gain insight into Zara North's character. I hoped to discover details I could work into Agent of the Crown, *because when I wrote that book, Zara was a background figure, and making her an essential part of* Servant of the Crown *meant she had to be better fleshed-out. But when the story was finished, I realized the information it contained was essential to the series (this was before* Exile of the Crown *was a thing). So I added it to the end of* Servant *and hoped it wouldn't feel too out of place.*

I apologize to the readers who listened to the audiobook of Servant; *I didn't know the short story didn't make it into that production.*

Takes place in summer 908 Y.B.

SHE'D HAD A LIFETIME TO LEARN HOW TO SCHOOL HER FACE TO REVEAL only the emotions she chose. Now Zara North wished she had learned how *not* to control herself, how to run screaming and laughing and sobbing through the corridors of the palace without fear of how it might affect the hundreds of thousands of Tremontanan citizens under her care. If her face showed no emotion today, it was because she was numb from the revelation Dr. Trevellian had quietly, inexorably handed her the way one might offer an unwelcome legacy from a long-dead relative.

It had to be a relative, didn't it? These things, these...the doctor had called it a gift, and maybe it was to him, but to Zara it was nothing but a curse, deadly to everyone except herself. But they had to come from *somewhere*, didn't they? Which of the faces in the long gallery two flights above had secretly harbored this, this *infection*, handed it off to child after child until it had sprung into full poisonous flower in her?

There was no one she could tell. Dr. Trevellian was a good man, but he wasn't a confidant except in medical matters, and this had gone so far beyond a simple medical matter that Zara went even more numb just thinking about it. She wished she could tell herself that she didn't know what to do, but Zara prided herself on her cold, analytical nature, and the solution to her problem was all too clear. Clear, but impossible for her to manage alone. She had to tell someone. The right someone.

She reversed her course and made her way down two flights of stairs to the Library. Alison had been right to insist on its being moved. In only five years the collection had grown to match the dimensions of the new room that rose three stories high, with wide balconies at each new story holding shelf after shelf of books. Unfortunately for Zara, Alison wasn't there. A stammering apprentice directed her back to the east wing.

Alison reclined on a sofa in the great drawing room with her arm over her eyes, her two children chasing each other around it, shouting words Zara couldn't make out. They broke off their game when they saw Zara and threw themselves at her, Sylvester jumping up and down for her attention, Jeffrey flinging his arms around her knees. "Auntie Zara, we're playing horses!" Sylvester shouted. Jeffrey made a sound very much like a horse whinnying. "I always win 'cause I'm the biggest!"

"Want to win!" Jeffrey demanded. "Auntie make me win!"

"Children, leave Aunt Zara alone," Alison said without moving.

"Come here now." Both boys detached themselves from Zara and ran back to their mother, and Zara felt a pang deep inside at their smooth faces, their agile limbs. *I will never have this. I never wanted children and now I would give anything to have my own baby screaming defiance at me.*

"I thought it would be nice to spend the afternoon with them," Alison said, not moving her arm, "but I didn't count on this awful headache. Children, why don't you play horses in the dining room. Sylvester, if I hear your brother complaining about how you never let him win, you and I will have a race, and the loser will go to bed early for a week."

"Not fair! You're bigger!"

"That's the point. Off you go, now, before Ellen comes for you."

The boys racketed off down the hall, neighing and whinnying. Alison let her arm flop to one side and stared at the ceiling. "I love my boys, but sometimes I think I was not cut out to be a mother."

"You are a *wonderful* mother," Zara said, more intensely than she'd meant. Alison sat up and stared at her, concerned.

"It's mid-afternoon. I've never known you to leave your offices before six o'clock. What's wrong?"

Zara turned and walked toward the empty fireplace, turned again and came back to stand behind a chair near Alison's sofa. She closed her hands on its back until her knuckles went white and the tendons stood out on the backs of her hands. Head bowed, she said, "There is so much wrong that it would be faster to tell you what is right. If there is such a thing."

"Zara, you're frightening me. Did something happen to Anthony?"

She shook her head. "He is well. I am well. I've never been more perfectly healthy in my life."

"I see Dr. Trevellian finally healed your leg. Did he say why it took so long? Granted that two days is better than however long it takes a broken leg to heal on its own, but I've never known his healing to be so slow."

Zara raised her head and regarded her sister-in-law. "What I am about to tell you cannot go further than the two of us, do you under-stand?" she said fiercely.

"What do you mean? Zara, you don't expect me to keep whatever this is secret from Anthony, do you? I can't do that!"

"I don't mean Anthony. This touches him as much as anyone. But *no one else*, understand?"

"Zara—" Alison whispered.

"Swear it, Alison!"

"I swear. I—sweet ungoverned heaven, you're crying. You never cry."

Zara reached up and felt the damp trail streaking her cheek. She shook her head as if denying it would make the tears vanish. "Dr. Trevellian didn't heal me. I healed myself."

Alison's mouth made an O of astonishment. "But...you can't possi-bly...Zara, you can't have inherent magic."

"Apparently I can."

Alison looked quickly around the room as if afraid someone had come in without them noticing. "But...healing...surely no one could object to that? Even if you are the Queen."

She felt her head shaking from side to side in negation, had to clasp her hands hard together to keep them from shaking too. "Not like Dr. Trevellian. Alison, I have never been sick a day in my life. I never bruise, I never have headaches. My body heals itself with no direction from me."

"Zara, to me that sounds like a good magical ability for a ruler to have."

Her eyes ached with tears she was afraid to shed, afraid if once she started crying she wouldn't stop. "Do you know what the doctor told me this morning? He said that aging is like hundreds of tiny injuries that happen every day, deep in the blood and bone where we can't see them. We're born dying, Alison, everyone except me, because my body heals itself over and over again, all those tiny wounds we don't even—" She covered her face with her hands and choked on a sob. Crying hurt. That was why she never did it. The unknown ancestor who'd bequeathed this dubious gift to her had taken her dignity along with the rest of her life.

She felt Alison tentatively put her arms around her. How closed off was she, that the people she cared most about were afraid even to touch her? She clung to Alison and shuddered with dry, tearless sobs.

"I understand," Alison murmured in her ear. "You'd live forever. Be Queen forever. It would be a nightmare."

And that was why she could tell Alison; she was quick to see the ramifications of any problem. The eternal reign of an undying Queen —what a disaster for Tremontane. She gently removed Alison's arms from around her shoulders and wiped her eyes. "The doctor doesn't think I'll live forever. My ability isn't perfect. It took two days for my healing to do what Dr. Trevellian's could have put right in a few hours. At any rate, I will still age, but far too slowly." She didn't tell Alison the other thing the doctor had told her, the cruel reality that her body would see any child she might conceive as an infection, and destroy it. That humiliation was too great for her to share with anyone. "But it would mean the end of the North family sooner than that, as soon as it became clear that I wasn't aging. Once the citizens of Tremontane knew their royal family was tainted by inherent magic...it might not mean our deaths, but it would certainly mean a demand for me to step down as Queen, let the Crown pass to another family. I think you can see the problem there."

"Civil war," Alison said. "None of the provincial rulers has a good claim to rule. Belladry Chadwick and Fern Harcourt would certainly be at each other's throats. You're right, no one can know about this." There were tears in her eyes as well. "So what are you going to do?"

"What I have to," Zara said. "I will have to die."

"It's going to be complicated," Alison said, "and require perfect timing, and we have to control every detail. That's why we came to you."

Davis Doyle sat behind his desk, regarding them both with wide, unblinking eyes. He lifted the bottle of whiskey as if to pour a measure into his cup, looked at it as if he didn't know what it was or why it was in his hand, and set it down again. "I," he began, then shook his head. "You want—Alison, this is insane. It can't possibly work."

"It will work, Mister Doyle," Zara said. "Alison and Anthony will make it happen. The doctor will make it look real. You need only provide the setting, something I expect you are good at given your occupation."

"We've given this a lot of thought," Anthony said, "and this really is the only way, Doyle."

Doyle looked around at his office in the Waxwold Theater. "The building is no problem," he said, "so long as the excuse for the new construction holds. There are just so many things that could go wrong...are you sure about this, your Majesty?"

"The alternative is that my death is real," Zara said. "I cannot quite bring myself to do that. An assassination, on the other hand, will be very convincing."

Doyle sighed. "We'll construct the trap door in box 3," he said, "try to keep it quiet, but if anyone starts nosing around we can give out that the royal family wants a private way in and out. You sure you don't want the assassin captured? He'd be guilty of attempted murder even if you did hire him to do the job."

Alison and Anthony exchanged glances. "We're sure," Alison said. "Just have it come out near the back door, just past the facilities."

"I'll do what I can. The Waxwold has a lot of extra space under the boxes because of the way we had to put in the stairs, but it will be crowded—sweet heaven, I can't believe I just said that. As if crowding were the issue."

"Thank you, Mister Doyle," Zara said, extending her hand. After a moment's hesitation, he took it. "I wish there were some way to repay you for this. I know I'm asking a lot of you."

"I don't think I want repaying for engineering my sovereign

monarch's murder," Doyle said. "Allie, Tony, I'll let you know when the construction's complete, and you can show your assassin how it works." He sighed. "I don't want to know where you're going to find anyone who's willing to go along with this."

"No, you don't," Alison said.

"You can't possibly be as calm as you seem," Anthony said to Alison, who was standing at the front of box 3, waving at people she knew.

"I'm not," she replied. "I'm trying not to think about what comes next. And being happy that I'm not wearing a corset. Those things are horrible."

"I ought to be the one, Alison—"

"We already determined you're not fast enough, and everyone will be looking for you when it happens. It has to be me, Anthony." Her voice sounded strong, but Zara could see her sister's lips tremble, and the sick, anguished feeling she'd been carrying around all evening grew stronger. How coldblooded was she, that she could ask such a thing of Alison?

"But you shouldn't *have* to." Anthony took her hand and drew her close to his side.

"None of us should *have* to do any of this," Zara said. She sat behind them, afraid if she stood the tremor in her arms and legs would be visible. She had thought three weeks would be enough time for her to become accustomed to her fate, but instead it had been like slow death. There were so many last times: her last Council meeting, her last visit with her mother—that had nearly broken her, and she had gone to the privacy of her bedroom and howled into her pillow until she was hoarse. The obliviousness of everyone around her maddened and relieved her by turns. She found herself more aware of Anthony now, of how confidently he moved and spoke, of the tenderness in his look and his voice when he addressed his wife and the joy in his eyes when he tossed Sylvester or Jeffrey into the air, both of them laughing. Was he ready for this new responsibility? Had she trained him well enough? *Yes,* she thought at supper—the last one—*he's ready,* and it eased her burden somewhat.

Now she looked at him standing with Alison near the front of the box. His hand curled around hers casually; five years of marriage and they still acted like newlyweds. Well, they'd earned that. It eased her burden more to know she wasn't leaving behind a Consort to mourn her. What a heartbreak that would be. She thought, briefly, *Suppose that waits in my future,* and quashed the thought. Time enough for planning for the future when this was all over. Dr. Trevellian had warned her that it was possible this could actually kill her; it was a chance she was willing to take for the sake of her country, but she hoped she would survive it. And then she could think about what came next.

The curtain rose and the lights went down, Alison and Anthony took their seats, and Zara made herself concentrate on the play. It was a tragedy, which was fortunate; she would have had trouble pretending to laugh in all the right places for a comedy. As it was, she barely heard the words because she was running through the plan in her head. Alison had been correct—it would require perfect timing, and they hadn't been able to practice all the steps as they'd wanted. She clasped her hands in her lap to still their shaking and prayed to ungoverned heaven that all would be well.

Too soon, the lights came up on the intermission. Anthony stood. "It's not too late to change the plan," he said. "We can find a way to fake your death."

"We've discussed this thoroughly," Zara said. "I must remain convincingly dead long enough for independent witnesses to affirm my demise. Drowning is far too complicated. An accident isn't complicated enough and could involve innocents. We tried to imitate a fatal illness, but no poison was capable of doing more than inconveniencing me. This is the only way."

"You know an assassination could destabilize the country. What if we succeed at this only to throw the country into the very turmoil we're trying to avoid?"

Zara took a deep breath. "I have faith in you both," she said. "We've planned how to organize the search. The 'assassin' will be found dead at his own hand rather than face trial—you have all the evidence to prove his guilt. No one else need die over this."

Anthony gripped the back of his chair hard. "Zara, if this kills you...."

"Then I will go to heaven, or hell, knowing that I have caused the two people I love most immeasurable pain," Zara said. "But if we do nothing, this family will suffer as much as the kingdom. That is the sacrifice we're all making tonight. Please."

Alison and Anthony exchanged glances. "There's really no other way," Alison said.

Anthony closed his eyes briefly. Then he took his sister's hands and raised her to her feet so he could embrace her. "I hope it works," he said. "Goodbye, sister." He let her go, then offered Alison his arm. "Shall we?" he said. Then, more loudly, he said, "I think I'm in need of the facilities," and opened the door.

"Take one of the guards," Zara said.

"Zara, I don't think that's necessary," Anthony said.

"We've had too many threats I have been unable to eliminate," Zara said. "Humor me."

"All right, sister dear." Zara heard him say, "Lieutenant, the Queen asks that you—"to one of the pair of guards standing sentinel outside the door before it closed on his words. She began to count. They'd timed this part, Alison pacing from the box to the facilities while Zara waited and counted as well. Now, when Zara reached a count of fifty, she stood and opened the door. "Please fetch my fan from the carriage. It's rather warm in here," she said.

"Your Majesty, I can't leave you unattended," the woman said.

Zara's throat tightened. Who knew what might happen to this guard for leaving her post tonight if Anthony couldn't engineer a pardon for her? "It will only take a few minutes, and I will be perfectly safe," she said. "Go now."

The guard hesitated, but in the face of the blue-eyed North stare she had to back down. Zara shut the door, then knelt by the trap door and opened it. Seconds later Alison emerged, climbing easily through. "I couldn't have done that in a corset," she said quietly. She was wrapped in a dark cloak she'd left wadded up in a corner of the props room. It completely covered her blue silk gown.

"I'm ready," Zara said. She took her seat and crossed her hands in her lap. How strange that they were still now that she was facing death.

She heard Alison take a deep breath, then felt the muzzle of a black powder pistol pressed against the back of her head. "I love you, Zara," Alison said. "Goodbye."

Then there was noise, and pain, and then nothing.

SHE WOKE, CONFUSED AT HER SURROUNDINGS; HER BED WAS TOO HARD, it was darker than it should be for 6:30 in the morning, and instead of the refreshing smell of hot coffee, there was only the dry, musty smell of a room long disused. She sat up and discovered that she was in some kind of shed, lying on a thin mattress in a wagon that creaked as she moved. Piles of hay lay haphazardly against the rear walls, and cracks between the gray, unfinished boards let in faint slivers of light. Why was she—?

Memory returned like a whirlwind, threatening to carry her away. She put her hands to her head to stop the world spinning and discovered that her black hair had been cut short, its ends now brushing her cheeks. She felt around the back of her head and found nothing amiss except a round, ridged circle of scar tissue, almost imperceptible through her hair. She breathed out slowly. Dr. Trevellian had been correct; even being shot through the head was not enough to kill her. She felt along her face and her forehead, pinched the bridge of her nose, and finally found more scarring along the outside of her right eye socket where the ball had exited. *That must have been very convincing*, she thought, then imagined Anthony's face when he saw the wreck her face would have been, and had to squeeze her eyes shut to keep from crying. There was no way he could have been prepared for that, no matter how well he knew what would happen. How could she have done that to him? To them? *It's not over yet. Time for tears later. Or never.*

She climbed down from the wagon and looked it over. It was old, but still in good shape, and would be sufficient for her journey. There were sacks and barrels and crates, not many, stowed near the seat of the wagon, which was unpadded and probably would not be comfortable over the days to come, but it was more important that she not draw attention to herself by looking unusually prosperous.

She went around the front of the wagon to unlatch the shed doors and push them open. The yard was mostly shadow in the pre-dawn light, and nothing moved except the horses drowsing in their stalls opposite the shed. Zara walked over to them and went down the line until she found the one she'd chosen the week before, a chestnut gelding with a white blaze on its nose that looked a little like her own profile stretched out, which had amused her. She stroked the blaze and the horse whickered at her companionably. "You and I'll get along right fine," she said, trying out the accent she'd been practicing in private since she and Alison and Anthony had made their plan. It still sounded wrong in her ears, like a bad actress in a play, reciting lines she'd learned by rote, but it was the best she could do. It would have to be enough.

She went back to the wagon and dug around until she found something to eat. The bread was a day old—well, Dr. Trevellian had had no idea how long it would take her to heal. She would have to find out what day it was. At least he'd managed to smuggle her out of the palace, hopefully without involving anyone else. Had Anthony been able to draw attention away from Alison so she could escape? Whom would they blame for the assassination? What had happened to the guard? She tore off more bread and wished she had coffee. Past time she weaned herself of the habit.

When the sun rose, she found someone to help her hitch the horse to the wagon, then drove out of the yard and down the road away from the city. Ravensholm. Dr. Trevellian had been able to transport her farther than she'd thought. She prayed that his part in the ruse had not been discovered either. She snapped the reins over the horse's head and he picked up the pace. Driving a wagon wasn't much different from driving her own carriage through the Park, fortunately. There were so many things she would have to learn, so many things she would get wrong, but at least she was certain that no one would recognize her outside Aurilien. That was the thing no one ever realized; the Queen was well-known, but few people saw her closely enough, and regularly enough, to be able to identify her in a crowd. Most Tremontanans saw her face only on coins, and that portrait was so idealized Zara hardly recognized herself in it. The farther east she went, the less likely it was that anyone would know the short-haired, travel-worn woman was Zara North.

She reached Savantry by nightfall, which meant she hadn't made very good time. At this rate it would be another two or three days before she arrived in Kingsport. She found an inn where she could stable her horse and wagon and went into the taproom and sat at the bar, too weary to think.

"What'll it be?" a voice said. She looked up at the barman, who was tall and wide and had a cheerful face with an enormous mustache.

"Beer," she said. She'd never had beer before, but it seemed the sort of thing a countrywoman might drink. A large ceramic mug appeared in front of her, foaming over, and she picked it up and took a healthy swig, afraid to look foolish by sipping at it. It went down smoothly and had a strange taste, but her stomach approved.

"You from the capital?" the barman said. She shook her head. "Too bad. Was hopin' for more news about the Queen. Seems everyone's got a story to tell and they ain't all true."

"What...are they saying?" Zara said.

The barman shrugged. "Says they caught the bastard what did it," he said, "some kid at the theater with a grudge against royalty. That's true for sure. He'll hang in a few days."

Zara buried her face in her mug again. That was wrong. They should have found the "assassin's" body after a short chase; no one should have been blamed for her death. Had Anthony been unable to take command of that search? "Makes sense," she said, "her being killed in the theater, that it was someone who knew the place well."

"The royal family's in mourning, o' course. Heard they shot a bunch of guards what let the killer get past. Damn if they don't deserve it, too."

That was definitely wrong. It had all gone wrong. She had to get out of there. "Sounds right," she said, and laid down a coin on the counter. "I don't suppose—I mean, maybe you've got a room I can rent?"

He showed her to the room, which was little more than a bed and a cupboard, and she sat on the bed and shook. That rumor had to be false. Anthony would definitely have spared the guards. If he could. *It has to look real,* she thought, *and what are a few lives against the welfare of the kingdom?* She stared blindly at the unpainted wooden wall. That she'd sacrificed her own life for that cause was not comforting.

In the morning she went out and bought a newspaper. Seven days since her death. *Could* she die, ever? Dr. Trevellian's assurances aside, it was a question she couldn't bear to entertain. She settled for reading the headlines. The supposed assassin's name was Fenton; she'd never met him, but there was no doubt Alison and Anthony, owners of the Waxwold Theater, knew him well. She had no idea why he'd been accused of the crime and the newspaper was not forthcoming with the details. The guards who had been on duty that night hadn't been shot; they were in prison, and their sentence had not yet been handed down. *Anthony will save them. I know he'll find a way.* New measures were being taken to protect the royal family, who had not emerged from the palace since the assassination. Zara folded the paper and threw it away, then went to hitch up her wagon. There was no more she could do, except let Zara North go.

She let her mind wander as the horse plodded eastward. She would need an occupation. That would be difficult; the only thing she was good at was running a kingdom, and it was unlikely anyone would ask her to do that. She thought briefly of joining an Eskandelic harem, running a principality behind the scenes, but the idea of having to share power with four or five other women wearied her, and besides, she didn't want to marry for duty. She never had, which was why she had no Consort to leave behind. She could learn a trade. She was good at needlework, thanks to her mother's training, but she'd never really liked it...though she no longer had the freedom to do only what she liked, did she? *Tailoring. Embroidery. Tatting lace.* If she had the ability to sense source, she could be a Deviser, but that was unfortunately out of the question. *Weaving?* That had potential. It looked so soothing, working the loom and watching the fabric grow by inches along the threads. She was old to be an apprentice, was too old even by her apparent age, but if she could manage a recalcitrant Council into voting her way she could certainly manage someone into taking her on.

Suddenly the wagon lurched and sagged, jolting her nearly off the seat and into the road. She scrambled to rein the horse in and hopped down to examine the problem. A wheel had slipped off the rear axle and now lay in the dirt a few feet away, thankfully undamaged; the axle too was intact, though the way the wagon's weight pressed down on it couldn't be doing it any good. She went to lift the wheel, got it upright with only a little effort, but the wagon was canted so sharply that she would need another four hands to raise it to where she could slide the wheel back on. She dropped the wheel and stepped away, wiping her hands on her trousers. Damn. She'd wanted a convincingly aged wagon, but not one that was actually falling apart. Now what was she going to do?

She looked along the road in both directions, not expecting to find help—the road had been mostly empty all day—so she was surprised to see someone on horseback approaching from the west. She stepped to one side and waited for the rider to draw closer. It was a man, she eventually saw, wearing a hat pulled far down over his eyes and a coat grimed with road dust. He came to a stop several feet from her and said, "You know, that wagon won't go 'less it's got all four wheels on."

Zara's eyes narrowed, and she was about to unleash a torrent of sharp-edged sarcasm at him when she realized he was grinning in a friendly way. She laughed a little self-consciously and said, "That's what I hear."

He dismounted and walked toward her. "Happen I can give you a hand," he said. He was a big man, broad in the chest and shoulders, and looked as if he might be able to lift the wagon with one hand and the wheel with the other. He took off his coat and folded it, laid it by the side of the road, and added, "Might want to shift that load though. Makes it easier to move the wagon."

Zara nodded and began handing out bundles and boxes that he set on the ground in a neat pile next to his coat. When the wagon was empty, he said, "You lift the wheel, and we'll see if we can't get it back on."

She felt flattered that he assumed she could manage the wheel by herself. She got it upright again and rolled it toward the wagon. The man crouched, got his hands under the frame, and with a grunt heaved it up until Zara could manhandle the wheel back onto the axle. He let the weight of the wagon settle back onto the wheel with another grunt. "Will it stay on?" she said.

"Hmm." The man looked around. "You need that crate?"

"I...no." She had no idea what was in it, other than something intended to help her set herself up in her new home, wherever that would be. She opened it and found dishes packed in straw. "I think I can wrap these in the quilt, if you need the box."

The man took hold of the empty crate and broke it apart as if it were made of matchsticks. "This should work," he said, showing her a length of wood that had been one edge of the crate. He wedged it into the hole where the pin holding the wheel in place had been. "Should hold long enough for you to get to Maraston, about two miles down the road," he said. "Someone ought be able to fix it right, there. But I'll travel with you that far, make sure you don't break down again."

"Thank you, Mister…"

He grinned again and held out his hand for her to shake. "Hank Hobson."

Zara realized she had never given any thought to a new name. She groped about and fell on the first thing that came to mind. "Agatha," she said. "Agatha…Weaver."

"Good to know you, Mistress Weaver," Hobson said.

"Miss," Zara said.

He smiled again, and this time there was an unfamiliar light in his eye. "Then it's *very* good to meet you, Miss Weaver," he said, removing his hat and bowing to her, just a little. His face was rugged, not exactly handsome, but there was something about him that made Zara blush for the first time in her entire life. "Where are you headed? After Maraston, I mean."

"What makes you think I'm not staying there?" Zara asked.

"Maraston's not a big place," Hobson said. "You look like someone who's got her sights on bigger things."

Zara blushed again, this time with frustration. Was it still so obvious, what she'd been? "I'm looking for a change, not rightly sure what," she said. "Where are *you* headed?"

"Sterris. It's a handful of miles south of Kingsport. Also not a big place, but I like it." He put his hat back on and tugged on the brim to settle it. "Not a bad place for a fresh start. If someone were looking for something like that."

"I reckon that's true," Zara said. "Of course, it would help to know someone there." She turned away, just a little, feeling awkward about meeting his eyes.

"You know me," Hobson pointed out.

"I've only just met you, Mister Hobson." She flicked a sidelong glance at him. "Of course, you always get to know people better when you share a road with them."

"That's true," Hobson said, keeping a straight face. "And as long as two people are going the same way, well, they ought at least talk to each other."

"It's the friendly thing to do," Zara said. *Sweet heaven, I'm flirting with a total stranger.* She felt like a stranger to herself, free of responsibilities to anyone, without the need to watch her words and her demeanor constantly. It was exhilarating.

"Miss Weaver," Hobson said, "that was my thought exactly."

Zara began gathering her things and stowing them in the wagon. "Then I think we should be moving on, Mister Hobson," she said. "We've got a long road ahead of us." *And I have a new life to begin.*

EXILE OF THE CROWN:
INTRODUCTION

*Z*ara's book, Voyager of the Crown, *gave me no end of trouble.*
It actually progressed well until I got to the point where Zara
and her friends embark on their plan to fight the pirate captain Ghazarian,
and then I got stuck. To try to jog things loose, I went back to Zara's roots,
thinking if I understood her better, I might find a solution for Voyager. *I*
ended up with four episodes in her life, enough to publish as a novella. (I
also ended up with two-thirds of what would become Ally of the Crown.)
It took another year and a half to find an ending for her novel.

The episodes fit between books: parts one and two are between Servant
of the Crown *and* Rider of the Crown, *and parts three and four are*
between Rider *and* Agent of the Crown, *with part four taking place just*
days before the beginning of the latter book. All are labeled here for the
convenience of readers who want to read in strict chronological order.

I loved the theme of the loom that connects these stories.

EXILE OF THE CROWN PART ONE: WINTER, 908 Y.B.

*S*he hadn't expected the noise. The thumping of the treadles, the clacking of the shuttle, the creaking groan of the batten, echoing off the walls and her skull until it was nearly tangible. She jerked on the picking stick, shifted her feet, repeated the motions. Maybe if she weren't so damned slow at the thing, it wouldn't bother her so much. Then again, Mistress Watkins wasn't deaf, and she'd been a weaver for more than thirty years, so probably Zara was being oversensitive. She gritted her teeth. She refused to let some contraption of metal and wood defeat her. She'd chosen this path, and she wasn't giving up.

She felt a tap on her shoulder. "That's enough for now," Mistress Watkins said, speaking in that carrying voice that wasn't shouting and yet was easily heard over the noise of the loom. Zara let go the picking stick and sat back, flexing her calves. "Good work."

"I'm not fast enough," Zara said.

"Patience, Agatha. You've already made more progress than I imagined. Guess it wasn't so stupid taking on an older apprentice. At least I don't have to worry about you running off to the big city, wasting my time and effort."

"I've had my fill of the big city. Sterris is about right for me."

Mistress Watkins' eyes twinkled. "Especially when you've got so much to keep you here?"

So it was back to that again. Zara slid off the seat and crossed the room to pick up her cloak. "I've nowhere else to be, that's certain. And I've got years of my apprenticeship to go. That's more than enough."

"You're breaking poor Mister Hobson's heart, you are. Might as well put him out of his misery."

"I'm not inclined to marry. Mister Hobson knows that. It's not my fault he's too stubborn to see sense."

Mistress Watkins moved around the room, tidying up even though it was Zara's job as apprentice to do that. "And yet I notice you never give him the kind of send-off I know you're capable of."

Zara put up the hood of her cloak to conceal her blush. "Is prying into my affairs part of the apprenticeship?"

That had been more acerbic than she'd intended, but Mistress Watkins didn't take offense. "That's part of belonging to a small town," she said. "We live in each other's pockets. This time of year more than most, as we start thinking about Wintersmeet and how we're all connected. I don't like seeing you lonely."

"I'm not lonely."

"You should be. We're all made to be joined, Agatha, and Hank Hobson...I'm just saying, don't go pushing away your happiness just because you're afraid it might turn on you."

"That's not—" Zara closed her lips on the rest of that sentence. "I just don't feel that way about him," she said instead.

"Don't you," Mistress Watkins said in a bland voice. "See you in the morning, Agatha."

Zara wrapped her cloak securely about herself and stepped into the wintry evening. Snow had been falling all day. Earlier it had roared around Mistress Watkins' home, nearly drowning out the sound of the loom. Now it fell in tiny flakes that caught on the dark gray wool of her cloak and quivered there briefly before melting from its warmth. She'd left it on the hearth all afternoon and it was beautifully, if irregularly, hot. She let out a breath that steamed in the frigid air. Mercy Johnson's pub, for a hand pie to take home with her, then—

"Well, Miss Weaver, what a coincidence!"

Zara let out another breath, this one exasperated. "Mister Hobson," she said. "It's hardly a coincidence when you're always here just as I leave for home."

Hank Hobson tipped his hat to her, making a small avalanche of snow fall off its brim between them. "I just happen to pass this way most nights," he said.

"And you just happen to stand outside this door long enough for the snow to accumulate on your hat."

"It's a comfortable corner. Would you deny me my comforts?" Hobson grinned and winked, and despite her irritation Zara had to control a matching smile. He was annoying, and stubborn, and persistent, and every time she left Mistress Watkins' house and he wasn't there she felt hollow inside. It was stupid, *she* was stupid, and she needed to give him a real push so he'd stop trying to court her, but...

"As we're both here, perhaps you'll let me escort you home?" Hobson offered her his arm.

"I don't need help walking, Mister Hobson."

"Oh, but I think I do. It's been a long day in the mines and I'm feeling a bit wobbly." Hobson's face, rugged and not quite handsome, creased in a comical expression of sorrow. "You're too kind a woman to let a man fall on his face if she could help it."

This time, she did smile, then cursed herself for being drawn by him, but by heaven, he was attractive. When he wasn't being ridiculous he looked at her in a way that left her shaken with its intensity. "I'm going to Mercy's," she said, then felt stupid at how inane that sounded.

"That's where I'm going!" he exclaimed, clapping a hand to his chest in pretended astonishment. "Now you've no excuse. You'll help me there, and I'll buy you a pint in thanks."

He really was too ridiculous for words. "Very well," Zara said. "Just one pint."

"I wouldn't get a lady drunk," Hobson said with a wink, and held out his arm again. This time, Zara took it.

Hobson was a good deal taller and broader than she was, but he matched his steps to hers, and he gave off warmth more steadily than a chimney. Zara had to resist the urge to draw him closer, because heaven only knew what he'd make of that. She regretted, as she often did, that she'd flirted with him in the first place. In those heady early days of freedom, of leaving Zara North in the dust, she'd forgotten— or maybe hadn't wanted to remember—the cruel reality of her inherent magic, that she was destined to live a long, long life, outliving everyone she cared about. Outliving Hank Hobson by a long way.

It wasn't fair to either of them to pretend they could make a normal life together, particularly a childless one—the other curse of her inherent magic. But when she'd finally made herself face the truth, and began distancing herself from him, he didn't take the hint. He wasn't rude, or aggressive, just...patient. Patient, kind, and funny, and occasionally serious in a way that made her heart flutter, and always there, just waiting for her to change her mind. She should have been angry about it, but there was a part of her—the weak, sentimental part Zara North kept firmly under control—that couldn't bear the thought of him leaving.

Ahead, warm lantern light turned the falling snowflakes gold, and a quiet rush of voices grew louder as they approached Mercy's pub. "Will you let me buy you supper?" Hobson said.

"Do I ever let you buy me supper?"

"A man can dream, can't he?" He held the door open for her with a bow and a sweep of his arm. Zara bit back another smile. *Don't encourage him. Eat something, have a drink, then you can be on your way.*

Mercy herself came out from behind the bar to greet them. "Agatha, Hank, you want the usual?"

"We're not together," Zara said. It was what she always said.

"Sure you're not," Mercy said, rolling her eyes. "I'll send food out directly, and a couple of pints."

"You see?" Hobson said. "Is it so bad, sharing a meal with me?"

"We're not sharing a meal. We're two people eating at the same table."

"Not much difference, Miss Weaver." He pulled out a chair for her. "And how goes the apprenticeship?"

"Well, I think. I'm still so slow, it's frustrating."

"That comes with time. And then you'll have the skill to match the name."

She'd chosen the name to match the skill she intended to learn, but she couldn't tell him that. "I'm not good at waiting for things."

"That, too, comes with time." He leaned back as one of Mercy's servers slid a couple of plates of sliced ham in front of them. "I, on the other hand, am *excellent* at waiting for things."

Zara didn't need to see the amused gleam in his eye to know what he meant. "Not everything comes for the waiting."

"But the best things are worth that chance."

"Isn't it worse when you wait for something only to discover it will never happen?"

"That's never happened to me."

Zara cut a very large piece of meat and stuffed it into her mouth so she wouldn't respond with something scathing. She needed him to stop pursuing her, but she didn't want to hurt him. *Maybe that's the only way left*, she thought. *Hurt him, send him running from you, it's not as if you don't know how to find someone's weakness and exploit it. He's just like every other man.*

"What are your plans for Wintersmeet?" Hobson said.

"A nice quiet evening in," Zara said. "What about you?"

"Midnight service at the bethel, then the big dance afterward."

"I didn't know you were religious."

"I'm not, much, but I'm far from family and I like the feeling of being surrounded by people on the solstice."

Zara couldn't wait to feel her bonds to her family at the solstice. It was all she had left. "Sounds nice," she said.

"The dance is the biggest social event of the year. You should come. Lots of friends, lots of food."

"I'm not really very sociable."

Hobson shrugged and began cutting his meat. "Just think about it."

He'd gone from flirtatious to indifferent in a heartbeat, and Zara felt unexpectedly guilty about her coldness. Then she felt angry. Her life was her business and nobody else's. Hank Hobson needed to keep his nose out of it.

They ate in silence, but when Zara finished off her pint and stood to go, Hobson stood with her. "I really don't need an escort, Mister Hobson," she said. Just as she always did.

"You're on my way home, Miss Weaver," Hobson said, "so why don't we walk together?" Just as *he* always did. She suspected he was lying about the way his path home went, but couldn't call him on it. And she didn't want to walk alone.

They walked down the street in silence, this time without their arms linked. It had stopped snowing, but Zara kept the hood of her cloak up to keep the back of her neck warm. Dr. Trevellian had for some reason cut her hair off while she was dead, and it hadn't grown back much in the last six months. Hobson was a hulking presence next to her; she was tall, but he was taller, and while Zara wasn't afraid of anything in this town, she still felt comforted to have him by her side.

"I was hoping to persuade you to meet me at the dance," Hobson said abruptly. "It's not good, being all alone at Wintersmeet."

"That's my business."

"And I want to dance with you," he continued, not put off by her sharp tone.

"Why's that?" She didn't know why her heart was beating faster.

"Because I like to see you smile. Because I bet you're a wonderful dancer."

"I don't dance much." She never danced at all, and now she couldn't remember why not. Too intimate, possibly, and the Queen couldn't afford casual intimacy with anyone without the rumormongers turning a simple dance into a full-on theatrical production.

"Then dance once with me, and sit the rest out." He grinned at her in the darkness. "I'd rather it that way, truth be told. I don't want competition."

"You don't have competition."

The grin fell away from his face. "I don't?" he said in a low voice.

"No—I mean—" Zara stammered, and he smiled mischievously at her. "Mister Hobson, will you please believe me when I tell you I'm not interested?"

Hobson stopped, and Zara nearly walked past her own front door. "No," he said.

"You're impertinent. When a woman says 'no,' that's what it means."

Hobson took a deep breath, serious once more. "That's not it," he said. "I'm not going to tell you you don't know your own mind. You're a strong, self-assured, beautiful woman, and I think you know what you want. And maybe friends is all we can ever be. But I've seen you step outside Mistress Watkins' door and look up the street to see if I'm coming. I've sat down to supper with you a hundred times since you came to Sterris and every time is a joy to me. So I don't think you've made up your mind for certain. And until you do, I won't give up hope." He bowed, then set off down the street, not waiting for a reply.

Zara stood with her hand on the frozen latch and watched him go. Her face was hot, her fingers burned with cold, and for the briefest second she thought about calling him back. Finally she pushed her door open and removed her cloak in the darkness. It didn't matter what she wanted. She couldn't make a life with him and it was wrong to try.

She stood in the black hall gripping her cloak, staring at nothing, for nearly a minute. Then without turning on the light, she went to her bedroom and lay down, fully clothed, on the bed. She needed to leave Sterris, and to hell with what she'd told Mistress Watkins. For the first time in her life, Zara knew she was too weak to face a challenge. Leave, find a new home, never look back. He'd thank her if he knew the truth.

No one worked on Wintersmeet Eve day. Zara spent the hours cleaning her tiny rented house, all three rooms of it. She didn't like cleaning—couldn't imagine a sensible person who did—but it was good, hard, mindless work, and when she was finished she had a clean house and a tired but satisfied body. A fresh start to a new year.

She bathed in front of the fireplace, then set out her simple meal and a bottle of good wine and ate until she was contentedly full. Then she dragged her chair over to the fireplace with the bottle and a glass and stared into the fire, sipping occasionally. Back at the palace they'd be dancing the night away in silver and white. Alison and Anthony always looked so good together, so happy, though their first Wintersmeet Ball together had been disastrous.

She remembered how Anthony had looked that morning—six years ago, now—how quietly he'd spoken, as if his life were in shattered pieces and the best he could hope for was not to lose any of them. *I want to be the man she thought I was*, he'd said, and what a man he'd become. What a King he now was. At least she didn't have any worries on that front.

She discovered to her surprise that the glass was empty and poured more wine. This would be her last. She couldn't get drunk—her body converted alcohol too quickly for it to do more than give her a pleasant full-body tingle—but she didn't like the idea of not being in control, even theoretically. She took a larger swallow, reached out with the poker and jabbed at the fire, drank again. It should be nearly midnight. She hoped.

Then she felt it, the unmistakable tugging as the magical lines of power shifted their alignment. And there they were, Mother and Alison and Anthony and her nephews, pulses of glowing light that were tangible rather than visible. Zara held her breath for those three seconds, grasping at the feeling even as it slipped away from her, tears running down her face at the aching loneliness it left behind. She never cried. It was painful and pointless and did nothing but leave her headachy and runny. She covered her face with her hands and sobbed.

Eventually she ran out of tears and drew one last ragged breath, then wiped her face with her hands and wiped her hands on her trousers. Enough of that. She was alone, true, but there was nothing wrong with that. In a sense, she'd been alone her whole life.

She'd thought to marry, once, just after her father's death, but that had been disastrous. Had she ever really loved Jonathan, or had she just thought she loved him because marrying without love, doing her duty to the Crown, had felt so cold? It didn't matter, because he hadn't loved her: *I want someone who needs me. Someone I can take care of. You aren't that.* And she hadn't met anyone since then she'd even considered sharing her life with.

Until now.

Zara slid off her chair to sit closer to the fire, close enough to feel it scorch her skin. It was madness. Hank Hobson would age and die while she stayed young. He would never become a father. And she'd be lying to him every day of their life together because no one could know her true identity. It would be the most selfish thing she'd ever done, selfish and cruel, and if she cared at all about him, she'd spurn him completely. He'd be hurt, but it would pass, and he'd move on, and so would she. Alone.

She came to her feet, pacing the small room. Alone. The idea of that long, long life stretching out before her, utterly alone, filled her with horror. *I don't care,* she thought, then said aloud, "I don't care. I don't care!"

She rushed to her bedroom and took her one dress off its peg on the wall. It was dull yellow and didn't suit her coloring, but she put it on and twirled around, enjoying how the sleeves fitted close to her arms and the skirt flared out around her ankles. She didn't have shoes to match, but there was enough snow that boots made more sense anyway. She threw her cloak over her shoulders and ran out her front door and up the street.

The place where Sterris's two main streets intersected was wide enough for a couple of oxcarts filled with ore to drive side by side, and it was there the townsfolk had set up lanterns on poles and cleared the street of snow. Light, and music, spilled down the street, and Zara ran toward it, pulled onward like a child's toy on a string.

She slowed as she reached the outskirts of the crowd. Now she was there, her excitement turned to apprehension. Most of Sterris seemed to be at the dance; finding Hobson in that crowd was unlikely. She turned down the offer of a beer with a smile and moved forward, feeling shy and awkward even though she knew a third of the people and all of them greeted her freely, as if there were nothing at all strange about her presence.

Then she saw him, standing a few yards away. Hobson was head and shoulders above the men standing near him, broad and power-fully built, and her heart began beating faster. She couldn't bring herself to go to him. This was stupid. She was making a huge mistake. But she couldn't turn around to leave.

He said something to the man next to him, and his eyes met hers. He looked startled, then smiled, a warm grin that she couldn't help but match. He clapped the other man on the shoulder companion-ably, then made his way through the crowd until he stood before her, his rugged face still creased in a smile. "Dance with me?" he said, extending his hand.

Zara put her hand in his. "It's why I came," she said, then shrieked in mixed surprise and delight as he put his arm around her waist and lifted her, spun her once and set her down. "Though I didn't expect *that*," she said, breathlessly.

"I aim to keep you off balance," Hobson said, drawing her along after him toward where couples were forming up for the next dance. "See if I can convince you to dance with me more than once."

"You know what that means in the big city," Zara said, curtseying to him as the music began. "Once is nothing. Two is an interest."

"And I am *very* interested in you, Miss Weaver." Hobson bowed to her in return, then took her in his arms. "Agatha."

His voice caressed her name, that name she'd taken at random, and it had never felt more like her own than right then. "You're impertinent," she said with a smile.

"I prefer to think of it as 'daring.'" He spun her away, then brought her back, his strong hands holding her steady. They were still ingrained with coal dust, and the sight was so unexpectedly arousing it made her catch her breath. "And daring usually wins the day."

"You think you've won something?"

Hobson's expression went from teasing to serious. "First prize," he said in a low voice, and Zara couldn't look away from him, couldn't think of anything to say to that. They danced in silence until the music ended, then stood, hand in hand, as men and women moved around them preparing for the next dance. Zara's heart was pounding. If he asked her for another dance, what would she say? One dance meant nothing. Two meant an interest. Two in a row was a declaration. Was that what she wanted? Was it what *he* wanted?

As if he'd read her mind, he drew her closer, raised her hand to his lips and kissed it gently. "I'd dance with you forever if you'd let me, Agatha," he said. "Say it's what you want, too."

The music started, something slow and swaying. She should walk away. But she knew if she did, if she walked away from him at that moment, he wouldn't follow, and he wouldn't be waiting at Mistress Watkins' door ever again. *This is what I want, and to hell with the future.* "Dance with me again, Hank," she said, and fierce joy lit his face. Once more he put his arms around her and drew her into the rhythm of the dance.

For the rest of the night she was never more than a hand's breadth away from him as they spun through dance after dance. She had no idea what her neighbors thought of it and didn't care. *My love,* she thought once as they came together after going down the line during a country dance and he smiled at her as if it had been an eternity they'd been separated instead of less than a minute. When they weren't dancing, she stood beside him, her hand in his, gazing at him in wonder. Maybe it was just the holiday, maybe by the dawn this would all be a fever dream, and she clasped his hand more tightly and prayed it wasn't true.

When the sky began to turn pink and the stars had faded, he walked her home. It felt strange, and wonderful, to take the same path they always took, familiar and yet utterly different. Neither of them spoke; Zara couldn't think of anything that wouldn't break this spell between them, and a tiny part of her was afraid of what would happen when they reached her door and had to say goodnight, or good morning, or whatever it was. What was *he* thinking? Was he as conscious of her nearness as she was of his?

At the door, she turned to face him. "Well," she said.

"Well," he repeated. His face was still, though a smile still touched his lips.

"I...it was an enjoyable evening," Zara said, then mentally kicked herself as his smile dropped away. That had definitely been the wrong thing to say. She'd once commanded the respect of hundreds of powerful men and women and never had she been caught without words—until now, when it actually mattered. "Oh, hell," she said, took hold of the front of his coat and pulled him close for a kiss.

His lips were cold only for a moment before the touch of hers warmed them, and then he was kissing her fiercely, pushing the hood of her cloak back and twining his fingers in her hair. She put her arms around him and drew him closer until she felt the heat of his body through her dress, the lean hardness of his muscles and the strength of his arms, circling her.

He slid his hands beneath her cloak to stroke her back, sending a thrill through her, a hot streak that flashed through her body and left her burning with desire. She kissed him again, and again, not caring that they were standing in the middle of the street where anyone could see, and heard him make a noise deep in his throat that made his kisses sweeter, more intense. "Don't stop," she murmured when he began to pull away.

"Not a chance," he said into her ear, kissing its curve. "Dear heaven, I've wanted you for so long."

"I was afraid," she confessed. She'd never admitted to fear in her life, but this was the one man in all the world who would never use her weaknesses against her. "It's never been easy for me to trust."

"You don't need to be afraid, Agatha. I love you."

She shivered with delight. "I love you, Hank," she said, and the words came so easily she was amazed she hadn't said them before.

He smiled, then kissed her lips again, softly. "What a way to begin the new year," he murmured.

She could have gone on kissing him forever, but her heart was screaming a warning. "Wait." All her secrets warred within her. She drew back enough to be able to look him in the eye, which was all the further his embrace would let her. "I...can't have children. That might matter to you."

He pursed his lips. "You sure about that?"

"As sure as I'm standing here. I'll understand—"

"I'm not changing my mind, Agatha. I love you for who you are, and if you think you can get rid of me that easily, think again."

"And—" She almost told him. But the truth of her identity wasn't hers to tell; it was a state secret, and one she would have to keep from him. And it wasn't truly a lie; she was never going back to being Zara North, and Agatha Weaver was who she was. She smiled at him, taking off his hat and smoothing his hair. "It's Wintersmeet Day now," she said.

"It's been Wintersmeet Day since midnight," he pointed out, and kissed her forehead.

"Lucky day to get betrothed," she said.

He blinked at her. "So I've heard. Agatha—"

"You said it, Hank. I always know my own mind. What I want to know is, do you know yours?"

Hank stroked her cheek, then kissed her once more, sweeter than honey. "I think Hank Weaver has a nice ring to it," he said.

"You'd take my name?" *Was* it her name? What would happen when they swore oath to one another? But the idea of giving up her family, those few brief seconds of contact at the solstices, filled her with nearly as great a dread as the idea of losing Hank had.

"You don't talk about it much," Hank said, "but I know your family is important to you. I'd be honored to join them."

Her heart felt full to bursting with joy. "Then marry me," she said. "Soon."

"Nothing wrong with today, is there?"

Zara laughed. "You're so decisive."

"I'm just afraid the most beautiful woman in Sterris is going to change her mind about me." Hank ran one hand through his hair, then settled his hat firmly on his head. "I want you sworn and sealed to me as soon as possible."

"And free to share my bed?" Zara teased.

"To share your life, sweetheart. Now and forever."

Zara leaned into him and laid her cheek against his shoulder. "A wonderful, long life together."

EXILE OF THE CROWN PART TWO: SPRING, 924 Y.B.

The loom had been silent for weeks now. The half-finished length of blue and violet cloth taunted Zara, reminding her of all the responsibilities she'd ignored since....

She sat at the loom and took the picking stick in hand. Its smooth, ridged wood fit her palm naturally. She'd had the thing for eight years, ever since the end of her apprenticeship, and it was worn on one side where she gripped it. She flicked it once, twice, sending the empty shuttle flying back and forth through the shed. Then, furious, she began working it so hard the *clacks* of the shuttle's metal-sheathed tips became harder, sharper, until a loud *crack* and a rough hiss told her she'd broken it. She flung the picking stick away to swing rapidly on its wire and dug the broken shuttle out of the loom. It was only cracked on one side, not shattered, but that was something she couldn't repair. Just like everything else.

She set it aside next to the spinning wheel and went into the kitchen. She wasn't hungry. Mercy kept telling her she had to eat, but she was reasonably sure her body wouldn't die even if she starved it. Not that she could imagine what *would* happen. Nothing good, probably. And she didn't really want to find out.

She found the remains of a meat pie Mercy had given her—Zara was a terrible cook, even when she wanted to eat—and sat at the table and ate. She'd moved the other chair to the far side of the room. It was hard enough sleeping in the big bed without any more reminders of—

She squeezed her eyes shut briefly, then took another big bite. Hank was gone. It was time she faced that fact. But she couldn't stop seeing his mangled body, damn them for bringing him home to her in that state. He'd gone down that mine every day for the fifteen years they'd been married without having anything worse than a broken finger happen to him, and then the tunnel collapsed, and just like that, he'd gone from being a living, vibrant man to a wrecked pile of flesh and bone. *He pulled two men to safety,* they'd told her, *he died a hero,* but that didn't change the fact that he'd died, period.

She pulled a piece of gristle from between her teeth and flicked it across the kitchen, not caring where it landed. He'd been dead for four weeks now, and for four weeks she'd felt dead too.

She finished her meal and washed the pie tin so she could return it to Mercy. The funny thing, the absolutely hysterically funny thing, was that this day had always been coming. She'd always known she would outlive him. She'd just thought he'd die in bed when he was ninety and not in a mining accident when he was forty-three. She dried the pie tin and set it aside. Mercy didn't need it right away, and it was one of those days where Zara couldn't bear her friend's pity.

She went back to stand by the loom. It just seemed like so much trouble, and for what? A length of fabric that would be cut to make a shirt or a dress that would wear out in a few years and be thrown away. From her perspective that was barely a blink of the eye of time. And yet people paid her to do it, and if she didn't, she'd be back to starving, though not to death. She'd finish the cloth. Just not today.

Instead she sat at her spinning wheel and picked up a tuft of grayish wool. Spinning was soothing in a way weaving was not; it was quiet, and mindless, and she could let her thoughts spin round with the wheel without dwelling on the painful ones. She had dozens of skeins that needed dyeing; maybe she should do that tomorrow. In between working the loom. Hank wouldn't want her to let her grief take over her life. Besides, she was still Zara North, and Zara North never cried.

A knock at the door startled her out of her reverie. She let the wool slip through her fingers and went to answer it. Probably someone else, some well-meaning someone, come to see how she was faring. She liked her friends, but she wished they'd find some other way to express their sympathy than constant, awkward visits in which they either didn't know what to say or said the wrong thing. Only Ed Kerwin, who'd lost his wife to disease six months before, was any comfort, and even he didn't know where to look when he stopped by.

"Yes?" she said to the man standing in her doorway. Then she went mute, because the stranger looked exactly like her brother Anthony. A young Anthony, and one slimmer than her muscular, broad-shouldered brother, but still him. The young man looked as startled as she felt. "Can I...help you with something?" she said.

"I hope so," the stranger said. "Are you...is your name North?"

She had to grip the edge of the door hard to keep from falling over. "Agatha Weaver," she said.

"You can't be," he said.

"I am. Have been all my life."

The young man's brow creased in thought. "I've seen you before. I know I have. A long time ago."

Suddenly it all fell into place. The blue eyes, just like hers— "I recognize *you*," Zara said. "You're Jeff—Prince Jeffrey North. Begging your pardon, your Highness, but what are you doing on my doorstep?"

The Prince's mouth fell open. "Dear heaven," he said. "*Aunt Zara?*"

Zara grabbed him by the wrist and towed him inside, shutting the door firmly behind him. "That's not a name you want to go throwing around in the street," she said. "And I'm Agatha Weaver."

"You're Zara North, I'm sure of it," the Prince said. "I remember you—I was just a little boy, but you were unforgettable. You died.

Why are you here? Why don't you look any different from when I was small?"

Zara let out a deep sigh. "Why don't you tell me first why you're so certain I'm your dead aunt?"

The Prince glanced around as if he expected to see lurkers hidden in her hallway. "I have inherent magic," he said in a low voice. "I always know where my family is. Not like at the solstices, when you can feel the connection but not where people are, or which bond belongs to which person; it's more like reaching out along the lines of power, and then I just...know. Mother and Father, Sylvester and Elspeth—and then there was...they're like tiny bonfires under the skin of the world, and they've been growing stronger and easier to see as I've gotten older. And I saw yours, all the way out here in the east, and I had to know who you were. Mother and Father always told us, at the solstices, that those extra bonds we felt were just a couple of distant cousins, but when I got older I knew that was impossible, because anyone sworn and sealed to the North family would be living in the palace. And then, four weeks ago, one of them disappeared, and I couldn't bear not knowing. So I came. Aunt Zara, why are you here? How are you alive?"

He was so earnest, and so like the boy she remembered, that Zara turned and went into the kitchen, not waiting for him to follow her. "Take a seat," she said, and after a moment he dragged Hank's chair over to the table and sat down opposite her. She examined the face that was so like his father's. He was only seventeen, as old as Anthony had been when their father died, but he carried himself with the calm certainty Anthony had taken years to grow into.

"I'll tell you the story, but on condition you swear never to tell anyone who I am," she said.

"I swear."

Zara nodded. Then she told him everything. What her inherent magic was and how she'd learned of it. How she and Alison and Anthony had staged her death. How she'd crossed the country to make a new life for herself. "You know better than anyone what it could mean to the North family if the kingdom knew it was tainted by inherent magic," she concluded. "It would be the end of our dynasty and the beginning of civil war as the Counts and Barons fought to take the Crown. You've got to keep my secret as well as your own."

"I understand," Jeffrey said. "You were brave to give up your life like that."

"It's not bravery if it's the only choice left to you."

"Still. I'm sorry."

"Don't be. I have a good life here." *Or had.* She hesitated, then said, "How are your parents? And little Sylvester?"

"Mother and Father are well. Happy. Sylvester's a pain. We don't get along. And Elspeth—but you never met Elspeth, she was born four years after you...left. She's sort of a brat, but she's smart and funny too, so I guess I don't mind her much."

"I'm glad to hear it. Wish I'd been there to see you all grow up."

"Can I tell them? Mother and Father, I mean."

"About me?"

"You said they already know you're not dead. I think they'd be happy to know how you're doing. Mother could even come visit—"

"No visits. You swore it, young man."

"But—"

"*No.*" She wasn't going to confess her weakness to her young nephew, how she didn't think she could bear seeing Alison and Anthony again, especially now Hank was gone. "Besides, you can't tell them you found me without betraying your own secret."

Jeffrey shrugged. "I was thinking of telling them anyway. I don't keep secrets from my parents. I just...I came here to see whether my talent was real or just my imagination. If it turned out there really was a North living all the way out here, that would be proof."

Zara hesitated again. It wasn't as if she hadn't considered this before. Anthony wouldn't be able to come without everyone watching him, but Alison...she went to Kingsport all the time, visiting her father, and it would be so simple to arrange a meeting. And then it would be another meeting, and another, and sometime one of them would slip, and then there would be a scandal, because Agatha Weaver on her own was nobody, but Agatha Weaver next to

Alison North looked too much like a North herself to keep the secret.

"You can tell them I'm well," she said, "but that's all. They know I'm alive at the solstices and that has to be enough. My life is none of your business, Jeffrey."

"Yes, ma'am," Jeffrey said, then looked embarrassed at his slip of the tongue. Maybe she hadn't left Zara North as far behind as she'd thought. "I promise."

"Good." She leaned back and regarded him again. "Did you speak to anyone here? Anyone recognize you?"

"I didn't need directions. And I don't think anyone recognized me." But he looked uncertain, and Zara's heart sank. A Prince of Tremontane, especially one who looked so much like the King, wouldn't pass unnoticed. Damn. She couldn't stay in Sterris any longer. Lost her husband, lost her home—anger gripped her, replacing the momentary despair.

"You fool," she said. "Didn't it occur to you that maybe there was a good reason this North wasn't in Aurilien in the bosom of her loving family? You just had to stir things up."

"I didn't mean any harm," Jeffrey protested.

"Not meaning it doesn't make things right. Get out. Go home and don't come back."

Jeffrey stood, but didn't move toward the door. "It's not just me," he said. "There's something else wrong."

"None of your business. Get out of here or I'll throw you out." Not that she could manage it; he was four inches taller and thirty years younger than she was. But his presence was shredding her nerves, and in a moment she'd begin shrieking.

"All right," Jeffrey said. "I'm sorry." He moved past her, and a moment later she heard the door open and shut. She stood and leaned heavily on the table, her eyes closed and her breathing coming heavily. Well. She'd known she had to leave Sterris, people were starting to talk about her youthful appearance; she just hadn't been able to face the truth. She ought to thank Jeffrey for pushing her in the right direction, but all she could feel was anger and pain coursing through her like glass shards in the blood.

She heaved a deep sigh and went to her bedroom. She'd winnow her things tonight, get crates in the morning, arrange for someone to disassemble and pack the loom—she'd have to work hard to finish that cloth before she left. Find her spare shuttle. The need for planning almost dispelled the memory of Hank's broken body. Maybe someday she'd be able to remember him as he'd been.

The front door opened. "Who is it?" Zara called out, trying not to feel irritated at the new intrusion.

"It's me," Jeffrey said, stepping into the kitchen. "I'm sorry."

"I thought I told you to get out. I distinctly remember saying that, *your Highness.*" She invested the last two words with as much disdain as she could muster.

"I know. But I couldn't leave without telling you one more thing." He took a deep breath. "We've never forgotten you," he said. "Mother and Father talk about you so often I feel like I know you—I know that's an impertinence, but it's how it is. I can't imagine what your life is like, but I know how I'd feel if I had to be separated from my family. Even Sylvester, who mostly makes me want to punch him. So I wanted you to know…."

"What?" Zara snapped when it seemed he'd run out of words.

"That you're not completely alone. That every solstice, we know you're alive and now I'll know to think of you. I know it's not much and it can't make up for your isolation, but I hoped it would matter to you."

"You're right. That's an impertinence." His mouth was set in a firm line, as if he'd resolved on an unpleasant task and was seeing it through despite his reluctance. He looked so like Anthony it made her heart hurt worse, and unexpected compassion led her to say, "Thank you."

Jeffrey looked surprised at this. "I just wish things could be different."

"So do I."

"Where will you go?"

He'd seen the truth, then. "Don't know yet. Maybe I'll see Eskandel for a while. But I don't need to tell you, do I?"

He grinned. "No. Does it bother you to know I'll know where you are?"

"A little."

"I promised I wouldn't tell."

"I believe you."

Jeffrey ducked his head. "You want to know what I remember?" he said. "I had a horse—a wooden horse with wheels for feet—and Sylvester stole it and threw it down the stairs from the north wing and two of the wheels came off. I was crying, and I remember...you came along, probably on your way to work, and you sat down beside me and asked me if crying was going to put the wheels back on. Then you took me to your office and showed me how to fix it—I can't remember how, except that it was with something you took out of your desk that wasn't an axle, but fit. And you said something about sometimes the best solution was the wrong tool for the right task. I didn't understand it at the time, which is probably why I remember it. It makes a lot more sense now."

She didn't remember that at all. "That's a lot of years to carry a memory."

"It's one of my earliest ones. You're not alone, Aunt Zara, and maybe someday you won't have to hide anymore."

"That's unlikely."

"I'd prefer to think of it as...hopeful."

For just a moment, her pain fell away, and she saw a future in which she was reunited with her family. Then the moment passed, leaving her with that aching emptiness again, but it wasn't quite so bad. "You go ahead and hang onto that hope for me," she said quietly.

"I will," Jeffrey said, and put his arms around her. It startled her so much that she reflexively returned his embrace instead of pushing him away, which was her second impulse, and a cruel one. "Goodbye, Aunt Zara."

"Goodbye, Jeffrey, and...tell your parents I love them."

Jeffrey nodded and released her. "Do you need anything? I brought a little money."

"I'll be fine, nephew. Now...go home."

She followed him to the door this time and stood motionless in the hall for a few moments after he'd gone. Then she went to her room and began taking Hank's clothing out of the dresser drawers. She hadn't been able to bear it before, but now it felt like a proper farewell. "So that's your nephew," she said to the air. "Last I saw him, he was a chubby toddler, and now he's a man grown. Did it bother you to reach ungoverned heaven and discover the secret I kept from you? I assume that's how it works. Maybe I'm wrong. But I like to think I don't have to hide from you now you're gone. I'm sorry I never told you. I thought it was safer that way, but maybe I should have believed you could keep the secret."

She straightened the folds of his spare trousers and patted the neat bundle of cloth. "I love you, Hank, and someday we'll be together again. I know I'm not much for religion, but you were, and maybe I can hang onto your faith for a while."

An hour later, she went to Mercy's pub and begged a couple of leftover crates, and packed up all the things she'd sell or give away. The house wasn't hers, but the furnishings were, and between that and all the little things she'd accumulated over the years, she should be able to make enough to store the loom for a few months, maybe a year. Or maybe she'd sell that, too. She wasn't ready to settle down again. Time to travel for a spell and see what the world had to offer. Time for Zara North to begin another new life.

OWEN

I originally thought Elspeth would be the heroine of what eventually became Rider of the Crown, *so I knew some details of what happened to her, one of which was Owen meeting her and Jeffrey. When I came to write this story, it turned out those details were wrong. I don't know why Elspeth continues to elude me as a POV character, but this story is all Owen's.*

Takes place from summer 927 to spring 928 Y.B.

DAY 1

The sound of pursuit was closer now. Oujan descended the overgrown slope as rapidly as he dared, leaping and sliding and keeping his footing through skill and desperation. The rich, lush scent of crushed greenery rose up around him, choking him. Good thing Hrovald's warriors weren't accompanied by dogs, because Oujan was leaving a scent trail a mile wide. On the other hand, those warriors had caught up to him far faster than Oujan had expected, so maybe it didn't matter.

He caught himself at the foot of the incline and ran, casting about in all directions for salvation. This forest, thick with summer's growth, would conceal him for a while, but however much of a bastard the usurper Hrovald was, his men weren't stupid. Oujan's only hope was that he could outrun and outlast them. Since he knew the full amount of the bounty on his head, it was a stupid hope. But if Oujan hadn't surrendered the night the old king had been murdered, he wasn't going to give up now.

Above the sound of his running footsteps and his labored breathing, he heard the rush of running water. A river, here in the middle of the forest? He must be more turned around than he'd thought. The only river he knew of anywhere near here was the Tjorbar, flowing south from the Spine of the World, but he'd thought he was a good ten miles away from its banks.

Oujan changed direction. If the ground was clearer near the river, he'd make better time, and Balderan willing, there might be a settlement, or, hell, he'd settle for finding an abandoned boat. Anything to stretch his lead on Hrovald's warriors.

He couldn't hear the warriors anymore. That meant they'd made it down from the heights, and Oujan was in serious trouble. He automatically put a hand to the hilt of his sword to keep it from swinging as he leaped a low-growing bush, and cursed when his hand hit nothing but air. He'd left his longsword behind when he'd failed to defend his king, and the short sword that swung at his other hip wasn't his. The memory tightened his throat, and he pushed himself to run faster, wishing he could outrun his past as he was outrunning his pursuit.

He came abruptly out of the trees and pulled up short, nearly falling over the riverbank into the Tjorbar's flood. The forest grew right up to the mighty river's banks, which dropped a good three feet to the surface of the water. Tree roots protruded from the banks, ready to trip running feet. Oujan would gain no advantage from following the river.

His other hope, that he might ford the Tjorbar and lose himself on its far side, died a terrible death as he regarded how wide it was. Wide, yes, but flowing as slow as molasses in winter, so swimming was a possibility. For someone who knew how to swim.

His feet carried him along the bank downstream as he went over possibilities. Hrovald's warriors were trained in the art of battle, but none of them had Oujan's skill at tracking or moving through the landscape. He still had the advantage, even if their numbers meant it wasn't much of one. They weren't so much following his trail as covering as much ground as possible and hoping he'd make a mistake. Staying with the river, searching for a ford...that was his best course of action for now.

Ahead, the river's course took a sharp bend to the left, and Oujan ducked back beneath the trees to avoid where the riverbank had been eroded by the current. Stumbling, cursing under his breath, he paused to listen. Still nothing but the wind in the trees and the water's chattering flow. The way his luck was going, he would come out onto the riverbank again to find Hrovald's warriors stopped for a drink. He shook his head and pressed on.

What little sky he could see through the great oaks' leaves was leaden with the weight of an oncoming summer storm. If it had arrived an hour earlier, it might have been his salvation, obscuring his trail enough for him to evade his pursuers. As it was, he was just going to die wet. He headed for the riverbank again, hoping the curve of the river's course would reveal a ford where there wasn't one before. Which was the same as hoping for a miracle. Given that he was the last of King Dyrak's warriors, the only one to survive the massacre, Oujan feared Balderan thought he'd already had one more miracle than he deserved.

He burst out of the forest to find himself unexpectedly on clear ground. The river's sharp bend had curved back on itself, a much slower, shallower turn to the right, and the riverbank sloped gently down to what was almost a pool carved out of the river's course.

And he wasn't alone. A sorrel mare, bright against the dark trunks of the oaks, bent her head to drink from the pool. Crouched nearby was a young woman, her hands cupped and overflowing with water. She looked up in surprise, but didn't move. She didn't seem afraid of him at all. Her large brown eyes watched him curiously, as if he were a woodland creature she'd never seen before.

Oujan's feet carried him forward without stopping. A horse. His pursuers were on foot. *Thank you, Balderan, for my miracle.*

The young woman stood as he drew nearer and said something in Tremontanese. "Sorry," Oujan said. "I'd promise to bring her back, but we both know that's a lie."

"Bring her back?" the young woman said in perfect Ruskeldin. "You're stealing my horse?"

Startled, Oujan came to a stop a few feet away. "You speak my language?"

"I speak several languages. Did you need me to say it in Eskandelic? Why are you trying to steal my horse?" The young woman— hell, she was barely more than a girl—still showed no signs of fear. She put out a hand to stroke the mare's nose, calming her.

Oujan stepped forward and reached for the reins. He didn't have time for a conversation in any language. "You'll be fine," he said. "I need this horse."

The girl grabbed the reins first and stepped out of Oujan's reach. "You look awful," she said. "You're not a bandit, are you? Mercier swore there weren't any bandits—oh, heaven, Jeffrey will be furious with him if I'm in danger."

Oujan's head spun. Who was this girl, that she could talk about bandits as if they were a minor inconvenience, like mosquitoes? "I'm not a bandit," he said helplessly. "I just need your horse."

"But you're running from something, I can tell." The young woman stood on tiptoe to peer past his shoulder. She was tiny, he realized, and beautiful, with shining fair hair that hung straight over her shoulders nearly to the small of her back. "Which means—"

A shout rang out through the trees. Oujan whipped around, scanning the forest. He saw nothing, but then someone else shouted, and he knew his luck had run out. He took two swift steps and grabbed the girl, ripping the reins from her hands. He had to go, now, before it really was too late.

The young woman gasped and struggled out of his grip. Oujan shoved her to the side and mounted. He looked down at the young woman, whose mouth hung open in astonishment but not fear. She would be fine. Someone like her couldn't be far from her companions, and she'd be facing a long walk, but nothing more dangerous than that.

Unless.

Unless Hrovald's warriors were better trackers than he'd thought. Unless they followed him closely enough to stumble upon this young woman the way Oujan had. Oujan examined her again, took in her slim figure, her beautiful face, and his heart sank. However intent Hrovald's men were on finding him, he had no doubt they'd be willing to take an hour or so to amuse themselves with this girl.

He wheeled the horse around and leaned down to grab her arm and haul her up behind him. "Hold on," he said, and kicked the mare into a gallop. The girl gasped and flung her arms around his waist, pressing herself close to him. Any other time, that would have thrilled him. Now, he could clearly hear the sound of shouting, and all his attention was on the ground before him.

The damp ground squelched beneath the horse's hooves as Oujan urged her onward. The open space narrowed, taking them beneath the trees again, and then widened out as the forest fell away and turned into broad, grassy fields. It was so unexpected Oujan turned to look behind him, wondering madly if he'd dreamed the great forests that bordered the Spine of the World. He half expected to see Hrovald's warriors burst out of the tree line, screaming and waving their swords. But the forest stared placidly back at him, the only movement a flock of gray birds that rose from the canopy and swooped and darted in a swirl before flying north.

"Kidnapping me is a bad idea," the girl shouted. "I thought I should warn you."

Oujan nearly fell off the horse trying to look down his own shoulder at his small companion. "What?"

"Whatever you're afraid of back there, I can promise there's much worse waiting for you if you don't let me go."

This was the strangest girl he'd ever met. "I'm not kidnapping you," he said. "I'm just borrowing your horse."

"What are you running from?" The girl sounded curious and, again, not even a little bit afraid.

Oujan laughed despite himself. The strangest girl, and the strangest conversation. "A lot of bad men who'd do worse to you than I have."

"I see. Turn right up there, away from the river."

"What?"

"It's the road to The Junipers. On the right. We'll be safe there." The young woman leaned past him and pointed. Oujan saw where the grassy plains were beaten flat into a pale dirt road that extended left and right. On the right, the road curved to follow an incline that rose to become a hill topped by more trees. On the left, the plains continued into the distance until they came up once again on the banks of the Tjorbar River.

Oujan glanced down at the young woman again. She was looking past him at the hill. Oujan couldn't see anything there that might be a protection. Worse, if her friends were hidden there, Oujan could be riding into greater danger.

Then a howling cry rose up behind them. Oujan twisted around to cast a swift glance at the distant forest. Tiny figures emerged from it, their swords glinting in the gray light. They ran as if they hoped to outpace the horse. Oujan cursed and urged the mare faster.

"What are you doing? I said, go right!" the girl shouted.

Oujan ignored her. Whatever waited for them on the top of the hill was no match for a full Ruskalder warband. Not to mention her friends might not be interested in hearing his side of the story, when it looked for all the world as if he'd kidnapped this girl.

He gazed into the distance, straining to see anything that might let him elude their pursuers. Aside from the tree-topped hill, the plains were bare and featureless and looked to extend all the way through Tremontane and into Eskandel beyond. Eventually, he would have to stop or kill the horse with riding, and he was under no illusions about the tenacity of his fellow Ruskalder. Hrovald's bounty was enough to keep those men chasing him forever.

Something shifted at his side, and to his astonishment, the girl drew the short sword from its sheath. "What are you—" he demanded.

Cold steel pressed into his side. "Go right," the girl said. "Do it now."

He almost laughed. Her grip on the sword was all wrong, and it would take nothing for him to knock it out of her hand. But the sheer bloody nerve of her gambit amazed him. He'd never known anyone like her. *Balderan, if this is Your miracle, far be it from me to reject it.* Oujan wrenched on the reins and turned right.

The road didn't go straight up the hill; it curved around its base and took a gentler path that nevertheless brought them ever closer to the summit. The slowness of their ascent made Oujan's heart beat painfully hard with fear. Every time they changed direction, he saw the Ruskalder advancing, silent now, their swords sheathed and their boots thrumming across the sodden field. Thunder rumbled as if the gods approached as well, interested in seeing how it all worked out. Oujan cursed inwardly. This wasn't a miracle, it was his final mistake, and he was going to get this extraordinary girl killed alongside him.

The road swerved to pass between the trees, which swallowed the two of them up. Oujan heard the mare's labored breathing and cursed aloud. The poor animal wasn't big enough to carry both of them, certainly not at speed. They were going to die sooner rather than later. Oujan urged her on anyway. They were going to have to take him by force. And he intended to kill every one of them if it meant saving the girl.

Then the road broke through the trees into a clearing, and Oujan nearly fell off the horse in astonishment. A great stone turreted castle rose up before him, filling the clearing as if the gods had dropped it there. Men in green and brown rushed toward them, shouting. Oujan brought the mare to a halt just as the first rank of soldiers formed up and brought an array of crossbows to bear on him. "Wait, no—"

"It's all right!" the young woman shouted. "He's with—"

A shout, a wooden clap, and something struck Oujan, knocking him backward. The girl lost her seat and fell, and he turned and made a grab for her even as pain blossomed around the crossbow bolt sticking out of his chest. She screamed, and for the first time, she sounded afraid. Oujan rolled awkwardly out of the saddle and crawled to put himself between her and the soldiers, but his hands weren't responding, and his legs felt numb. He collapsed on his side, breathing heavily and watching the butt end of the bolt rise and fall with his breathing, like it was a part of his body.

The girl was above him—above him? When had he fallen?—and had him by the shoulders. Her lips moved slowly, but no sound emerged, which was sad because he'd come to like her voice. He blinked at her. "Don't let them shoot you," he said, and the Tjorbar River swelled over him, pulling him down into its black, freezing depths.

DAY 2

Oujan woke to the sound of something whistling, a thin, high-pitched sound that came and went like wind blowing over a hollow reed. He drew in a deep breath, and the whistling stopped; let the breath out, and heard a longer, slightly deeper whistle that ended when he ran out of air. He lay flat on his back on a bed whose mattress was softer than he was used to and smelled of lavender. A bed. He couldn't remember how he'd gotten there.

His chest hurt with a sharp ache, and he reached to touch it and discovered his hand—both his hands—were tied to the bed frame. Terror shot through him, and he jerked hard at his bonds and felt them give not at all. His feet were bound as well, as he found when he tried to roll over. No. He'd been captured, and Hrovald—

Oujan made himself lie still, though his heart beat fast enough it made the ache sharper. Whoever had captured him, it wasn't Hrovald's men, because they wouldn't have taken him alive. Or was he wrong, and Hrovald's anger and humiliation were so great he'd ordered Dyrak's last warrior brought back to Ranstjad so he could torture and murder Oujan himself? Oujan closed his eyes and sniffed. The air was still clear and fresh, warmer than summer in

Ruskald, and it smelled of juniper and rainwater. This was Tremontane, not Ruskald.

He wasn't sure that was much better. If he hadn't been captured by Hrovald's men, the only other possibility was that the girl's friends —those green and brown soldiers, whoever they were—had drawn the wrong conclusion about his sudden appearance with her. Which meant he might be in even worse trouble, if she was as important as he was starting to believe she was. Some Tremontanan Count or Baron's daughter? He tried to remember what little he knew of Tremontanan geography. This was Barony Marandis, he thought, but that was all he knew.

He opened his eyes and craned his head. He was naked from the waist up, and his chest was bandaged. The room was small, but clean, with a couple of windows too small for anyone but a child to climb through letting in watery post-storm light. Its walls were painted a light cream, contrasting with the heavy black beams crossing the ceiling. If he stretched his neck, he could see a door across the room from his bed, also of the same black wood.

He relaxed and stared up at the ceiling. They'd tied him up *and* treated his wound? That made no damn sense. Why not just let him die, if they thought he was dangerous enough to be bound? Or, alternatively, why lock him in here if they wanted him to live?

The rasp of the door latch opening made him tense against his bonds again and jerk his head up as far as he could manage. The door swung open, and the girl entered. She wasn't alone. A tall, dark-haired man a few years younger than Oujan followed her in. The girl looked worried. The man's face was so expressionless it made Oujan nervous. Someone that committed to not giving anything away might do...anything. Oujan was painfully aware of his helpless condition, but he kept his own face still. Showing fear might be fatal.

The girl said something in Tremontanese that the young man responded to with an off-handed gesture. To Oujan's surprise, the girl scowled at her companion and said something else that sounded sarcastic. Then she turned to Oujan. "I'm really sorry about this," she said. "Jeffrey is being irrational. I told them you were protecting me, but they didn't believe you weren't a filthy kidnapper."

"Let me go," Oujan said.

"I told them that, too." The girl let out a sound somewhere between a grunt and a snort. It was such a perfect sound of angry derision Oujan almost smiled. "They're 'investigating.' They want to know why you attacked us. You and your warband."

"Those were not my men!"

She made the sound again. "Obviously!" She turned and addressed her companion, flinging up her hands and speaking rapidly. The young man listened, his expression not changing at all. When she wound down, he spoke a few words, gesturing at Oujan. To his astonishment, the girl blushed.

"I forgot we weren't introduced," she said. "My name is Elspeth. This is my brother Jeffrey. What's your name?"

"Oujan," Oujan said.

"Oujan," the girl repeated. "Jeffrey wants to know why you're here, if you didn't intend to kidnap me."

Oujan looked at Jeffrey, whose calm demeanor was starting to grate on him. "Untie me, and we can pretend to be civilized," he said.

"You're not really a captive," Elspeth said. "They tied your hands because you fought the doctor who treated your wound, and they tied your feet because you kicked me."

Oujan's eyes widened. "I...I am so sorry. Did I hurt you?"

"A little. But it's all right, I know you didn't mean to. It just didn't help matters any because they already thought I was your captive." She turned to Jeffrey and spoke at length. When she finished, Jeffrey examined Oujan's face. The young man had the brightest blue eyes Oujan had ever seen. Then Jeffrey drew a belt knife and cut Oujan's hands and feet free. Oujan rubbed his wrists and tried to sit up, but Elspeth put a restraining hand on his shoulder.

"You're still injured," she said, "and it's better you lie still, or so the doctor says. And now I really would like to know who you are and why you were being chased by all those warriors."

Oujan tried to sit up again, felt the sharp ache in his chest increase, and lay back instead. "I should go," he said, and felt stupid —but it was true; his presence here would only bring down more trouble on Elspeth and her impassive brother.

Elspeth laughed as if he'd made a joke. "You're safe at The Junipers," she said. "The soldiers killed five or six of the Ruskalder, and the rest fled. They won't try that again, not if Dyrak wants to maintain the peace."

That made no sense. Oujan wondered if he wasn't still addled from being shot in the chest. "They'll keep coming. You can't protect me forever."

Elspeth sat on the edge of his bed. "Oujan, did you do something to Dyrak? That was a lot of warriors chasing just one man."

Did he do something to Dyrak. Oujan laughed, winced, and touched the bandage. "It's not a short story," he warned her.

Elspeth spoke to Jeffrey, who turned away and returned carrying a chair, which he set nearby and seated himself in. "We like long stories," she said.

Oujan nodded. "Dyrak is dead," he began. "How much do you know about Ruskalder politics?"

Elspeth said something to Jeffrey that included the word "Dyrak." Jeffrey's eyes widened, and he spoke forcefully to Elspeth, who waved his words away. "Jeffrey knows a lot about Ruskalder politics," Elspeth said. "Go on."

With many pauses for Elspeth to translate, Oujan told the whole story. How King Dyrak of Ruskald had been betrayed by his chieftain Hrovald, who had attacked Ranstjad in the night and slaughtered the king and his family. How Oujan, one of Dyrak's elite warriors, had fought until there was no hope left, then fled. He didn't go into detail about how he'd humiliated Hrovald in his flight; he was almost embarrassed about that, and these two Tremontanans didn't need those details. And how Oujan had made his escape southward over the Spine into Tremontane, followed by Hrovald's warriors.

"Tradition is that anyone who fights for the old king is a traitor to the new one," he concluded, "and Hrovald fears if he leaves any of us alive, we will be a rallying point for anyone who wants to challenge him. So he needs me dead."

Elspeth translated this for her brother, who was leaning with his chin propped on one hand, intent on Oujan as if he could understand Ruskeldin. He said something to Elspeth, who said, "Those warriors who ran, they'll tell Hrovald where you are."

Oujan nodded, sending a twinge of pain through his chest. Jeffrey stood and spoke at length. Elspeth began translating before he was finished speaking. "You're not safe, not with that injury," she said, "and Jeffrey apologizes for the misunderstanding that wounded you. He says we owe you my life—"

"How is that?"

"If you'd left me in the forest, and those men had found me..." Elspeth shrugged. "Anyway, it's our fault you're in a weakened condition, and we owe it to you to protect you while you heal. But that means you have to come back with us. We're leaving for Aurilien in a few days, and you're welcome to stay with us until you're healed."

Oujan stared at Elspeth. "That's very kind, but it's unnecessary. I'll be on my way as soon as you give me back my clothes."

"Your clothes are ruined. And that's beside the point." Elspeth leaned forward, her shining blonde hair swinging free past her shoulders. "I don't want you falling into those warriors' hands just because our stupid soldiers overreacted. You won't be well for a long time. Please, Oujan. Let us help you."

Oujan looked past her at Jeffrey, who had sat upright and was tapping his fingers on his thigh as if deep in thought. He said something to Elspeth, who brightened and turned back to face Oujan. "That's a good point! Jeffrey says, if you want to strike at Hrovald— and I think you do—you have a better chance of doing it if you let us help you. Jeffrey's never liked Hrovald, and he says he owes you a debt for revealing that Ruskald has a new king for him to deal with."

"I don't understand. Why would Jeffrey care?"

Elspeth's eyes widened. "Oh, I forgot," she said. "I don't think I said...Oujan, my brother is the King of Tremontane."

A sharp pain that had nothing to do with his injury shot through his chest. Oujan stared at the beautiful girl who had, just like that, become a stranger again. "Then," he managed, "that means you are…"

"Crown Princess Elspeth North," Elspeth said.

Why her words filled him with a sense of loss, he didn't know. "Your Highness—"

"Just Elspeth. Please." Elspeth's cheeks were pink again. "You see why we can protect you?"

Oujan struggled upright and managed to prop himself on his elbows. His breathing became labored and his chest hurt worse. Elspeth was right; he didn't stand a chance on his own. "Hrovald will not be happy if he finds out you've sheltered me," he said. "I don't think you understand how vindictive he is."

Elspeth repeated this to the King, who shrugged and said something that made Elspeth laugh. "He says Hrovald will have enough trouble bringing the rest of the chieftains in line, and it's not as if Tremontane and Ruskald were friends before," she told him. "Don't worry about Tremontane. Just—come south with us. Until you're healed."

Oujan looked from Elspeth to Jeffrey—the King, why hadn't Elspeth mentioned that sooner?—and back again. Elspeth's enormous brown eyes pleaded with him. He wondered how many men she'd turned that look on, and a flash of irrational jealousy shot through him. "I'll come," he said.

Elspeth smiled and put her hand over his. "Lie back and rest. I'll have someone bring food in a bit. We leave for Aurilien in three days."

Oujan nodded and lowered himself back onto the mattress. Jeffrey said something, nodded at Oujan, and left the room. "What was that?" Oujan asked.

"He said 'welcome to Tremontane,'" Elspeth said. "I think he was being funny."

"I can imagine," Oujan said. Some welcome. A crossbow bolt to the chest. Heathen Tremontanans challenging the gods' prohibition against projectile weapons. But it meant he was safe, for now. "Thank you."

"I really am sorry they shot you." Elspeth patted his hand. "Dr. Worthing didn't come with us, or you'd be healed already." Her smile went mischievous. "But that means you're stuck here, and I can't say I'm sorry about that."

She turned and left the room. Oujan stared after her. What did that mean? A rush of warmth spread over his face. He barely knew the girl, and she was treating him like an old friend. She fascinated him more every minute. Fascinated, and... He scowled and closed his eyes. Forget that she was a princess; she was far too young for him, and he had no business being attracted to her. He'd recover eventually, and head farther south, and she would become a pleasant memory. He made himself relax into sleep.

DAY 5

Three days later, he rode beside Elspeth and the King as the procession headed south. His chest still hurt, but he'd pretended to Elspeth he was better than he was, and she hadn't made him ride in the wagon like an invalid. Elspeth chattered like a bird about everything that caught her fancy. But it wasn't idle chatter; she was bright, and clever, and Oujan found himself fascinated all over again by her.

"I'm a student at the University of Kingsport," she told him, "studying languages. I have a knack for them—is my accent all right? None of my instructors are Ruskalder."

"Your accent is perfect," Oujan said. "I would have assumed you were Ruskalder if you hadn't spoken Tremontanese when we met."

She smiled more broadly. "Thank you. Maybe I could teach you my language! I'm sure Jeffrey would like to speak to you. He only speaks Veriboldan in addition to Tremontanese."

The King, riding on Elspeth's other side, turned his head at the sound of his name. Elspeth spoke briefly to him, and he nodded, smiling slightly, and replied.

"Jeffrey says he ought to speak Ruskeldin, since we're so often at odds with your country." Elspeth shrugged. "I think it's ridiculous that we have to fight all the time, though less ridiculous if it's Hrovald who's the King. He—or maybe I shouldn't criticize."

"Hrovald murdered the true King, so criticize away," Oujan said.

"He wanted Ruskald at war with Tremontane, Jeffrey says." Elspeth's lovely face scrunched up in a scowl. "Why would he want that? I've heard that Ruskalder all love war and battle and want to conquer the world, but I don't know if I believe it."

"That's not true. Balderan wants us to honor our battles, and to face challenges head-on. That's not the same as loving war."

"That's what I thought. Is Balderan your god, then? I'm afraid I don't know enough about religion to know the names of the lost gods. I realize your beliefs are different from mine."

"Balderan is one of the Three. I suppose you don't believe in anything, if you think the gods are lost."

Elspeth shook her head. They'd come out of the forest and were crossing the wide plains, and insects chirred and leaped around their horses' hooves. "We believe in ungoverned heaven binding our families. No one knows what happened to the gods, why they left, or were taken, but that doesn't mean we don't respect their memory."

The conversation made Oujan uncomfortable. He'd worshipped the Three his whole life, but in a casual, off-handed way, and Elspeth sounded as if her beliefs were more grounded than his. "That seems so strange. I'm sure my religion is as strange to you."

"I have friends who study history, and religious history is part of that. They say we have more in common than we realize." Elspeth looked more closely at him. "Your eyes are glassy, and you're sitting awfully still. Are you sure you're well?"

He wasn't feeling well, but he didn't think he would fall off his borrowed horse. "Well enough for this."

"You'd better be honest with me. There's no shame in riding in the wagon."

Oujan would rather cling to this horse than ride in the wagon. "I know. I'm fine."

Elspeth said something in Tremontanese. "That means, 'I am too stubborn for my own good.' Here, now you say it."

Oujan laughed and repeated the syllables. The King twitched, then burst out laughing. He said something, smiling wryly, and Elspeth said, "Jeffrey says he understands stubbornness because he's lived with me for seventeen years. I think that's rude, don't you?"

"You're seventeen?" She was older than he'd thought, though not by much. He quashed the irrational hope that rose up inside him. That still made her ten years younger than him. And she was still a princess.

Elspeth nodded. "I know, I look young for my age. I hate it. People are always underestimating me, or treating me like a child."

"I promise not to do that." Promise, where did that come from? He was leaving in a few days; what he said or did wouldn't matter.

Elspeth smiled more brightly. "You never have. It's why I like you."

"You barely know me." The irrational hope was harder to ignore when she looked at him that way.

"I don't think it takes long to decide if someone will be your friend. Now, let's continue."

"Continue? With what?"

"Language lessons. Jeffrey wants to be your friend, too."

Oujan looked at the King, who was watching their conversation curiously. Friends with a King. He wanted to laugh at the strange turn his life had taken. Instead, he said, "All right. How do you say 'Thank you' in Tremontanese?"

DAY 26

Elspeth pointed at the fountain spraying water ten feet in the air. "That?"

"Fountain," Oujan said in Tremontanese.

She pointed at a rosebush. "That?"

"Flower. Or rose."

"And what's beyond that?"

"Wall."

They were sitting on a bench in the royal family's private garden, practicing Oujan's Tremontanese vocabulary. In three weeks he'd gone from barely being able to say "please" and "thank you" and "how do you say" to being able to carry on a halting conversation in a foreign language. Elspeth hadn't acted surprised, just said, "Being immersed in a language, surrounded by people who don't ever speak yours, makes learning that language much faster. And you have a knack for languages, too."

Now he said, "Not I know what is...I say, this." He pointed at the soft green grass, cut to an even lawn that looked like velvet.

"Grass. Or lawn." Elspeth leaned back and closed her eyes. "It's such a beautiful day. I hope Jeffrey is free for dinner. He's always so busy."

"He is good King, I think." To Oujan's surprise, once he'd started learning the language, he'd discovered he and the King had much in common—a love of hunting, an interest in politics, a fondness for historical epics. And Jeffrey was good at making people feel comfortable around him—when he chose. Oujan had seen him formal and distant, and had seen him unbend, and wished he dared ask Jeffrey what made the difference. They were friends, he thought, but there were things Jeffrey made clear were off-limits.

"He is. He never expected to be King, so I'm not sure he realizes how good he is yet. He doesn't like to talk about himself—but you know that."

Oujan nodded, though she wasn't looking at him. "Why do he say Owen and not Oujan?"

Elspeth opened one eye and squinted at him. "Owen is Oujan in Tremontanese. Like Hrovald is Harold. There are name equivalents of all sorts throughout all the languages we know. In Eskandelic, for example, Oujan is Uvan. And your surname...I know the Ruskalder use occupations for surnames. What would you call yourself?"

"All the warriors of the king are Hjagar." Saying the word in his own language felt odd, after speaking Tremontanese for so long.

"Hjagar. Pursuer...no, hunter. Owen Hunter." Elspeth smoothed her hair behind her ears, a restless gesture. "It's such an odd notion. I don't know why the names change. My teachers say it's a reflection of how all our languages have a common ancestor. Don't you think it's interesting to imagine everyone speaking the same language once?"

"I think I am Owen—it is to say, I like..." He struggled to find words to express himself, and switched to Ruskeldin. "I feel as if I've left Ruskald behind. That I could be condemned for fighting for Dyrak, for doing what I was sworn to do...it's a betrayal of me, in a way, and I feel as if my own country is alien now."

Elspeth sat up. "So, does that mean you want to stay in Tremontane?"

Owen shrugged. Her eyes were uncomfortably intent on him. "I don't know. I just know I wouldn't want to return to Ruskald even if Hrovald dropped dead tomorrow."

Elspeth moved closer to him. "I want you to stay," she said. "Jeffrey wants you to stay. We don't have many friends like you."

With an awkward laugh, Owen said in Tremontanese, "You to have friends, being King and Princess. I am just one man."

Elspeth shook her head, not drawn by his levity. "Everyone's always so...*respectful*. They always know we're royalty, and that keeps them at a distance. You...it's like we've known you all our lives, and you've just returned after a long absence."

Her words stunned him. She was right. He never thought of them as anything but Jeffrey and Elspeth, and whenever he considered moving on, it was with a sense of terrible loss, as if he'd be giving up his family all over again.

He looked at her, sitting very close now, her head tilted to face him and her long blonde hair shining in the sun, and his breath caught. He was a fool. She thought of him as a friend, and he...damn it, she was completely off limits, and would have been even if he hadn't become so close to her and her brother. What a betrayal of their friendship.

"So, you'll stay, yes?" Elspeth was saying, and he wrenched himself back to the present and smiled in what he hoped was a friendly, non-romantic way.

"You to ask so nice, I cannot say no," he said.

"Good," Elspeth said, and kissed him.

A rush of passion swept over him, and without thinking twice, he drew her into his arms and returned her kiss. It was better than he'd dared dream, holding her and kissing her and feeling her respond as if she, too, had been waiting for this moment. The realization was like a slap to the face, bringing him back to himself. He disentangled himself from her and said, "Elspeth, no."

Her lips were still curved in anticipation of his kiss, and the sight inflamed him further, but he scooted back and took hold of her hands to stop her touching him. "This is wrong," he said. "You know and I know it is wrong."

"Why is it wrong? Because you're not Tremontanan? Or because you're not noble?" Elspeth glared at him. "None of that matters."

He switched to Ruskeldin. "Because I'm ten years older than you. You're just starting out in life, Elspeth—"

Her glare intensified. "You said you'd never treat me like a child. I'm an adult by both our countries' standards, Owen. And I know what I want."

"Well, it's not what I want," he lied.

Elspeth recoiled, and the hurt in her expression made him again feel as if he'd been slapped. "But you kissed me," she said. "I thought..."

"I reacted as any man would." Owen released her hands and stood. "Elspeth, it's impossible. I'm sorry. This is just...I'm just an interesting stranger, that's all, and what you feel will pass—"

She rose to her feet in one swift movement and struck him hard across the face. The sound of the slap cut across the burble of the fountain. "Don't you *dare* tell me how I feel," she snarled. "I'm not some starry-eyed waif who falls in love with every mysterious stranger who crosses her path. I love you, Owen, and I think you care about me more than a little. And I don't...I don't give a damn about anything else."

Owen drew in a deep breath and let it out slowly. "I don't feel the same. I'm sorry." His heart ached as if he'd once again been shot, but he kept his face impassive. He would be the worst of friends if he took advantage of her youth and inexperience, no matter how his heart cried out for her.

"You're lying," Elspeth said flatly.

He shrugged. "Believe what you want. I think I should go."

Her anger faded, replaced by uncertainty. "Go...where?"

Anywhere would be better than here, looking at her. "I don't know. Eskandel. I can't stay here."

"Owen, you don't have to leave."

She was so beautiful. And she loved him. It was more than he could bear. "Thank you for your hospitality," he said, resorting to formality, "but I shouldn't impose any longer." He turned and walked away, heading for the garden door. She didn't follow him.

Inside, he climbed the many steps to the east wing, where the royal family lived and where he'd stayed the last three weeks. Cursing himself, he went to his room and sat heavily on the sofa in the sitting room. Most of the east wing rooms were the same, Jeffrey had explained—little groupings of sitting room, bedroom, dressing room, and bath. It was more luxury than Owen had ever had even in the king's house in Ranstjad, more luxury than he'd seen in his whole life. And he'd have traded it all away to be able to hold Elspeth again and tell her how much he loved her.

It was simply impossible. Age, rank, nationality were all against them. He would be taking advantage of her if he gave in to his feelings, and he couldn't bear to treat her that way. So he had to leave. Maybe he didn't have to go as far as Eskandel...no, remaining in Tremontane would be too painful so long as it meant he was anywhere near Elspeth.

He rose, feeling like an old man, and went into his dressing room. He had clothes—Jeffrey had pressed money on him, saying, "It's nothing much, and you can hardly go around half-naked. What would the servants think?—and he thought about leaving them behind, but that was a stupid, juvenile gesture, a rejection of their friendship. He emptied his rucksack that he'd carried with him all the way from Ruskald and began packing. What could he do in Eskandel? He'd figure some way to support himself.

He fastened the straps and shouldered the bag, taking one last look around the bedroom. It had started to feel like home. He shuddered and turned away.

When he pushed open the door to the sitting room, Jeffrey was there, sitting on the sofa with his arms extended across its back and one ankle crossed over his opposite knee, the picture of a young man at his ease. "You were going to leave without saying goodbye?" he said, arching one dark eyebrow.

"No," Owen said automatically. "It is to say...no, I give—say goodbye. I leave now."

Jeffrey lowered his arms and sat forward. "Why are you leaving?"

Had he spoken to Elspeth, or not? Owen didn't know what to say. He settled on, "I am heal, I am well, I do not stay longer. It is danger."

"Not for me. For you, certainly, if you leave Aurilien. Unless you think Hrovald has given up searching for you?" Jeffrey tilted his head to look up at Owen. "But that's not the reason, is it? Owen—"

He thought about protesting that Elspeth had kissed him first, realized that was a dishonorable response, and said, "I do not belong."

Jeffrey's face went still, closed-off the way it did when he was suppressing a strong emotion. "Owen," he said, "you're my friend. I... it's probably stupid and sentimental to say this, but I think you're the best friend I have. That means you belong here. I don't—" He turned his head away, looking at the bare fireplace. "But I won't make you stay if you really feel you shouldn't."

Owen looked down at Jeffrey, wondering how much it had cost his proud, self-sufficient friend to say that. He dropped his rucksack and sat on the chair opposite Jeffrey. "Do Elspeth say to you what happens?"

Jeffrey glanced his way. "She just said you insisted on leaving. But I can tell when she's hiding something. You fought, didn't you?"

Owen shrugged. Fighting had been part of it, yes, and he didn't want to tell Elspeth's brother that he'd fallen hopelessly in love with her. "It does not matter."

Jeffrey raised an eyebrow again. "Whatever passed between you,

you can make it right. Owen, if you go...look, just don't go, all right? I don't have so many friends that I can afford to lose one of them. Even if he is a proud and bloodthirsty Ruskalder warrior."

"I do not know what is bloodthirsty. You mean I drink blood?" Owen made a face.

Jeffrey laughed. "It's just an expression. And a joke. You are the least bloodthirsty man I've ever known." He rose from his seat. "Stay for supper at least. Talk to Elspeth. Whatever happened, I'm sure she doesn't want you to leave."

A hundred protests rose up in Owen's chest. Jeffrey walked to the door and paused with his hand on the frame, not looking back. "And, Owen," he said. "If you're afraid I'll be angry that you've fallen in love with Elspeth, don't be. I'd rather you than any of the nobles of Tremontane." He left, shutting the door quietly behind him.

Owen sagged back against the sofa and closed his eyes. So it was obvious, was it? He had to admit it was a relief that Jeffrey didn't hate him, because if he was honest with himself, Jeffrey was the best friend he'd ever had, too. But Jeffrey's approval didn't change anything. He was still an unsuitable lover for a Princess of Tremontane, and he really ought to leave before things became any more awkward.

But he didn't want to.

Setting aside the fact that the thought of leaving Elspeth made his heart contract painfully, he didn't want to lose Jeffrey's friendship. He also wasn't keen on the idea of putting himself within reach of Hrovald's warriors again, though he wasn't so much of a coward that he'd hide in the palace for the rest of his life. So the question was, could he stay here, seeing Elspeth every day and treating her with casual friendliness?

He let out a deep breath. Elspeth's attraction to him had to be a passing thing. He wasn't handsome, didn't have a title or a fortune, and this was just because they'd met in such a spectacular fashion. If he stayed, if he went on treating her like nothing more than a friend, she'd eventually lose interest, and they could go on as they had begun. He could endure that if it meant not losing what he'd begun thinking of as home.

He stood and carried his rucksack back to the dressing room and returned his clothes to the wardrobe. He'd give it three days. If being near Elspeth was impossible, he'd know by the end of that time and he could make a different decision then. And if not... He paused with his hand on the wardrobe door. Home. It wasn't such a strange idea, after all.

Day 72

Owen leaned his wooden practice swords against the rack and wiped sweat from his forehead. His recent opponent did the same. "That Ruskalder two-weapon style is tough to defend against," the man said. "Thanks for the lesson."

"You do well," Owen said, nodding. He'd been surprised at how readily the Tremontanan soldiers stationed at the palace had accepted him. It was tempting to imagine Jeffrey making it a royal command—be nice to the King's friend, even if he is a filthy Ruskalder—but he guessed it was just that Tremontanans saw things differently. No Ruskalder would admit to weakness, even in the form of not knowing a particular fighting style; no Ruskalder would approach a practice bout as anything but a serious battle. But these Tremontanans worked together with no sign of jealousy or pride, one soldier showing another a move that had defeated the second, individuals breaking down a battle strategy for a small group, none of them afraid of having their knowledge turned against them. It was so different from Ruskald.

He stood and watched the practice field for a few minutes, admiring how well the Tremontanan soldiers drilled together. That was another thing Ruskalder didn't do; in battle, it was every man for himself. Owen could see benefits and drawbacks to each approach. Maybe he should suggest some things to George Donaldson, who had the charge of the palace soldiers. Donaldson always gave him skeptical looks when he came to the practice field, but he looked that way at every new soldier, so Owen didn't think it was personal.

After a while, growing bored, he returned to the east wing, where he bathed and changed his clothes. It was still a few hours until supper, so he thought he might go to the Library and make progress on his reading. Jeffrey and Elspeth's mother, Alison North, had been teaching him over the past month and a half, and the reading had improved his Tremontanese considerably.

When he passed through the east wing drawing room, with its many comfortable sofas and the giant fireplace of river stones, unlit at this season, Elspeth looked up from where she sat. The sight of her made his heart beat faster. He gave her a pleasant smile that concealed his emotions and said, "I am going to the Library, what is it you do?"

She eyed him for a moment before staring back into the empty fireplace. "I was going to a party, but I changed my mind."

"Oh? It is not a good party?"

She shrugged. "I don't know. I'm just not in the mood to socialize." She rose and stretched. She wasn't dressed for a party, wore trousers and a loose green shirt, but she was beautiful whatever she wore. "Do you mind if I go to the Library with you?"

Owen's heartbeat sped up even faster. "Of course I do not mind. You will choose for me a new book."

"I'm sure Mother can do that." But she followed him out of the east wing anyway.

They walked together, side by side, down the varied corridors of the palace. Owen never had any trouble finding his way around, what with how different the halls were. They were as good a beacon as if they'd had directions written on the walls. He wanted to ask Elspeth, as he often did, why the palace construction was so erratic, but despite her superficial friendliness, the closeness they'd once had was gone.

He'd done his best. He'd treated her like a sister and hoped she would take the hint. But they'd never regained the friendship they'd had before the day she had kissed him. And no matter what he did or said, his feelings for her hadn't changed. He still loved her.

He glanced furtively at her, at the curve of her profile, at her slightly furrowed eyebrows that said she was thinking about something, and wished he could kiss her. But no, even if all the other objections were swept away, she was no doubt angry that he'd rejected her, and he had no hope at all. He told himself it was for the best, but he was having trouble believing it.

They crossed the Rotunda, a vast empty space with a tiled floor that rose several stories to a domed roof. The roof was painted with scenes from some past King's life, someone who'd been powerful, to judge by the many deeds depicted. Owen suspected they were fictional. No one was that amazing.

Elspeth stopped, and Owen went on a few steps before realizing she wasn't with him. "Is something wrong?" he asked.

"It's the Ruskalder ambassador, Jafvran," Elspeth said in a low voice. "I think he's seen you."

A jolt of fear went through Owen before he reminded himself Jafvran was no danger to him. He looked in the direction Elspeth faced and saw a white-haired Ruskalder man staring back at him. He was surrounded by warriors, and as Owen watched, Jafvran muttered something to them. Every one of the warriors came to attention and strode in Owen's direction.

Owen put Elspeth behind him. He was unarmed, but he wasn't helpless, and if those warriors wanted a fight, he would give it to them.

"Owen, stop," Elspeth said, sounding like herself for once. She stepped out from behind him. Exasperated, Owen grabbed her arm and once more put her where he could protect her.

The warriors, all eight of them, circled Owen and Elspeth. "Traitor," one of them said in Ruskeldin. "And coward. You hide in the Tremontanan King's palace like a rat cowering from the hawk. You should face us in battle and win an honorable death."

"If I'm a traitor, I can hardly have an honorable death, can I?" Owen said. He kept his voice calm and his hand on Elspeth's arm.

The warrior sneered. "Death in battle restores all honor."

"But a life well lived is better than honorable death." Owen stepped forward, putting himself nose to nose with the warrior.

He saw the man's eyes shift, realized the warrior was looking at something past his shoulder, and then Elspeth screamed his name, wrenching away from his grip. He whirled around in time to see another warrior's short sword plunge into Elspeth's stomach as she moved to intercept the blow meant for Owen.

Owen's vision went red. He threw himself at the soldier who'd struck Elspeth, bearing him to the ground beneath his weight. With his left hand, he grabbed the warrior's long hair and slammed his head to crack sickeningly against the hard tile floor of the Rotunda. With his right, he went for the warrior's longsword, drawing it from its sheath. He leaped to his feet and plunged the sword into the man's body until it struck tile, down and then up toward the warrior's breastbone.

He tore the sword free and attacked the next closest warrior, whose sword was half-drawn. With a snarl, he drove the longsword deep into the warrior's belly and twisted, taking fierce pleasure in the man's scream of agony. He shoved the man off his blade to fall atop his comrade's bloody body and turned to face his next opponent. The red haze across his vision had faded. Everything was sharp-edged and clear and moving as slowly as everything always did when he was in a battle rage.

The other warriors closed in, but Owen was past caring. He thrust, slashed, darted back and found another target. Distantly, he was aware of shouting, but this was battle, and paying attention to anything that wasn't right in front of you meant death. He gutted another warrior, disarmed him of his short sword, and used both his stolen weapons to drive back someone who dared try the same tactic on him.

Then the warriors were gone, fallen or retreated, he wasn't sure which, and he lowered his bloody swords and tried to catch his breath. The shouting had gotten louder, and he shook sweat from his eyes and focused on what was nearest: Jafvran, screaming at his warriors to retreat to protect him; soldiers in Tremontane colors, approaching Owen warily; Jeffrey, a few feet away and shouting things Owen couldn't understand; and several bodies lying sprawled around him. One of them was much smaller than the others.

Elspeth.

Owen flung the swords away and knelt beside her. Blood spread from beneath her hands, which clutched her stomach. She was paler than usual and her eyes were closed. "Elspeth," Owen said. He tried to lift her hands so he could see the wound more clearly, but she shook her head, making it flop slowly from side to side, and clutched herself more tightly.

Her lips moved, but he couldn't hear her. "What?" he said in Ruskeldin, leaning close to put his ear nearly to her mouth.

There was blood on her lips. "...watch...your back..." she whispered.

He felt as if the sword had stabbed him, after all. "Elspeth," he said hoarsely. "You idiot."

She smiled, and lay still.

"Elspeth!" he screamed. He grabbed her by the shoulders and clutched her to him. He was aware of someone kneeling beside him —Jeffrey, with his hand on Owen's shoulder, shouting at him. His grasp of Tremontanese deserted him, and Jeffrey's words washed unintelligibly over him. Then Jeffrey punched him in the face.

Owen jerked back, his grip on Elspeth's body loosening. He stared at Jeffrey, stunned by the blow. Jeffrey grabbed his shoulder again. "Dr. Worthing is coming," he shouted. "It's not too late. What happened?"

Not too late. Owen realized the body he held was still breathing, though the movement of Elspeth's chest was so slight it was no wonder he'd missed it. "She saved my life," he said in Ruskeldin, then repeated the words in Tremontanese when Jeffrey looked confused. "It was—" He looked past Jeffrey at where Jafvran had stood. The Ruskalder were gone. "The Ruskalder ambassador, he ask his men to kill me. Elspeth is in the way."

Jeffrey's lips tightened in fury. "He'll pay for this." He touched

Elspeth's shoulder. "Accident or no, that's an assault on the heir to the Crown. That is the end of our diplomatic relationship with Ruskald. And if I could justify hanging him and every one of his warriors, I would."

Owen barely heard him. All his attention was on Elspeth. She was so small and so still... His eyes burned with tears that wouldn't fall. "It does not help her," he pointed out, though he still felt deep satisfaction at having killed the man who'd hurt her.

Jeffrey looked away. "I know."

The Rotunda was crowded with people, soldiers in green and brown, servants in North blue and silver, men and women in varying degrees of formal wear, all of them surrounding Owen and Jeffrey and Elspeth and murmuring words Owen couldn't make out. Five Ruskalder soldiers lay dead around him. He didn't remember killing that many. Maybe the murmuring was fear of him. Good. Fear meant no one was likely to attack him again, for Elspeth to get in the way—

Someone pushed through the crowd and went to his knees beside Owen. "Excuse me," Dr. Worthing said, putting his arms around Elspeth. Owen fought him for half a breath before coming to his senses and releasing her. Dr. Worthing laid her gently on the floor and took her hands in both of his. He bowed his head, and the entire Rotunda went still.

Owen watched, though there was nothing to see. Elspeth didn't seem to be breathing. He reminded himself that Dr. Worthing was a competent healer, possessed of the *cadhaen-rach*, inherent magic. The doctor had healed Owen's wound when they arrived in Aurilien, leaving him feeling as if the injury were six months in the past. He knew what the doctor could do. But he didn't think Dr. Worthing could raise someone from the dead. And Elspeth looked dead.

He closed his eyes and prayed, not to Balderan, but to ungoverned heaven. It felt fitting that he address his prayers to what Elspeth believed in, even though he felt stupid about praying to a place instead of the gods. *Don't take her*, he begged. *I can't bear it.*

He heard Dr. Worthing shift position, and he closed his eyes tighter. If Elspeth was dead, he didn't want to know about it until he had no choice. Then Dr. Worthing stood, and Owen couldn't take the suspense. He opened his eyes.

Elspeth still lay there, perfectly still, but her chest was rising and falling naturally and she looked, not dead, but asleep. Jeffrey had stood as well and was talking quietly to the doctor. Owen took one of Elspeth's hands, sticky with blood, and gripped it tightly. For a moment, her fingers moved, clutching his, and then they relaxed.

He saw movement out of the corner of his eye and realized Jeffrey was crouched beside him. "She's lost so much blood," Jeffrey said, "but the doctor says she will recover. I've called for someone to take her to her rooms—"

"No," Owen said, and took Elspeth in his arms. "It is for me to do. She saved my life."

Jeffrey nodded. They both stood, and Owen surveyed the crowd surrounding them. Everyone looked afraid, though he couldn't tell if it was fear of him or fear for their Princess's life. It didn't matter. She was alive.

He carried her through the halls, feeling like a man in a dream that stank of blood and sweat. He and Jeffrey started to gain a following about halfway to the east wing. By the time they were there, it was a following of twenty people, all of them silently intent on Elspeth. Owen laid her on her bed and stood there, looking at her, until a short, round woman with a fierce expression shooed him and Jeffrey away. "She doesn't need men staring at her while we get her cleaned up," the woman said. Owen came to his senses and went back to the east wing drawing room.

He sat on the hearth and stared at his hands, streaked with blood. Jeffrey took a seat nearby and said, "Can you tell me what happened?"

Owen nodded. He heard himself tell Jeffrey everything, from seeing Jafvran to the horrible wrenching agony of watching that warrior stab Elspeth. "He mean—meant to kill me in the back," he said. "Elspeth saw it and put herself in my way. She is stupid."

"It was a damn fool thing to do," Jeffrey agreed. "But typical of her. She's impulsive where her...her friends are concerned."

Owen's mind was still with Elspeth, lying motionless in her bed. "I cannot stay," he said.

"You have somewhere else to be? Owen, this had better not be about you going after Jafvran and the rest of those warriors. I can't let you enact vigilante justice on their bodies."

Owen didn't know what "vigilante" meant, but he could guess at Jeffrey's meaning. "I bring this on you," he tried to explain. "On Elspeth. She does not die if I am not here."

Jeffrey swore explosively. "Don't you dare think that way," he said. "It's not your fault Jafvran saw you, it's not your fault he let his warriors attack you, and it's definitely not your fault Elspeth thought you were worth saving. All of this is on Hrovald, ultimately. And how do you think Elspeth will feel if she wakes up and you're gone?"

He hadn't thought of that. "Relieved?" he ventured.

Jeffrey laughed. "She would hunt you down and give you a tongue-lashing the likes of which no one's ever seen before. Besides, I don't think you want to go."

Owen shook his head. If he left, his last memory of Elspeth would be of her still, bloody body. "I will stay."

"Good." Jeffrey stood. "Go get cleaned up. I'm going to find out where Jafvran went. Did you kill the man who stabbed Elspeth?"

Owen nodded.

"Then I won't have to demand he be handed over to face our justice. That would be tricky, diplomatically. But I won't be surprised to learn Jafvran is already on his way back to Ruskald. I'll have to send a letter formalizing his expulsion...damn, but I wish I could kick him all the way back to Hrovald, then kick Hrovald."

Owen watched Jeffrey walk away. He felt numb inside, his thoughts sluggish. Get cleaned up. He could manage that.

He took his second bath of the day and dressed in clean, unstained clothes, then lit a fire in his sitting room and burned the clothes with Elspeth's blood on them. Then he lay on his bed and let his thoughts drift. She would recover. Everything could go back to how it had been...

...but it really couldn't. Holding Elspeth's lifeless body close to his heart had been a revelation. He'd lied to himself for so many weeks, convinced himself that age and rank and nationality mattered more than what he felt. Maybe it was wrong of him to love her; maybe he was taking advantage of her youth and inexperience. He didn't care. He loved Elspeth North.

He drifted off to sleep, wearied from the fight and the emotional distress, and woke to find the room in near-darkness. In the next moment, he shot to his feet, startled to find someone seated on the bed beside him. "I'm sorry," Elspeth said in Ruskeldin. "I should have thought how you'd react."

His heart, which had lurched in fear, sped up until he could hear his pulse thrumming through his ears. "What are you doing here?"

Elspeth shifted. She was wearing a white nightdress, and that and her fair hair were all he could see of her in the dimness. "I was afraid you would leave. I know you must blame yourself for what happened."

Owen sat on the edge of the bed, half-turned to face her. "What were you thinking, putting yourself in the way of that sword? Elspeth, I can take care of myself."

She shrugged. "I saw him aim the blade at your back, and it infuriated me that he would make such a cowardly attack. And then I stepped into its path. I really didn't think it through."

"No, you didn't. Swear you'll never do anything so foolish again."

There was silence for a few moments. Then Elspeth said, "I don't think I can promise that. Not if it means letting you get hurt."

Owen's breath caught. "You think I give a damn about my safety?" he demanded. "That I wouldn't give my life to see you protected from all harm? Elspeth, I don't—you can't think like that."

To his surprise, she laughed. He couldn't remember the last time he'd heard her laugh. "Owen," she said, "listen to us. Fighting over who gets to sacrifice for the other."

He had to laugh in turn. "I win," he said, "because I am bigger and stronger, and you will just have to sit by and let me give my life for you."

"I don't know if I could bear that," Elspeth said. "You're not leaving, right?"

He sighed. "I should. But Jeffrey convinced me I had a duty."

He heard her take a sharp breath. "Duty? Is that all?" She sounded angry, and hurt, and his heart ached as if she'd stabbed him.

"No," he said. "It's not."

Elspeth went silent.

Owen closed his eyes. "I'm sorry," he said. "I'm too old, or you're too young, and I have no business taking advantage of you—no, let me finish," he said when he heard her draw in another breath to protest. "It's not right, you and I, it doesn't make any sense. I am no one a Princess of Tremontane should even consider falling in love with. And yet I am drawn to you, over and over again, no matter what's right or wrong. I love you. I never want to leave you. So, please, tell me to go and never return, because I can't bring myself to do it."

Silence fell between them, still and dense and cold. Then he heard her shift, rustling the bedclothes, until he felt the heat of her body next to him. He didn't open his eyes. He couldn't bear to look at her.

A small hand took his, warm fingers curling around his cold ones. Elspeth put her head on his shoulder. "So what you're saying," she said, "is that you will only go if I tell you to."

Owen nodded.

"Which means, if I tell you to stay, you'd have to do that instead."

He nodded again.

Her other hand rested atop their joined ones. "Stay with me," she whispered. "I love you. Stay with me."

His heart felt as if it might overflow with joy. "Elspeth," he said, and she lifted her head and kissed him. He put his arms around her and kissed her in return, pulling her close so he could feel her body against him, her warm, living body that fit itself so perfectly to his. Elspeth moved then, shifting so she was sitting on his lap, and he shivered with pleasure and ran his hands down her sides to the small of her back.

She put her hands on his shoulders and pushed, gently. "Lie down," she whispered between kisses.

The thought of lying with her, of taking off her nightgown and feeling her skin against his, nearly drove him mad with desire. With his last scrap of self-control, he took hold of her wrists and said, "We can't do that."

She moved from kissing his lips to kissing his cheek, which he suddenly realized was scratchy with beard growth because he'd forgotten to shave that morning. "I just want to lie next to you," she said.

He hadn't really understood what an innocent she was in some ways until that moment. "We wouldn't stop at that," he assured her, and kissed her one last time.

"Oh," Elspeth said. He thought she sounded embarrassed. So he put his arms around her again and held her close, this time thinking only of how glad he was that she was alive and that she loved him.

"There's nothing wrong with wanting more than kisses," he said, "but in my country, a man does a woman honor by waiting to share that intimacy until after they're married."

Elspeth drew in a sharp breath. "Is that a proposal?"

He'd meant only to reassure her that her desires were normal, and her question caught him off-guard. "It...I..."

"I'm sorry, that was presumptuous of me," Elspeth said. "I should have said, Owen Hunter, will you marry me? I'll understand if it's too sudden."

Happiness threatened to carry him away. "I didn't know women were allowed to propose marriage," he teased.

"This is Tremontane. Women can do all sorts of things."

He tightened his arms around her. "I would love nothing better than to marry you, Elspeth."

She sighed with pleasure. "That's fortunate, because I would have felt very foolish if I'd misunderstood your intentions."

His intentions were rapidly becoming physical again. "I will walk you back to your room, and we will say goodnight, and in the morning we will plan to be married. I suppose that requires a lot of preparation?"

"Yes. I'm sorry. Can you bear to wait until Wintersmeet? The solstice? There are so many things to do, and I'm supposed to visit a friend in Veribold in a month or so—I'd rather get all those things out of the way, so we can be married with no other demands on our time."

The solstice was two and a half months away. An eternity. "I can wait that long."

Elspeth laughed, a sound that thrilled through him. She slipped her hand into his. "Just a few months," she said. "I suppose, technically, you should ask Jeffrey's permission to marry me. He won't say no. He knows what I'd do to him if he did."

"He already said yes, weeks ago. At least, he said he'd rather I loved you than that any of the nobles of Tremontane did."

Elspeth squealed and swatted Owen's chest. "Giving me away like I was a prize!"

Owen smiled and kissed her one last time, slow and sweet. "The implication was that I was your prize, love."

"Oh. In that case, I don't mind." She rested her head briefly on his shoulder. "I love you, Owen. Promise you won't leave me."

He drew her beneath his arm. "I will never leave you," he said. "And I swear to protect you from all harm."

Day 239

Owen's horse didn't seem to mind that he'd demanded it carry two people. Though Elspeth was so small and light, he wasn't sure the horse even noticed her weight. She felt like a bundle of bones in his arms, more fragile than he'd ever known her, and he was almost afraid to hold her close, in case those bones snapped.

They hadn't spoken all day, all through the long ride, except when they stopped to eat. Owen didn't like the dark circles under her eyes, like she was already exhausted, but the war camp hadn't had a carriage, and riding was the only option that would get Elspeth back to Aurilien before battle was joined. He intended to buy or borrow a carriage somewhere when they stopped for the night. He would do anything if it meant protecting his love.

Ahead, faint smoky pillars against the blue early spring sky indicated a town. According to the map he'd consulted before leaving this morning, it should be Carlsford, abutting the Snow River they rode beside. Carlsford was much bigger than the village where they'd had dinner, big enough for a good inn with good rooms. Elspeth had endured the rough journey, fleeing Ranstjad and Hrovald's soldiers, without complaint, but Owen was sure she was on the brink of collapse. A night in a real bed was what she needed.

Inwardly, he cursed himself again. He should have ignored Jeffrey's stupid, cautious assessment of the situation and gone north to rescue Elspeth the instant they knew where she was. If he'd retrieved her immediately, she wouldn't have been exposed to lung fever with such disastrous results. And that bastard Hesketh wouldn't have—

He still couldn't believe it. Sweet, compassionate Elspeth, befriending Hrovald's sniveling son and having that "friendship" turned on her in such a terrible, violent manner. She was too small to fight back, too small to stop him, and Hesketh had raped her. Owen remembered getting his hands around Hesketh's throat and the feeling of bone snapping. It had eased his heart at the time, but now the memory was cold and empty. Killing Hesketh hadn't changed things for Elspeth. It hadn't undone the past. Owen had never faced anything he couldn't fight until now.

Elspeth stirred in his arms. "Is that Carlsford?"

"It is," he said in Ruskeldin, too tired to use his still-halting Tremontanese. "How do you feel? Are you in pain? It looks to be only another mile or so away."

"I'm just tired. And hungry. But I'm always hungry." Elspeth shifted her weight to sit up straighter. "Are *you* all right? You've been so quiet."

"Just...thinking. About the journey. Making plans." He didn't want to tell her his main preoccupation was wondering if she would ever again be the carefree, laughing young woman he'd fallen in love with. He feared she would take that as a criticism, or worse, believe he'd only loved her until she was attacked. He'd known men like that, obsessed with women's virginity and convinced a woman who'd been raped was somehow impure. As if a woman's character and strength were kept between her legs. How ridiculous.

No, what worried him was the possibility that what had happened to her would go on hurting her for the rest of her life. That wasn't something he could do anything about. He didn't even know what was expected in a situation like this. Should she talk about it? Pretend it hadn't happened? They were married now; was she ready for sex with him? He certainly wasn't going to demand it of her, had told her that when he asked her to let Jeffrey marry them, but he didn't know if he should do anything to encourage her, or never bring it up, or...

His confused, angry thoughts carried them all the way into Carlsford, which was too big to be called a town and too small to be a city. Owen was used to Aurilien, which was old and showed the signs of different architectural styles over the centuries in its varied buildings. Carlsford looked much newer, with none of the wattle-and-daub construction common to the poorer parts of Aurilien. Its buildings were mostly of small red or gray bricks decorating flat façades rather than leaning out over the streets to take advantage of the space, with plenty of large, multi-paned glass windows that reflected the last sunlight with a ruddy glow. The result was warm and welcoming, and Owen's heart lifted. They would figure this all out together.

He bypassed the first two inns they came to, judging them not large enough to provide the right amount of comfort. The third was large enough, but bustling to the point he suspected there weren't many rooms left. Taking a side street, he finally came to an inn three stories tall, with a large stable yard and Device lights flanking the doorposts. Gratefully, he steered the horse through the gate and helped Elspeth down. She staggered when her feet touched earth, and he put a hand on her elbow to steady her. "Sorry," he said.

"I'm fine. I'm just shaky." Elspeth stepped away from his supportive hand, making him feel cold and lost again.

Owen turned the horse over to one of the stable hands. Too late, he saw the stalls were almost entirely occupied. The inn was busier than he'd thought. But Elspeth shivered, and he decided it was a bad idea to move on looking for something better.

The inn turned out to be even more modern than the town, with the front door opening not on the taproom, but on a narrow, high-ceilinged room with a tall counter in front of a staircase wide enough to let four people walk side by side. An elderly woman sat behind the counter. She looked more like a shop assistant than an innkeeper, with her white wraparound apron and her tightly pinned hair, but she gave Owen and Elspeth a pleasant smile and said, "Welcome to the Bradbury Inn. How can I help you?"

"My wife and I wish a room for the night, and supper," Owen said in Tremontanese. Saying "wife" gave him a strange, disoriented feeling, as if they weren't actually married. Speaking their vows in front of Jeffrey and some of the officers was so different from the elaborate ceremony Elspeth had planned. If not for the unmistakable feeling of the marriage bond, Owen might have believed it all for show.

"Of course, sir," the woman said without hesitation, even though Owen's accent clearly marked him as foreign. He was glad she wasn't one of those who hated Ruskalder, like the man who'd grudgingly served them dinner at noon. Owen was tired and emotionally overwhelmed and didn't need to fight yet another battle.

The woman led the way up both flights of stairs to the third floor and opened a door nearly at the end of a long corridor. She handed Owen a key—another Tremontanan peculiarity, putting locks on doors in public places—and said, "Supper is served from five o'clock until eight-thirty. The taproom is open until midnight. Please let me know if there is anything you need."

Owen nodded. Elspeth had already entered the room, so he only said, "Thank you," and followed her. His heart sank. The room was small but well-furnished, and it smelled pleasantly of lilacs. It was quiet, and when he looked out the window, he saw it overlooked the stable yard and not the street. It even had a tap instead of a pitcher of water, another luxury Ruskalder inns never had.

No, the problem was the bed. It was nice enough, with a brightly colored blue and green quilt and pillows not flattened by much use.

But it was barely wide enough for two people, and Owen knew immediately it was a mistake. He loved Elspeth, and he didn't want to impose on her physically...unless it was what she wanted...damn it, he just didn't know what to do for her.

Elspeth stood in the middle of the room looking at the bed. "I can ask for a different room," Owen said. "Maybe...one with two...Elspeth..."

"I'm not going to fall to pieces just because we're sharing a bed," she said irritably. "You have to stop treating me like I'm breakable, Owen."

He didn't want to point out that she looked breakable. "I'm sorry. I don't know what you need."

Elspeth let out a sigh. "Food, right now. And then I want to sleep. We don't have to leave early, do we?"

"We can stay here for a few days if you'd rather." Jeffrey had given him a very full purse when they left that morning, full enough to take them all the way through Tremontane and Eskandel if they'd wanted.

"No, I want to be home." She glanced at him over her shoulder. "Owen?"

"Yes?"

She hesitated, then shook her head. "It's nothing. Let's eat."

They sat in the very full dining room—dining room and separate taproom, so strange—and ate in silence. Owen searched for things to say and came up empty. He'd thought, when they were first reunited, that everything was normal between them. They'd talked and even laughed together. But after they'd made it back to the Tremontanan Army camp, everything had changed. And now this awkwardness between them had grown until Owen felt like screaming.

He watched Elspeth pick at her food, and said, "Is it not what you like? We can ask for something else."

She shook her head. "It's fine. I'm hungry, but I don't have much appetite—I know that doesn't make sense."

It didn't make sense, but he nodded. "Try to eat."

"I *am* trying, Owen," she said, and the sharpness in her voice warned him not to say anything else. He found he didn't have much of an appetite, either.

When their meal was finished, he steered her out of the inn rather than returning upstairs. "Where are we going?" Elspeth said.

"To buy you some clothes. A nightdress, at least. You look like you're wearing someone's castoffs."

"Because I am wearing someone's castoffs." This time, she sounded tired rather than snappish, but it still hurt Owen's heart to hear her sound so unlike herself.

They found a shop just closing up, but Owen convinced the shop-keeper to sell to them by handing over a few extra guilders. More guilders got them a nightdress, a pair of trousers that almost fit Elspeth, two shirts, and assorted toiletries. After accepting their pack-ages, Owen and Elspeth left the store, and Owen turned to return to the inn.

"Shouldn't we get things for you?" Elspeth said.

"It's too late. Everything's closed. But my clothes fit me better than yours did, and I sleep naked."

Elspeth's eyes grew wide, and Owen felt like kicking himself. "In my undershorts," he amended. "Elspeth—"

"I'm not fragile," Elspeth said hotly. "We're married. It doesn't matter." She strode ahead of him, her too-large boots clapping against the cobbles of the street. Owen followed her more slowly. It felt as if he were feeling his way through a dark room filled with glass vases that would break if he so much as brushed against them. They needed to talk. He didn't know what to say.

Elspeth waited for him outside their door, which he unlocked. The sun had nearly set, so he fumbled around looking for the Device lamp, which glowed brightly when he turned it on. Elspeth took the bundles from him and set them on the clothespress at the foot of the bed. "I know it's early, but I want to sleep."

"You should. You look exhausted." Owen turned to go.

"You're leaving?" Elspeth said. She sounded confused, and sad, and it broke his heart.

"I just want a drink before bed," he said. "I'll be back soon. Go ahead and sleep."

Elspeth nodded. Owen let himself out and shut the door. He turned the key over in his hand, examining it. The lock was one of those odd ones he'd only ever seen in Tremontane, with a knob on the inside, so you needed a key to open it on the outside but could lock or unlock it just with the knob on the inside. Hesitantly, he locked the door. He wasn't sure Elspeth would think to do that, and the idea of someone bursting in on her while he was gone filled him with rage. He put the key in his pocket and went downstairs.

The taproom was noisier than the dining room, and fuller, with almost all the tables occupied and most of the stools as well. Owen pushed politely past two men who looked like farmers and got the attention of the barman to order a pint.

"Not from around here, eh?" one of the farmers said.

Owen's pulse sped up. The man's voice had had an edge to it, one Owen was familiar with. It said the speaker didn't much care for foreigners, specifically Ruskalder foreigners. Owen knew the citizens of Barony Daxtry, where they now were, interacted with Ruskalder frequently. He also knew most of those interactions were hostile.

"I am not," he said, hoping to shut off that line of conversation.

"Not sure how a Ruskalder can afford a place like this," the other farmer said. "Don't you all live in shacks with your pigs? Henry, isn't that what you heard? That Ruskalder sleep with their pigs?"

Owen suddenly felt very weary. These stupid men were likely drunk and itching for entertainment and willing to get into a fight because they were bored. "All right," he said. "We will go outside and you will show me how Ruskalder sleep with pigs."

The two farmers eyed him warily. "Beg pardon?" the first man said.

"It is that you want to fight me," Owen said. "I am a Ruskalder warrior and you are not, but you wish to test yourself against me. I promise it will not end well for you. But I am tired and I am angry and fighting you will give me something else to think about. So we will go. And when I have beaten you both senseless, I will finish my drink." He stepped back from the bar and gestured.

Now the farmers looked nervous. "Hey, mister, we don't want trouble," said the second farmer. "We were just making conversation."

"Rude conversation," Owen said. "Insulting conversation."

The first farmer looked more closely at Owen, sizing him up and not liking the conclusions he drew. "I take it back," he said. "Forget I said anything, huh? You look like hell."

Owen hadn't been near a mirror in days and had no idea how he looked. Now he glanced at the mirror over the bar and was stunned. He looked as haggard as Elspeth, his hair matted, his eyes bleary, lines dragging down the corners of his mouth. Suddenly all he wanted was to go up to his room and hold his wife close, not kissing or making love, just holding each other so he could remember not everything was awful.

"I will go," he said, slapping a few coins on the counter. "Please to have a drink, and do not insult anyone else, because I do not think a fight is a good idea for such as you." He walked away before they could say anything else.

Upstairs, he unlocked the door and let himself into the dark room, locking it again behind him. He stood for a minute by the door, letting his eyes grow accustomed to what little light came through the window. He assumed Elspeth was asleep, so when he could make out shapes, he moved quietly to the room's one chair and sat to remove his boots.

Then he stayed, uncertainty keeping him rooted to the chair. He could join Elspeth in bed, but he didn't want to startle her if she really was asleep. It was such a narrow bed, too. Maybe he should stay in this chair, which was surprisingly comfortable. It wouldn't kill him to sleep sitting up one night. He leaned back and stretched out his legs. Really very comfortable.

From the bed, he heard, "Owen?"

He sat up. "Yes?"

"Are you coming to bed?"

His heart beat faster. "I...thought I would sit for a while."

Elspeth said nothing. Then, to his horror, he heard a quiet sob.

He was on his knees beside the bed in an instant, reaching for her hand. "What's wrong?" he said. "Don't cry."

"You can't even bring yourself to share my bed," Elspeth said in a choked voice. "I thought it didn't matter to you that I'm not...that Hesketh..."

"That is *not* how I feel," Owen said. He rose to sit on the edge of the bed, holding tight to her hand. "I don't know what you need, Elspeth. I would give my life to make you happy, but this—I can't make this right. I feel so helpless. Elspeth, love, tell me what to do."

Elspeth shuddered, bringing her tears under control. "I don't— no, I'm not going to say that," she said. "I'm tired of feeling like a victim, Owen. I'm tired of feeling like being raped defines my life. But I'm not ready for sex, and that feels just as bad. Like I'm making you suffer for my weakness."

Owen felt for her shoulder and followed it up to where he could cradle her cheek in his hand. "Don't worry about me. I promise I'm not secretly resenting you for...I don't know, for denying my marital rights or something stupid like that. We have our whole lives ahead of us, Elspeth, years and years for sharing that intimacy. There's no rush. But..."

"What?"

He let out a deep breath. "I would very much like to sleep beside you. I want to hold you and reassure myself that you are alive and well and not trapped in Hrovald's house. I think it might be something we both need. But I will be just as happy to sit in that chair all night, if *that's* what you need."

To his surprise and delight, she laughed. "That chair looks so uncomfortable."

"It's not bad. I've slept in worse places."

Elspeth sat up. "Join me here, then, and tell me about these worse places."

Owen let go of her hand and stood. Then, after a moment's hesitation, he took off his shirt and trousers and slid into bed beside her, taking her in his arms. She smelled sweaty, like he probably did after the journey from Ranstjad, but he didn't care. He rested his head against hers and felt his tension melt away at the touch of her body, the feel of her hair against his cheek.

"There was a time," he said, "when my warband was traveling with Dyrak to visit all the chieftains—a big circuit, understand?— and we were at one of the smaller towns. The chieftain didn't have room for all of us in his barracks. So we had to sleep in a barn. Several barns, really."

"That doesn't sound so bad."

"It wasn't. The bad part was that the barn I slept in was also home to a pack of the farmer's dogs. He must have had eight or ten of them. Big, floppy-eared mutts that *loved* visitors. Every time we settled in to sleep, a dog would come snuffling around, looking for someone to scratch behind its ears. I don't know why the dogs never slept, but we sure didn't."

Elspeth laughed. "That does sound unpleasant. But it could be worse."

"It was worse. We found out when we left the next morning that the dogs had fleas."

That set her laughing harder. "Oh, Owen," she said when she finally wound down, "I'm sorry I didn't just talk to you. I felt so embarrassed and uncertain—"

He kissed the top of her head. "And I felt confused and angry— not at you, love—and I should have talked to you, too."

She snuggled closer. "When you walked into Hrovald's house, I couldn't believe it. I'd wanted you for so long, it didn't feel real."

"I felt so awful when I finally recognized you. I didn't think you could ever change enough that I wouldn't know you anywhere."

Elspeth yawned. "I feel better now. Stronger. I always do when I'm with you."

Her words made the last of Owen's burden lift away. "Sleep," he told her, "and we'll take our time in the morning, and everything will be fine."

"Eventually," Elspeth said, sounding drowsy. He held her and stroked her hair until they both fell asleep.

The room faced west, so when morning came, it was as a soft, blue-edged glow that suffused the room, waking Owen gradually. Elspeth still slept, and he craned his neck to look at her. She looked healthier than she had in days, her skin rosy, her long dark lashes resting on her cheek like a fringe, her chest rising and falling gently as she breathed. Her short hair framed her face like a golden halo. Her beauty continued to astonish him as if he were seeing her for the first time, though it had been most of a year since they'd met. He closed his eyes and let out a deep, satisfied breath.

Elspeth stirred. Then she rolled over to face him. He opened his mouth to tell her good morning, but before he could speak, she put her arms around his neck and pulled him close for a kiss.

Startled, at first he didn't respond. She kissed him again, her lips soft and insistent on his. "Owen," she murmured, "don't tell me you've forgotten how."

"Is this a good idea?" he asked.

Elspeth looked up at him, her brown eyes enormous. "I don't know," she said. "But I want to feel something other than fear. I love you, and I want you to touch me—you, do you understand? Not anyone else."

He thought he did understand, a little. He brushed her hair back from her face. "I love you," he said, though the words felt inadequate to express everything he felt. "I—"

She silenced him with a kiss, which he returned with all his heart. Her hands gently touched his chest, hesitating on the light scar tissue where the crossbow bolt had struck him. "We're neither of us unmarked," she murmured, "but we're still ourselves."

"Still ourselves," he replied, and then they no longer needed words.

***

Later, Owen traced the curve of her back, all the way to her bottom, and felt her shiver. "Too sensitive?"

"It tickles. Why, is that something you enjoy?" She ran her fingers over his chest, and he let out a quiet moan of pleasure. "I guess it is."

Owen regarded her as she continued stroking his chest, his eyes half-lidded. "Let's stay like this forever," he suggested.

"I'm too hungry," Elspeth said. "Aren't you hungry? I feel as if I could eat an entire cow. Cooked, of course. I'm not *that* hungry."

"That's a relief." Owen disentangled himself from her and stretched. "Food, and then I have to see about hiring a carriage. That horse ride was too hard on you."

Elspeth stood and began dressing. "I would say I'm strong enough to ride, but I'm sensible. Not like you, wounded and pretending you could stay upright on a horse—do you remember that?" She laughed. "I watched you so closely that day, ready to grab you if you fell, though of course you'd just have taken me down with you."

He'd almost forgotten that. "I wanted to look strong and manly in front of a beautiful girl."

"You mostly just looked pale and pinched around the lips. And handsome."

Owen paused in the act of pulling on his trousers. "You must be thinking of some other Ruskalder warrior. The best anyone's ever called me is moderately attractive."

Elspeth's lips quirked in an impish smile. "I thought you were handsome from the moment I first saw you."

His eyebrows climbed to his hairline. "What, bedraggled from running through the forest, with five days' beard growth and no doubt smelling to the heavens?"

She crossed the room to stand in front of him, dressed only in her undershorts and one of the new shirts. "And still worried about my safety even though you were desperate and I was a stranger. You ran toward me, intent on stealing my horse—"

"Borrowing."

"And I knew," Elspeth went on, "that my life would never be the same." She kissed him lightly on the lips. "We've made a good start, Owen, but I still...it's going to take time for me to be fully myself again. I hope you'll stay by my side, because I don't think I could bear to do this alone."

Owen took her in his arms and held her close to his heart. "I will never leave you alone again." It was a promise he felt no fear of making. For the first time in months, he felt nothing but peace.

JEFFREY/RIDER OF THE CROWN:
INTRODUCTION

(*Rider of the Crown*, Spring 928 Y.B.)

I had trouble writing the second section of Rider of the Crown, *in which Imogen comes to Aurilien to be the ambassador of her people. It just didn't work, and I couldn't figure out why. Of the many things I tried before settling on the final form, the one that I'm still pleased with, despite the fact that technically it's another failure, is the version I told from Jeffrey's point of view.*

Because the first Tremontane novel I wrote was Agent of the Crown, *King Jeffrey was originally nothing more than Telaine's powerful uncle who was more or less a background figure. (Her Aunt Imogen was even less of a character, because at the time I was still focused on the protagonists of the series being directly descended from one person, and I thought Telaine's mother Elspeth would be the main character of the second book. Foolish of me.) So when I realized that Imogen and Jeffrey rather than Elspeth and Owen would be the central couple, I had to do a lot of rethinking. And in the first draft of Rider, Jeffrey was too distant to be a compelling romantic interest for Imogen. So telling the story from his point of view gave me much-needed insight into his character.*

And, as it turned out, it was fun. I got to explore my own pain at

Jeffrey's father Anthony's death vicariously through this second son who'd never been intended to rule, who was the youngest North ever to take the Crown, and who was muddling through learning who he really was and what kind of King he would be.

This section has the first ten chapters of Jeffrey's version of the "Tremontane" section in Rider *of the* Crown, *as well as a handful of later scenes I wrote from his point of view. Those first ten chapters are a window into that original, scrapped version, and I've left intact things I changed later, such as Jeffrey keeping his magical talent a secret from his mother and the absurdly small sizes of the armies (something I played with as a response to something else I was reading at the time). The other sections were written after I discarded those ten chapters, hence Imogen living in the embassy.*

I don't know why it took me so long to realize that Imogen as ambassador would never be given rooms in the palace, and to understand what a powerful role her tiermatha plays in her life. It turned out making those two changes was key to figuring out the story as it exists in its current form. But Jeffrey as he appears in this section remains one of my favorite characters.

JEFFREY: CHAPTER ONE

"You are not going," Jeffrey said in a low, level voice, "and I don't want to hear another word about it."

"Then you will not," Owen said, anger making his Ruskalder accent thicker.

"Don't play that game with me, Owen. It would be suicide."

"You have a plan? Tell it to me. I want to hear this great plan and then I will give up on my foolishness."

Jeffrey swore and turned away from his friend. "Hrovald can't keep her forever," he said. "He knows it will be war if he stops pretending she's his guest. We wait, and then we send in a neutral party—*neutral*, do you hear me?—to bring her home. There's no reason—"

"Every reason!" Owen shouted. "She saved me. She kept me sane. She is to be my wife. I cannot bear it that she is trapped in that madman's house, enduring whatever he chooses to do to her—"

"Hrovald isn't going to touch her. And don't think your right to defend her trumps mine as her brother and her King. Damn it, Owen, she's the heir to the throne! Yes, I want her back. Hrovald has the whole country by the throat as long as she's there. But he's going to go on pretending this is all an innocent twist of fate for as long as he can. Give me time to figure something else out. Don't go after her yourself."

"It is what he asked for," Owen said. "It is easy. I give myself to him and he lets Elspeth come home."

"He'll kill you."

"And if she is not here? How will my life matter?"

Jeffrey threw up his hands. "Heaven save me from lovelorn romantics." He paced the confines of his tent, which was big, but not big enough for him to vent his frustration and anger. Owen watched him pace, standing at ease with his hands behind his back as Dyrak's soldiers had been wont to do. Owen had served Dyrak for years before Hrovald staged the coup that put himself on the throne and made Owen a wanted fugitive.

Owen would never say what he'd done to earn Hrovald's personal animosity, but whatever it was, it had made Hrovald furious enough that when the crown princess of Tremontane fell by accident into his hands, the only thing he wanted in exchange for her was Owen Hunter. One man, when he could have extracted a legion of concessions from Tremontane's king for the return of his sister and heir. One man who was Jeffrey's best friend and his sister Elspeth's betrothed husband.

"Two weeks," he said, turning back to Owen, "two weeks for me to figure out an acceptable alternative. She's been gone for five months. Two weeks isn't much to ask. Please, Owen. Swear to me you won't do this. Elspeth won't thank you for sacrificing yourself."

Owen said nothing. His lips were set in that hard, straight line that said he didn't want to see the sense of what Jeffrey was saying. "*Please*," Jeffrey repeated.

"...I swear I will not do anything foolish," Owen said finally.

"Thank you," Jeffrey said. "Would you give me a minute alone? Marcus and Diana will be here soon and I need to prepare some notes for our meeting." Owen nodded curtly and left the tent. Jeffrey put his hands on the edge of the table in front of him and bowed his head, and exhaled slowly.

He'd known where she was the whole time, of course. Had known it even before the message came from Hrovald, the delicate but oh-so-clear statement of his demands. He'd had to pretend to be worried all that week before the message arrived, couldn't even reassure his mother that her youngest child was alive and, he hoped, well. The magical talent that let him know where any member of the North family was at any time had to be kept secret; it was a small thing, certainly no threat to anyone, but suspicion of inherent magic was still strong enough that his fitness to be king could be called into question if anyone knew the truth. And he felt his grasp on the Crown was shaky enough as it was.

He missed his father so much. Three years gone, and it no longer hurt the way it had, but there was never a day that he didn't wish his father were there to advise him. Though, of course, if his father were there, he'd be king and Jeffrey wouldn't need advice. He'd been the superfluous younger brother all his life, then Sylvester announced he was adopting into his wife's family and abdicating his position as heir, and less than a year later Anthony North dropped dead of an aneurysm and Jeffrey, unprepared and uncertain, was suddenly king of Tremontane.

It wasn't as if he was totally untrained. He'd received the same instruction as Sylvester, had the same tutors, and Father had treated them both as if they were equally capable of doing the job. But it was different, growing up without that *expectation*, and even if he had the training he sure as hell didn't have the…the what? The certainty? Yes, that was it. The certainty that he knew what he was doing, that he deserved to be where he was.

"Your Majesty," Marcus Anselm said, ducking through the tent door. He was one of the few men in the camp who were as tall as Jeffrey, but where Jeffrey was slim, Marcus was built like a brick wall. Behind that façade, however, was a sharp mind and quick eyes that missed nothing. Jeffrey's father had built an impressive array of advisers that Jeffrey had been grateful to inherit; Marcus Anselm, general in chief of the army of Tremontane, was one of the best of that cadre.

"Marcus. What's the news?"

"There's some restlessness among the troops now that the weather's turning warmer. They're devoted to the princess, you know, and they were willing to fight through that unexpected snowstorm to get to this position, but now they're ready to move on Ruskald. I'm going to institute some drills, some war games to keep the edge without driving us over one, if you take my meaning."

"It would help if we could advance our position," Diana Ashmore said as she entered. She had an elegant face with a long, straight nose and eyes that were too close to it, giving her an air of superciliousness that was belied by her calm, friendly voice and pleasant smile. "Give them a sense of accomplishment."

"I won't cross the border into Ruskald until it's absolutely necessary," Jeffrey said. "We're all still pretending this isn't a hostage situation. If we're the first to aggress on their territory, it gives Hrovald an advantage, and we have so few advantages I'm unwilling to let any of them slip through our fingers."

"I understand the situation, your Majesty, I'm simply pointing out an obvious solution," Diana said. Her barony of Daxtry abutted directly on Ruskalder territory, and she was responsible for the part of the army that guarded that border. Of the three, she probably had the most direct experience fighting Ruskalder, but Jeffrey felt she was sometimes bolder than a situation warranted. Even so, her advice was worth listening to.

"It hasn't come to that," Marcus rumbled. He and Diana were not friends. "And pray heaven it doesn't."

"You're not afraid of fighting Ruskalder, are you?" Diana said, sounding amused.

"Don't try to twist my words, Diana. You've only fought border skirmishes. You've never seen the Ruskalder army *en masse*. They outnumber us by nearly two to one, and their warriors are bloodthirsty savages. The only edge we have are our rifles and those new projectile Devices, and that's not much of an edge. So no, I am not afraid of fighting Ruskalder, I am afraid of going against them head to head. I'd prefer a war of attrition if we can manage one."

"And I'd like to avoid war altogether," Jeffrey said. "Diana, what news from your scouts?"

"The border is still clear," she said. "We haven't seen any Ruskalder, either scouts or warbands. We have seen a couple of Kirkellan warriors riding the border, but they've ignored us so we've ignored them."

"Is there any danger they'd throw in with the Ruskalder if it came to war?"

"I doubt it. Their *matrian*, Mairen, has some kind of treaty with Hrovald, but it's a mutual non-aggression pact and I don't think they'd feel obligated to back him if he attacked us. If *we* attack *Hrovald*, that's another matter."

"Damn." The Kirkellan weren't numerous, but they were fearsome warriors who rode enormous horses that were almost warriors themselves. If they had to go up against the combined might of the Ruskalder and the Kirkellan, Jeffrey might as well hand over the Crown right now and save them all a lot of bloodshed.

"Let's not borrow trouble," Marcus said. "I'll take care of the army's restlessness, give you time to come up with a plan. Hrovald's not going to come marching around the mountains tomorrow morning."

Jeffrey nodded. There was a scuffle outside the tent as if the guards had prevented someone entering. "I need to see the king! It's important!" said a girl's voice.

Jeffrey lifted the tent flap. One of the pages in North livery stared up at him. She seemed too young to be a page, but then they all seemed too young these days, even though Jeffrey himself wasn't more than twenty-two.

"Your Majesty, the scouts reported a disturbance on the north line," she said, and for a moment Jeffrey absurdly heard that as "North line" and wondered what new threat had come to his bare and branchless family tree. "Owen Hunter and two scouts took horses and rode away before anyone could stop them. They crossed the border into Ruskald."

Jeffrey stared at her in astonishment for a couple of heartbeats, then he closed his eyes and cursed, fervently and violently. When he opened his eyes the girl was looking at him in terror. "Thank you," he said, and she took it for a dismissal and was out of his sight like lightning. He turned back to look at Marcus and Diana, both of whom shared the same look of horror. "Spread the word," he said. "We move out at first light."

AT DAWN TWO DAYS LATER, JEFFREY LAY AWAKE ON HIS COT AND focused his attention on the spot of light that was his sister. He'd never tried to explain how his talent worked to anyone, mainly because there was only one other person who even knew he had it, and she lived on the other side of the country, in hiding to protect her own talent. But it was as if he could see the whole world at once, not from above as a bird does, but from underneath, as if it was part of his skin. The Norths lay sprinkled across it like bonfires.

There was Elspeth, still presumably at Hrovald's house—he could only sense geography, not manmade things like cities or national boundaries. There was his mother, waiting in the place he knew Aurilien to be; he really ought to send her word of what had happened, but he hated to have to tell her, yet again, that Elspeth hadn't been recovered. There was...Mistress Weaver, far away on the coast; he didn't dare even think her true name inside the privacy of his own head. That was all. His father was dead, his brother wasn't a North anymore. Four Norths where once there had been a palace full of them.

He hadn't slept that night. They'd moved the camp across the border into Ruskald, some fifty miles north of its previous position, and if nothing happened Jeffrey planned to push it another twenty-five tomorrow. Every mile was another poke in Hrovald's eye, and eventually he'd have to respond. Marcus assured him they were ready, and Jeffrey hoped it was true.

Maybe Owen would succeed. He'd taken companions, so he was going to try the plan he'd proposed: walk into Hrovald's house and offer himself in Elspeth's place, send her out to the others and have them bring her back. The hell of it was, it would work. Hrovald was so personally invested in seeing Owen die that he wouldn't care about his captive princess anymore. And Elspeth would lose her husband, and Jeffrey would lose the best friend he'd ever had.

Surprising that they'd all become so close, so quickly; Owen had stumbled into their lives less than a year before, but it was as if he was an old friend they'd merely lost track of. Jeffrey had always been solitary, and his friendship with Owen had been unexpected and desperately needed. The thought that he was going to throw his life away made Jeffrey wish he could transport himself to the shining bonfire that was Elspeth and stab Hrovald through the heart. The resulting confusion as the chiefs of the Ruskalder battled for the crown would be a side benefit.

He sighed, rolled out of his cot, and began to wash and dress for the day. His head ached a little thanks to the sleepless night. Today was going to be miserable, not like the last five months hadn't been equally miserable.

He splashed cold water on his face, ran his damp fingers through his black hair, and looked at himself in the mirror. He looked too much like his father. Maybe that was a good thing, maybe it meant his councilors and the government officials responded to him out of some residual respect his father had left hanging in the air around him. Or maybe it was a bad thing; maybe they looked at him and expected him to be as good as his father because the resemblance was so striking. Maybe he should grow a beard.

Someone clapped outside the tent door. Jeffrey left his curtained-off room at the back of the tent, buttoning up his coat, and pushed open the flap. "Morning report, your Majesty," Marcus said, and Jeffrey stood back to let him enter. "Morale is high, maybe a little too high since we've had to discipline several soldiers for over-exuberance, but I'd rather cheerful troops than morose ones as long as we're not actually on the battlefield. Cheerful can turn into dead far too easily there."

"Excellent. Be prepared to move out again in the morning, if we still have no word."

"Yes, your Majesty. And I...had another thought."

Jeffrey braced himself. Marcus's thoughts often led to more work for him.

Marcus went to the map table and shuffled pages around until he found one of the region. It showed the area they were currently in, with the borders of Ruskald, Tremontane, Veribold, and the Kirkellan territory called the Eidestal. "We're here," he said, pointing at a spot within the Ruskald border. He traced a line south. "This is all Ruskalder territory," he said, "at least on paper. Their borders dip down south between Tremontane and Veribold in this long finger, right?"

"I do know how to read a map, Marcus."

"Then try to imagine this." He traced a line from the northern Veriboldan border to the edge of the mountains that formed the border between Tremontane and Ruskald. It cut off that fingerlike extrusion of Ruskald from the rest of the country.

"This area," Marcus said, tapping the long finger of land, "has always been a nightmare of national security. There's just too much for Diana's people to cover, and we can't let the army mass along this border without making Ruskald—and, frankly, Veribold—nervous. I've thought for years that if this were part of Tremontane, we'd be in a much better position to defend against Ruskald."

"You're suggesting we just take it? With our army that's half the size of Hrovald's?"

"I'm saying that as long as we're aggressing on their territory, we might as well go for broke."

"Marcus," Jeffrey said in an even tone, "you know I respect you like you were my own uncle, but I think you're insane."

"It's not as bad as you think. Most of this territory is unoccupied. Frankly, the only reason Ruskald holds it is that Veribold doesn't care and Tremontane has been preoccupied with internal issues. But now we're in a position to stake a claim that's better than Ruskald's."

"And you don't think this will upset the Veriboldans?"

"Like I said, they haven't made a move themselves."

Jeffrey thought about it. "It's true they prefer having us for neighbors to Ruskald," he said. "At least that was the impression I got from Bixhenta, the last time we spoke." He paced the tent, mulling it over. "Do you have a plan for this?"

"Two plans, contingent on whether we meet Hrovald in a pitched battle. But they both start with us moving to...this position." His finger stabbed down on the map. "That will give us the best chance of controlling the territory no matter what happens with Hrovald."

Jeffrey traced the imaginary line Marcus had minutes ago. "Talk to Diana," he said. "If this works, she'll be the one whose boundary extends into the disputed area."

"That's not a good idea. Daxtry would be county sized, then. Bigger than county sized."

"I'm not going to think about how to divide up territory we don't have yet," Jeffrey said. "Diana's still going to be on the border and it will be her soldiers at the head of the line if Hrovald comes after us. Consult with her, and prepare to move out tomorrow morning."

After Marcus left, Jeffrey continued pacing. Annexing territory when he didn't even know if he could get his heir back. At least it gave him something to do. He resolved to stop staring at the little bonfire in his head until she was back. It would only drive him crazy. Though one could argue that he was already crazy for listening to Marcus's plan in the first place.

"Owen hasn't come back, and neither has Elspeth," Jeffrey told his advisers two evenings later, his heart like lead in his chest. "We're going to act as if his mission has failed. Tomorrow I will send messengers to Hrovald requesting Elspeth's return, authorized to negotiate on my behalf. There's no way to know what his response will be, but I predict it will not be positive. The army is to stand in readiness to advance. If Hrovald refuses to return the crown princess, we will march on Ranstjad and attack."

"What about the territory?" a man asked.

Marcus replied, "If the princess is returned unharmed, we'll go home. If not, when we've defeated the Ruskalder army, we'll maintain a presence in this area—" he pointed to the map—"in preparation for permanent settlements."

"*When* we defeat the Ruskalder army?" Diana Ashmore said under her breath.

"I try to think positively, Diana," Marcus said frostily.

"I'm trying to think practically, Marcus. Do we have a plan of attack?"

"Of course I have a plan of attack—"

"That's *enough*," Jeffrey said, silencing both of them. "Tomorrow, after the messengers are—"

The tent flap opened. Jeffrey, who'd given orders that they weren't to be disturbed, looked up angrily and saw Owen, whose face was emotionless. "*Owen*," Jeffrey began, a hundred possible angry words rising up inside him. Then Owen's small companion, someone too thin with short blonde hair, stepped forward, arms outstretched, and all those words vanished into the distance. "Sweet heaven," he whispered as she walked into his arms, "*Elspeth.*"

JEFFREY: CHAPTER TWO

"*E*lspeth," Jeffrey repeated, and bent to kiss her shining hair. She felt like a bundle of bones in his arms, far thinner than he remembered her being, and he was afraid to hold her too close in case some of those bones snapped under his hands. "Sweet heaven, what have they done to you?"

"She was very sick," said a woman who stood at Owen's side. Her accent was thicker than Owen's and her Tremontanese more tentative. "She is still not well completely. I promise that I cared for her the best—as best as I could. We had to cut her hair because of the fever. I am sorry."

Jeffrey looked more closely at her. "Who are you?" he asked. She was tall, as tall as he was, plump and heavily built. Direct hazel eyes met his. She looked as if she'd been in a fight, as did Owen, who had a trace of dried blood in his hair.

"This is Imogen of the Kirkellan," Owen said. "It's because of her that we escaped Hrovald's city alive."

Jeffrey looked from the young woman to Owen and then down at Elspeth's bowed head, tucked into his shoulder. There was no way Hrovald would simply have let them walk out of his house. Whoever this woman was, she had worked a miracle.

Jeffrey came around the map table, his hand outstretched. His leaden heart had turned lighter than his sister's golden hair. "I owe you everything," he said. "Anything I can do for you—you brought me my sister and my best friend—anything at all, it's yours."

She took his hand reflexively, her eyes once again locked with his. "I need nothing," she said, sounding a little overwhelmed by his intensity. "I cared for Elspeth because she needed me. I must go to my mother soon. She will want to know how Hrovald wanted to take the Crown of Tremontane."

Jeffrey released her and turned to Owen. "The Crown?" he said.

Owen glanced around the room. "This should be private," he said. Jeffrey nodded, then gestured to his officers and advisers. They filed out of the tent without a word. Jeffrey seated Elspeth on a camp stool and knelt in front of her. She did look as if she'd been ill. She was so thin and pale it broke his heart to look at her.

Owen stood behind Elspeth and put a protective arm around her. "Swear to me you will not yell, or rage, or tear around throwing things until you hear all," he said.

Jeffrey made an exasperated face. "You went off against my express command and it's sheer luck you made it back alive, let alone with Elspeth," he said. "Don't think that succeeding at your insane mission means I won't rip you a new one."

"That is not what I mean," Owen said. "Swear."

"Fine. I swear not to throw a fit. What is so dire?"

Owen lowered his voice. "Hrovald's son raped Elspeth."

For a moment, Owen's words made no sense. Then their meaning was entirely too clear. His ears rang with them until the sound of his own blood pounding through them deafened him. He stood in a swift movement and opened his mouth to shout, to swear, to somehow give voice to the fury that pulsed in his veins. Owen glared at him, and he shut his mouth and looked down at his sister. Elspeth's chin quivered, and her eyes filled with tears, and he had to turn away from her devastated face. And all this time he'd thought she was safe.

He wished he'd marched on Hrovald's house the second he knew where Elspeth was. Never mind that that was impossible; his little sister, this sweet, clever, funny girl who had never hurt anyone in her life had...he couldn't finish the thought.

Behind him, he heard Elspeth having a conversation with the young woman, Imogen, in what sounded like Kirkellish. Then he heard Elspeth laugh. If she could still laugh, maybe she could heal. It eased his heart, somewhat. "Did you kill him?" he asked Owen. Owen nodded, and that eased his heart a little more. If Hesketh couldn't die at his hand, it was fitting that he die at Owen's. He cleared his throat, and said, "Are you telling me this has something to do with Hrovald trying to conquer Tremontane?"

"He planned to say that Hesketh's...physical relationship with Elspeth meant they were married, and then wait for her to give birth to Hesketh's child, who would then be an heir to the throne."

"It doesn't work like that."

"If he was able to kill you in battle, it would have."

Jeffrey glanced at Elspeth again. "So is she..."

Elspeth buried her face in her hands. Owen's arms tightened around her. Imogen said, "She is not carrying a child."

Jeffrey looked at her, startled. He'd forgotten she was there. "How do you know?" he asked.

Imogen rolled her eyes. "She had her..." She seemed to be looking for the right word. She switched to Kirkellish and said something to Elspeth that made her gasp in relief.

"She says I had my monthlies while I was ill. That was after Hesketh...it means I'm not pregnant!" She hugged Owen tightly. Jeffrey sagged onto a camp chair and rubbed his face.

"I don't know if I can stand any more surprises," he said, and one of the guards stuck his head through the door and said, "Your Majesty, there's a fight going on near the horse lines."

Imogen said something harsh in Kirkellish and ran out of the tent. Jeffrey, mystified, followed Owen and Elspeth, who hurried after her. They ended up at the enclosure, where a maddened Kirkellan horse that looked to Jeffrey to be about eight feet tall screamed and thrashed, tossing a woman who was clinging to her reins back and forth over the ground. Imogen, completely heedless of the danger, ran into the enclosure, picked the woman up off the ground, tore the reins out of her hands, and tossed her to one side as if she weighed no more than a child.

Jeffrey watched in amazement as the Kirkellan woman threw herself over the horse's back and lay full length along her neck and body, her face near the mare's head. Jeffrey could see her talking into the horse's ear, stroking her mane, holding on even as the horse reared a little and shook her head. Jeffrey was sure it was only a matter of time before the horse sent Imogen flying, but instead it began to settle down, stopped screaming, and went from stamping its feet to moving restlessly and then, finally, standing still. Imogen kissed the side of the mare's face and continued to stroke her mane. She said something soothing in Kirkellish, then slid off the horse's back and laid her cheek against its neck.

It dawned on Jeffrey that there were several more horses here than usual, and that they were all enormous. "There are a lot of Kirkellan horses here," he said aloud, and Imogen turned to look at him.

"This is my *tiermatha*," she said in Tremontanese, gesturing at several Kirkellan warriors standing nearby. "They are also—were also ones who brought Elspeth home." She turned back to face them and said something angry in Kirkellish. Jeffrey thought it wouldn't be pleasant to be yelled at by the formidable young woman, but she didn't seem angry with them. One of the Kirkellan women started explaining something, pointing at the horse and then making a gesture and a buzzing sound—she was talking about that experimental grooming Device, the one the stable mistress was so enthusiastic about. Imogen replied in a calmer voice and pointed at him, and twelve Kirkellan warriors turned to look directly at him. What was she telling them?

The stable mistress, who'd been the woman hanging onto the horse before Imogen had tossed her out of danger, came limping up to Imogen at that point. "Your horse is dangerous," she said. "She shouldn't be with the rest of the animals. Who knows what she might do? I want you to—"

"What is your name?" Imogen said, cutting her off.

"You have no right to make demands of me—"

"What did you put on my horse?"

"It was a simple grooming Device. What kind of creature overreacts like that?"

"The Kirkellan do not use the Devices," Imogen said, raising her voice. "The Kirkellan take care of the horses with the own hands as heaven intends it to be. You put a buzzy thing on my horse and scared her and you are now wanting to make it her fault that she is scared? I will find this buzzy thing and I will make you eat it unless you apologize to Victory right now."

Jeffrey grinned. This was a woman he wanted to get to know better. She'd rescued Elspeth and Owen, had dragged a terrified horse back to earth with nothing but her own two hands, and now she was threatening the stable mistress in her own domain. She didn't seem to be afraid of anything.

The woman was red with fury. "Apologize? Me, apologize?"

Jeffrey decided it was time for him to intervene. "Madam, for a stable mistress you seem remarkably ignorant about Kirkellan horses," he said with amusement. "You should know better than to use a Device that I happen to know is untested outside the field on a horse that doesn't belong to you. I suggest you do as the lady tells you and apologize to the horse."

The woman looked confused. "The horse?"

Imogen glared at her and nodded in Victory's direction. The horse nodded as if she understood the conversation.

The woman looked from Victory to Imogen and back again. "I'm sorry," she said in a stunned voice. "It won't happen again."

"Thank you," Imogen said, and led Victory to where her stable mates waited, patting her on the neck. Jeffrey watched her for a while until it became clear she and her friends were talking about him. One of the men was eyeing him with a frankly sensual appraisal that made him feel uncomfortable. He turned and bumped into Owen, who had Elspeth under his arm. "Would you invite Imogen to eat with us?" he said. "I know she said she didn't want anything for bringing you home, but I'd at least like to speak to her a little more."

"I'll ask, but she might not want to leave the *tiermatha*," Owen said. "They're a close-knit bunch. I think she's in charge, but it's hard to tell with the Kirkellan; rank isn't nearly as important to them as it is to either of our people."

"Well, make an effort," Jeffrey said, "and *you*, Elspeth, are coming with me to lie down before supper. You look exhausted." Elspeth started to protest, but at a look from Owen she went with Jeffrey without complaining. Apparently there were things she'd do for her betrothed that she wouldn't do for the brother she'd known all her life.

He took her to his own room inside the king's tent and made her lie down on the cot, covered her with a blanket and pushed her short hair back from her face.

"Stay with me," she pleaded when he made as if to leave. "I don't like being alone."

He dragged a chair over and sat beside her, holding her thin, light hand. "We were all so worried," he said. "It took a week for us to even learn you were still alive. Mother and I were frantic."

"I was safe. Imogen took care of me. She is my dearest friend."

For a brief, angry moment, Jeffrey wondered why Elspeth's dearest friend hadn't protected her from Hesketh. Something of his thoughts must have shown on his face, for Elspeth clutched his hand tighter—it was like having a baby bird cling to his fist—and said, "No, don't blame her. Everyone was so sick, and people were dying, and Imogen had to take care of them all. Some of her *tiermatha* almost died. I thought Hesketh was my friend—I felt sorry for him—no, I don't want to talk about it. I'm glad Owen killed him," she said fiercely. "I want it to be over."

"I can't fix this for you," Jeffrey said, frustrated.

"I don't know how to fix it for myself. But Imogen said, remember that I am still the same Elspeth. The rest will have to come in time."

"Your Imogen seems very wise," Jeffrey said with a smile.

"She is. She was so patient with me when there were things I didn't know. They barely even have Devices, Jeffrey, and Hrovald treats women like things, and he teaches his soldiers to feel the same way. I was frightened, the whole time I was there, but I felt safer when Imogen was near me. I wish I was more like her."

"Well, I for one am glad you are exactly like Elspeth," Jeffrey said, tweaking her nose, and she laughed, then coughed a little.

"No, don't worry, I'm not sick anymore, but the coughing afterward is normal. It's annoying, but it doesn't hurt," Elspeth assured him when he gave her an alarmed look. "And I'm hungry. I try to eat all the time and I feel as if I'm not gaining any weight. Imogen looks at me as if I'm going to snap in half."

Jeffrey felt his desire to know his sister's new friend increase. Half the words out of Elspeth's mouth had something to do with Imogen. The smell of hot meat and bread filled the air, and Jeffrey peered out of the gap in the partition. "I'm feeling rather hungry myself," he said. "Let's eat, and then I'll have them make up a bed in the other room and you can sleep. I want to send you south as quickly as I can, so Mother can care for you."

"Was she too terribly panicked?" Elspeth said as Jeffrey held the flap for her.

"You know what she's like. She looks like she's calm, but then you watch her reading and she stares at the same page for twenty minutes. She's spent a lot of time alone, these past months, that or staying at the Library until after midnight, copying out old documents. It will relieve her so much to see you safe."

Elspeth sat at the table and helped herself to a hot roll. "I'm sorry I gave everyone so much distress," she said. "I should have waited for that storm to pass before setting out for home. And I *really* shouldn't have asked the driver to cut across Ruskald to Daxtry, but I was so impatient to see Owen again..."

"It's done, and there's no point thinking about what might have been," Jeffrey said. He looked up as Owen pushed the tent door open and entered, followed by Imogen. She seemed perfectly composed and not at all overawed at being in the king's tent. But then, she'd been at Hrovald's house when Elspeth was there—come to think on it, what had a rider of the Kirkellan been doing, living at Hrovald's house?

"Thank you for coming," he said, pulling out a chair and holding it for her. She looked at him quizzically, then sat down. "Help yourselves. We don't bother with ceremony here; no point, when it's a war camp rather than the palace." Imogen and Owen both loaded their plates with sliced meat, sautéed onions, bread and hunks of cheese. Jeffrey poured out mugs of dark ale for everyone except Elspeth, who didn't like the taste.

Owen and their guest ate as if they were starving, which might have been true when you considered that Owen had probably only brought enough rations for three, but had returned with an extra thirteen people in tow. The Kirkellan were perfectly capable of hunting for themselves, but rabbit roasted over a tiny fire wasn't the same as the robust fare the camp kitchens turned out every day. Elspeth picked at her food until Imogen glowered at her, at which point she dug in more heartily. It seemed everyone had more of a hold on Elspeth's obedience than her own brother.

They ate in silence for a while, then Elspeth said, "Is Victory all right?"

Imogen swallowed. "Yes, she was just scared. Sometimes she is silly when she is scared. I am sorry I yelled at that woman."

"Don't be," Jeffrey said. "Her behavior was inexcusable. I still can't believe you went in there with the horse thrashing around. That was incredibly brave."

"You do not like horses," Imogen said, fixing him with those hazel eyes again.

Jeffrey was taken aback. "Who told you that? I never said I didn't like horses," he said.

"Elspeth said it," Imogen said, blushing.

"Well, you don't," Elspeth said, her mouth half full of food.

"I never said that. Just because I'm not a rider like—" *like my father*—"like other people. I think horses are beautiful."

"I would like you to meet Victory," Imogen said, "maybe in the morning."

"I—thank you," Jeffrey said. From what he knew, the Kirkellan treated their horses in many ways as if they were people. "Are you leaving for home in the morning?"

Imogen nodded. "My mother should hear the news of the *banrach* immediately."

"Excuse me, I don't understand that word."

"It's a horrible custom that says Imogen has to be married to Hrovald for five years," Elspeth said. "As part of the peace between the Kirkellan and Ruskald."

Jeffrey laid his fork and knife down. "*Who* did you say your mother was?"

"Mairen of the Kirkellan."

Good heaven. The matrian *of the Kirkellan.* "You're married to Hrovald?" He knew he sounded overly incredulous, but he simply couldn't imagine Imogen sharing Hrovald's bed. The very idea revolted him.

Imogen blushed. "I am not married anymore. It is not a marriage like a...there is no sex, it is not that I slept with him—"

"It's a marriage in name, Jeffrey," Elspeth explained. "It made Hrovald and Mairen related, like brother and sister, some kind of family members anyway. It meant they had the same claim on each other's loyalty as any blood relatives would." Imogen said something in Kirkellish, and Elspeth nodded. "There are rules about what can break it, and Hrovald broke the *banrach* when he was going to use me...use me to make a claim on the Crown of Tremontane. It would—"

She turned to Imogen and said something, and Imogen responded at length. "She says that since Tremontane and the Kirkellan are not at war, Hrovald would have been forcing them to take sides against us on his behalf. The Kirkellan only agreed not to go to war against Ruskald, not to be their auxiliaries in a war they started against someone else."

That was essentially the situation as Jeffrey had understood it. But if Imogen's understanding was correct, Mairen's treaty with Hrovald was void, and that left the Kirkellan as open to Ruskalder attack as

Tremontane was. An idea flickered into life. "It seems we have more to talk about than I thought," he told Imogen. "Would the *matrian* be interested in a treaty with Tremontane? It sounds as if you burned your bridges thoroughly when you left. Hrovald's the kind of man who would pursue war simply to avenge himself on you and Owen. Though I'm not sure who he'd be angrier at, the woman who humiliated him or the man who killed his heir."

Imogen looked at Owen, who nodded. Jeffrey added, "We would be willing to support you against Hrovald. And I could use someone to put pressure on Hrovald's western flank so he can't prosecute full-out war against us. I think we have more in common with each other than either of us has with Ruskald, if you'll pardon my presumption."

Imogen looked at her plate for a moment, then back at him. "I cannot make a treaty myself," she said, and Jeffrey nodded. "I can take your offer to the *matrian* and ask her. But I think, me, that it is a good idea. I do not know if we can make a treaty before Hrovald brings his army against you, though."

"Oh, I have an idea for that," Jeffrey said.

JEFFREY: CHAPTER THREE

"It's called a telecoder," Jeffrey explained as Imogen walked around it, staring at it intently in the lamplight. "They're usually about the size of your horse, but this is an experimental model for the military. Portable. Go ahead, you can touch it."

Imogen reached out a finger and ran it along the shining brass of the arm, then pushed the thumbplate and jerked her hand back when the arm moved. "It is meant to do that?"

"Yes, that's how it works." Jeffrey set the dials for it to communicate with its counterpart, sitting on a table five feet away. "The arm has a needle underneath, and when you press where you just did, it touches this tape—" he held up the dangling length of narrow paper —"and makes a mark. And the machine it's connected to makes the same mark, or it does when it's turned on." He turned a knob at the back of each machine. "Would you like to try?"

Imogen didn't look convinced. "It is...complicated." She said the last word as if she were trying it out on her tongue.

"The Devices are complicated, but the idea is simple. Look. If you have your hand on Victory's reins, and you pull them on the left side, Victory's head turns left, yes?" Imogen nodded, then understanding bloomed on her face. She reached out and tapped the thumbplate a few times, watching the other Device come to life and tap out the same rhythm simultaneously. She smiled and tapped it again. "It is like magic," she said.

"Just Devisery, though I'm told that's a little like magic."

"We do not have many Devices. Hard to find...what is it that makes them go?"

"Source."

"Yes, hard to find source in the Eidestal." She removed her finger from the thumbplate. "This is good. You will give us one, yes?"

"That's the idea."

"But I do not understand how to talk if this makes dots and lines and longer lines."

"We have a code—do you know what a code is? Our code turns the marks the telecoder makes into letters and words. I'll send some people with you who know how to use it, and they can translate what the *matrian* says from Kirkellish into code, and here we'll decode the message into Kirkellish and translate it to Tremontanese."

Imogen looked skeptical. "It is a lot to ask, to trust a Device."

Jeffrey ran his hands through his hair. "I know," he said. "And to trust the technicians—the Device operators—and to trust me. Imogen, I wish we had more time. I would ride to the Eidestal myself and Mairen and I could work this out face to face. But there isn't any time. I swear to you that this Device does what I say it does, and that I intend to deal honestly with the *matrian*. And since I can't say that to her face, I have to say it to you. Do you believe me?"

The golden lamplight threw shadows across her face. It was impossible to tell what she was thinking. She bent her head to look at the telecoder again. "I believe you, king of Tremontane," she said. "And it is my...reputation I am putting in your hands. The *matrian* will blame me if you are the liar."

"Everything I've told you is true," Jeffrey said, taking her hands in his. She looked at their joined hands, but said nothing. "And I think you can convince the *matrian* of that."

She nodded and once again met his eyes. "It is a good plan," she said. "You will give me your...proposal, yes? And my *tiermatha* will ride at first light."

"Thank you, Imogen," he said, and let go of her hands, which fell to her side. "Do you have a place to sleep? Is your...your *tiermatha* comfortable? And your horses?"

She smiled, and in the half-shadows of the lamp it looked crooked with humor. "We have a rest place," she said. "And I still have nothing we need that you can give me for a life. Two lives."

"I suppose there's no way to repay that debt, really."

"No. And I did not do it for you. I did it for them. And for me." She nodded at him and left the Devisers' tent. He stared at the tent flap long after she'd gone. Would her word count for enough, with the *matrian*? With her mother? He remembered that steady gaze, the grip of her hands, and thought that it just might.

TWO DAYS LATER HE HOVERED AROUND THE REMAINING TELECODER, watching its unmoving arm the way a terrier watches a rat hole. Imogen should be there by now. She could be giving his proposal to the *matrian* right now. At any moment the telecoder could start chattering with...well, he had to hope it was good news, didn't he?

Their advance scouts had reported that Hrovald's army was on the move, that it would be here in the next two or three days. Such a narrow margin, two versus three, a small difference upon which success or failure rested. He paced more, not caring that his presence unsettled the technicians. They didn't need to be composed until the message came through. Until then, their king was going to pace.

"Your Majesty," Diana Ashmore said, entering the Devisers' tent, "you're not going to make the message come through any faster by waiting here for it."

"You know if I walk away, that will be the moment it arrives."

"And someone will bring word when that happens. Besides, it will need to be decoded and translated before you can read it."

Jeffrey said nothing, but stopped pacing in favor of standing next to the Device and staring at it, willing it to move.

"Your Majesty, I did have something to discuss with you," Diana said. "In private."

Jeffrey looked up from the telecoder. "Are you trying to get me out of here with a ruse?"

"No, your Majesty, but I'm sure the technicians will welcome your absence."

Jeffrey looked at the nearest technician, who didn't meet his eyes. "Fine," he said, and brushed past Diana out of the tent. "What is it?"

"In *private*, your Majesty."

Jeffrey sighed and walked with her to his own tent. "Is this private enough for you, Baroness?"

"You don't need to be testy, Jeffrey."

"I know. I'm sorry, Diana. Tell me what's on your mind."

Diana went to the table and pulled out the map of the area. "We've already occupied this much of the disputed territory," she said, gesturing. "Tomorrow my forces will rejoin the body of the army, but they haven't had any trouble holding this area."

"Isn't that because there isn't anyone there?"

"What I'm saying is that they can cover all the territory without losing contact with one another. I believe that if—when—we defeat Hrovald's army, they'll be able to maintain that level of alertness indefinitely."

"That's good to know. But it sounds like you have something else in mind."

"I do." Diana looked up from the table. "I want you to extend the boundaries of Daxtry and make it a County. I think I've proved I can maintain my own Barony as well as the demands of keeping up our military presence along the border. It makes sense to maintain a continuity of rule when there's going to be so much turmoil in the coming months, what with consolidating our hold on the entire territory."

Jeffrey looked at the map. "That's a lot of territory, Diana," he said. "I'm not saying you can't do it, but what you're suggesting would make Daxtry the largest county in the kingdom. Do you think the other Counts and Barons will sit quietly and let that happen?"

"I think, if you are behind me, the others will fall in line. They respect you."

They do? If they did, he didn't see it. What he saw was a roomful of nobles, all of whom disagreed with him on some issue or another, none of whom accepted anything he had to say without turning it into an argument.

He shook his head. "I don't think it would be that easy. And honestly, Diana, I'm not convinced it's a good idea myself. But it's worth considering. You've done excellent work here on the frontier and I'm not sure you always get the recognition you deserve. I'm not going to parcel out land we haven't conquered yet, but I promise I'll give your proposal serious consideration."

Diana looked surprised. "I—it's not what I hoped to hear, but thank you, your Majesty."

"Thank *you*, Diana. Was there anything else?"

"Actually, yes, if—"

A page threw the tent door open. "Your Majesty, the message is coming through!"

Jeffrey ran from the King's tent to the Devisers' tent, brushing past a dozen people and almost running into four or five more. He arrived, breathless, to see one technician reading the message off the tape while another wrote down the decoded text. He clenched his fists and willed himself not to pace or hover or do anything else that might disrupt the technicians' work. Finally the second technician handed off the paper to a third person, who sat at a desk, her lips moving slightly, as she translated the document from Kirkellish to Tremontanese. Jeffrey couldn't stand it any longer. He went and stood behind the woman and read over her shoulder as she wrote.

GREETINGS TO KING JEFFREY OF TREMONTANE FROM MAIREN OF THE KIRKELLAN. MUTUAL AID TREATY IS DESIRABLE HOWEVER NEGOTIATIONS WILL NOT COMMENCE UNTIL IMMEDIATE THREAT

The translator stopped to change pens. Jeffrey's heart sank.

Mairen wanted a treaty, but wasn't willing to negotiate until after Hrovald's attack? She wanted to see how things would play out. So much for Imogen's ability to convince her mother of the urgency of the situation and the mutual benefit a treaty would bring to both their countries.

Jeffrey squeezed his eyes shut and swallowed a handful of curses. He heard the translator's pen resume its scratching trail across the paper. He almost couldn't bear to look. No, it was his duty to look. Taking on unpleasant responsibilities was a King's burden, his father had said. His father would have been more convincing. He opened his eyes and followed the translator's pen.

IMMEDIATE THREAT IS PAST. AS TOKEN OF GOOD FAITH KIRKELLAN WILL SEND ONE THOUSAND HORSES TO ARRIVE IN TWO DAYS. OTHER TERMS OF TREATY IN ABEYANCE. IMOGEN SPEAKS HIGHLY OF YOU AM LOOKING FORWARD TO MEETING IN PERSON SIGNED MAIREN OF THE KIRKELLAN ACKNOWLEDGE RECEIPT.

One thousand horses. In Kirkellan terms, that meant one thousand mounted warriors. *One thousand* well-trained, saber-wielding warriors on *one thousand* well-trained, enormous horses. That would increase the size of the army by almost half again its current strength. Jeffrey found he'd stopped breathing and his vision was getting blurry; he made himself take a deep breath and wipe the silly grin off his face. "Send a reply," he told the technicians. "Um...message received, thanks to the *matrian* for her generosity and anticipate coming to mutually beneficial terms after defeating Hrovald." That might even happen, now. *One thousand mounted warriors.* "Oh, and my, um, Warleader wishes to coordinate attack with yours, message to follow." At least, Marcus would as soon as he heard about it.

Jeffrey reached out of the tent, collared a page, and sent her flying to bring Marcus to the Devisers' tent. Imogen spoke highly of him, did she? It was nice to think he'd made as much of an impression on her as she had on him, though he couldn't remember doing anything particularly noteworthy.

Marcus came through the door, panting. "What's wrong?"

"Nothing's wrong. Everything is right. Mairen's sending a thousand warriors to join the attack."

Marcus's mouth fell open. "A thousand…"

"A thousand mounted warriors. They'll be here in two days. We just have to hope to heaven Hrovald's army gets stuck in the mud or something. I told the *matrian* you'd want to coordinate their attack with their Warleader."

"Damn. That's not going to be easy. I hope they have maps. Wait, *I* don't have maps. You, boy—no, I can't explain which ones I want."

"I'll go. Marcus, we may actually survive this."

"Let's not get overconfident…but just between the two of us, you're right."

Jeffrey kept his pace to something less than a run, but his thoughts went racing ahead of him. They'd need to choose their battlefield with their allies in mind. That meant moving again. Thank heaven Elspeth was well out of it; he'd married her and Owen the day before, and with luck they'd be in Aurilien before battle with the Ruskalder was even joined. Not that that would matter if they couldn't stop the Ruskalder. If the Tremontanan army fell—but there was no point thinking like that. They would win. They *had* to win. Everything that came after could wait.

MARCUS'S CHOSEN BATTLE SITE WAS A PLAIN AT THE BASE OF A LOW RISE to the west. They took up positions that put the rise on their left and gave them room to maneuver in all other directions. The rise was important. With the commanders and Jeffrey gathered in the king's tent, Marcus drew up his plan of attack.

"The Kirkellan are coming to us from the west. They'll use the rise to conceal themselves until they're ready to attack, which will hopefully rattle the Ruskalder into making mistakes. Depending on when they arrive, they'll either attack the left flank or the rear, with smaller parties taking the fight to the front lines. Our problem is that we don't know how soon they'll get here. Ideally, they'll arrive before

Hrovald does and we'll be better able to coordinate, but we're planning for the worst contingency, which is that they arrive after battle is joined. Our strategy, therefore, allows for our allies' presence, but doesn't depend on it.

"Here—" Marcus drew several lines—"and here are where the riflemen will be. From this position they'll be able to start firing when the Ruskalder are about two hundred yards from our front lines." A murmur went up at this, and Marcus grinned. "And you all were annoyed at how much practicing they did. Our best riflemen can shoot a fly off your nose at four hundred yards and can shoot three times a minute. They'll soften up the front lines for the infantry."

"Where are the cavalry in all of this? They're not being pushed aside just because we have other horses coming—horses we know nothing about, I might add?" said the captain in charge of the cavalry.

"Our light cavalry functions differently from the Kirkellan heavy cavalry, Dorcas. Your soldiers will harry the Ruskalder on the eastern flank. We want to surround them on both sides, but if the Kirkellan don't show up right away, you're going to be the sole flanking force." The captain nodded, stiffly, her mouth still set in a hard line. Jeffrey didn't know her well, but Marcus trusted her, and Jeffrey now wondered if her pride would interfere with her ability to do her duty. They needed their cavalry on the right flank to press Hrovald's army hard, not a glamorous job or one that allowed for individuals to gain glory. Jeffrey made a mental note to discuss the potential problem with Marcus.

"The infantry will hold the line here," Marcus said, drawing a long slash across the board. "The end of the line will move to follow our flankers. We want to enclose Hrovald's army like this, keep them bottled up. The important thing to remember is that Hrovald doesn't have a unified force as we do. His chiefs all maintain their own smaller armies, somewhere between three and five hundred men apiece, and though Hrovald directs the overall strategy, his chiefs dictate how their men will carry it out. We're going to exploit that autonomy by trying to break the army into its constituent parts. We may be able to force some of those smaller armies to retreat, depending on how they're organized. I'll be directing our tactics from here—" he drew an X to the rear and center of the other lines —"where I can observe the motion of the enemy troops and direct our action along the army's fracture lines, as it were." He laid down his piece of charcoal and dusted his fingers off on his jerkin. "Any questions?"

"How soon do we expect to join battle?" asked a man to the rear of the group.

"Our scouts tell us they'll be here sometime tomorrow no earlier than noon."

"And we have no sign of the Kirkellan warriors."

"Not as yet."

"Isn't it possible that they won't get here at all?" The man glanced from side to side as if looking for support, and there were murmurs among the others. A couple of people shifted and looked away from Marcus and his battle plan.

"Mairen of the Kirkellan has said she will send aid," Jeffrey said, "and I have faith that she will keep her word."

"Begging your pardon, your Majesty, but we know little of the Kirkellan besides their reputation," said the same man. "It is not their people Hrovald is trying to destroy."

"What is your name, Colonel?" Jeffrey asked.

The man blanched. "Uh...Charlton Eggers, your Majesty."

"Colonel Eggers, if Hrovald defeats us tomorrow, he will assuredly turn his armies against the Kirkellan next. Mairen knows that. She is aware that in this action, we are her first line of defense. You said we know little of the Kirkellan other than their reputation. This is true. We know that they are honorable warriors—too honorable to allow others to fight their battles for them. Colonel Eggers, the Kirkellan *will* come to our aid because this is their battle too. General Anselm will be watching the battle. I will be watching the horizon. And I guarantee that when our allies arrive, I will ensure that every man and woman on that field knows it."

There was more murmuring. The colonel's face regained its color. He inclined his head in a bow. "Thank you, your Majesty," he said.

"If there are no other questions...?" Marcus surveyed the room. "Then return to your commands and prepare for battle. We will form up at mid-morning, and may heaven guide our swords."

When everyone had filed out, Marcus said, "That was some speech."

Jeffrey colored. "Too much?"

"Just enough. They look to you, you know."

"Do they? I feel like a figurehead, most of the time. It's not as if I'm a soldier."

"You're not a figurehead. You represent what they're fighting for. Their homes. Their kingdom. You're smart, you're articulate, and soldier or not, you know how to command respect."

Jeffrey went even redder. "That's a lot of praise."

"And not false praise, either. You hand out enough of it, I figure you ought to get some back." He clapped Jeffrey on the shoulder. "And it doesn't hurt that you're a good-looking young man. Hell, half the soldiers on the field would follow you based on that alone."

Jeffrey laughed. "They would not. They're professionals."

"Professionals with good eyesight." Jeffrey punched him lightly on the shoulder, and Marcus grinned. "Come to supper with the commanders. It'll boost their morale. No, no more compliments; they just like to see that you aren't unapproachable."

"I'll do that if you stop telling me how great I am."

"Well, it *is* hard to take you seriously when the tail of your coat is tucked into your trousers like that." Jeffrey craned his head to look over his shoulder and cursed. Marcus left, roaring with laughter.

Jeffrey adjusted his clothing and sat down where he could see Marcus's strategy board. Marcus was smart; this would work. It had to work. He leaned his elbows on the board and put his chin in his hand. No battle plan survived contact with the enemy. It was the thing no one had said that everyone had no doubt been thinking. This all looked good on the board, but so much could go wrong. And the truth was, as much as he trusted Mairen to keep her word, he wasn't at all sure the Kirkellan would make it in time to be of any help. The scouts should have seen some trace of them, yes?

He wondered if Imogen would be one of the warriors in the army. She led that *tiermatha* of hers—it occurred to him that he had no idea how the Kirkellan arranged their fighting forces. Tiny groups of thirteen couldn't make a huge difference, could they? Or did they combine for large battles like this one? He both hoped and feared that she'd come. Hoped, because he wouldn't mind seeing her fight; feared, because he didn't want to see her die. Surely the *matrian* wouldn't send her daughter into combat. Or would she think of it as an honor, or a duty? So much he didn't know about the Kirkellan, and no guarantee that they'd all survive for him to learn it.

JEFFREY: CHAPTER FOUR

*T*he engineers had built a platform that raised Marcus's command post enough above the ground that he and his aides could see most of the battlefield clearly. The army spread out not too loosely from east to west, over two thousand soldiers in ranks seven or eight deep. The cavalry moved restlessly at the eastern end of the line, too few, to Jeffrey's eye, to effectively press the flank, but four hundred was all they had, so it would have to be enough.

He couldn't see all the riflemen, who were behind the lines on ground as high as they could find, but the few he could see reassured him; they were relaxed and ready to shoot. They were the Tremontanan army's best edge over the Ruskalder, and Jeffrey hoped they were as good as Marcus claimed. Jeffrey surveyed the distant horizon through a self-focusing telescope Device. No movement to either the north or the west. He lowered the Device and said, "It's past noon."

"It's not as if we agreed on a schedule," Marcus said. "Tell Hughes to tighten up his formation," he said to a page. "And pass the word for everyone to break out rations and get some rest. We'll see them coming in plenty of time." The young runner nodded and swarmed down the ladder.

Jeffrey raised the Device again and looked to the west. Their platform wasn't tall enough for him to see over the crest of the rise. He'd know of the Kirkellans' arrival just moments before Hrovald's army did. He closed the Device and began to pace. Marcus eyed him skeptically. "That's a bad habit of yours," he said. "Tells everyone you're uncertain. Cut it out or I'll tie you to a chair."

"You don't think that would be more demoralizing?"

"No. Stop fidgeting or go somewhere else. Take a ride. Write a letter to the Dowager Consort. She'd probably put it in a vault with all the other important papers from Tremontane's history."

Jeffrey scowled at Marcus, but stopped pacing. He took up Owen's relaxed pose, legs apart, hands behind his back, and thought of other things. Elspeth and Owen would be home. Owen had threatened to return as soon as Elspeth was safe, but Jeffrey was certain he wouldn't be able to leave her alone once she pleaded with him with those big brown puppy eyes that had always gotten her everything she wanted from their father and had earned her more than one spanking from their mother. Right now Jeffrey would be grateful to discover Owen was not immune to their effect.

He dropped his pose and walked around to the rear of the platform. Three horses waited there, watched over by an older page. Three horses for the last part of the plan, the desperate final action that would mean all was lost: three horses to take him, Marcus, and Diana back to Aurilien to defend that city against Hrovald's invaders. It would be a pointless action; Aurilien was currently defended by nothing but the few soldiers of the Home Guard, all of them top fighters but none of them able to fight off a full-sized army. But Marcus insisted that the King of Tremontane would not be slaughtered like an animal on the battlefield. No, he could be slaughtered in the comfort of his own home instead. *I refuse to think like that.* He went back to the front of the platform, took out the Device and looked at the distant horizon again. It was like pacing, only much slower.

There was movement on the horizon.

At first, Jeffrey thought his impatient eyes might be mistaken. He continued to watch until it was clear that what he saw was not an illusion, but people marching toward them. His heart began beating faster. He lowered the Device and said, in a low voice, "Marcus."

"I see it," Marcus said. He had a Device of his own, with two lenses instead of one, and he looked out across the field as if nothing were out of the ordinary. "I'll give the word in five minutes. Give the soldiers time to finish eating and stretch a bit."

Jeffrey once again looked at the western horizon. Still nothing. He tried to remain calm. "They'll come," he said, not aware that he'd spoken aloud until Marcus said, "No sense watching for them anymore. Right now the fight's down to us."

After a few more minutes, Marcus sent a handful of runners to the commanders in the field. Jeffrey watched as a ripple passed over the army, word spreading from the rear to the front and soldiers standing from where they'd sat to eat their cold dinner. Jeffrey tried to imagine what they were feeling: fear, anxiety, anticipation, eagerness? He turned his Device on the front line and saw only the backs of their heads, men and women with their faces turned resolutely toward the foe they couldn't yet see.

Jeffrey went back to watching the Ruskalder approach and wished he had a better sense of distance. The Device confused everything. He put it aside and began watching with his own eyes. They were still too far away to make out individuals; the Ruskalder were a solid mass that seemed to go on for miles, though Jeffrey knew there were only about four thousand men in the army and wouldn't be spread out nearly that far. He found his hands were clenched so tightly on the Device they were sweating, and he closed the thing to a flat disc and put it inside his coat.

Marcus was still looking through his Device. He cursed. "They're spread out farther along the line than we are," he said. "You, tell Dorcas Higgins to move her people farther east. They're going to have to drive the Ruskalder farther in," he told Jeffrey when the page had gone. "That rise is going to save us on the west. It's steep enough that it will make moving around our people difficult. We're going to have to flank them or be enveloped ourselves."

And still the Ruskalder came on, close enough now to see them as individuals dressed in leather armor Jeffrey hoped was inferior to the Tremontanan soldiers' leather and steel gear. Some of the Ruskalder wore leather caps, but most were bareheaded. They carried dual swords, long and short, though none of them had drawn weapons yet. Jeffrey couldn't take his eyes off them. They moved like predators. Jeffrey hoped the army didn't find them as intimidating as he had to admit he did. But no, the Tremontanan army was better armed, better armored, and almost certainly better trained to fight as a unit. The Ruskalder weren't going to find them prey at all.

Hrovald. This was all his fault. Jeffrey pulled out his Device and swept the army. There. No, that wasn't Hrovald, it was one of his chiefs, but the man had a banner that set him apart from the others. "Do we focus on the banners?" he asked Marcus, who stood silent and unmoving beside him.

"Yes and no," Marcus said. "The banners mark the locations where the armies are joined. If I give the word, the commanders know to have their soldiers strike for them, but if there isn't a way through, going after the banner is just a way to get more of us killed."

Jeffrey went back to looking over the Ruskalder army. "I see him," he said, and Marcus didn't need to be told whom Jeffrey was talking about. "Left of center."

"There he is," Marcus agreed. "Pity we can't just go straight for him. I bet most of these chiefs would turn and run if he wasn't there to control them."

"All of them would," Jeffrey corrected. "The chiefs would go for secure ground so they could make a play for Ruskald. Fighting us would simply lose them valuable men they might need to bring against their rivals. And all of them see themselves as potential kings."

Marcus grunted. "Now I *really* wish we had a shot—" He lowered his Device and ran for the rear of the platform, climbed rapidly down the ladder and ran off toward one of the riflemen's embankments.

Jeffrey watched him go, light dawning. If Hrovald came close enough, maybe one of the riflemen could take him out. He went back to watching Hrovald. It was a good idea, but not something they should count on. Jeffrey knew Hrovald to be both intelligent and cunning. Jeffrey would be very surprised if Hrovald couldn't figure out the limit of the riflemen's range and stay well out of it.

Marcus came back a few minutes later, breathing heavily. "I know what you're going to say, there's not much chance of it," he said, "but if we aren't prepared for the possibility, we're going to kick ourselves later." Jeffrey nodded his agreement.

Then there was nothing they could do but watch the slow, steady advancement of the Ruskalder troops. They seemed to give off a dark menace that trailed behind them like an insubstantial cloud. Jeffrey kept his Device trained on Hrovald, who rode one of the few horses in the army—not even all the chiefs rode—and was accompanied by another rider who bore a banner with the emblem of Ruskald, a fist holding a knife, point down.

Jeffrey's hands shook with anger. He felt impotent, standing here on a platform well out of danger, not allowed to take up a sword in defense of his country or able to meet Hrovald on the field of battle to take his revenge for what had happened to Elspeth. He thrust the Device back into his coat, not bothering to close it, and found a camp chair. He needed to regain control. He needed to look strong and certain even if none of those soldiers was able to look back and see him standing here. He still wasn't sure if he was a good King yet, but he sure as hell could look the part.

"You all right?" Marcus said, laying a hand on his shoulder. Jeffrey nodded. He took a deep breath, stood, and said, "It's time."

They both went to the front edge of the platform. Any minute now. A cry went up from the left and, like an echo, another from the right, and suddenly the air exploded as the riflemen took their first shots. Men at the front of the Ruskalder army dropped; their comrades cried out in surprise and fear. Another round of firing, more dead or wounded Ruskalder on the ground, and the enemy army charged, some stumbling over the bodies of their fallen fellows, but none hesitating. More shooting, this time ragged as some riflemen reloaded faster than others. More Ruskalder dropped. Jeffrey turned his gaze on their own front line, which held firm. Out of the corner of his eye he saw movement, and turned, dreading that their men had started to flee, but it was Captain Higgins's cavalry, making their wide curving turn to enclose the eastern flank of the enemy army. Light flashed off their raised, curved sabers as they stretched out in a long line to stop the Ruskalder from coming around behind the soldiers on the east side and enveloping them completely.

A last salvo, and the Ruskalder met the Tremontanan front line with a clash, and the Tremontanans staggered back, temporarily overwhelmed by the momentum of their enemy. Jeffrey realized his hands were clenched into fists, his nails driving into his palms, and forced them to relax and open. The noise drifted up to them, shouts and screams of pain and the sharp sound of metal on metal. Jeffrey didn't understand what he was looking at, couldn't tell if they were winning or losing or even if it was too early to know anything like that. Marcus was so intent on what he saw that Jeffrey didn't like to disturb him. He turned his attention back to the cavalry, which seemed to have succeeded—no. No. The Ruskalder had managed to get a line around them and were now attacking them on all sides. Horses and riders fell. The remaining riders pulled back, trying to escape the trap they were in, and regrouped to flank again. Marcus cursed, and sent a runner off in that direction. Soon Jeffrey saw the infantry on that side moving back and east to support the cavalry, which spared them, but at what cost to the main body of the army? Jeffrey could see the Ruskalder pressing them hard on that side, and saw also that the front line on that side was beginning to sag.

He looked around the rest of the field. The Tremontanans were holding their own on the west, he thought, though it was entirely due to that rise, which, as Marcus predicted, the Ruskalder were reluctant to tackle. Jeffrey didn't understand that; it wasn't that big a hill. But he didn't care. He relaxed his fists again, feeling the sharp pain from his nails cutting into his flesh.

The cavalry on the east had recovered, but only just, and the entire line had been pushed back toward the platform. Marcus was sending messengers rapidly now, and then he said, "Look," and pointed toward the eastern side of the field, where a wedge of Tremontanan fighters had inserted itself between two parts of the army, surrounding the enemy who were pressing the cavalry most fiercely. The enemy pulled back, the wedge retreated, and the front line made ground against the Ruskalder.

"Excellent," Jeffrey said, and Marcus grunted. It didn't sound positive. "Wasn't that good?" Jeffrey asked.

"They were meant to drive that wedge all the way forward and envelop those troops," he said. "The fighting's just too fierce over there. It's...not good."

Jeffrey stared at him. Marcus looked grim. No, worse than grim, he looked impassive. Jeffrey turned away, his heart leaden. "Not good" meant disaster was coming, in Marcus-speak. With shaking hands, Jeffrey turned his Device on the western horizon. There wasn't anything he could do for his army. There wasn't anything he could do for *anyone* at this point. All he could do was watch the horizon, as he'd sworn to do, and hope. He watched until his eyes watered, put down the Device and rubbed them. It was pointless. He lifted the Device to the horizon.

A single Kirkellan warrior stood there, his or her horse perfectly still, watching the battle.

Jeffrey lowered the Device and watched the rider turn and ride away. "No," he said, "no," and it was a curse on his lips. How dare they taunt him? Mairen had *promised*, and he, like a fool, had believed her. He bowed his head and squeezed his eyes shut. They had been betrayed—no, he'd been betrayed, and he'd betrayed his soldiers by giving them false hope.

He looked up at the rise again. There was the Kirkellan, just standing there. Or was it a different one? Who cared? As if it made a difference.

Another rider joined the first. Then a third. Then, before his eyes, the horizon was filled with horses and riders. He dropped the Device, heard it tinkle as the lens shattered. He looked around madly. A signal. They needed a signal. "Marcus, we need a rallying call," he said, grabbing the general by the collar and turning him to look at the western rise.

Marcus swore, then grabbed a runner. "Tell the buglers to sound the call to arms," he said, and at that moment five hundred mounted warriors charged over the top of the hill with a shout that no one could fail to hear. They plunged down upon the rear of the army, and the shout was replaced by screams and a thundering crash of horses riding down infantry who could not escape.

Jeffrey kept a tight hold on himself to keep from jumping up and down and cheering. He saw the second wave of riders, this one much smaller, come over the rise toward the Tremontanan front lines. Wave after wave swept past the Ruskalder; bright javelins spun and flew, impaling warrior after warrior until, miraculously, the Ruskalder broke and fled.

With a cheer, half the Kirkellan gave chase. The other half pulled up and milled around, looking confused...no, looking around. One of them raised a javelin and shouted an unintelligible command, and the entire force of about one hundred riders rode toward the rear of the Tremontanan army, then around and behind it. As they passed the platform, the lead rider raised her javelin high as if in salute. Jeffrey's heart lifted. He would know that rider anywhere.

He watched her lead her troop all the way to where the embattled cavalry still struggled. In a complicated maneuver, the Kirkellan horses took up the Tremontanan cavalry's position, pushing the Ruskalder back. They moved as if it were a dance, horses trading positions as needed, shoving the line bodily away from the Tremontanan army, who rallied behind them and began to do some pushing of their own. The Ruskalder gave way slowly, then all at once turned and scrambled over one another to get free.

"Marcus," Jeffrey said.

"Don't be too excited yet. Hrovald hasn't given up," Marcus replied, but as Jeffrey turned his gaze on the main Kirkellan force, he saw the entire western side of Hrovald's army break away and retreat. It was more orderly than the scrambling dash Imogen's warriors had forced on the eastern side, and Jeffrey could see two of the banners leading the way, but it was a retreat nonetheless. This time Jeffrey did cheer, just once, before Marcus gave him a look that was meant to remind him of his station.

"And...there he goes," Marcus said, and Jeffrey saw Hrovald's banner drop and Hrovald turn his horse to follow his fleeing army.

"Should we pursue him?"

"We'll get too spread out. Unless you think killing Hrovald would be worth the risk?"

"You're asking me about military tactics?"

"This isn't military. This is politics. Your Majesty." Marcus invested the last two words with a heavy meaning.

Jeffrey considered briefly. "Hrovald's lost the respect of his chiefs. The two that broke and ran, there on the west, it's possible that was a show of defiance and a warning that one or both of them might challenge him for the throne. In any case, he's going to be too busy consolidating his power to come against us any time soon. By the way he's moving, I judge we'd lose a lot more soldiers and risk not capturing or killing him at all. So I say, have them pull back."

Marcus nodded. "Send word to fall back," he told two of the runners, then looked back at Jeffrey. "Well done, your Majesty," he said, and bowed. Jeffrey felt uncomfortable, but accepted his gesture.

"Now I have to meet with Mairen and see if we can't put together something more permanent than the loan of her warriors," he said. "I wonder how many of them we lost."

"I doubt she'd hold it against us," Marcus said.

Jeffrey shook his head. "No, she won't, but we ought to pay our respects to their dead as well as our own." He looked out over the field and now saw the fallen bodies that peopled it. "War's over. Time to bury our dead and see if we can't build a peace for their sakes."

JEFFREY: CHAPTER FIVE

They set up the negotiation tent halfway between the army camp and the temporary camp of the Kirkellan. Jeffrey was astonished at how quickly they had built what was effectively a tent city. It was far more permanent looking in two hours than the Tremontanan camp had been in a month. The *matrian*'s own tent was visible from a distance, though her banner didn't currently fly over it. That meant she was on her way here.

Jeffrey gestured his honor guard to stand a little farther away. A page stood next to an improvised flagpole, holding a flag in the Tremontane colors. Since Jeffrey knew little of the Kirkellan customs regarding respect and hospitality, he decided to wait to fly his flag until the *matrian* arrived.

And...there she was. Her honor guard was a little more impressive than Jeffrey's, consisting of two large fellows in furs and armor who looked as if they were perfectly capable of ripping one of Jeffrey's arms off if that became necessary. Mairen herself was a short, round woman with short dark hair and alert blue eyes. She stopped a few feet away from Jeffrey and nodded at him. "King of Tremontane," she said in lightly accented Tremontanese.

"*Matrian* of the Kirkellan," Jeffrey replied.

"You have not raised your flag," she said.

"I didn't know if that might constitute an insult, as if I were claiming right of precedence."

Mairen smiled. "That you thought so is respectful enough." She gestured at the page holding the Tremontanan flag, who quickly fastened it to the line. Mairen herself raised the line enough to fasten her own flag there, then hoisted both to flutter in the slight breeze.

"Will you enter?" Jeffrey asked, and politely held the tent flap for her. She smiled again and entered without comment. He followed her. The honor guards remained outside.

Inside was a table and two chairs, ink and pens and paper, and nothing else. Jeffrey and Mairen sat opposite each other. "I'm glad you speak my language," Jeffrey said. "I'm afraid I only speak Veriboldan."

"I speak that too," Mairen said. "We trade with Veribold regularly. It is an interesting society."

"I agree," Jeffrey said. "Though despite having a Veriboldan ambassador in Aurilien, we know very little about them."

Mairen nodded. "As we know little about Tremontane, and as I imagine you know little of us."

Jeffrey smiled and bowed his head. "We would like to know more of the Kirkellan. I am grateful for the assistance you've given us. I hope your losses were not too heavy."

"Warriors die doing what they love," Mairen said, "but it is a loss nonetheless when one of them leaves us for heaven."

"We feel the same."

"Then we already have something in common," Mairen said with a smile. "Tell me, king of Tremontane, how it is you envision our countries' relationship in the future?"

He'd given this a lot of thought. "Mutual defensive aid. We share a common enemy and I am afraid Hrovald will come after your people next. I realize the Kirkellan have defended themselves successfully against Ruskald for many years, but from what I understand you entered into a peace treaty that may have been skewed in Hrovald's favor, which—forgive me—suggests that you are not in as strong a position in relation to Ruskald as you might like."

"And where does your information come from?" Mairen sounded a little angry, which made sense because Jeffrey had just as much as told her that her warrior people couldn't take care of themselves.

"Imogen of the Kirkellan rescued my sister and my friend from Hrovald. She spoke of the treaty and the *banrach* and the reasons behind both. I found her both intelligent and wise. If I misunderstand the situation, it's because of my failings, not hers."

Mairen subsided. "You can hardly expect me to admit to weakness before someone I'm negotiating with."

"But I am admitting weakness when I say that without your warriors' help, my army would have fallen. And you didn't take advantage of that weakness. I believe you to be honorable and I think you'll do the honorable thing by me, as I intend to do by you."

"That takes courage. I salute you for it."

"Thank you. May I ask, in return, how you see our countries' relationship?"

Mairen clasped her fingers together and laid her hands on the table. "I agree that we can benefit one another in terms of defense," she said, "but I believe we have an opportunity here that we should not pass up. I am...disturbed by my people's isolation from the wider world. Our trade with Veribold is limited to those on the edges of society; we do not have a diplomatic relation with them. And you know what our relation with Hrovald is. I think a diplomatic and economic relationship with Tremontane would benefit us both."

"Not to be insulting, but in what way can the Kirkellan benefit Tremontane? Our trade goods are more varied and highly refined, and our societies are very different."

"We have one thing that no one else does, and that is our horses," Mairen said. "I have seen the animals you use. They are small and weak and my sources tell me that they do not have nearly the power ours do."

"They suit us well."

"But they could suit you better if they were bred with ours."

The idea captured Jeffrey's interest. It was true that Tremontanan horses were slim and lightweight, and the repeated failure of Devisers to invent a self-propelled carriage and their resulting dependence on horse-drawn conveyances meant a limitation on commerce and travel. "You wouldn't mind us, um, diluting the breed?"

"We've bred our horses over the centuries to be exactly what we need in the environment we live in. We would expect you to do the same. And I think, also, that a cultural exchange would make both our countries more aware of the possibilities outside our separate boundaries. We might begin with an exchange of ambassadors, and see what happens after that."

Jeffrey nodded slowly. "I agree, *matrian*."

"You should call me Mairen."

"And I would like you to call me Jeffrey." They clasped hands.

"Then I think we should draw this up," Mairen said, "if you don't mind doing the writing."

"Not at all." Jeffrey drew pen and paper toward him. "Tell me if I'm missing anything."

It took them two hours to come up with an agreement, and another hour for scribes to make a fair copy of Jeffrey's untidy handwriting twice. Each signed both documents, then waited for the ink to dry. "I'm glad you didn't offer another *banrach*," Jeffrey said. "I'm afraid I would have had to refuse."

"I think Imogen might have rebelled if I did," Mairen said with a chuckle, "though she seems to like you well enough."

"I like her too," Jeffrey said. "Aside from the debt I owe her, I think she's an impressive young woman and I enjoyed talking to her. Hrovald would have had a hard time cowing her."

"Which is why I sent her. She is strong-willed and strong of body, and intelligent. I am grateful she did not have to complete the term of the *banrach*, though. Too much time in Hrovald's house and even Imogen would have changed."

Jeffrey's stomach tightened again at the thought of Imogen living with Hrovald. "I wish we'd been able to kill him."

"So do I. Imogen had the chance, but she let it go—a poor decision, but the only one she could make at the time."

"She didn't mention that."

"She may be a warrior, but I think she has trouble with the idea of taking a life in cold blood. I would never say this to her, she would be insulted, but there is a part of her that is no warrior."

Jeffrey picked up the documents and handed one copy to her. "I will send my ambassador to you when I get back to Aurilien. You will wait here?"

"For another four weeks, until it is time for us to move to the summer hunting grounds. As agreed, we will lend some of our *tier-matha* to patrol the territory you have annexed until the winter. I will send my ambassador and her retinue to you tomorrow, along with a company of riders to enrich your—what did you call it?"

"The Home Guard."

"Yes. To be part of the Home Guard while the army is reinforcing the annexed territory, again to return to us before the snows fall."

"And I will direct trading caravans to the Eidestal during the summertime. They'd probably want to go anyway, now that they wouldn't be crossing Ruskald to reach you."

"Then we are in agreement, Jeffrey of Tremontane."

"We are, and thank you, Mairen of the Kirkellan."

They shook hands again, then retrieved their flags and went to their respective camps. Jeffrey went straight to his tent, flopped down on his cot, and covered his face with his hands. Negotiating exhausted him and made him hungry, but right now exhaustion was winning.

He felt confident about the treaty, though he wasn't sure Tremontane wasn't getting the better end of the deal. That would depend on how excited people back home would be at the prospect of breeding Kirkellan warhorses with their smaller ones. And George Donaldson was going to have kittens when he found out Jeffrey had just doubled the number of soldiers he was responsible for, back home, and that the new ones didn't even speak Tremontanese. Well, George would just have to live with it. Mairen had been awfully accommodating about sending them. Did she think they'd be protection for the ambassador?

A Kirkellan ambassador in Tremontane. Where would they put him, or her? No, *her*, the *matrian* had said *her*. Could they set her up in a house in the city, like the Veribold and Eskandel ambassadors? That might be too much culture shock for a woman raised as a nomad who'd never lived in anything but a tent before. The palace? Same problem, really. He groaned. Why hadn't he thought of all this before he agreed to an exchange of ambassadors?

He sat up and ran his fingers through his hair, then tried to finger-comb it back down. The ambassador could wait until tomorrow. Right now he had to meet with the commanders of the army to discuss the occupation of the territory. No. Right now he had to *eat*.

THEY WERE STILL DISCUSSING THE OCCUPATION OF THE TERRITORY THE next morning, a discussion which only ended because the king's tent started coming down around them as the camp was dismantled. Jeffrey led everyone out of the collapsing tent and said, "Marcus, I'm going to leave the rest of it to you. All I insist on is that you not push the occupied territory any farther north than it is. We're not so in need of land that we have to snatch as much as we can from Hrovald. I'm satisfied with the line we've drawn, so no excuses, understood?"

"Yes, your Majesty," Marcus rumbled, glancing sharply at Colonel Stubbs beside him, who'd been the one most vocal about taking more territory. Stubbs made an exasperated face, but said, "I understand, your Majesty."

"Your Majesty, I—" began Colonel Williams, but Jeffrey silenced him with a gesture.

"Sorry to cut you off like that," he said in a low voice, "but I know what you were going to complain about and they're almost here. Some of them might even speak Tremontanese." The ambassador and her retinue were approaching. Jeffrey raised his hand to salute the rider at the head of the long column of Kirkellan, then grinned broadly.

"Imogen!" he said. "Are you the ambassador, then? Mairen said... but this really is wonderful. I know Elspeth will be thrilled to see you. Oh—you're injured."

Imogen sat her horse like a statue, a bandage wrapped around her head. As Jeffrey spoke, she unbent barely enough to give him a half-smile. She didn't seem very happy to be there. *Looks like Mairen put pressure on her again. I'll have to make sure she feels comfortable in Aurilien.* "It is nothing," she said, putting her hand to her head. "It is —they bleed much. But it is almost healed."

"I'm glad to hear this. So, I remember your *tiermatha*, and this is the company Mairen promised to send with you. Are you their, um, captain?"

Imogen shook her head, turned and gestured to a couple of women behind her. "These are Rhion and Fionna," she said. "They are...leaders of part of the company that was mine in the battle. It is to say, the company is in two parts, and Rhion leads one and Fionna leads the other. I have only my *tiermatha* now." She smiled, a real smile, not forced or cold. "Ambassador is much work, I think."

"Depends on how you do it," Jeffrey joked. When she looked blank, he added, "I am pleased to meet Rhion and Fionna both. This is Colonel Fred Williams, commander of the Home Guard. He'll be your superior officer," he added, addressing the two women by reflex even though their blank expressions told him they spoke not one word of Tremontanese.

Imogen was frowning again. "You say he is better than them?"

"No, I didn't—oh, no, 'superior officer' doesn't mean superior like better, it means he's in command. Like you were in command of Rhion and Fionna during the battle."

Imogen's face cleared. "I understand," she said, and turned in her seat to say something to Rhion and Fionna. Both women grew steadily more concerned the longer Imogen talked. Then Rhion burst out angrily and at length. Williams said, "I told you I thought this was a bad idea, your Majesty."

"Just give them time to get used to it." He hoped he was right about that.

Imogen turned back and said, "It is all right. She is concerned about the language."

"See?" Jeffrey said. "Nothing to worry about."

Imogen was speaking to the two women again. Eventually, they looked at one another, and Fionna said something that made all three women laugh. "She says it will be an adventure," Imogen explained.

Williams didn't look happy. He turned to look at Jeffrey, who raised an eyebrow at him, daring him to complain further. "All right," he said, "I'll keep an open mind. But I hope they learn to speak our language."

"Maybe it is you who will speak ours," Imogen said tartly, and Jeffrey felt a twinge of unease. Despite his words, he was starting to worry again about the wisdom of this plan. He'd accepted a hundred warriors who couldn't communicate with anyone except each other and an ambassador who kept getting angry and didn't seem to want to be there. She hadn't even dismounted, and he was getting a crick in his neck having to look up at her all the time. It looked as if he was the one who would have to be the diplomat.

"Imogen, this is General Marcus Anselm, Colonel Stubbs, Colonel Williams you've met, and Diana Ashmore, Baroness of Daxtry. She's been responsible for our defenses along the old Ruskalder border. Colonel Stubbs is Marcus's second in command. They'll stay here and Colonel Williams will return with us to Aurilien. Marcus, I'll have those other telecoders to you by the end of next week. Diana, we'll see you in Aurilien in a week or so, yes? Keep me apprised of any developments. I want to know if the Ruskalder even waggle their furry buttocks in our direction."

He looked around for his horse and saw a page leading it toward him. *I hope I don't look like an idiot mounting this thing, not in front of all those Kirkellan who probably could ride before they could walk.* He mounted without assistance and without looking too foolish. His father would have given them a real show. "Let's move out," he said, prodding the black gelding in the ribs, and led their little procession across the fields in the direction of Aurilien.

It took them most of three days—three long, unpleasant days and two even less pleasant nights—to reach Aurilien. The Kirkellan, naturally, kept to themselves, pitching their own low-roofed tents and cooking for themselves. Jeffrey, with his spacious three-room tent, his pages, his personal guard, and even a cook felt awkward and soft beside them. Imogen remained distant and irritable. He tried to invite her to dine with him and Fred, on the grounds that she was the ambassador, but she refused every time.

After supper every evening, he lay on his cot, fully clothed, and listened to her talk and laugh with her *tiermatha*, and felt alone and jealous of their camaraderie. Maybe he'd been wrong about her. It wasn't as if they'd had all that much contact, but he had thought she might be a friend. He couldn't wait to get back to Aurilien.

He now wished Owen had resisted his bride's big brown puppy eyes and come back to the camp. Fred was a good man, but too class-conscious to be a comfortable companion. He thought about trying to join the *tiermatha* around their fire, but knew it would be a mistake; he couldn't fit in and would just feel more awkward and alone than ever.

They left the plains behind after the first day and traveled south through forests, birch and maple giving way to ash and oak, all of them budding pale green and filling the air with the scent of new growth. Jeffrey breathed in the fresh air and felt himself relax despite his forbidding, silent companion. He didn't know why Imogen continued to ride by his side when she could ride with her damn *tier-matha* and share in the jokes he couldn't understand. Maybe she had some sense of her duties as an ambassador even if she didn't want to perform them, though why she'd think riding next to him was one of those duties was beyond his comprehension. She never said anything, and after the first day, when all his efforts to draw her out were rebuffed, he didn't say anything either.

On the afternoon of the third day, they came out of the forest to see Aurilien some miles off, and Imogen gave a low gasp. Jeffrey couldn't blame her; the city's beauty amazed him every time he came home. It sprawled across the lowland plain like a lazy, sleeping cat, its golden wall failing to restrain the low-roofed buildings that spilled over into the green wooded landscape surrounding it. There was the palace, at the top of a rise where centuries past forts and castles had stood. Jeffrey's father had once shown him a place where the foundation of one of those castles was still visible, deep in a basement that dripped with condensation. Jeffrey had dug out a piece of the mortar and kept it in his pocket for weeks until he'd forgotten it, left it to dissolve in the laundry. That the golden city should be built on such a fragile foundation now struck him as absurd.

He realized he'd stopped his horse and forced everyone to pile up behind him, then realized further that he'd stopped because Imogen had. "Do you like it?" he said quietly, not sure if she'd respond. "I so rarely leave the city that I forget what it looks like from out here. From inside, you only see pieces of it, and it's not so...so...it's had hundreds of years to become what it is, and it never fails to amaze me. I hope you'll like it. I know it's different from what you're used to."

She turned to look at him, and finally she was the Imogen he remembered. "It is beautiful. And powerful," she said. She turned away, blinking hard, and Jeffrey realized all in a rush that she wasn't angry, she was homesick. His heart went out to her. He hoped they, he and Elspeth and Owen, could help her feel welcome.

The road wound back into the forest, still a little chilly in the early spring air even though it was afternoon and sunlight bathed everything in its warmth. Here there were birds courting and challenging one another, and small animals darting between roots or up tree trunks, and occasionally a small deer would flit across the road. Imogen's head turned constantly to follow the birds, which in turn followed them from tree to tree. A squirrel scampered onto a low-hanging branch, almost at Imogen's eye level, and she laughed and reached out to touch it, almost stroking its fur before it danced away.

When they emerged from the trees, the city wall loomed beyond a small settlement of those low-roofed houses. It was less overwhelming than the sight of the whole city had been. The road, which until then had been packed earth, was now covered with broad stones that had been traveled so often they were pressed deep into the ground, their faintly curving tops all that was visible of them. Jeffrey glanced down at his own horse's shod hooves, and Victory's unprotected ones, and wondered how hard Tremontanan paved streets would be on Kirkellan hooves. Would they accept horseshoes? Jeffrey decided to leave the worrying about that to the experts.

Men and women and children came out of the houses to stare at them, then to cheer as they realized who was passing. Jeffrey waved at them, forcing himself to smile. They deserved to see a happy, confident king, one who'd been victorious over the Ruskalder even though that was all down to his experienced generals. What had Marcus said? He represented what they'd fought for? Well, he would do his damnedest to be what they needed, even though he felt like a fraud.

Beside him, Imogen sat stiffly, not acknowledging the cheers. Jeffrey found himself growing angry with her. Why had she agreed to be the ambassador if she wasn't going to act like one? She might as well have stayed with her people. Homesickness or no, if he could bear the cheering, she could.

The crowds grew as they neared the gate, drawn to the king's banner that went before their extraordinary procession of over one hundred giant horses. Jeffrey felt his smile grow strained. His father had never said what this was like, being the focus of so much adulation. But then Anthony North had been confident. He'd known who he was and what he was capable of. His son wasn't nearly so certain.

"You are not well," Imogen said in a voice that was just barely audible over the shouting. Jeffrey jumped a little. He wasn't used to hearing her voice.

"I'm fine," he said, continuing to wave. "Three years and I haven't gotten used to this. I feel—" He shook his head just a little as if to negate his words. "I'm not good with crowds, is all."

He turned to smile at the people on Imogen's side of the road. She looked at him for a long moment, her expression unreadable. Then she smiled, startling him almost to the point of forgetting to wave, turned away and began waving at the crowds, who cheered her. She looked back at Jeffrey and said, "We can be not good with crowds together, I think," and went on smiling and waving as if she was genuinely happy to see each person there.

Jeffrey followed her example, completely surprised. Had she misunderstood what he'd said—or had she understood him perfectly? At any rate, he hoped this meant she'd given up on being angry, or homesick, or whatever it was, because he wanted her for a friend.

JEFFREY: CHAPTER SIX

*T*he gate guards in green and brown saluted them as they passed. Imogen leaned over to Jeffrey and said, "Why is it some wear those colors and some wear the other? The blue and the silver?"

"Those are the colors of Tremontane," he explained. "Green and brown for the mountains. Blue and silver is for the house of North, my family. The ones who wear it are in service to my family, not to the kingdom."

"The blue and the silver is prettier," Imogen said, and Jeffrey laughed.

"Don't tell anyone, but I agree," he said. He went back to waving at the crowd, and Imogen joined him. If anything, the throng of people lining the street was larger than the one outside the city, their cries deafening. Jeffrey waved and smiled until his face hurt and his arm was sore.

Within the wall, Aurilien was beautiful but less grand than when it was seen from a distance. Jeffrey always thought of it as a very cheerful city, the buildings standing straight instead of huddling together waiting for something to attack them as in other cities, such as the much older Kingsport. The roofs were gently sloped, the wooden walls whitewashed or painted neatly, the doors stained dark colors to contrast with the lighter walls. Signs painted with pictures declared what was available inside: a foaming mug for a tavern, a candle for an inn, a bar of soap for a bathing house. People leaned out of upper story windows to cheer their King. Jeffrey wondered idly what he'd do if one of them decided to throw something at him. Keep smiling, probably.

The crowds thinned somewhat as they passed into a district where the buildings were made of stone rather than wood, and Imogen gaped at these tall, ornate houses with steps leading up to their wide doors and glass windows four or five feet across that lined their faces three or even four rows high. Plants grew in stone pots at the foot of these stairs, some of them flowering, some like tiny trees. Horses pulling carriages pulled to one side as the procession passed, and men and women looked out of them and cheered and waved handkerchiefs.

Imogen leaned over to him and said, "I do not think those horses are happy."

"They're treated very well," Jeffrey said, hoping it was true.

"They think there are better things they can do, like be ridden properly. Why do those people not ride instead of being pulled in carts?"

"Um...not everyone in Tremontane can ride, Imogen. And I don't think our horses are as smart as yours." He wondered if he was slandering Tremontanan horses, but Imogen was actually talking to him instead of acting like a statue, and he didn't want her to turn to stone again.

They turned onto Queen's Way Road, four times as wide as the other streets, and it seemed this was where the rest of the city had come to wait for them, and cheer, and wave. More carriages lined the road, people inside cheering, drivers sitting on top cheering, horses indifferent. Small children ran alongside the procession, though not too close to the Kirkellan horses, whose hooves were as large as some of the children's heads. Imogen waved down at them, and they beamed at her. Jeffrey wondered how much of what was happening those children understood. How many of these people knew why they were cheering? Were they happy about the successful defeat of the Ruskalder army, or were they cheering a king they thought had engineered that defeat? It was impossible to tell for certain.

They passed through a fifteen-foot-tall ironwork gate, flung wide to welcome them, and started up a long curving road covered in flat, rectangular stones fitted neatly together in patterns that followed the curve of the road. The road ended at a circular area about one hundred feet across, also covered with the rectangular stones, at the edge of which stood stairs leading up to the palace. The building, if you could call something so immense by such an ordinary word, was pleasantly irregular, with wings added upon wings upon older wings, and Willow North's tower near the center of the palace complex looked older than all of them. Soldiers in green and brown stood at the foot of the wide steps and at the door at the top of the steps, which was open.

Colonel Williams saluted Jeffrey and shouted for the riders to continue on through the open area to where the road emerged and curved around the side of the palace. Rhion and Fionna looked uncertainly at Imogen, who waved them on. The *tiermatha* looked as confused as Rhion and Fionna. Imogen hesitated for a moment, then waved at them to join the line of riders following Williams. One or two of them looked as if they wanted to protest, but wheeled their horses around and led the *tiermatha* away. This time, Jeffrey saw Imogen blinking back tears. He tactfully looked away as he dismounted, then came around to offer her a hand. "Welcome to Aurilien," he said.

She hesitated, then accepted and somewhat awkwardly, more awkwardly than he'd ever seen her, dismounted. "I must stable Victory," she said. The tears were gone as if they'd never been.

"I know," Jeffrey said. A groom came toward them and Jeffrey handed her his reins. "She'll take you—us—to the stables," he said, amending his statement when he saw the lost look return to her face. *So,* now *she wants my company*, he thought, somewhat irritably, then felt ashamed of himself. She was lonely, and he wasn't going to be spiteful.

The stables were a series of long enclosed stalls surrounding a wide yard of packed earth. A forge, currently cold, lay at the far side of the yard. One of the slim Tremontanan horses trotted around the yard on a long line held by a man who stood near the center. Jeffrey couldn't see the point of the exercise, but then he knew almost nothing about horses. Sounds of movement and an occasional whinny came from one of the buildings. The groom went unhesitatingly toward that building and went inside; Imogen and Jeffrey followed.

The young groom disappeared into one of the stalls; an older woman stuck her head out of another. "Your Majesty," she said, surprised, "how can I help you?" She looked at Victory and her mouth hung open. She looked at Imogen, dressed in her Kirkellan clothing, looked at the horse again, then started miming something Jeffrey couldn't make out at all.

"I speak your language," Imogen said, amused.

"That's a relief," the woman said, smiling wryly. "I couldn't for the life of me figure out how to mime 'oats'. Come this way, milady, and I hope you don't take this the wrong way, but we weren't expecting such a big horse."

"She is Kirkellan."

"I know, but I've never seen one up close, milady."

"I am just Imogen."

"You're a diplomat, so you're milady while you're here, milady, and I'd better not hear of my people saying otherwise."

"Very well. I am milady and you are?"

"Kate Fanshaw, milady, and I have the keeping of the stables at the palace. I think we have a stall she'll fit into. What's her name, milady?"

"She is Victory, and thank you for asking."

The stall was big enough, more than big enough, and Victory made a whickering noise of approval. Imogen removed her tack and wiped her down, then brushed her, checking her legs and hooves for injuries and murmuring softly to her. It was like watching a mother care for her enormous child.

"You seem well suited to each other," Jeffrey said, surprising Imogen, who seemed to have forgotten he was there. "How long have you had her?"

"I do not have her. Victory and I are friends since she was— almost since she was foaled."

"Good heaven, she's unshod," said Fanshaw. "May I look at her hoof?"

Imogen stroked Victory's nose and whispered to her, then said, "You can to—I mean, yes, do look."

Fanshaw gently lifted Victory's left front hoof and traced its contours. "I never realized your horses go unshod."

"They do for most of the year. For the winter they have the shoes." Imogen brushed Victory's light red mane and laid her cheek against her soft nose.

"You may want to see about having her shod now. Everything around here is paved. She won't like that."

"You have a...a person who puts the shoes on the—on horses?"

"A farrier? Two or three. Come back sometime and I'll introduce you. They're very good."

Imogen gave Fanshaw an approving look. "Thank you," she said, and finished putting away Victory's gear while the horse stuck her nose deep into the hay trough. "I will come again soon." Jeffrey watched her stroke Victory's mane again, then lift her gear onto her shoulder. "What is it?" she asked him, and he realized he'd been staring at her.

He couldn't remember what he'd been thinking. "Nothing," he said. "Let me call someone to carry that for you."

"I am—I can carry it for me," she said, her knuckles whitening on the grip, and he let the subject drop.

"Now that Victory is in her new home, shall I show you yours?" he asked.

Imogen nodded, then shook her head and said, "I rather you

show me where the Kirkellan will stay, so I know where to find my *tiermatha*."

Jeffrey nodded and led her around to the front of the palace again, wondering if she expected her *tiermatha* to go everywhere with her. How was she supposed to attend diplomatic functions trailed by twelve fierce warriors who looked capable of disemboweling someone with a dinner fork? And yet...was it his job to tell her how to do hers? She wouldn't be much good as a Kirkellan ambassador if he told her what to say or do. He sighed. He just had to hope she'd get over being homesick and probably resentful and learn to serve her people. Something in that rang an echo in his head, but he couldn't think why.

"You are unhappy with me," Imogen said.

"What? No, I'm not," Jeffrey said, uncomfortably aware that this wasn't exactly true.

"You made—" Imogen gave a sigh. "That is a not comfortable sound. You think I should not want to see my *tiermatha*."

How much lying should he do? "I know how important your *tiermatha* is—are?—to you," he said carefully. "You would not be Imogen if you didn't care about them. I am worried that...you don't want to be here. To be an ambassador."

Imogen stopped. "You do not know that," she said. She put her gear on the ground and crossed her arms across her chest.

"I can guess. You wanted to go home, didn't you? And Mairen told you you'd be the ambassador because you speak Tremontanese, and you resented it. So I think you're resisting it, and that worries me."

Imogen looked away from him, toward the palace wall. "I speak Tremontanese, and you and I are friends," she said in a low voice. "If we are not friends, Mairen had find—would have found someone else."

Jeffrey was staggered. "So you don't want us to be friends? Isn't it a little late for that?"

Imogen laughed, still looking away. It sounded bitter. "I am not nice to you because I felt it was your fault I am here," she said. "I am angry at Mother. You are right. I do not want to be here, but I promised I would be a good ambassador and I break my promise already." Her voice wobbled a little. Jeffrey closed his eyes and sighed again. "There," Imogen said. "That is the disappointed sound you make."

He stared at her, disbelieving, then started to laugh. After a while Imogen turned back to look at him. Her face was a mixture of irritation and confusion that made him laugh harder. "That's not disappointment," he said when he regained control of himself. "That's the sound I make when I don't know what to do. Imogen, I know you're sad and frustrated and now you're lonely because everyone you know is gone, but being resentful isn't going to make things better. I—" He almost said, *I know because my father left, too,* but the words stuck in his throat. He said instead, "Isn't there anything good about being here?"

She looked blank, then smiled mischievously. "Elspeth says you have good Devices."

Jeffrey laughed again. "Anything *else*?"

She pursed her lips, thinking. "Kate Fanshaw is nice to Victory. Nicer than Hrovald's person was."

"Imogen..."

She laughed. "Yes. I have friends. And you are one."

"Thank heaven for that. And you have...let me count...one hundred and eighteen Kirkellan friends who will be happy to go riding with you or fight with you or whatever it is you do for fun in the Eidestal."

"And I will be a good ambassador when I learn what that is."

"Didn't Mairen tell you what to do?"

"She said, tell people about the Kirkellan and listen to them talk about their—I mean themselves. But there should be more than that."

"Not really. You can find out what other countries want and what the Kirkellan can give them, and make agreements about that. But mostly you want other countries to like yours so they'll be friendly if you ever need anything from *them*."

Imogen nodded thoughtfully. "I think I can do that."

"So do I. Now, do you want to see your *tiermatha*, or do you want to leave that great bundle of yours somewhere? Because I really can get someone to take it to your rooms for you."

Imogen thought about it. "It is heavy," she said, "and I think I can still be Kirkellan if someone else carries it."

Jeffrey looked around and snapped his fingers at a passing page. "Take this to the ambassador's quarters," he said, "wherever that is. Ask someone in the east wing for help." As the page stumbled off under the weight of Imogen's gear, he told her, "I thought you might be more comfortable among friends, so when I sent word you were coming I told them to set you up in the east wing. Elspeth and Owen will be there, and me and my mother—I think you'll like her."

"If she is like her children I think I will like her too," Imogen grinned, and together they proceeded toward the main entrance of the palace.

Jeffrey had grown up in the palace, but now he saw it anew through Imogen's amazed eyes. There was color everywhere, in the soft rugs that covered the floor, in the walls painted different colors in every room they passed, in paintings hung on the walls that contrasted with sculpture in white marble or warm, rosy wood. Imogen ran a finger across the bare shoulder of a naked marble woman only two feet tall, poised as if to take flight from the pedestal she perched on. "Is it that people in Tremontane often wear no clothes?"

Jeffrey looked at the statue and laughed. "Some of our artists celebrate the human form by showing it unclad. If that woman were full-sized and alive, she'd be very embarrassed to be caught naked like that."

He pointed down a hall to a door where two guards in North livery stood sentinel. "This door leads to the east wing. That's where you'll be staying. I thought I should show you the way to the barracks from here, so you can find it yourself later."

He took her down a series of passages, all carpeted in dark blue with walls painted white and gold, then opened a door on a much less ornate, much narrower hallway that appeared to be in the older part of the palace. The walls were stone rather than painted plaster, and the floor was worn in the middle as if generations of palace inhabitants had walked this way every day for years. They had the hallway to themselves until they came to the end, where a guard in green and brown saluted the king and opened the door for him.

They came outside into a cacophony of shouts and chanting and the clacking of wooden swords. When Jeffrey's vision adjusted to the bright sunlight, he saw an exercise yard filled with men and women engaged in swordplay, calisthenics, hand to hand combat, and other training activities. Beyond the yard lay a wide green expanse hundreds of feet across, surrounded by tiers of seats painted bright green and white and covered by tapering roofs. Tiny figures ran around the edge of the open space delineated by the tiers. "What is that?" Imogen asked, pointing.

"That's the parade ground," Jeffrey said. "The army does drills there, and we have other things, races and contests of skill, that people come to watch. George, how are you?" he said, extending his hand to a curly-haired older man wearing a sleeveless tunic stained with sweat. "Meet the Kirkellan ambassador, Imogen. This is the army's training master, George Donaldson. George, has Fred come by yet?"

"He was here about ten minutes ago. Over a hundred Kirkellan warriors, he said. Sounded a little—" Donaldson glanced at Imogen, then went on, "We'll do our best, but I don't mind telling you I'm a little worried at having over a hundred people barracked with us who don't speak our language."

"They will learn. Or perhaps you will learn ours," Imogen said, a little belligerently.

"I'm sorry, I didn't mean to offend," Donaldson said stiffly.

Imogen glanced at Jeffrey, and her belligerence faded. "No, I am the sorry one, I am worried about the language problem too." Donaldson relaxed just a little. "Can I work here? With your people?" The people in question had mostly stopped working and were watching Imogen. She did stand out, Jeffrey thought, and probably would even if she weren't dressed like a Kirkellan warrior. He wondered what she'd look like gowned for a reception. It was hard to imagine.

"You, madam ambassador? I—" Now Donaldson looked astounded. "I beg your pardon, but is that something you should do?"

"I am Kirkellan warrior too," Imogen said.

"Yes, but you're a diplomat, and they're just soldiers. If they hurt you—"

Imogen laughed. "If they hurt me, then I deserve it," she said. "And more likely I will hurt them. Though I try not to because that is bad..." She trailed off and waved her hand as if to convey a thought.

"Bad form?" Jeffrey said, amused.

"That is good enough. Bad form to hurt others for not being careful, you or them."

Donaldson looked confused, but nodded as if he understood. Probably he just wanted the strange conversation to end. Jeffrey covered his mouth to conceal a smile. "I assured the *matrian* that the ambassador could have as much training as she desires," he said. "Try to get over your class consciousness just this once, George."

"As if I haven't kicked your ass repeatedly since you were a kid, *Jeffrey*," Donaldson said amiably. "And I admit it, milady, I'd like to see you fight." He gave her a look of admiring appraisal. "Come by any time and we'll give you a workout."

"Thank you," Imogen said. "I would start now, but I think the king is tired of showing me places."

"Not at all," Jeffrey said, realizing that he was enjoying himself. Imogen wasn't at all shy about showing her emotions, amazement or irritation or amusement, and he found it interesting to show her something new and see what she thought of it. "Though I thought you might want to wash, since we've been on the road for so long."

"I will come back later," Imogen assured Donaldson, and after one last look around the training yard, she went back the way they'd come, leaving Jeffrey to bid Donaldson goodbye and hurry to catch up.

"I think he must be good at what he does," Imogen said.

"He is. What makes you say that?"

"He wanted me not to fight because I am a diplomat, not because I am not a warrior. He could look at me and see what I can do. That is a not common talent."

"He taught my brother and me to fight. Sylvester never cared for it, but I got to be pretty good, if it's not bragging to say so."

"It is never bragging to be honest, only to say you are better when you do not know you are," Imogen said. "Maybe you and I will fight sometime."

"I don't think I'm up to your weight class," Jeffrey said without thinking, then immediately said, "Oh, heaven, that was rude."

"It was rude?" Imogen said. "I am heavier than you. That is not rude. It is unfortunate for you, I think."

Jeffrey choked on a laugh. "I mean in my culture it's rude to comment on a lady's weight."

"That is strange. Will a woman be less fat or too skinny if you say nothing?"

"I, um, I never really thought about it. I suppose it's rude because, um, if a lady is heavy and she doesn't want to be, it's rude to point out something she can't help."

"I understand that better than the other. But I am a fat girl and I like how I am."

Jeffrey, looking at Imogen, thought he might have said "well padded" rather than "fat girl," then wondered why he was trying to make the distinction. "I like how you are, too," he said.

"Thank you. Will those soldiers let me in?"

"They will. I'll make sure the guards on sentry duty all know who you are." They passed between the soldiers and entered the east wing. A short hallway opened on a sitting room with a high ceiling and a vast fireplace made of river stones in which coals had been banked to a warm glow. The parquet floor was covered with plush rugs; chairs and sofas upholstered in North blue raw silk were arranged near the fireplace, lamp Devices scattered throughout the room. Three other hallways led off the room at each of the other corners. One had light coming from it; the other two were dark.

Jeffrey went to the fireplace and pulled a rope dangling from the ceiling. "I don't know what rooms you've been assigned," he said, "though I don't know why it matters, they're all pretty much alike." He pointed at one of the dark hallways. "My mother lives down that hall, but she's in Kingsport until tomorrow—" A man in North livery emerged from the well-lit hallway, bowing so the bald spot on the top of his head was visible. "Can you tell me where madam ambassador will be staying?"

The man bowed again and silently led the way along the other darkened hall, past rows of doors that all looked alike even to Jeffrey, who'd grown up here. He wondered if they ought to put up a sign so Imogen could find her way back without having to try every door on her side of the hallway. "That's my room, there," he said, pointing, as if that mattered to her, "and Elspeth is across the way—"

The door opened and Elspeth herself emerged. She gave a little shriek and flung herself at Imogen. "I'm *so glad* you're here!" she squealed. "When Jeffrey said you were the ambassador I was just so thrilled! We're going to have so much fun, you and I, I promise, it won't be all stuffy dinners and receptions!"

Imogen hugged the girl back. "I am glad to see you too. I did not know there would be stuffy anything. I still do not know how to be an ambassador, but I will try." She looked at Jeffrey and smiled, and he smiled back at her, feeling lighthearted all of a sudden.

"I know where her rooms are, so you can stop following her around, Jeffrey, I know you have work to do," Elspeth said.

"I—you're right," he said. "I will see you both at supper, then, and —" But they'd gone into Imogen's room and shut the door, leaving Jeffrey feeling a little adrift. He went to his own room, deciding to wash before getting back to work. In fact, it was late enough he might not even go to his offices until tomorrow. Anything that had built up while he was gone could wait a few more hours, and the more he thought about it, the more itchy and dirty he felt. A long bath, and then a long supper with his family and Imogen. He felt better already.

JEFFREY: CHAPTER SEVEN

*T*he next morning, he regretted the sense of responsibility that brought him to the north wing, the executive wing, of the palace early. He'd only been gone a little over three weeks and it seemed as if nothing had been done in his absence. He prodded a stack of documents with his finger. So much for competent subordinates. No, that was unfair. All of this represented hard work by those subordinates; it wasn't their fault that their monarch had to sign off on so much of it.

He drew the first piece of paper toward himself and read it. His father had impressed on him the importance of always knowing what it was he was putting his name to. It wasn't so much, he'd said, that people would try to trick you into enacting a bad law, it was that your name was a promise, and you'd better know what promises you'd agreed to keep, as a king. He signed the first document and moved on to the next. And the next three. And the five after that.

His appointments secretary, Arthur, knocked on the door. "Your Majesty, you have a meeting with the council in fifteen minutes." He handed the king his daily schedule.

Jeffrey nodded his thanks, put down his pen and massaged his right wrist and palm. Not even half done. Well, they'd waited three weeks, they could wait a little longer. The council meeting, unfortunately, could not. He never looked forward to council meetings and he looked forward even less to this one, because the top item on the agenda was the new territory they'd conquered. The sooner those lands were put under someone's administration, the easier it would be to maintain them, and they wouldn't come under the direct supervision of the Crown anymore. As if he needed more things to worry about.

There was the Devisers' Guild—or the putative Devisers' Guild, anyway—that wanted permission to separate from the failing Scholia, though he wasn't sure why they thought they needed government permission for that. Three Baronies and a County wanted funds to upgrade roads that crossed provincial boundaries, and all of their lords and ladies had kicked the request up to him on the grounds that it was a kingdom-wide matter. He was supposed to review sentencing for a handful of capital cases, which he especially hated as it made him feel that he held those men and women's lives in his hands. Which, technically, he did.

And then there were the petitioners. By heaven, there were always petitioners, men and women who didn't think their provincial lords could or would give them justice, so they came straight to him. He had subordinates from the Justiciary who looked over the cases first, to weed out the obviously frivolous complaints, but in the end it always came down to him. They all, without exception, had this image of the Crown as being something romantic and all-powerful. The truth was that it was almost all paperwork.

He shoved back his chair, left the office and took the back way to the council chamber, in case someone lurked along his regular route with another responsibility to hang around his neck. The back way was damp and cold, the unplastered stone of the walls and the uncarpeted stone of the floor making the narrow, low-ceilinged passageway feel even more claustrophobic. His boots tapped along the worn flagstones, echoing hollowly back at him. It was part of a network of passages linking all the oldest parts of the palace, and he liked it because it was one place he could almost guarantee no one would find him. Though at this time of year, it hadn't yet lost the chill that emanated from the stones all winter long. Well, it didn't have to be comfortable. It only had to be private.

The back way came out through a not-quite-secret door in the council chamber. The vast round room had little in common with the passage Jeffrey had just emerged from, though they were nearly the same age. The paneled walls were painted a soft rose and had oak wainscoting stained a warm red-brown, carved along the top with oak leaves picked out with gold. The dark red carpet covered the floor from wall to wall and was plush enough that if a person stood still long enough, he would leave his footprints behind when he walked away. The double doors matched the wainscoting and had brass handles shaped like oak leaves. Devices lit the chamber from the domed ceiling high above. Except for the worn, round, black oak table in the center of the room, it didn't look like a room in which heated debates over tariffs took place. It looked like a lady's private parlor from which all the furniture had been taken for cleaning.

The chamber was empty. Jeffrey checked his watch; he was early. He took his seat in the chair that almost looked like a throne and rubbed his left hand across the smooth, worn wood of the round table, polished by hundreds of hands before his. He didn't think he had much control over this council. Most of them had been appointed by his father, except for the chief of Internal Affairs, Micheline Branston, whose predecessor's term had expired the previous year. They were all polite, but they also all treated him indulgently, as if he were only playing at being king. It didn't help that he often felt that way himself. He worried that the day would come when they would decide they didn't have to listen to him anymore. He worried even more that that day was today.

New territory. It didn't matter that it was undeveloped, empty land—or maybe he was wrong, maybe it mattered even more that it was untouched and waiting for the right hand to turn it into an economic marvel. Every one of the councilors had a stake in who received the land and how it was parceled out, even if few of them were likely to receive a title as a result of those decisions.

Diana had already said she wanted a chunk of it for Daxtry. Hugh Harstow, chief of Commerce, would see the new land—or, rather, the provinces formed from it—as a source of revenue. The Foreign Affairs chief, Maxwell Burgess, would look to develop a different relationship with Veribold and...actually, he wondered how Burgess felt about their new diplomatic ties to the Kirkellan. He was as upper class as you could get without a title and had a tendency toward snobbery. Jeffrey might have to keep an eye on him with regard to how he treated Imogen. He didn't want Burgess souring their relationship with their new friends, and he certainly didn't want him snubbing their ambassador.

Elspeth should be out shopping with Imogen right now, getting her a dress for the concert tonight. Elspeth had thought it would be a good idea to introduce her into society gradually, in preparation for Elspeth's wedding reception next week. Imogen was yet another worry on his list. How much of a shock would Aurilien be, when her only other experience with city life was Ranstjad? He wanted her to like it here, and he didn't know what he could do to make that happen. So he just worried, pointlessly, and caught himself drumming his fingers on the table and made himself stop. Imogen would be fine. Elspeth would make sure of that.

The double doors opened. "—there isn't any other way to look at it, Lex, it was a clear violation of policy. Good morning, your Majesty." Helena Rowland inclined her head to him; her conversational partner, Lex Stoddard, did the same, but more perfunctorily. Helena was chief of Communications, a position his father had held before ascending to the throne; Lex was chief of Transportation and one of the many thorns in Jeffrey's side. At least Helena was respectful. Lex, a skeletally thin man in his late fifties, made no secret of his feelings that the kingdom would be better off if Jeffrey gave more of his responsibilities to his councilors and spent his time...Lex was never clear on what he thought Jeffrey ought to be doing instead of ruling, but he probably didn't care so long as it was something that kept the King out of the council chamber.

"I disagree, Helena, there's plenty of room for misinterpreting that particular clause. Harstow, you agree with me, yes?"

"I think I've told you before, Stoddard, that I dislike being accosted when you are in the middle of a conversation," Hugh Harstow said. The chief of Commerce was in his early thirties, young for his responsibilities, though his brown hair was already thinning and he'd begun to develop a middle-aged paunch to go with his middle-aged attitude. His red, wet lips thinned in disapproval of Stoddard's approach; disliking Stoddard was one of the few things Jeffrey and Harstow had in common. "I have no way of knowing the facts with which you want me to agree."

"We're talking about who takes precedence when a telecode must be carried across municipal lines for delivery," Stoddard said. "It's obviously a matter for Transport jurisdiction."

"Don't be ridiculous, Lex," Helena said. "The message originates with the telecoder office and we're responsible for it. And I resent that your bullies thought they were allowed to strong-arm—"

"I object to that characterization. They were merely carrying out their duties."

"And I fail to see that this has anything to do with me," Harstow said, passing by them and taking his seat. "Good morning, your Majesty."

"Good morning, Hugh." Jeffrey raised his voice and said, "Helena, Lex, it sounds as if you have an item for our next meeting's agenda. Until that time, set your differences aside, please, because we have important business to discuss today." He put the faintest emphasis on "important" and saw Helena blush and Stoddard bite back a harsh reply. The two took their seats, which were unfortunately adjacent to each other. Jeffrey considered rearranging the seating, then realized there was no way to arrange his councilors that would keep them from fighting with each other.

Micheline Branston and Jonathan Crabtree, respectively chiefs of

Internal Affairs and Finance, were the next to arrive, and finally, when Jeffrey had almost decided to convene the meeting without him, Maxwell Burgess came in, breathing heavily as if he'd been running. He was a shortish, fattish, blondish man who was never on time to council meetings but always on time to diplomatic functions, so Jeffrey never chastised him. This was everyone who'd be attending that day; Diana Ashmore and Emmeline Mathers, chief of Defense, were still with the army, his mother was on her way back from Kingsport, and the two Counts who represented the provinces were still on their estates.

"Thank you all for attending," Jeffrey began. "I'm sure you know there's only one item on the agenda today—the disposition of the new lands acquired during the recent conflict with Ruskald. Since we're still securing those lands, some of you—" he looked at Micheline, who'd been vocal in her opposition to parcel the new lands out —"have objected to making any determinations yet. And I agree."

This got a murmured reaction from them, and glances were traded across the table. Jeffrey made mental note of who looked at whom and filed it away for later analysis. "It would be premature to make those decisions without due consideration. However, today I will be hearing proposals for the disposition of these lands, which I will consider and then present my decision to the full council in a week. I've summoned the Counts and Barons and we should have a full convocation at that time."

He hoped so, anyway. His sister-in-law Catherine, Baroness of Silverfield, was expecting her second child, and Sylvester had sent word that she wasn't well. Jeffrey had deliberately set the date for final deliberations as far off as he could, to give her plenty of time to travel, but there was no guarantee she'd be able to manage the journey.

"So," Jeffrey said, "I am entertaining proposals as of right now." He beckoned to one of his aides to bring maps, fine vellum, pencils and note paper. "Here is the region we are debating." He spread out a map showing the previous boundaries of Tremontane and its counties, Ruskald, Veribold, and a squiggly line indicating Kirkellan territory. He then laid a sheet of nearly transparent vellum over the map and traced the new boundaries. "What shall we do with our new acquisition?"

No one spoke at first. Had he been too forceful? Then Micheline reached out with her own pencil and said, "The most obvious possibility is to extend the borders of Daxtry and Avory and make them both counties." She drew in a faint line.

"Darker, Micheline, make it darker," Jeffrey said. "Thank you. There's our first proposal."

"You want to give Diana Ashmore that much territory?" Lex Stoddard said. "That's half again as big as the smallest county is now!"

"Lex, we're not debating the merits of these proposals right now," Jeffrey said. He handed the vellum off to one of the aides and whipped out another one, quickly sketched the boundaries, and stood back. "I'll make my decision after I've considered all the options."

"*Your* decision?" Stoddard said incredulously. "Shouldn't this go up for a vote?"

Jeffrey raised an eyebrow at him, but inside his heart was pounding. *This is where it happens. Either you're the King or you aren't.* "This is not a question of taxation or building roads," he said. "This decision will alter the face of this country, a country for which I have the ultimate responsibility, and as Tremontane's King the decision is mine alone. Yes, I am asking for the input of this council because I value your advice. Altering our borders is a serious thing. But I would like to remind you all that as your King I do not need your permission to do it. I intend to make the decision I judge is best for this country, with or without your help." He set his hand down flat on the map, centered on Tremontane. "So I suggest you continue with your proposals."

He fixed each of them with his gaze, something he'd seen his father do to great effect in council meetings. He had no idea if it worked. He was afraid he'd sounded petulant, or worse, arrogant. But they seemed to have trouble meeting his eyes, and eventually Harstow cleared his throat and said, "It seems to me that the kingdom would benefit by creating two new Baronies, here and here, along our new border with Veribold. I admit to having some personal interest in the question, as my department will benefit from the increased trade, but it's still a sound proposal."

"Thank you, Hugh." Jeffrey added new boundaries and his heart rate gradually went back to normal. "Anyone else?"

At the end of the meeting, Jeffrey had seven or eight vellum sheets rolled under his arm and, he thought, a measure of respect from his councilors he hadn't had when he walked in that morning. He was glad his mother hadn't been there, though he would have appreciated her perspective on his performance. It was just difficult to maintain his image as a responsible ruler in front of the woman who'd seen him run naked through the halls of the palace, laughing at having eluded his nanny's grasp, when he was five.

Alison North had represented the Arts and Heritage department five times since it had been instituted under Zara North and had, despite her disdain for politics, a deep understanding of how the council worked. Her advice mattered more to him than that of the rest of the council combined. He wondered if she'd return in time for the concert. He really wanted her to meet Imogen. Not that it mattered, because she'd almost certainly refuse to attend; she didn't go to any more social functions than she had to.

He took the short route back to his office, nodding politely at those he passed, who bowed to him in return. Back in his office, he dumped the vellum sheets in a corner and sat down. The windows shed a dim light over his desk; it seemed a storm was coming in. The desk's highly polished surface reflected his face poorly, making him look haggard. At least, he hoped it was a poor reflection.

He tidied his hair with the help of this imperfect mirror and dragged the pile of papers needing signatures toward him again. He'd finish these, then...what was on his schedule? It seemed he'd be eating his dinner at his desk again. And possibly his supper, too, if he wanted any time to go over those boundary proposals today. He sighed and inked his pen. Yes, his life was glamorous. No wonder everyone wanted to be him.

HIS SUPPER CONSISTED OF A PLATE OF COLD SLICED MEAT AND CHEESE and a long slab of bread. He sliced the bread open and filled it with the meat and cheese. Some supper. He had to assemble it himself. He checked his watch and cursed through a mouthful of food, which sent crumbs of bread and cheese spraying across his desk and over the last sheet of vellum. He set his improvised meal aside and shook the vellum free of crumbs, then managed to knock his wine glass over with his elbow, spilling red wine over his desk, over the blotter, and onto his lap.

Holding the vellum high above the disaster, he cursed again and at length. He looked at the vellum, then tossed it aside to flutter to the floor. He wasn't going to accept that proposal anyway. He rescued the stacks of paperwork, realizing too late that the wine had soaked into the bread and his meal, such as it was, was ruined. So were his trousers, probably, a light brown suede he'd rather liked until they were streaked with purplish-red as if he'd had some gory accident. That was it. He was done for the day.

He ruthlessly dumped the mess in Arthur's lap and again took the back way around to the east wing, not wanting anyone to see the condition he was in. No doubt he smelled like a drunk, too. The sitting room was empty, the fire banked low. He checked his watch again. Elspeth and Imogen were probably at supper, which gave him plenty of time to change for the concert and get something else to eat.

He stripped out of the ruined trousers and washed thoroughly, not wanting to smell even the tiniest bit like alcohol, then with the help of his valet dressed in semi-formal pressed black trousers—he'd had enough of light colors for one day—and matching waistcoat over a ruby-colored linen shirt. Coat, cravat, and pearl stick-pin that was a gift from his maternal grandfather completed his ensemble.

His valet went over his coat with a fine-bristled brush as Jeffrey examined himself in the mirror. His father had had more muscle to him, and although Jeffrey had also inherited his father's broad shoulders, he never felt as if he filled them out properly. He twitched his coat to fall more naturally across those shoulders, then went to join the ladies in the dining room.

He came up short in the sitting room because Elspeth was there, dressed for the concert, staring into the embers of the fire with her chin in her hands, an angry look on her face. "Have you eaten already?" Jeffrey said with some dismay. His stomach rumbled loudly as if it knew it wasn't going to be fed any time soon. "Where's Imogen?"

Elspeth made a sound somewhere between a snort and a growl. "She's not coming," she said, and made the noise again.

"What do you mean, she's not coming? Is she sick?"

"No," *snort-growl*, "she's just being stupid."

Jeffrey grabbed his sister's hand so she was forced to look at him. "Elspeth, what's going on?"

She yanked her hand out of his. "She's being stupid because she doesn't want to dress in Tremontanan clothing and she wants to go to the concert in her own clothes."

"I don't understand. Why did you spend all that time shopping today if she wasn't going to wear what you bought?"

Elspeth leaped to her feet. "We didn't go shopping! How was I supposed to know she didn't have anything to wear? Did you know she only has the one set of clothes and she washed them in the bathtub today? She wasn't wearing anything at all when I went to help her dress!"

An image of Imogen naked with her hair cascading over her shoulders flashed across Jeffrey's inner eye in breathtaking clarity for about two seconds, which was long enough to make him forget whatever he'd been about to say.

Elspeth added, "She never said she didn't have clothes, so I assumed everything was fine!"

Jeffrey threw up his hands. "Elspeth, she just got here from the Eidestal! Where under heaven was she supposed to get Tremontanan clothes? What were you *thinking*?"

"Oh, yes, why don't you yell at me too! She yelled at me just because I told her people were going to laugh at her for wearing the wrong clothes. Which they will!"

"No, they won't. They'll just think she's a foreigner."

Elspeth made the noise again. "Jeffrey, you don't know anything about women. If Imogen goes in her Kirkellan clothes, those leather pants and that shirt she sewed herself, everyone will always think of her as a barbarian. She'll never be anything else."

"But that's what she is. Kirkellan, I mean, not a barbarian."

Elspeth threw up her own hands now. "You are both so *stupid!*"

"And you're being a brat. And rude." Jeffrey turned away. "I'm going to tell Imogen she can wear whatever she wants."

"Jeffrey, don't you dare. If you like her at all, you won't let her do it." Elspeth started to cry. "I'm sorry, I'm just so mad and frustrated and I know it's wrong to cry because it's manipulative, but you're going to...to *destroy* her reputation!"

Jeffrey hesitated. Elspeth could be frivolous and she could be petty, but she had a good grasp of social mores. If she said Imogen would be hurt by appearing in her own clothes, she was probably right. "Damn it," he said. "I was hoping at least one thing would go right today."

"I feel really bad now about calling her stupid," Elspeth said, wiping her eyes. "I felt guilty because I didn't think about her all day. I was at a party, and...I should have been here to make her feel at home."

"She probably would have been just as upset, no matter when you told her she had to wear Tremontanan clothes," Jeffrey said. "She's very homesick, you know. I don't think she wants to let go of who she is."

"I don't see why she can't be herself in a gown and nice shoes," Elspeth said, sniffling.

"She can't be a *warrior* in a gown and nice shoes. And a warrior is what she is."

"It's not everything she is."

"Maybe, but I think she has to decide that for herself."

"Do we still have to go to the concert?"

Jeffrey's stomach rumbled again. "Unfortunately, yes. I did promise we would make an appearance. And we'll have to make Imogen's excuses for her."

Elspeth tucked her hand into her brother's arm. "It had better be a good concert."

It wasn't.

JEFFREY: CHAPTER EIGHT

*J*effrey was early to the breakfast table the next morning only to find someone else had been even earlier. Imogen sat alone at the long table, picking at scrambled eggs with her fork. He felt a rush of relief and pleasure that she hadn't run off in the night. "Good morning!" he said cheerfully, then remembered last night and what had started it all, and said, "Did you...are you all right? Elspeth told me what happened. I'm sorry we were so inconsiderate."

"I am all right," she said, not looking at him. "I was...inconsiderate too. I yelled at Elspeth."

"I do that all the time," Jeffrey assured her, helping himself from the sideboard and taking a seat across from her so they'd be able to look at each other without turning all the time. Assuming she decided to look at him. "Usually she deserves it."

"I have a brother who deserves to be yelled at," she said with a little smile, though she still wasn't looking at him. It occurred to him that *she* might be feeling a little guilty, too. He really wished he understood her better.

"Have you spoken to...no, you wouldn't have, Elspeth always

sleeps as late as she can manage. I know she feels bad about what she said to you."

"Did she say to you the things she said to me?"

Jeffrey took a moment to parse this. "Only a little. You didn't want to lose yourself, was that it?"

Hazel eyes finally met his. "That is it, yes. You understand."

"A little." He didn't, really, didn't have any experiences to compare to hers, but he *was* starting to understand how much her identity meant to her and how hard it was for her to be in a place she felt was trying to take it from her. He wondered what her life in Ranstjad had been like. Hrovald would not have liked having a woman warrior in his house.

"Ah, good, Jeffrey, I'm glad to see you."

"Mother! When did you get back?"

"Late last night. Your grandfather sends his love, by the way." Alison North loaded her plate with scrambled eggs and toast and sat down next to Imogen. "Imogen and I had a lovely conversation last night. Isn't it lucky she didn't go to the concert?" She directed a look at Jeffrey that said volumes about why Imogen hadn't gone to the concert and what Alison was going to do to her children about it when she got them alone later.

"I am glad," Imogen said.

"You need to eat, Imogen, you'll want your strength today. Jeffrey, shouldn't you be at work?"

Jeffrey ignored her. "What are you doing today that needs so much strength?"

"Shopping. For clothes." Imogen glared at him, daring him to make an issue of it.

It was an obvious trap, easily avoided. "With Mother? You'll have a good time, then. Mother doesn't like shopping for clothes. She has several clothiers who all know her and know what she likes, in and out and done in fifteen minutes."

"I'm sure it will take longer than that, Jeffrey. But Imogen doesn't need much." Alison poured herself a cup of coffee and loaded it with cream and sugar until Jeffrey was surprised the spoon didn't stand up by itself. "Jeffrey, would you mind clearing your schedule at dinnertime so you can eat with the rest of us?"

"Of course." He wiped his lips with his napkin and rose. "Anything else I can do for you ladies?"

"Just make sure you wear comfortable shoes today," Alison said cryptically, and Jeffrey, realizing he wasn't going to get any more than that out of her, made his escape.

"I have your schedule, your Majesty," Arthur said, rising as Jeffrey approached. "And your desk has been scrubbed and the blotter replaced, and I took the liberty of having Domestic go over the rug under your desk."

"Thank you, Arthur," Jeffrey said, accepting the paper his secretary held out for him. He really should arrange some sort of bonus for the man. "I'll be dining with my family today, so this afternoon's schedule will have to be rearranged."

"Of course, your Majesty," Arthur said, not showing any dismay. *A big bonus.*

He shoveled a few more tons of paperwork off his desk, then spent the rest of the morning hearing petitioners in the throne room, which was big and dark and was never used for anything except intimidating those who dared approach the King personally. He hated it, but could never quite bring himself to upset tradition by insisting the hearings be moved to a smaller, more friendly venue. The reasoning was that anyone who could endure the cold echoes of the throne room must have a serious request, but Jeffrey thought it just weeded out anyone who wasn't bold-spirited. *Someday*, he told himself after turning down yet another petition, *just not today. Or tomorrow. Or the next day. But someday.*

He was a little late getting away from the last petitioner, who'd turned out to have a case worth his attention, and hurried back to the east wing dining room to discover it empty. The door to the kitchen opened as he stood there—he never had figured out how the kitchen staff knew exactly when he arrived—and servants came out bearing steaming platters. "Has my mother been here?" he asked.

The woman at the head of the line said, "No, your Majesty, we never serve the food until you arrive."

"Yes, and I'm sure I've told you not to wait for me if there are others ready to dine," he said, but it was clear no one else had arrived before him. "I'm going to find my family. Sorry about the false warning, but I should be back soon. And thank you, all of you, your service is always exemplary."

So. Either everyone was much later than he was, or they were all busy elsewhere. He felt a little annoyed. Elspeth he could see forgetting the time, but his mother was always punctual. He left the dining room, then stopped, at a loss as to where to begin looking. What if they were still out shopping? His stomach rumbled. How long should he wait before giving up and having his dinner by himself? Not very long, he decided.

He heard music coming from somewhere down the hall, tinkling, echoing music that sounded as if someone had captured a string quartet and stuffed it into a giant glass bottle. He followed the sound to one of the unused parlors—really, they were all unused now that it was just the three of them failing to fill the east wing to capacity—and pushed the door open.

"...one two three, one two *back*, no, forward, not back," Elspeth said. "Mother, I don't think this is working. I keep forgetting I'm supposed to be the man." Elspeth and Imogen stood near the center of the room, hands clasped and arms around each other's waists. Alison sat to one side, her hand on the knob of a music Device.

"I do not understand why it is that the man and the woman have different steps," Imogen said.

"Because if they both did the same steps, they would either walk away from each other or walk into each other," Alison explained. She pushed the large brass button that shut off the Device playing the music. "Oh, Jeffrey, thank heaven. Where have you been?"

"I don't mean to sound petty," Jeffrey said, "but I did clear my schedule to have dinner with all of you and no one's in the dining room."

"Dancing first, dinner after," Alison said. "Come here, dear. Elspeth just can't keep up with Imogen."

"And you already know the man's part," Elspeth said. She retreated to her mother's side of the room. Imogen trailed after her.

"Is this why you wanted me to clear my schedule?" Jeffrey said.

"Imogen is learning to dance, and she needs a partner, so come over here before the food gets cold." Alison pointed at Imogen. "Back to the center, Imogen, and let's try this one more time."

Jeffrey looked at Imogen. "I'm not a very good dancer," he said.

"Don't be ridiculous. You're a perfectly good dancer. You just don't like to do it," Alison said.

Jeffrey went to the center of the room. Imogen joined him there and held out her hand stiffly. He took it and turned it over, examining it. "You should at least act as if you're pleased to dance with your partner," he said with a grin.

"I am tired and this is not enjoyable. But I am thankful you will help."

"One dance, and then we can eat." He waggled his eyebrows at her, making her laugh. "There, that's better already."

"Hands on waists, right hands clasped, keep your elbow up, Imogen, and—" The tinny music started up again, and Imogen and Jeffrey both moved at once and bumped up against each other, then laughed together.

"Let's try that again," he said, "and this time do it backwards from what Elspeth incorrectly taught you."

"As if you could have done better, Jeffrey."

"At least I wouldn't have taught her the man's part, tiny." This time, they swung gracefully into the music, and after the first few steps Imogen stopped looking at her feet and could meet Jeffrey's eyes. "Much better," he said. The tiny lines of tension around Imogen's hazel eyes disappeared.

"It is more fun this way," she said, and he laughed.

"I've never danced with anyone as tall as me before," he said. "It's interesting. In a good way, you understand."

"I do because I was dancing with Elspeth and she is tiny as you say."

"Hey! It's not my fault you're both giants. Everyone around me is a giant. Except Mother."

"Your father never complained about dancing with me," Alison said.

The memory of watching his father and mother dance sent a pang of sadness through him. Imogen looked at him curiously and said, "Do I step wrong?"

He controlled his face. "No, it was just a passing thought, nothing to do with you. You look very nice in your new clothes, by the way. Very much like a Tremontanan lady."

Imogen flushed. "How did I look before?" she asked, a little angry.

Oops. Jeffrey said, "Ah...also very nice?"

"I did not look nice. I looked like a warrior."

He raised an eyebrow at her. "Which suited you very well, as I recall."

For some reason, this made Imogen blush. Alison said, "Jeffrey, stop implying that Imogen's Kirkellan clothing made her look like a savage and pay attention. Imogen, keep your elbow up."

"I did *not* think you looked like a savage," he assured Imogen. "All right, you end by turning away, then coming back together—no, further away, let's try that again—right." She turned and came face to face with him again, her hazel eyes dancing with pleasure. "I think you've got it."

"I think I should not dance with a shorter partner," Imogen said with a laugh.

"Then I'll have to dance it with you," he said. "I'd dance with the Veriboldan and Eskandelic ambassadors too, but they're both male and the ambassador from Eskandel has a very jealous harem."

"I do not know what harem means."

The king turned to look at Alison. "Mother will explain it to you."

"But not over dinner," she said.

"Definitely not over dinner," Jeffrey said, and took Imogen's hand and bowed over it. "Please join us, madam ambassador."

JEFFREY TRIED TO AVOID HIS COUNCILORS DURING THE NEXT FEW DAYS and was so successful he wondered if they might be avoiding him too. He'd winnowed out the proposals that were either impractical or clearly skewed in one of his lords' favor, which left him with three. Of the three, there was one he thought was a clear winner, and after two days of consideration he almost decided to make the announcement without waiting for the full council's presence. But no, he'd called them all to Aurilien; the least he could do was tell them in person. They needed to know he respected them, even though it was clear many of them didn't respect him very much. He turned his attention to other things.

On the third day he came to his office rather later than usual, having slept poorly and dreamed of things he couldn't now remember except that they'd been unsettling and exhausting. Arthur was talking to a young man Jeffrey didn't know, who was perched on the edge of Arthur's desk. "I'm just saying the language doesn't have to be a barrier," the young man said, leaning in close to Arthur. "Some things you don't need talking for, right?"

Arthur grinned and winked at his friend, then noticed the King standing nearby and straightened. "Excuse me, your Majesty," he said, and the other young man stood quickly and bowed. He didn't seem embarrassed to be caught in such an informal pose.

"I assume you're talking about the Kirkellan?" Jeffrey said.

"Yes, your Majesty," Arthur said. He exchanged glances with his friend and a sly smile touched his lips for just a second. "We—that is, many of the staff have been out to watch them exercise their horses. It's...captivating."

Jeffrey grinned, for a moment just another young man who could appreciate the fairer sex—or, in Arthur's case, his own sex. "It sounds like you're finding ways to communicate," he said.

"Oh, yes, your Majesty," the stranger said with a twinkle, then seemed to remember to whom he was speaking. "That is—we're all interested in building bridges between our cultures."

"I understand perfectly," Jeffrey said, repressing a smile. "Perhaps I should take the time to visit the training yard myself."

"You won't regret it, your Majesty," Arthur said, then he too recollected himself and handed Jeffrey a sheet of paper. "Your schedule, sir."

"Thank you." Jeffrey glanced over it. There wasn't anything this morning that wouldn't keep. "Clear my schedule until dinner," he said, handing it back. "I think I have a...diplomatic appointment instead. Bridge building, as you say."

He took a little time to change into some less formal attire, dispensing with the services of his valet for once, and went down the long, stony corridor that emerged into the training yard. To his surprise, the yard was empty. The parade ground, on the other hand, was crowded with horses and people, and the lowest tiers surrounding the grassy oval were packed with spectators, who suddenly cheered and applauded some activity Jeffrey couldn't see through the crowd massed on this side of the oval.

He went forward and elbowed his way through the crowd, whose members elbowed back until, stunned, they realized who it was they were prodding. Jeffrey nodded and smiled politely at the shocked faces until he reached the front of the crowd and could see what was going on.

The parade ground had been transformed. Stacks of hay bales dotted the field, all of them bearing targets at heights varying from waist to eye level. Here and there javelins stood, stabbed into the ground like pins in a vast green pincushion. At the far end of the oval, white wooden stiles in lines stood sentinel over what remained of the smooth grassy turf, which was now torn into clots of earth scattered on both sides of a rough, grassless path.

Past the stiles the path turned in a wide curve to become a long stretch of bare earth, down which a Kirkellan horse and rider now thundered. They passed a point marked by two poles topped with flags, and another cheer went up from the watching tiers and from the crowd surrounding the field. Another horse, responding to a shout from his rider, took off toward the bales of hay. The rider snatched up a javelin from among several stuck into the ground, wound up and flung it at one of the targets as her horse wove between them. So it was a game, or a training exercise, and by the looks of things it was popular entertainment as well.

The horse came out from between the hay bales and went at the stiles. It clipped two of the five, knocking them over to the accompaniment of the crowd's groans, then came around to the straightaway and finished with the rider pulling up just short of the flagpoles. Her companions laughed and called out in Kirkellish; she made a rude gesture at them, laughing in turn.

There was a line of horses waiting to take a turn in the gauntlet, and Jeffrey saw George standing near its head. He made his way toward the training master, shouting, "I can't believe you let them tear up your baby like that!"

George turned at the sound of Jeffrey's voice and smiled wryly. "That damn language barrier again," he said. "I didn't know what they were asking for until it was too late. I figure, what the hell, we can always put down fresh sod next spring."

"Why haven't I heard about this before?" Jeffrey gestured, and as if in response another horse started off down the gauntlet. "Seems like half the palace is out here today."

"You have actual responsibilities. Most of these people are hangers-on, I think, people who'd be at some other race if they weren't at this one. I can't believe we don't have bookmakers yet."

"That's surprising." The rider and horse came down the last stretch to much applause. "It's impressive. For such big beasts, they can get up quite a turn of speed if they want to."

"I want to see some of our animals run the track. Need to get some jumpers out here, though the ambassador would still beat every one of them. That horse of hers is astonishing."

"I hear ambassador and now I think, that is me," Imogen said, bringing Victory up beside them. She looked so natural up there that Jeffrey felt a rush of pride on her behalf. "You are here to watch us ride?"

"I am," he said. "George tells me Victory is a jumper."

"She is the best."

Another rider passed Imogen and said something to her that made her laugh. The man added a comment that Jeffrey, despite not speaking the language, interpreted as a challenge. Imogen replied in the same tone, and they shook hands. "He is saying he does not think Victory can take all the—what do you say? Stiles? He thinks she cannot jump all five without kicking them. No one does this yet today, but that is because Victory does not run yet. So we have a bet. You will watch and cheer?"

"I will."

"Then we will win." She grinned at him, that brilliant smile that he saw so rarely. He felt a pang of guilt. She belonged on that horse, with those warriors, not here in Aurilien...but Mairen had said there was a part of Imogen that wasn't a warrior, and maybe she needed to learn what that part of her was.

Another rider took his turn, and then Imogen and Victory were at the starting line. The cheer that greeted her arrival was deafening. Imogen stood up in her saddle and waved at the spectators, who were on their feet. Their response made Jeffrey irritable. He wanted to see her race, not play to a crowd of wastrel good-for-nothing third sons and daughters.

Imogen settled back into the saddle, checked the fit of her boots into the stirrups, and shouted to Victory, who started slowly but gained momentum until she was practically flying across the field. Imogen weaved through the hay bales without bothering with the javelins and came around and set Victory's head at the stiles. Jeffrey found himself holding his breath. Victory gathered herself and sailed over the first hurdle, then the second, as the spectators counted them off. Jeffrey thought he saw the third stile rock, just a little, but the count went on until, one last time, Victory flew gracefully over the hurdle and everyone including Jeffrey himself screamed, "*Five!*" The cheering redoubled. Victory came around the straightaway at speed, crossing the line between the flags before Imogen reined her in. The other rider came up to her and they had a conversation which ended with both of them laughing.

She came back to where George and Jeffrey were standing and dismounted. "It is too bad. I felt her kick the stile. I wanted Victory to win that bet."

"But it didn't go over," Jeffrey said.

Imogen shrugged. "It is still not a perfect run. Victory will do better next time. And it is not much of a bet. He is interested in that woman over there." She pointed at a dark-haired soldier who sat in the lowest row of seats, watching the fun. "I tell her so for him."

"What was he going to do if you won?"

"He offered to do the same for me." She laughed. "With gestures and his few words of Tremontanese. But I am not interested in any of these." She indicated the entire field, and Jeffrey, surprisingly, felt relieved. If George was right, none of these men were worthy of her. "I can speak to them myself if I am. Some of them are handsome." Jeffrey's heart sank a little.

"Wait until Elspeth's reception," he said lightly. "You'll see many men who are much better. Smarter, more handsome, funnier..." He wondered why he was trying so hard to sell her on the virtues of unknown men. It wasn't as if the other courtiers were much better than anyone here. Maybe he should be encouraging her to...or maybe he should keep his damn opinions to himself, and stop interfering in her life.

"I hope so," Imogen said. "I have a gown that will make them...I do not know the word. It is a beautiful gown and I look beautiful in it."

"I can't wait to see it," Jeffrey said. "Will you be riding again today?"

"No, I have had my turn. Too many people want to ride and there is not enough time. I will ride with Victory for her exercise instead."

He almost asked if he could come with her. The thought surprised him. He wasn't a great rider, and though he didn't hate horses as it seemed everyone around him believed, he didn't love them the way Imogen loved Victory or even the way Elspeth loved her gentle mare. It was just that Imogen was, for once, relaxed and confident instead of being irritable and insecure, and he wanted to have at least some interactions with her when she wasn't thinking about how much she'd rather be anywhere than here. He wanted her to like Aurilien, wanted her to like being the ambassador, wanted her to like him too, and he thought that if only he could show her the good things about Tremontane, she might not feel so alone. Though watching her in the crowd today, surrounded by the other Kirkellan, it seemed the last thing she felt was alone.

So he said, "If you go outside the gates, stay within sight of the city. I'd hate to send a search party after you."

She grinned. "I am finding my way for many years before I come to your city, King of Tremontane. I promise I will not be lost." She mounted and rode off past the training yard and down the path leading out of the palace.

"Remarkable woman," George mused, watching her go. "You should see her fight."

"Has she been down here often?"

"Twice now. She and that big guy, Revalan, first time they took up swords I thought for sure one of them was going to die. But apparently that's how they blow off steam. Why in hell did anyone pick *her* for an ambassador? She's more like a warrior queen."

"The *matrian* says there's more to her than fighting and she wants her to learn what that is."

"Well, she's got the makings of a champion show jumper, I can tell you that."

"I think the *matrian* had something a little less closely related to combat."

"If you find out what it is, I'd like to know. I think that young woman could do pretty much anything she put her mind to."

Imogen disappeared behind a distant curve. "I hope you're right," Jeffrey said.

JEFFREY: CHAPTER NINE

*J*effrey dismissed his valet and examined his reflection—black coat with blue and silver waistcoat, black hair and blue eyes to match. Could he do away with knee breeches? Did the King have that kind of power over fashion? His mother had ruthlessly made the corset disappear, when she was Consort, but he doubted his influence extended that far. He extended one leg and looked at it critically. He still couldn't see the appeal, though he'd heard about ladies swooning over a well-turned calf. Since ladies made an effort to swoon over him anyway, he had no idea if it was his calves or his Crown that did it.

No one else was in the sitting room when he entered, so he took a seat and gazed at the logs glowing cherry-red in the fireplace. He enjoyed these receptions. There were always people to talk to, and while there was dancing, it wasn't the most important part of the evening. At dances, he had to sit majestically in his not-a-throne next to Alison and occasionally ask one of the safely married women to take a turn around the floor with him. He never dared dance with the young, unmarried ones, since gossip always had him betrothed to whatever woman he stood up with before their dance had even finished. Jeffrey had begun to wonder how he was ever to find a wife, if he wasn't allowed to get to know anyone of the right age and social status. Maybe he should disguise himself and go into the lower city, court an inappropriate woman and make her the Consort. No, his face was too well known, and why should he think such a woman would make him any happier than one of his own class?

Alison came around the corner and sat next to him, kicking at the silvery skirt of her gown. "I'm not looking forward to the next council meeting," she said. "Have you already made a decision on the disposition of the new lands?"

He shrugged. "I have a preference, but nothing's settled yet."

"Well, whatever you decide, the peers and the councilors will make a lot of noise about how wrong you are."

"Am I doing the right thing?"

Alison turned in her seat to look at him. "That sounds like a question unrelated to the topic."

"I'm never certain, when I'm dealing with the council and the nobles, whether they respect me or are just putting up with me because fate dropped me onto the throne."

"That's almost self-pity."

"I'm serious."

"So am I. Jeffrey, I know this isn't what any of us expected, but in the past three years you've grown into your role far more than I think you realize. I can assure you that the council members respect you. It's a pity Anthony never let you children observe some of his council meetings. His councilors were every bit as vocal in their disagreements with him as yours are."

Jeffrey felt a little of his load lighten. "What did he do?"

"Sat and waited for them to finish talking, then told them what was going to happen." Alison smiled. "Sometimes he didn't wait for them to finish. You have something of his presence, you know. And something of his trouble. No one expected Zara to—well, you know the truth. Even with everything we arranged, your father was completely thrown by his ascension to the throne. It was a long time before he felt comfortable as king."

"I never saw it."

"You were awfully young. And he was good at hiding his insecurity. I was probably the only one who saw it." Alison paused. "It's a pity you don't have someone you can share the burden with."

"I have you."

"You know what I mean, son. I wish you'd think seriously about marriage."

Her words were so close to what he'd been thinking about before that he laughed. "I think about it often. I'm not sure what to do about it. You should make me a list of eligible young women and I could close my eyes and point."

"Don't joke about this," Alison said with such intensity that Jeffrey was startled. "Marriage isn't something to be entered into for the wrong reasons. Even more so when you're talking about a Consort. Your father's rule would have been very different if he hadn't married me, and I say that with no false modesty. We had a wonderful marriage. It's why I haven't pushed you to simply pick a girl and marry her, no matter how badly you need more heirs. I want you to have a marriage like mine. I think Elspeth does."

"Then, in all seriousness, how am I supposed to meet this paragon?"

"I don't know." Alison sighed. "Perhaps it's time we stopped caring about what people say."

Jeffrey groaned. "I don't like dancing."

"It's an excellent means of social interaction that makes no promises. And you're good at it."

"But I don't like it."

"Stop whining." Alison smiled at her son. "I could always make you a list."

Jeffrey stood. "I suppose it's as good a start as any. But not tonight, please? Every Count and Baron in the kingdom is here tonight and I have to make them feel as if this reception is as much for them as it is for Elspeth."

"Are you talking about me?" Elspeth said, swaying into view on Owen's arm. They too wore North blue and silver, Owen looking very much like a Ruskalder who'd been thrust into someone else's clothes.

As far as Jeffrey knew, no one ever harassed Owen for being from Ruskald despite Tremontane's being at war with that country. He thought it might be the romance of the thing: Owen fleeing a tyrant's wrath, falling in love with a beautiful princess and marrying her. Or it could just be that he was big enough, and dangerous-looking enough, that no one wanted to pick a fight with him. Either way, Jeffrey was glad his best friend wasn't suffering social stigma just for having been born in the wrong country.

Elspeth smiled up at her husband, flashing her dimple at him, and he smiled back and leaned down to kiss her. "You should be talking about me, it's my reception," she continued. "Isn't Imogen ready yet? I'll go get her."

"No, Imogen is here," Imogen said, and Jeffrey, mouth open to reply to Elspeth, found he'd forgotten what he meant to say. She was stunning. Red silk draped every curve of her body, flowed from shoulder to waist and then to a full skirt that shimmered when it caught the light. Her brown hair was piled high on her head, revealing a long neck with a faint scar that ran over her collarbone and under the neckline of her gown. He wondered absently if it felt different from the rest of her skin, realized he was still staring, and blinked to break the spell.

"You were right about your gown," he said. "It's beautiful."

"And so are you," Elspeth said, hugging her.

"I like how I look," she said, turning to make the skirt swirl, "and I am still me."

"You are yourself however you dress," Alison said. "I wish we had an escort for you."

Jeffrey almost offered before he remembered that he was the king, that it was his duty to escort the Dowager Consort (not that his mother would allow him to use that appellation in her presence) and that it would look very strange for the king of Tremontane to escort a foreign ambassador to a diplomatic event, however beautiful the ambassador might be. Instead, he said, "Oh, I think Imogen will be far more impressive entering by herself. No one standing nearby to distract from the effect." He bowed to her, and she smiled and blushed a little, which made her look even better. No, on the whole it would be better if he didn't escort her tonight.

"Well, let's go. I don't want to miss any more of my reception than I already have," Elspeth said, and Jeffrey and Alison led the way, Elspeth and Owen following and Imogen bringing up the rear.

They had to rearrange themselves when they reached the ball-room so that Imogen could enter first—"Elspeth cannot be near me because I think no one will look at her when I am there," Imogen said, and Elspeth squealed a little and punched her arm. Jeffrey privately agreed with her. Elspeth had her mother's beauty, that doll-like prettiness and those enormous brown eyes, but Imogen was... Jeffrey couldn't find words to finish the sentence. She was extraordinary, that's what she was.

He and Alison waited just out of sight at the top of the stairs for Ivor the herald to announce Imogen's name, and were mutually grati-fied to hear a hush come over the room as she walked down the stairs. They grinned at each other before moving into position for the far more formal announcement of the king of Tremontane and the Dowager Consort's entrance. They crossed the room to sit in the high-backed chairs atop a carpeted dais, and then Ivor announced Elspeth and Owen, to cheery applause.

Elspeth looked so much better now, Jeffrey thought, still too thin, but not as breakable as she'd looked those first few days of her return. Owen looked at her as if she were his entire world, which was probably true. Jeffrey concealed a smile. Elspeth was preening like the butterfly he sometimes thought she was. It was always a surprise when she said or did something that reminded you that beneath that butterfly exterior was a clever mind and a kind heart. They looked so happy together that Jeffrey felt jealousy stab at his heart. Never mind what his mother said; the likelihood that he'd end up like she had, or like Owen and Elspeth had, was, well, unlikely.

The crowd made room for Owen to lead Elspeth to the center of the floor, her long blue skirt sweeping behind her so she appeared to be floating on his arm. Jeffrey looked at his mother as Owen and

Elspeth danced alone, Owen only a little clumsy, and said, "They make a handsome couple."

"They do," Alison said shortly, and Jeffrey, seeing the lines of tension around the corners of her lips, forbore to comment further. Alison hadn't danced once since the death of his father, and although Jeffrey knew that she, too, no longer felt his loss as sharply as she once had, he also knew that nothing reminded her so painfully of Anthony North as a formal dance. He also knew that there was nothing he could do to make it better.

So he sat and watched the happy couple and calculated how few dances he could get away with that night. He could already see a number of young women whose attention was on him instead of on the newlyweds. Maybe he should take his mother's advice and dance with some of them. But which ones? He had no way to choose between them. Then he thought with amusement that it hardly mattered; they were probably interchangeable.

The music faded, and again a murmur of quiet applause went up. The floor filled once again with couples dressed in their finest. Jeffrey cast his gaze around the room. More than half the provincial lords and ladies were here, though it was early yet and he thought more would appear as the night wore on. All his councilors were present. The reception was meant to double as a welcome for those attending the full council meeting in two days. Jeffrey intended to use it to take a sounding of current sentiment among the attendees.

He didn't have to look hard for Imogen, whose extraordinary red dress made her stand out in the crowd. It seemed Maxwell Burgess had her in hand and was introducing her to Serjian Ghentali, the Eskandel ambassador. Prince Ghentali was nice enough, but it was his harem who, in Eskandelic tradition, ran the show, and Burgess should have introduced her to them first. Imogen seemed to be enjoying her conversation with Ghentali, though. Jeffrey wished he could eavesdrop on their conversation. What did Imogen think of her first taste of diplomatic life? He made himself look away. Imogen was none of his business. She'd be fine. Right now he needed to make some contacts of his own.

He stood and then had to wait for the Veriboldan ambassador to pass in front of him and take his seat next to Jeffrey's. He was very old, his thin hair white and worn long around his shoulders, and his bright green eyes were so sunken in wrinkles he appeared to be peering out of a dark mask. His thin lips were made thinner by the way he pressed them together, as if to keep words from escaping. He wore a long black robe of fine silk over a tunic and skirt of green figured silk, tied with a golden cord. The tips of his bare toes protruded from the bottom of his skirt, the nails lacquered bronze, as were the nails of his right hand.

"Good evening, Bixhenta," Jeffrey said, addressing his words to the woman who accompanied the Proxy of Veribold. "Welcome to my sister's reception."

The woman, who was in her fifties, was dressed like the Proxy, though her robe was green and her tunic and skirt were a muddy brown, and her nails were unpainted. Her name was Paoine. She bent to speak into the old man's ear, listened for his response, and said, "The Proxy of Veribold extends his greetings to you as well, king of Tremontane."

Jeffrey bowed politely, keeping his laughter to himself. He knew Bixhenta spoke Tremontanese as well as anyone; Bixhenta, on the other hand, did not know Jeffrey spoke Veriboldan. What Paoine had actually said was -*The young king looks well tonight*-, and the Proxy had replied -*It's a wonder those good looks haven't gone to his head*-.

"I hope you'll receive the ambassador from the Kirkellan," he continued. "She is interested in meeting representatives from other countries, and I believe she is most anxious to make your acquaintance, as Veribold shares a border with the Eidestal and have been trading partners with the Kirkellan for many years."

Paoine began whispering in the Proxy's ear before Jeffrey was finished speaking. -*We're going to be forced to treat with the barbarian girl*-.

Bixhenta nodded. –*I imagine she can be fobbed off with some polite but meaningless words. Those Kirkellan aren't long on brains*-.

Now Jeffrey had trouble controlling his anger. "If you'll excuse me, Bixhenta, I must greet my guests," he said, and walked away without waiting for a reply. It was hard treating with the Veriboldans under any circumstances, with their demands to be treated according to strict Veriboldan propriety, but Bixhenta was also a snob, and Jeffrey didn't think Imogen would fare well against him.

Jeffrey wandered the room for a few minutes, shaking hands and greeting people. Had he said being the king was mostly paperwork? It was also mostly remembering people's names, and that was something Jeffrey was good at. Talking to people was where he felt most comfortable, most like the King everyone believed him to be.

He nodded and waved to a Count and Countess who were too far away for him to gracefully talk to—*must remember to speak with them later*—and stopped to have a quiet word with Micheline Branston, who as chief of Internal Affairs was responsible for security that evening. Almost all the peers of the realm gathered in one place; if he'd had any enemies, now would be the time for them to strike.

He wondered if he actually *did* have enemies, someone other than Hrovald, anyway. Maybe he needed some kind of spy network of his own, something to match the one Foreign Affairs ran outside Tremontane's boundaries. It was an interesting possibility. He added it to the list of things he'd consider later.

And *there* was a familiar face. "Sylvester!" Jeffrey clasped his brother's hand with a smile. "So you came, after all."

"We arrived this morning," Sylvester said. "Catherine's not here tonight. Still very unwell, and the journey didn't make things better."

"I'm sorry to hear that. I'm afraid it couldn't be helped."

"Catherine knows her duty better than anyone, as do I," Sylvester said, and there was a trace of bitterness in his voice that made Jeffrey's heart sink. So they were going to have that old argument again. Probably the best Jeffrey could do would be to postpone it for a less public venue.

"I take it you brought Charles?"

"Yes, he's with his nanny back at our townhouse, with Catherine. *He* thought the journey was wonderful. But he's barely three, he thinks sleeping under his bed with the blankets hanging down on all sides is marvelous."

"I hope you'll all come for supper one night, if Catherine's up to it."

"Wouldn't miss it. So, little brother, still enjoying the Crown?"

The Crown you should have worn, if you hadn't abandoned us. "Is 'enjoying' the right word? It's difficult. I'm busy all the time. What of you? Are you still enjoying being Catherine's right-hand man?"

Sylvester's eyes narrowed. "I think being her support is the most important thing I could have done with my life."

"Well, obviously, since it's the life you chose." Jeffrey knew he was picking a fight, the one he'd wanted to avoid, but being called "little brother" pushed all his buttons, as if he were a Device that was wound up and only needed a nudge to start running.

"Meaning that you didn't have a choice in yours."

"I'm not complaining."

"Are you sure?"

Jeffrey looked away from his brother's brown eyes, his fists clenched. "If I were, there wouldn't be much point to it, would there?"

"I told you I was sorry for how things turned out."

Jeffrey bit back something unforgiveable. Elspeth would kill him if he started a fight at her reception, and he would look uncontrolled and rash, not good characteristics to take with him into a full council meeting. "I know," he said more calmly, "and I apologize for implying that you chose wrong." *Even though I think you did.*

"Well, it's over and done, little brother, so I think we should enjoy the evening, don't you? I haven't seen Elspeth at all. You'd think that oak tree she married would make her obvious, right?" Sylvester scanned the room, then said, "Good heaven, who is *that*?"

Jeffrey turned and saw Imogen, standing alone and looking a little lost, and his heart lightened. "That's the Kirkellan ambassador. Let me introduce you."

Imogen's eyes widened when Jeffrey introduced Sylvester as his brother. "I do not know you have a brother," she said. "He has your face, Jeffrey, and Elspeth's eyes."

"And otherwise I look nothing like the rest of the family," Sylvester said with a smile. "Madam ambassador, might I have the pleasure of this dance? I will tell you stories of Jeffrey and Elspeth you can tease them with later."

"Don't believe anything he says, Imogen," Jeffrey said.

Imogen looked doubtful. "I think I know this dance, but you will have to help me with the steps," she said, accepting Sylvester's hand. Jeffrey watched them dance away and suddenly felt a little lost himself. He looked around for more people to talk to and saw Diana Ashmore deep in conversation with Maxwell Burgess.

"I hope you're not talking business, you two, because this is meant to be entertainment," he said as he approached them, claiming a glass of sparkling wine off a passing tray.

"As if I haven't watched you taking the measure of the peers since the first dance," Diana said, saluting him with her own glass.

"That's how I entertain myself. Max, how is our Kirkellan ambassador doing?"

"She's surprisingly good at her job, considering this is the first time she's had to be in public. I left her with Ghentali's harem and I think they had an enjoyable conversation. Not sure what kind of relationship the Kirkellan can have with Eskandel, there being most of Veribold between them, but she's charmed them and that's about half of what diplomacy is all about." He sounded a little surprised that the barbarian ambassador was doing so well, but he hadn't snubbed Imogen or sneered at her, so Jeffrey forgave him a little snobbishness.

"That's good to hear," he said. "Has she spoken with Bixhenta yet?"

"No, I was about to introduce them when *someone* found her a dance partner."

"I was being polite. And I wanted to get Sylvester off my back."

"Try not to start a fight," Diana said.

"I was very well behaved. And now I'm going to take a seat, unless you'd care to dance, Diana."

"Thank you, but I have some people I'd like to speak to."

"Of course. I'm sorry I interrupted your discussion."

"Nothing to interrupt," Burgess said. "Would you be sure to speak to Ghentali at least once tonight? I think he's feeling neglected because his harem's attracting all the attention."

"I'll remember that. Good evening, you two."

He returned to his seat and reminded himself to sit up straight instead of slouching as he always wanted to do in this throne-like chair. Alison glanced his way and said, "Not tired yet?"

"I was talking to Sylvester."

"Oh, Jeffrey."

"Don't take that tone with me. He started it."

"I have no doubt you were equally to blame. Why can't you just let it go? Sylvester followed his heart and his conscience. There's no point going over what might have been."

"I wouldn't if Sylvester didn't keep pointing out how glad he is that he 'did the right thing'."

Alison made an impatient sound. "Jeffrey, you sound like a six-year-old right now."

"He makes me feel like a six-year-old. At least when I was six and he was eight I could beat him up when we disagreed."

"Let it go, son. He may not be a North any longer, but he's still family, and we don't have enough of it to cast off what we have."

Jeffrey scowled, but nodded, and said, "Catherine's not well. Will you visit her tomorrow?"

"Of course. She was sick like this with Charles, too. It will pass, though I imagine right now she feels as if it will never end."

"I—wait, mother, I think Imogen's coming to talk to Bixhenta and I want to listen."

Alison rolled her eyes. "Eavesdropping is a crude habit."

"Yes, and I'm glad you taught me how to do it."

Jeffrey looked around the room, pretending to be unaware of Imogen's approach, but watching her avidly out of the corner of his eye. Burgess had coached her well; she approached Paoine, not Bixhenta, bowed at the waist and said, "I am Imogen of the Kirkellan."

Paoine inclined her head. "I am the Voice of Bixhenta, Proxy of

Veribold," she said. "He bids you welcome in the name of our country."

Imogen said, "My people are grateful for the relationship with Veribold we have made over the years."

Paoine bent and spoke into Bixhenta's ear. *–The fat girl is too young for her position. The Kirkellan do not respect us by sending her here.-*

-Pretend as if we care about her people. We need their trade.-

Paoine said, "The Proxy acknowledges the link between your people and ours. We respect your efforts in keeping the Ruskalder at bay, though Veribold needs no protection."

"If our positions were different, I am sure Veribold would do the same for us."

-Brash.-

-She is bold.- Bixhenta smiled, just the faintest twitch of the thin lips that Jeffrey almost didn't catch.

Paoine said, "Veribold does many things for the Kirkellan already. We hope you do not suggest we do more."

"I am just...acknowledging our relationship that is one of more than trading partners. Which is *tradition*," Imogen said, emphasizing the word just a little. "We are especially grateful for silk. It makes the best undergarments."

Jeffrey choked. Undergarments? Bixhenta's proud patrician heart would explode at the thought of Veribold's most prized commodity being used for barbarian underwear. But the wrinkles around Bixhenta's eyes only deepened briefly, and he said, *-Undergarments. How is it we have never thought of such a use?-* Paoine began to speak, but Bixhenta took hold of her sleeve and said, *-If they're so clever, I wonder what uses they will find for our other trade goods? I wish to arrange a meeting.-* Paoine's eyes widened, and she said, "The Proxy would like to discuss further trade opportunities between our people. He will meet with you at another time to review current policy and establish mutually beneficial alterations."

Imogen said, in a pleased voice, "I am happy to meet with the Proxy when it is, um, convenient for him. I am certain the *matrian* is —no, will be pleased to hear our relation with Veribold is still strong." She bowed from the waist again, this time directly at the Proxy, and he surprised Jeffrey by inclining his head in her direction. He'd never seen Bixhenta unbend so much.

Now Imogen seemed uncertain about what to do next, or possibly how to end the conversation gracefully. Jeffrey was at her side in two long strides, and said, "Please excuse use, Bixhenta, the ambassador has promised this dance to me." He put his arm around Imogen's waist and steered her away from the Proxy and toward where couples swirled across the floor in a tapestry of color.

"This is not a dance I know," Imogen protested.

"I know. I just wanted to get you out of there diplomatically. And speaking of which, congratulations on your first diplomatic victory."

"You *were* listening. You made that sound."

"I was trying not to fall over laughing. If I'd known all it would take to get Bixhenta to loosen up was to talk about underwear, I'd have done it a year ago."

"I only said what was true."

"And he knew it."

"Then it was only by accident that I make an agreement with him."

"A part of diplomacy is making use of happy accidents. I think you have a talent for it."

Imogen smiled and blushed. He liked it when she blushed; it made her eyes look brighter. "I am enjoying it," she said, "the talking to people. I have met many people and most of them are interesting. Even if some of them are interesting by what they do not say."

"Really? What do—wait, I know this song. This dance we *both* know." Jeffrey extended his hand with a smile, and Imogen took it. It really was different dancing with someone whose eyes were level with your own.

"No, don't look at your feet, look at me," he said, and Imogen lifted her chin and met his eyes. "You're actually more likely to trip if you look at your feet while you're dancing."

"If I trip, you will catch me," she said.

"I certainly will."

Her gaze left his and drifted past his right shoulder, and a puzzled look came over her face. "I think you Tremontanans take your marriage vows seriously."

Jeffrey returned a puzzled look of his own. "We do. We make oath to each other and the lines of power that cross the country bind those oaths. It's a serious thing, marriage. Why do you bring it up?"

"I meet—met the Countess of Cullinan and her consort tonight. And now she looks at another man and there is sex between them." Jeffrey choked, and she made an impatient face. "It is to say, they have sex in the past and when they look at each other the memory is there." She swung them around, causing Jeffrey to miss a couple of steps, and said, "It is the man at the foot of the steps. In light green."

Jeffrey looked, and said, "That's her steward, the man who manages her estates. I'd heard there was something between them, but it's the sort of rumor that could be spite as much as truth. You knew that with just a look?"

She shrugged. "Yes."

Jeffrey shook his head in amazement. "Imogen, you have more than just a talent for diplomacy."

She smiled as the dance came to an end. "And now I have a talent for dancing as well."

"You do. Would you care to sit? There's a chair for you with the other ambassadors."

"I am tired with the diplomacy. King of Tremontane, can the ambassador of the Kirkellan leave now?"

"If you want." Again the impulse to offer himself as an escort back to the east wing struck, and again he suppressed it. He still had people to talk to; it wasn't all that late yet. "Maybe Mother is ready to go. I don't think you'll find your way back on your own."

Alison was, in fact, ready to leave and happy to take Imogen with her. Jeffrey felt a little deflated, watching the two of them leave; much as he enjoyed political conversation, it was nice to have people you could talk to without worrying about subtext. He sat for a while, watching the currents, then stood and wandered back into the crowd.

JEFFREY: CHAPTER TEN

*E*lspeth's peals of laughter rang down the hall and through the closed door of Jeffrey's rooms. She was certainly up early for someone who'd danced until 3 a.m., particularly someone who rarely rose before ten if she could help it. Jeffrey followed the sound of her mirth into the sitting room, where she and Imogen sat side by side on a sofa, two piles of envelopes between them. Elspeth clutched one in her hand, giggling; Imogen looked confused and unhappy and angry.

"Are you laughing at Imogen?" Jeffrey asked, angry himself. Elspeth waved the envelope at him and shook her head, still overcome with laughter.

"These all came for her this morning," she explained, "and she can't read Tremontanese so she asked me to, to..." She began laughing again, and Imogen exclaimed in Kirkellish and stood, knocking over both piles.

"Elspeth, Imogen isn't in on whatever has you laughing like a drain," Jeffrey said. "Imogen, can I read these for you?"

She glared, then scooped up half of one pile and shoved it at him. "I do not think it is funny," she said.

Jeffrey removed a note from a cheap paper envelope and glanced at it. "This says Marcus Browne would like the pleasure of your company at dinner tomorrow, 1 p.m." He handed it back to her. "This one is an invitation to a poetry recitation...this one is for supper...this one is, hah, an invitation to watch the Kirkellan race at the track..."

He squared them in his hand and tapped them against his thigh. "It seems your appearance at the reception last night has made you popular," he said lightly, but inside he was seething. He knew most of those names, and none of them were people he thought Imogen should associate with—lazy, womanizing gadabouts who, if they took her out for a meal, would probably expect her to pay the tab.

"There are *more*, Jeffrey!" Elspeth giggled. "Lots more! Some of them are diplomatic invitations, but most of them are from Imogen's admirers! Isn't it wonderful?"

"Elspeth," Jeffrey said, trying to keep his inner seething from turning hotter and more angry, "are you laughing at the idea that Imogen might have admirers? That's an awful thing to do to a friend."

"I do not know why I should not have admirers," Imogen said angrily.

Elspeth's hilarity vanished. "Oh, Imogen, I'm so sorry, I didn't mean that at all. I was laughing because I think it's wonderful that you made such an impression on everyone last night. But you have to admit some of these are pretty funny. 'I adore the limpid pools of your eyes, like the coffee I had for breakfast,' how perfectly awful!"

Imogen scowled and sat down on a different seat. "I do not know whether they are good or not," she said, "but I do not like these—I do not know the word. These men who do not know me thinking I am interested in them."

That relieved Jeffrey's mind considerably. "Well," he said, trying to be fair, "they're inviting you to do things with them because they want to know you better."

"I do not know how to behave. And I do not know if I will like them. I do not even remember these men."

"Well, Jeffrey and I know most of them. Do you want us to help you choose?"

Imogen looked at Elspeth, then turned to Jeffrey. "Will you tell me which ones I will like?" she asked him. "Because I think since you are a man, you will know the good ones."

He looked at the handful of envelopes he held. None of them were good ones. None of them were men he'd tell her to go to dinner with, or a concert, or even walk across the street with. *Me*, he thought, *I want you to like* me, and knew he was lost.

"Well, most of these are people you should probably ignore," he said, trying not to listen to the little voice screaming at him from inside his head, "but I'm sure some of them—let me see the ones you have, Elspeth."

"I know which ones to throw away, Jeffrey. Oh, Michael Petty, he's nice. Shame about the ears, but really very nice."

"Michael Petty is a terrible choice. He'll drag you to a museum and then lecture you about the artist and what she was thinking and eating when she planned whatever awful piece you're looking at. Definitely not him."

"What about Anton Crowder?"

"He's almost engaged to Penelope Winterbourne. I don't know what business he has sending invitations to other women."

"Well..." Elspeth leafed through the rest of her stack. "I suppose you're right. There really isn't anyone good enough for you, Imogen."

"Oh," Imogen said. "I feel strange. I am—was not interested in these men, but now you say none of them are good enough for me and I am disappointed."

"I'm sure there will be other invitations," Jeffrey said, secretly giddy with glee that he'd successfully defended against the first wave of comers. "And since I wouldn't want you to feel completely neglected, why don't you—the two of you—come out to dine with me at noon?" He included Elspeth at the last minute. No sense declaring himself before he knew if Imogen even thought of him as more than a friend.

"We're both busy," Elspeth declared. "Sorry."

He tried not to look too deflated. "Oh well, I suppose I'll just have to eat alone. At my desk. By myself."

Imogen took the envelopes from his hand. "We will think of you all alone at your desk and feel sorry for you," she said with a mischievous smile, and his heart beat faster.

"That will make me feel *so* much better," he said, and made his retreat to the dining room before his face could betray him. He piled sausages and eggs onto a plate, wolfed his food, and retreated to his office without meeting anyone except Arthur, who was detestably cheerful when he handed over the day's schedule and said, "I left you some time for training, your Majesty, you were saying just the other day how you miss it." Jeffrey managed not to growl at him before locking himself in his office, falling into his chair and covering his face with both hands.

So.

It had been obvious for days, hadn't it? He just hadn't seen what was in front of him.

And now that he knew how he felt about her, he couldn't stop thinking about her. How her eyes sparkled when she was happy, the sound of her laugh, the way she'd looked in that gown, the way she looked in her own clothing...yes, he was lost, and he had no idea what to do about it.

He didn't know how to court an ordinary woman, much less one like Imogen. Could he just go up to her and say, "Imogen, I'm interested in you, let's spend some time together and see what happens"? He felt this was a bad idea, not least because it offered the possibility of a straightforward "No" answer. If he spoke Kirkellish, he could ask her *tiermatha* what to do, though they might just beat him to death for daring to think of Imogen that way. He could ask Elspeth—no, that would be a *terrible* idea, because she'd tell Imogen, and then they could both laugh at him.

He groaned. He'd always thought, without really considering the idea, that because he was handsome and a King he could pick any woman and she'd fall in love with him, with no work required on his part. He'd been a fool twice over.

JEFFREY: FIRST DATE

*J*effrey shrugged into the dark green frock coat with his valet's help. Was it a little too dark? A little too green? The waistcoat of gold brocaded satin was probably too much. He should change. "I think the vest—" he began.

"Your Majesty has already discarded a dozen waistcoats," Stephen said, "and if you wish to make your appointment, you will not discard a thirteenth." He produced a lint brush and began swiping at the sleeves and shoulders of the coat.

"I suppose you're right," Jeffrey said, holding his arms a little extended from his body. "What about the trousers? They're too informal."

"They are appropriate for attending the theater, as I'm sure your Majesty knows, having set that fashion."

"Right. They look fine, don't they?"

"I am certain the young lady will appreciate the effort you've made."

"It's her first visit to the theater," Jeffrey said. "I want her to enjoy herself." It was only partly true. What he wanted was to impress her, encourage her to look at him favorably. If he could continue to find ways to discourage her other suitors.... He turned away from the mirror. *Other* suitors. That put him solidly among their number, didn't it? Even if he was courting her secretly. Even if he couldn't quite bring himself to say *Imogen, I feel so much more than friendship for you, do you think...?*

He straightened the front of his coat, unnecessarily, as Stephen's carefully neutral face suggested. His valet only looked that way when he felt his royal master's insecurities were in danger of ruining his royal appearance.

Two guards waited outside the east wing, not paying attention to their counterparts who were stationed there tonight. Jeffrey always wondered if they chatted a bit before he appeared. He'd never know if they did; they were all so formal around him, even the ones who'd known him since childhood and had formerly saluted him with cheery ease. He tried to relax his shoulders and walk more naturally between them. "You look as if you're headed to your own execution," Mother often teased him, but he didn't really know what that looked like, just that he felt like a man-shaped wooden crate, trapping his fears and doubts well inside so no one would know how completely inadequate he felt himself to be. Father had—

He breathed in deeply and held the breath for a few seconds, then let it out in a long, silent stream, carrying that painful memory away. Kingship had come naturally to his father, who'd always carried himself with an easy confidence that could turn as quickly to commanding his counselors as it did to laughing with his children. Jeffrey's earliest memory was of being tossed in the air by those powerful, gentle hands, of that baritone voice assuring Mother that no, he wasn't going to drop the boy, then pretending to drop him and laughing at Mother's horrified shriek. Then being clasped between them as Father embraced her and feeling secure and loved. He'd cherished that memory, made himself relive it every night for a month after Father's death to keep other, more recent memories away. It almost never worked.

The carriage was waiting near the front steps of the palace. That couldn't be good for the horses, having to stand and wait for him. He hoped they at least walked around the city while he was in the theater instead of standing in the traces for three hours. Imogen disliked seeing horses harnessed to carriages; she never said anything, but he'd seen the distaste in her eyes the first time she'd had to ride in one. Of course, she was accustomed to riding free across the Eidestal, an image that captivated his imagination. She was like no woman he'd ever known before, carefree and quick to laugh and determined to learn everything she could about this strange society she'd been dropped into by fate. That was something they had in common; neither of them had been prepared for their current role.

He made his shoulders relax again. He'd never really forgiven Sylvester, though he'd smiled and said all the right things when they met at their father's funeral. But then, Sylvester had always put his needs before anyone else's. That night he'd come to Jeffrey's room to tell him he was leaving: *Catherine is Baroness of Silverfield, her brothers are selfish pigs, Jeff, you've met them. She can't leave the Barony to one of them. I love her too much to make her change for my sake—that would be selfish.* As if adopting out of the North family, renouncing his claim as heir to the throne, was any less selfish.

And Jeffrey had had less than a year to get used to his new status before he was thrust into one he'd thought he would have decades to prepare for. Years of guidance by— He rotated his shoulders again. It was the coat, that's what it was, the damned coat was too tight across the shoulders. He'd throw it away after tonight.

The carriage came to a stop, then rocked a little as one of the guards stepped down from her perch. Jeffrey made himself breathe calmly, slowly. This was an ordinary visit to the theater with a friend, and it would be enjoyable, and she'd agree to see another play with him, or have dinner, just the two of them, and gradually he could work himself up to declaring himself openly. He rubbed his palms on his trousers and hoped he hadn't left a mark. He'd spent three years avoiding the women who threw themselves at the King of Tremontane and had completely forgotten how to court a woman on his own terms. *Friends*, he thought, *we're friends*, and pretended that was all it was.

The guard opened the door, and Imogen climbed in. She was wearing that red dress she'd worn at Elspeth's reception; she couldn't know how much he liked it, could she? It was the perfect color for her skin and her amazing hair, thick and dark with ruddy highlights that he had fantasies about running his fingers through, pinned up loosely at the base of her neck tonight. She took a seat opposite him and smiled, and he tried to smile back, but it was that thin twist of the lips that was all he'd been able to manage for three years, and heaven alone knew what she made of it.

"You look lovely tonight," he said. *Beautiful, you fool, you should have said beautiful.*

"Thank you," Imogen said in that Kirkellish accent that made her words sound like water over stone. "You look lovely too." She blushed. "It is to say, handsome."

"The credit is entirely due my valet," Jeffrey said. "Did I see another carriage leaving the embassy just now?"

"One of my *tiermatha* is courting with a soldier. A Tremontanan soldier. She is courting your way."

"You know, it never occurred to me that might happen, but it makes sense, doesn't it? Your people thrown together with our people, I mean."

"It is still hard when they do not speak the same language, but Saevonna is learning."

"I suppose love finds a way no matter what language you speak." *By heaven, I hope so.*

"I do not know that it is love," Imogen said, a little startled.

"Did she dress in Tremontanan clothes?"

"Yes."

"Then if she changed her dress for him, learned his language, and went courting his way, I would say that's something more than mere affection."

A look of consternation crossed Imogen's face, and Jeffrey replayed his words in his head, looking for something that might have disturbed her. Did she think it was wrong for the Kirkellan to give up their lives for a Tremontanan romance? Would *she* be unwilling to pursue a relationship with *him*? Maybe this was a huge mistake. Well, if it was, he hadn't declared himself and neither of them had to be embarrassed. It could just be two friends at the theater. The idea made him feel hollow.

Then Imogen shrugged, and said, "I think we will have to see. It is only supper."

"True." Or maybe it wasn't a mistake, and he still had hope. The hollow feeling spread, making him feel as if he were spinning between possibilities. *Time enough for that when we know each other better. One step after another.*

He helped her down from the carriage and saw, as he had before, the curious twist at the corners of her mouth that said she didn't entirely understand the custom. How *did* she see them all, with their elaborate (by her standards) dress and manners and their houses and businesses that were so unlike the world of the nomadic Kirkellan? "That's the name of the play," he said, observing her interest in the glowing marquee. "*Two Came to Kingsport*. It's one of my favorites."

"I look forward to it," Imogen said. "This building is beautiful."

"My mother founded it, before she was Consort and Royal Librarian and couldn't give it enough of her time. I've been coming here my whole life."

The doorman pushed open the brass door and held it for them, bowing his head respectfully to his King. The first guard passed through, her eyes restlessly moving across the crowd while her partner hovered protectively behind them. Jeffrey tried not to let impatience overflow. Having a guard permanently attached to him was one of those things he'd had to adapt to, but he'd never considered what a damper it might be on a courtship. He'd already started going over legitimate reasons to escape them, assuming Imogen would someday be interested in being alone with him.

He cast a quick, covert glance at her; she was staring about with undisguised interest at the softly upholstered walls and the Device sconces lighting the antechamber to the theater. "This way," he said, tugging on her arm, and they ascended the shallow stairs to the passage curving around the wall of the theater and the door of box 3. One of the guards stepped inside, then after a minute returned and said, "Please go ahead, your Majesty."

Jeffrey drew Imogen through the door and held one of the seats for her. "The guards do not come to the play?" she said as the door closed on the man and woman.

"No," he said, sitting next to her, "they have to stand out there for hours and never see a single play. I feel a little sorry for them."

"So do I," Imogen said, and the lights went down, the curtain went up, and the play began.

It was surprisingly easy to relax and enjoy the play, though Jeffrey divided his attention between the stage and his beautiful companion. Imogen roared with unrestrained laughter, completely enthralled by the broad physical comedy, even if she didn't understand the subtle wordplay. Her pleasure was almost as enjoyable to him as the show itself. When the curtain dropped, she said, "That cannot be all there is. Miriam still has not found her shoes."

"This is intermission. You can use the facilities and stretch your legs if you like." Jeffrey stood and stretched a little himself. "One of the guards will escort you."

He sat back down in his chair when she was gone and realized he was smiling, a genuine, natural smile so surprising that he touched his lips in wonder. He hadn't laughed so hard in...well, a very long time. Come to think on it, he couldn't remember the last time he'd been to the theater. Had he really been so busy? His father had always had time for the theater, for his family. The smile disappeared. Just one more reminder that he wasn't Anthony North.

Someone rapped on the door, and Diana Ashmore said, "Jeffrey? Do you mind if I come in?"

Jeffrey closed his eyes and sent up a wordless prayer to heaven. They'd been such good friends, once, and then he'd become King and suddenly her interest in him had gone from friendly to romantic. She'd been subtle about it, at least at first, but in the last several months she'd done everything she could to convince him she was the best choice to be Consort. And she *would* be an excellent Consort; she was intelligent and politically astute and charming and she did seem to like him, though he doubted she was actually in love with him. But Jeffrey had seen how his parents looked at each other, and he wasn't going to settle for "like." "Of course," he called out, and the guards opened the door.

"It's a wonderful performance, isn't it?" Diana said. She sat in Imogen's chair and looked out over the audience—positioning herself, Jeffrey realized, so anyone who looked up would see her in the royal box. "And you have a wonderful view. I can't believe I've never been in here."

"I didn't realize you cared about theater, or I would have invited you," Jeffrey said, and immediately cursed himself for that slip of the tongue. *Don't encourage her, fool.*

Diana's eyes brightened, and she laid her hand caressingly on his knee. "There will be other plays, Jeffrey," she cooed. "And I think you owe me something after yesterday."

"It was the right decision, Diana. You know that."

"Of course. But I won't say I wasn't a little disappointed." Her smile didn't quite reach her eyes. Jeffrey didn't respond. There was nothing he could say that would change the fact that the new territory wasn't hers to govern.

The door opened again. Imogen took a few steps into the box and then stopped. "Hello," she said. Jeffrey felt a little sick now. He definitely didn't need Diana interfering in his secret courtship.

"Oh, Imogen, what a pleasant surprise to find you here," she said. "Jeffrey, how kind of you to introduce the ambassador to one of Aurilien's great cultural treasures. Do you mind if I share your box for the second act? I'm with friends who don't appreciate the theater as much as I do. Help me convince him, Imogen," she added, looking over her shoulder at Imogen and smiling a pleasant smile.

His stomach was knotting itself around his spine. He couldn't think of a single thing that would get Diana out of the box that didn't include telling both women this was meant to be courtship. "Of course we don't mind," he said. "Imogen, the second act's about to start, why don't you take your seat?"

Imogen looked at Diana. Diana's smile looked triumphant now. "I will enjoy this," Imogen said, and sat on Diana's other side. Diana took Jeffrey's hand and squeezed it, then didn't let go immediately. He gently extricated himself and tried to ignore her, focusing on the play, but he was aware only of Imogen, sitting too far away from him and laughing as if she didn't mind her seat at all. This was turning out to be one of the least comfortable nights of his life. He'd never been so close to telling Diana she didn't have a chance with him, would never have a chance with him, and he wasn't sure if it was good sense or cowardice that kept him from doing so.

When the curtain came down a final time and they finished applauding, Diana still didn't rise. "Thank you *so* much for sharing your escort, Imogen," she said. "You understand how attached old friends can be." She put her hand on Jeffrey's knee and patted it. Jeffrey wished he could grab her wrist and shove her away. How much longer was he going to continue to let her treat him as her personal property?

Imogen smiled brightly at her. "I am sorry for you," she said, "because it is hard for you to find your own escort." She looked so innocent that it took Jeffrey a moment to hear the slap in those words. "Perhaps you should find *other* friends to be attached to."

Diana's face was frozen in the act of saying something. Her eyes went narrow. "You—" she began angrily, then glanced at Jeffrey and turned it into a smile. "We really should go together sometime, Jeffrey," she said, and kissed him lightly on the cheek in the manner of an old friend. The smile she bestowed on Imogen as she left was not even a little bit friendly. Jeffrey had to swallow a laugh.

When the door shut behind Diana, he said, "That was unexpected."

"She was rude first."

"I know. That wasn't a criticism. I had no idea you could be so...catty."

"I do not—did not like her behaving as though *I* am intruding on *her* evening."

Jeffrey smiled, just that thin little smile, but inside he was turning joyful cartwheels. *She thinks this is an evening together. She wants to be with me. Sweet heaven, what do I do?* "I apologize," he said. "I shouldn't have asked her to stay. I hated to tell her no tonight when I essentially told her the biggest 'no' you can imagine yesterday."

"I know she is your friend, but she is not a nice person sometimes."

Not a nice person, ever, I think. "She certainly has been more obvious in her, um, bid for my affections lately." He touched his cheek, imagining Diana's kiss as a brand scorching his skin. "Shall we go? I doubt Diana is waiting around downstairs to accost me again."

"And if she is you can have your guards carry her away," Imogen said, and the picture of Diana being hauled away by the guards, screaming obscenities at him, made Jeffrey laugh.

Jeffrey assisted Imogen into the carriage and sat down opposite her. "I hope you enjoyed the play," he said, and immediately felt stupid. Couldn't he think of anything more substantial to say?

"I did," Imogen said. "There are others?"

"There are two other theaters, and then each theater will put on new performances every few months. We could go to see another, if you like, sometime."

"You do not mind?"

I wish I could spend every minute with you. "Not at all. I want you to enjoy the best Aurilien has to offer."

Imogen nodded. Jeffrey cast about for something else to say and came up empty. He watched Imogen for a while, concealing his interest by looking in every other direction. She didn't even sit like any other woman he knew; she was alert, her body relaxed but ready to act if that was necessary, her eyes scanning her surroundings and no doubt observing a hundred things Jeffrey missed. Even Diana, who for all her personal shortcomings was an excellent swordswoman, didn't look as much like a warrior as Imogen did. He recalled what Mairen had said of her, that there was more to her than her warrior nature, and thought *She may look like a lady, but she's never let go of the warrior.*

"May I ask you something you might find insulting?" he said before he could stop himself.

Imogen's gaze came to rest on him. "You will ask and then I will not be insulted even if it is insulting," she said with a smile, but her body was tense, and he wished he hadn't said anything. Too late now.

He leaned forward, hoping by that gesture to make his question more personal. "Mairen told me there was a part of you that wasn't a warrior," he said. "I've seen you become a diplomat and a part of Tremontanan society, and I think maybe that's what she was talking about. But it seems to me you're still clinging to the warrior part of you, and not allowing yourself to see what it's like to truly become this new self. I was wondering why that is."

Imogen drew in a harsh breath, then turned away to look out the window. Jeffrey wanted to kick himself. He hadn't meant that as an attack, but she'd reacted as if he'd punched her. "I apologize," he said. "I shouldn't have asked such a personal question." So much for courting her. Ever.

Imogen shook her head. "It is a true question," she said, swiping tears from her eyes that made his heart ache. "I made a promise to learn and I did not keep it."

"Why is that?"

"*That* is a personal question."

Jeffrey was grateful she couldn't see him blush in the light from the street lamps. "You're right," he said. "Don't answer that."

She sighed, a little shakily. "I am fighting with myself, all the time I am here. I think I know, inside me, I am only a warrior because I know nothing else, and I am afraid I will want to be another thing when I know what that is."

"Would it be so bad, being a diplomat instead of a warrior?"

"I am leaving behind everything I know."

She sounded so forlorn that Jeffrey moved to sit next to her, not quite daring to take her hand, but offering her comfort the only way he knew how anymore. "That's never easy," he said. "Especially when you're leaving your life behind for something you know nothing about."

"That is it. I must learn new things and do new things and I cannot know if I am right until after I have done them."

"I understand that."

"Do you? I do not see how." Her words were angry, resentful that he'd tried to usurp her experience, and pain struck him so unexpectedly that he had no defenses against it.

"I was never meant to be King, Imogen," he said. "I was the...have you ever heard the phrase 'the heir and the spare'? I was the spare. I didn't have to learn to rule. I was going to go into business—the theater business, actually—and I had my whole life planned. Then Sylvester...left, and that was the end of every one of my plans. I'd never even imagined myself as heir."

To his surprise, Imogen took his hand. Her palm was warm and smooth and he couldn't help it, he closed his fingers around her hand and held onto it. "And then you were King," she said quietly.

"And then I was King," he echoed. "Another role for which I was unprepared. Imogen, I'm not going to tell you I understand what you've experienced. I just know what it's like to be thrust into a life you aren't prepared for, that you could never have imagined."

"But what do I do?" She was close enough that he could see her eyes clearly despite the dim light. "I do not want to be a stranger to me."

"If it's what you're meant to be, you'll find you know yourself better than ever," he said. "At least, that's what Mother says. I haven't yet learned for myself if it's true."

She smiled at him. "You have not yet realized that you are a good King."

I could never be as good as my father. "I haven't destroyed Tremontane yet. That must mean something."

"And I think you are a good man. Maybe that is more important."

He became conscious, again, of her hand in his, of how close she was, of how her eyes were on a level with his, and before his brain could override his heart, he reached up with his free hand to caress her cheek. Her eyes went wide. "Jeffrey," she said, faintly. Her skin was soft, like rose petals, not at all what he expected of a warrior, and he stroked her cheek again, marveling at her beauty. Her lips parted as if to say something, then she leaned forward and kissed him.

He let go of her hand and put his arms around her to draw her closer, returning her kiss. She smelled of roses and, very faintly, of horses, and the two scents mingled in the air, making him want to go on breathing the smell of her forever. He explored her mouth with his kisses, gently, though his body was telling him to push her up against the side of the carriage and let her feel the passion that surged through him.

She had her arms around his neck now and was running her fingers through his hair, which inflamed him further, and he slid one hand down her back to the base of her spine and stroked her there. Then the carriage bumped to a stop, and his teeth grazed her lower lip, which made her laugh. It was such a merry sound that Jeffrey smiled, a real smile, and said, "I don't think I'm ready to stop, are you?"

Imogen shook her head. "It has only been two minutes. That is not enough."

Jeffrey disentangled himself long enough to rap on the carriage roof. "Go once around the Park," he said, and the carriage jerked back into motion. He took her into his arms once more and said, "I would apologize, but I have been thinking about doing that for several days now and I feel absolutely no regret."

"If you have been thinking about it for several days, I do not know it," Imogen said.

"I've learned to be good at concealing what I feel, after three years of dealing with my Council. I didn't want to burden you with my interest, if you weren't interested in *me*."

"So you are courting me when you ask if I want to see the play."

"I hoped it wasn't obvious. I panicked a little because of those damned invitations. I knew they would just keep coming and I would eventually run out of reasons for you to reject them. So I decided to court you secretly, give you time to get used to the idea before I declared myself. That way, if my charms didn't appeal to you—"

She interrupted him with a long, tender kiss that made him temporarily forget what he was saying. "You appeal to me," she said. "I thought you should know."

"Fortunate for both of us, then," he said with a smile. "At any rate, either you would be receptive to my courtship, or we'd be two friends who happened to enjoy the same social activities. Either of those outcomes would be acceptable."

She raised her eyebrows at him. "Really?"

He leaned forward until their foreheads touched. "No," he said. "I was never going to be happy until I held you in my arms, just like this."

"I think you know how to talk to women."

He laughed, thinking back on how nervous he'd been earlier. "Just you." He kissed her forehead. "So, if two minutes is too short, what would be long enough?"

"If you always kiss like you do then, I do not think I could put a number on that."

He kissed the scar that emerged from the neck of her gown to extend across her collarbone. "I do have to take you home sometime, you know."

"But sometime is not...oh, Jeffrey, do that again."

He nipped at her earlobe, then kissed behind her ear. "I should warn you," he said, "that I intend to take full advantage of you being trapped in this carriage with me."

She laughed, a low, throaty sound that made him wish the carriage were a little roomier, and said, "If take advantage means you kiss me again with your wonderful mouth, I like it." He laughed, and kissed her beautiful lips, making speech impossible.

The carriage once again came to a stop, startling Jeffrey, who'd completely lost track of time. Imogen drew back a bit and regarded him with those lovely dark eyes. "Sometime is now," she said. "I wish it was not true."

He stroked her cheek one last time. "Will you dance with me at the Spring Ball tomorrow?"

"Of course."

Her near-indignation, that he might think she wouldn't say yes, made him laugh. "Just one dance, though," he said. "I'm not ready for the world to know about our changed relationship, madam ambassador."

"This is a thing you are ashamed of?"

"No, but the implications of the King of Tremontane being romantically involved with an ambassador of a foreign country are...complicated."

She withdrew her arms and crossed them over her chest. "Then you should not have kissed me," she said.

He felt like he'd been slapped. Imogen was no longer smiling; anger creased her forehead, and her lips were pinched and set tight. "Imogen," he began, then registered how her eyes were creased with amusement and her lips were compressed because they were holding back a laugh. "You're teasing me," he said with relief.

She flung her arms around his neck and kissed him, a light, playful kiss. "I think you should not have your own way all the time."

"I think there's little danger of that with you around," he said. "I'll walk you to your door."

He waved away the guard—they were only going half a dozen steps up the embassy stairs—and tried not to cling to her arm, instead grazing her knuckles with a kiss. "Good night, my dear... ambassador," he said with a smile, and waited for her to shut the door behind herself before getting back into the carriage and directing the driver to return to the palace. He could still feel her lips on his, could still smell the sweet-musk scent of her, and that wide, unfamiliar smile spread across his face.

He could never have anticipated this. They'd only been apart for a minute and already he couldn't wait to see her again. *I'm falling in love with her*, he thought, and shivered with joy. True, she was the ambassador, which made things tricky; he'd have to come up with ways they could be alone that didn't look suspicious. Mother would definitely notice something was up if he wasn't careful.

He counted days in his head. A little more than eleven months, and her term as ambassador would be up, and he'd be able to court her publicly. He wished he could do it now, declare to the whole world that Imogen of the Kirkellan had kissed him, but he was the King and he didn't have the freedoms Prince Jeffrey North had once had. For the first time in almost four years, he felt no resentment over that thought.

JEFFREY: THE SPRING BALL

"You seem a little restless," Mother said. "Usually I'm the one who wishes I were elsewhere."

"I think it's the boundary decision," Jeffrey lied. "I'm a little weary of people wanting to talk to me about it."

"They aren't asking you to change your mind, are they?"

"No. They want to discuss their candidates for the new Baronies. I wish I dared just make a decision quickly, shut them all up, but this is a major turning point for Tremontane and whatever I decide is going to have long-term ramifications. So I can't hurry, however much I might want to."

"Which is why you're hiding over here."

"I'm sitting where everyone can see me, Mother."

"You know people are reluctant to approach you when you're sitting on that chair. It intimidates them. You'll have to leave it some-time." She was teasing him, but he could tell when she meant her words. "Why don't you dance?"

"Because I hate dancing." There was only one person he wanted to dance with tonight, and he couldn't see her anywhere. Couldn't see any of the *tiermatha*, so she probably just hadn't arrived yet.

"It's an important part of the social contract, Jeffrey."

"Then maybe you should dance," he snapped, and regretted it instantly. Alison North's face went still and even paler than usual. "Mother, I'm sorry—"

"You're under more strain than I realized," she said quietly. "I'm sorry I teased you."

"No, Mother, I should never have said that. I'm sorry."

"There's something else, isn't there?"

"No. I'm just—you're right, I'm under pressure about the new Baronies. But it's no excuse."

"You're right, though. I should dance. It probably looks bad that I don't."

Jeffrey took her hand. "Mother, everyone understands."

"Do they?" Tears glimmered in her eyes. "Jeffrey, I just can't bear it. I know it's weak—"

"It's not."

Behind him, he heard Bixhenta say something in that dry voice of his, and then Imogen spoke, and his heart began beating more rapidly. Mother's eyes narrowed. "What's wrong?"

He withdrew his hand carefully. "I've just thought of something else I have to do," he said, sounding exasperated. "As if I weren't busy enough."

"Really?" Mother sounded skeptical, and he tried to relax. She was the one person who could see through his cultivated demeanors, though he was sure she wouldn't be able to guess what had him on edge tonight.

"Yes, and I've also decided that I'm tired of hiding," he said with a smile, and stood. "I'm going to mingle, and I'm going to deflect anyone who wants to propose a candidate for the Baronies, and I might even dance. At least then no one will bother me."

Mother nodded. "You should dance with Imogen," she said, levelling a cool gaze at him. He returned it with equal coolness.

"Is she here? I haven't seen her," he said, which was entirely true. He bowed to her, and set off in search of the only woman he intended to dance with that night.

He'd had a restless night, reliving those wonderful kisses, and then he'd overslept, and then he'd been unable to focus all day, thinking of her. Had she thought of him at all? Did she know how she'd captivated him? He'd spent an hour in his office, pretending to work, but actually coming up with plans to be alone with her again. There was a concert in a few days that his family was scheduled to attend; he could invite her to that. Suppers at the palace—well, that wasn't exactly private, but it was an excuse to see her, and he wanted to spend time with her whether or not that meant kissing. Had his love life always been this complicated? Had he ever *had* a love life? This was far more difficult than deciding on two new Barons or Baronesses.

He finally saw her, talking to a member of her *tiermatha*, and commanded his heart and his feet to slow down. The Kirkellan woman saw him first, and he gave her a polite nod before smiling at Imogen. He was certain it was a foolish smile, but he couldn't stop himself. She wore white and pale green tonight, with her hair arranged elaborately atop her head, and the smile she gave him warmed him all over. "Good evening," he said to both women.

"Good evening, your Majesty," the unfamiliar woman said in passable Tremontanese. This might be the one Imogen had said was courting with a Tremontanan soldier.

"Good evening," Imogen said, looking away. Jeffrey could understand that. If anyone could see his eyes right now, they wouldn't have a secret, they'd have a scandal.

"I hoped to dance with you, madam ambassador," he said, offering her his hand. She hesitated—why hesitate?—then took it, still without meeting his eyes, and allowed him to lead her to the center of the ballroom. He'd chosen this dance deliberately, not only because it was one of the few they'd practiced together, but because it allowed him to hold her close without anyone thinking anything of it.

All the tension that had built up in him that day drained away when he put his arms around her and felt her arms encircle his waist. *I love her*, he thought, and it was such a stunning realization that he almost missed the first steps of the dance. She was what he wanted, she was the only person he could truly be himself with, and he wished more than ever he had some way to declare it openly.

"Are you enjoying yourself?" he said. It was banal, but he wasn't just going to burst out in a declaration of love, not in the middle of the dance floor.

"It is a nice dance," Imogen said.

"That doesn't sound very enthusiastic."

"I talked to Diana. It was not a nice talk."

"I'm surprised the two of you have anything to talk about."

"She thinks I steal you from her. We had a fight. I did not break her hand which I think is good for me that I show...restraint."

He laughed a little too loudly at that, drawing the attention of other couples dancing nearby. "Restraint indeed. I'm sorry she feels so hurt, but I'm not going to follow her wishes just to make her happy."

"That is what I tell—told her. She did not like that."

"I'm surprised you *didn't* get into a fist fight, talking like that."

"She is crazy but not stupid enough to fight a Kirkellan warrior with no weapon. She is thin enough I can break her with my one hand." He laughed again, quietly this time. "Do not laugh, I am serious."

"I'm sorry. I'm not laughing at you, just at the image of Diana snapping like a dry twig."

"It is funny, I think."

Jeffrey let out a slow, deep breath. "I've been completely useless all day," he said. "I haven't been able to stop thinking of you."

"I have thought of you as well." Her eyes were roving the ballroom, looking everywhere but at him. He could see his mother, sitting in her chair, watching them. How much could she tell, at that distance?

"I'm glad," he said. "I'd hate to be the only one who found last night memorable." It felt as if they were dancing in an invisible sphere, their words audible only to themselves. "Will you attend the violin concert next week with my family? I'm sure I can find a coach that only seats four to take Mother and Elspeth and Owen home, and then I'd have to escort you myself."

"I cannot," she said.

He hadn't expected that. He probably should have remembered she was an ambassador and couldn't just come running when he called. "Really? That's too bad. Well, I can think of some other pretext so we can be alone together. There's always another play, of course... the trouble is I'm watched almost everywhere I go, so privacy is hard."

Imogen took a deep breath. "It is to say I cannot go with you to be private. We cannot be a relationship."

He knew he hadn't fallen because he could feel the pressure of his feet on the floorboards, the slight jolt that went from his toes to his knees every time he took a step. He welcomed those little pains, because the rest of him was numb, as if he'd stepped into a frozen sea and been swept off his feet. He opened his mouth, but nothing came out. Not that his numb brain could think of anything to say to that.

Dimly, he heard her continue, "I am ambassador and you are King. I cannot—it is that I am the face of the Kirkellan to all the nations and not just to Tremontane. If I am with you I cannot treat with Bixhenta and that is why I am here, to treat with the nations and to be...I cannot remember the word, but it is when you do not put one above the other."

"Impartial," Jeffrey said. He could barely hear his voice, coming from somewhere beyond that frozen sea.

"That is the word. Impartial."

Now he was glad she wasn't looking at him. He hoped no one was looking at him. He must look like he'd been stabbed through the heart. It certainly felt as if she'd done so. Well, she was a warrior; at least she'd struck cleanly, no dancing (*hah!*) around the problem and killing him by inches. "I understand," he said, and was surprised that his speech was intelligible. "I apologize. I should have realized I was putting you in an untenable position."

"I do not understand 'untenable.'"

"It means I expected more from you than honor would allow." He could tell she'd finally turned to face him, but he couldn't bring himself to meet her eyes. Once again he saw Mother looking in their direction. It felt like too much effort to deflect her. "It's all right, I understand," he said.

"You do not sound all right."

You tore my heart in half. Should I sound all right? "I just regret not recognizing the problem sooner," he said. "I should never have pursued you."

"But...Jeffrey..."

The icy waters were receding, leaving him once again in control of his face, and he looked at her and managed to hold onto a polite smile. There were tears in her eyes, and he wished more than ever that he could comfort her, kiss her until her tears vanished. "We made no promises," he said, "and you have nothing to reproach yourself for. I hope you will still be my friend, Imogen."

She nodded, silently, and at that moment the music came to an end, and he stepped away from her and made his bow. Imogen wound her hands into the fabric of her gown and didn't return it. Then she walked away, and he watched her take a few steps, then moved off in the opposite direction.

He stayed for several more hours. He spoke with a dozen people, all of whom had "suggestions" for who should rule the new Baronies, all of whom he deflected skillfully. He danced again, three times, avoided Diana, drank just enough to feel dizzy without losing his ability to reason. Mother left two hours before he did; she didn't speak to him, but he could tell she knew something was wrong.

He didn't know when Imogen and the *tiermatha* left, didn't look for her at all, but at some point he could feel her absence and it eased the numbness around his heart, just a little, because it meant he didn't have to make an effort to avoid her *and* keep up the pretense that nothing was wrong. Finally, when he judged he'd been enough of a presence, he left and, trailed by his guards, went back to the east wing.

"You're dismissed," he told Stephen, who'd been sitting up waiting for him and looked surprised at the unusual command. Jeffrey undressed himself, struggled a little getting out of the tightly-fitted frock coat, and carefully put away all his clothes. No sense making more work for Stephen after telling him to leave. He stood in front of his mirror in his undershorts and looked into his own eyes. How stupid people were, to have looked directly at him tonight and not seen the pain that filled him.

He looked over the rest of himself, then closed his eyes and shuddered. He looked so much like his father. There'd been that one day, shortly after the funeral, when he'd been in the drawing room and he'd heard his mother come in and gasp, and he'd looked up just in time to see the agony cross her face as she realized he wasn't Anthony. It had felt just the same as it did right now, that icy numb sharpness like a blade through the chest. Amazing that it never got any easier, losing what you loved most in the world.

He turned out the light Devices and lay on his bed, not turning down the covers. She was right. She couldn't stay impartial if they were courting. That didn't make it hurt any less. She was the woman he wanted, the woman he loved more than anyone else, and she was the one woman he wasn't allowed to have.

Eleven months, and you can court her, he thought, but eleven months was a long time, and it wasn't as if she didn't have hundreds of men lining up to escort her places. Some of them were even decent fellows, handsome and smart and interesting, and heaven alone knew if she'd even still care about him in eleven months. Damn. He was a king, he was supposed to have his pick of women—no, that was a stupid way to think. King was just a costume he put on; Jeffrey North was a man, and a man who was so good at hiding who he was that he had no chance of meeting a woman who might fall in love with the real him.

He crawled under the covers and put the pillow over his head. Thank heaven he didn't have to see her often. He could learn to treat her with the same politeness he showed everyone outside his own family, that cool friendliness that charmed people without promising anything. What he wanted was irrelevant; she needed him to keep his distance, and he would do anything for her, even if it broke his heart. Which it would.

JEFFREY: THE PLOT

*J*effrey read the page a fourth time, hoping a different solution would suggest itself. Nothing came to mind. Well, it was probably too much to hope that the Baroness of Marandis had suddenly become stupid. Lady Rosalind Wemberly had a keen mind and a good appreciation of the King's responsibilities, which was why she only sent the most tangled problems his way. Which further meant, unfortunately, that any problem she was unable to solve was fiendishly complex and meant a long-term headache for Jeffrey.

He sighed and laid the paper down. The Ruskalder refugees trickling into Tremontane through the Rockwild Range most often ended up in Barony Marandis, where the easier passes were. Giving citizenship to ordinary people was easy enough, but when the refugees were a ruling chief of Ruskald and his family, it became a matter of international diplomacy. On the other hand, giving Hrovald a poke in the eye appealed to Jeffrey. Yes. Make Knoten of Hvartfast a Tremontanan citizen, and do it publicly so Hrovald's spies couldn't help but know it.

Someone knocked on the office door, and the door eased open

before Jeffrey could issue an invitation. "Your Majesty," Arthur said, "Mister Burgess would like a word with you."

Jeffrey put the paper away. "Max," he said as Burgess entered, "what can I do for you?"

"It's what I hope I can do for you, your Majesty," Burgess said. Perspiration shone on his forehead, and he mopped his brow with his sleeve as he came to stand in front of the desk. Jeffrey eyed him curiously. He'd never known Burgess to be so visibly distraught.

"Well, have a seat," he said.

Burgess shook his head. "It's—I'm not sure where to start," he said. "Just read this." He removed a folded sheet of paper and a length of telecoder tape from inside his dull brown coat and extended the paper to Jeffrey. Mystified, Jeffrey unfolded it.

"It's about troop movements in the new territory," he said. "I don't see what's odd about that."

"This wasn't a telecode from the Army," Burgess said. "It was private information, sent by Mairen of the Kirkellan to the Kirkellish ambassador here in Aurilien."

"To Imogen? Why would she care?"

"Why indeed." Burgess leaned against the desk, focusing his intense stare on Jeffrey. "Madam ambassador met with Bixhenta twice in the past two weeks. She sent a telecode request—" He waved the tape in Jeffrey's face— "and received this reply before returning to the Veriboldan embassy the second time. Her telecode was written in Kirkellish, but that clumsy attempt to fool us didn't work."

"I don't," Jeffrey began, then stopped and read the paper again. The message said only that the Kirkellish *tiermathas* were patrolling the newly conquered territory along with companies of Tremontanan soldiers, and that...*oh*. "This says the Veriboldan border is not patrolled, only the new Ruskalder border." A cold, sick feeling washed over him. "What are you implying, Max?" he asked, though he already knew.

"I'm saying Imogen of the Kirkellan is a spy for Veribold," Max said.

His words snapped Jeffrey out of the cold funk. Imogen as a spy for anyone—it was ridiculous. He would as soon believe his mother had decided to spy for Ruskald. "Max," he began, but Burgess overrode him.

"I've been watching the ambassador for some time now, ever since she became friendly with Bixhenta," he said. "She has cultivated an acquaintance with Prince Ghentali of Eskandel as well. He has given her gifts, treated her with high regard—I understand he intends to offer her a place in his harem."

All Jeffrey's instincts were ringing warning bells inside his head. Burgess knew full well a prince never offered marriage; that was the decision of the harem. And of course Imogen had built relationships, because that was why she was in Tremontane. Jeffrey's suspicions rose. Not of Imogen, whom he would trust with his life; no, it was Burgess who was behaving strangely.

Carefully keeping his expression neutral, he leaned back in his chair. "What do you think the Kirkellish ambassador has in mind?"

"I don't think the plot is hers," Burgess said. "She's too young and naïve to plot independently. No, I think she's Bixhenta's catspaw. He's sent a number of telecodes from the embassy to Haizea, and I'm sure Veribold is preparing to exploit that hole in our defenses. We're spread thin occupying territory, we're still guarding against Hrovald's potential return...we're ripe for invasion."

"That could devastate us," Jeffrey agreed. "Have we seen movement along the Veriboldan border?"

"There hasn't been anyone in the area who could observe." Burgess wiped his forehead again. "We need to move troops south to defend that border. Bixhenta has refused to respond to my inquiries, and I don't dare press for fear he'll learn we know the truth."

The warning bells were getting louder. "And Imogen?"

Burgess's intent stare focused on him again. "She should be taken into custody, to prevent her warning Bixhenta that we're onto him."

Burgess had an answer for everything, didn't he? And he'd been quick to suggest moving troops. But why? Jeffrey's instincts weren't enough to tell him more than that he would have to act very carefully.

Whatever Burgess had in mind, it was something that had him nervous, and Jeffrey couldn't afford for him to bolt.

He pushed back his chair and stood. "The ambassador is meant to have dinner with my family today. It will save us the trouble of trying to extricate her from her embassy if we take her into custody now." Just saying the words made him feel sick again. Imogen would believe he thought she was a traitor. He couldn't warn her even if there was time, because she was straightforward enough it was unlikely she could react properly. The sick feeling turned into anger. Burgess was going to pay for forcing Jeffrey to arrest the woman he loved.

He signaled to a handful of North guards to follow him as he and Burgess passed through the North wing. They scrambled to catch up, but Jeffrey didn't slow his stride. The more he thought about the situation, the angrier he became. There was a plot, yes, but if Imogen was innocent, that meant Burgess was the guilty one. But guilty of what? He didn't have enough *facts*, damn it, and when it came to foreign policy, Burgess was the one he went to for information. He had no choice but to go along as if he believed Burgess and hope he solved the mystery before whatever Burgess had set in motion came to fruition.

Imogen and Elspeth were both in the east wing drawing room when he arrived, soldiers in tow, Burgess panting heavily from the exertion of keeping up with Jeffrey in a rage. "Jeffrey! And Mister Burgess," Elspeth said. "Jeffrey, I'm starving—does this mean you're ready for dinner?"

"Not now, Elspeth," Jeffrey said. All his attention was on Imogen, who was dressed in a lovely muslin gown and held an embroidery hoop loosely in one hand. She wouldn't meet his eyes, but then it had been some time since the two of them had been able to act naturally around each other. He loved her, and he was about to betray her. His lips pinched into a thin, angry line. Burgess would have to do it. Jeffrey couldn't guarantee he could keep the charade going if he spoke.

"Madam ambassador," Burgess said, "would you stand, please?"

Imogen stuck her needle in her fabric and laid the hoop down. "What is this about?"

Burgess took a step forward and raised his chin high. "Madam ambassador, you are accused of espionage against Tremontane for having given confidential military information to the Proxy of Veribold."

Imogen's rosy complexion paled. "I do not understand," she said.

Burgess removed the telecode tape from inside his coat. "Madam ambassador, did you receive communications detailing Tremontanan troop movements from the Kirkellan camp?"

Now she looked at Jeffrey, the swiftest glance. He kept the hard, cold expression on his face out of sheer willpower. "I did," she said, "but I did not—"

"Following your first meeting with Bixhenta, you used the palace telecoder to send this message to the Kirkellan camp. You met with him a second time after receiving an answer."

"How do you have that? I burned it."

"The palace telecoders keep a duplicate of all messages sent and received," Jeffrey said, speaking in a low, angry voice. "The message you carefully concealed from the operator wasn't hard for our translators to decipher."

Burgess said, "The message is a request for information about troop movements in the occupied territory. The reply clearly states the Tremontanan border with Veribold is undefended and there is no one in the area who could raise an alarm when Veribold invades."

Imogen stared at Jeffrey, fear growing in her eyes. "Bixhenta told me to investigate the truth and not to just believe his words," she protested. "I did not tell him what I learned. He want me to, but I do not."

The look she gave him made his heart ache. She was afraid, but it wasn't enough to satisfy Burgess that Jeffrey believed him. He would have to twist the knife deeper. "Investigate the truth of what?" he asked. "That Tremontane lies open and ready for invasion? I fail to see what need you had of that information."

"Bixhenta refuses to speak to us," said Burgess. "I take that for confirmation. If he were innocent, he wouldn't need to hide in his embassy; he would want us to know the truth."

Imogen looked from Jeffrey to Burgess. "It is a mistake," she insisted. "I did not tell him."

"And there's this," Burgess said. He took Imogen's crystal pendant in his hand and yanked on it to break the chain. It cut into her neck and she cried out in pain, making Jeffrey clench his teeth harder to keep from protesting. "We asked Ghentali about his 'gift'. He confirmed it is a ten-carat diamond and he gave it to you 'out of friendship.'" His sarcastic emphases made Jeffrey's heart beat more painfully. "I wonder what secrets you sold to him to deserve what I can only call a princely gift."

She shook her head. "It is his birthday," she said. "He say he gives gifts to all."

"I didn't receive a gift. Neither did your escort, Mister Weatherby, who confirmed Ghentali's account. It seems very few of the Eskandelic ambassador's guests received a gift from him, and none were given anything nearly so valuable as this." Burgess tucked the telecode tape and the diamond into his coat. "Madam ambassador, I am placing you under arrest."

"*No!*" Elspeth exclaimed, grabbing Burgess's arm. "Imogen would never do anything like that. You're wrong!"

"Don't interfere, Elspeth," Jeffrey said in a flat, hard voice. "This has nothing to do with you."

"But—"

"I said *enough!*" he shouted, turning his glare on her. She flinched and dropped Burgess's arm. That was another thing Jeffrey intended to make Burgess suffer for, forcing Elspeth to cringe before her brother.

"Jeffrey—" Imogen pleaded.

"I don't want to hear anything from you," he said, maintaining that cold, horrible voice. "You may have helped Veribold invade my country, which makes you my enemy."

"But I did not do this—"

"Shut up. I'm done talking to you." He turned to Burgess. "Have her taken to the prison. I'll interrogate her later. We might be able to contain the damage if we find out exactly what she told Bixhenta."

"Madam ambassador, I would prefer not to bind you. Will you agree to go quietly?" Burgess said.

Imogen looked at the four guards. Jeffrey could see her assessing her chances against them and prayed she would be sensible, because if she got into a fight with the guards, he would defend her, and everything would fall apart. "I will go quietly because I am innocent and I will show you," she said.

As the guards led her away, Elspeth burst out crying. Jeffrey ignored her. "Max, I want a full report on my desk in one hour. Every detail, everything we even suspect Veribold knows. Elspeth, stop crying."

"You *bastard,*" Elspeth said between tears. "How could you do that to Imogen? I know you care about her!"

"I care about this country," Jeffrey said. "Imogen is a traitor, and traitors mean nothing to me." The words tasted like bile, and he sent up another prayer, this time that Imogen would forgive him. "Don't wait dinner on me. I have work to do."

He spent the next several hours reading Burgess's reports, teasing the meaning from between the lines. A picture began to form. Everything Burgess told him focused on one thing: bringing the troops south to defend against a Veriboldan invasion. The more he read, the more convinced he was that Burgess was acting on someone else's behalf. That chilled him more than the thought of treason did. Treason by Burgess was one thing; treason by some unknown force was terrifying.

He sent Burgess on an errand that would keep him out of the office for an hour or two and spent the time going over possibilities. Frame Imogen. Draw the troops south. The two were incompatible as far as a coherent plan went. Burgess was Diana's good friend, and if Jeffrey postulated that Burgess wasn't the loyal man Jeffrey had believed him to be all these years, he could see Burgess going along with a plan Diana concocted to discredit or harm Imogen. But pulling the troops south wasn't necessary to frame Imogen, and

Jeffrey couldn't imagine who aside from Hrovald would benefit from that. And Jeffrey had seen no evidence that Burgess was working with Hrovald.

He picked at the supper brought to his desk, a headache conspiring with his emotional turmoil to kill his appetite. He'd learned as much as he could squeeze out of Burgess without alerting the man that his plot was uncovered. Time to let him stew, wondering why Jeffrey hadn't given the order to move the troops. It was too late to visit the prison, though he wanted more than anything to see Imogen and beg her forgiveness. First thing in the morning.

He slept poorly, waking from incoherent dreams to memories of how Imogen had looked at him with that expression of betrayed trust, and dragged himself out of bed half an hour after dawn when it was clear he would get no more rest. He called for breakfast to be brought to his bedchamber and ate rapidly, not tasting the excellent meal. He hadn't seen his mother since Imogen's arrest and had no desire to find out what she thought of his behavior by eating in the dining room.

After a quick visit to his office to see whether Burgess had cracked yet, he left for the cells. He hadn't been there before, though he knew where they were because the path to the Judiciary led past them. He walked down the long, long corridor, fruitlessly going over things he might say to Imogen. She might know some detail that would tie the whole plot together. Or she really was as innocent as he believed, and knew nothing. She would be furious with him, probably wouldn't want to hear anything from him, and maybe this was pointless. Maybe he should leave her alone until he could release her and reveal everything.

He shook his head to clear it. No. He owed it to her to explain, even if all she did was scream at him for abusing her trust. He would explain, and then he would return to his office and give his notes one last pass. And then he would drag Burgess in for questioning and make him suffer.

The guards at both ends of the prison cell corridor saluted him and let him through without argument. The corridor smelled of stale smoke, though the lights on the walls were modern Devices, and of someone's supper. The cold light of the Devices turned his skin chalky and greenish, and the dark skin of the guard who waited beside the cells looked dull purple.

"Your Majesty," she said, "how can I help you?"

She was unexpectedly well-spoken for a guard, which startled Jeffrey. "I, ah, I'm here to speak to the Kirkellish ambassador," he said, regaining his poise with some effort.

The guard nodded. She walked down the row of oak doors, their windows small and barred with iron, as if anyone could possibly fit through them. Tiny sliding doors at the base of each slab of oak mystified him; again, they were too small for anyone to fit through, so what was the point?

Imogen's cell was the fourth on the left. The guard unlocked the door and opened it for him. "Leave her to me," Jeffrey said, glaring at the guard though she hadn't said anything. She swallowed, nodded, and backed away. Jeffrey entered and shut the door behind him, and heard the lock turn.

Imogen sat on a low iron cot that almost had to be too short for her. She looked disheveled, as if she'd slept in her clothes—of course she'd slept in her clothes, it wasn't as if prisoners were allowed nightwear. She sat hunched slightly, drawing in on herself for protection. Her expression was so miserable he had to turn away. She didn't make a sound, but he held a finger to his lips to silence her anyway as he listened for the retreating footsteps of the guard. He was certain the guard was circumspect, but he couldn't risk anyone overhearing this.

After nearly a minute, he judged they had as much privacy as was possible in the cells. He turned to face Imogen, whose expression had become confused and angry. It broke his heart. "Imogen, I am so sorry," he said quietly. "I couldn't think of anything else to do."

"I am innocent," Imogen insisted.

"I know." He took a step in her direction, then stopped, his fists clenched at his sides. Going to his knees before her and begging her forgiveness was a stupid idea his heart insisted was essential. "Somebody wants me to believe Veribold is on the verge of invading us, so I'll draw the troops south. They want it badly enough they drew you into the plot, made it look like you were working with Bixhenta. Max was so insistent..." He blew out a deep breath. "I had to pretend I believed him, Imogen, because I need to find out why he's so desperate for me to believe the lie."

Imogen shook her head. "It is Burgess who planned this because Diana hates me."

"I thought of that, but the plot Max 'uncovered' goes much farther than you. He might be working with Diana, but honestly, I don't see what she'd gain from this." He began to pace, came up almost immediately against the cell wall, and stopped. "I think you looked like a good candidate to pin it on because we're...friends, and I'd be off balance thinking you'd betrayed me." He laughed, one short mirthless sound. "Max's bad luck that he picked the one person outside my own family I'd never believe it of."

Imogen's shoulders relaxed. "You believe me."

The hope in her eyes should have reassured him, but it only made him feel worse. "Imogen, I would sooner doubt myself. I'm sorry, but I wouldn't have warned you even if I'd had time. I couldn't count on you reacting properly. I didn't mean anything I said to you in the drawing room. It was all part of the plan." He took another step toward her, then returned to pacing in a tight circle. "I swear I'll make Max pay for this."

"You are certain he does this?"

"I'm certain. He's smart, but he's sloppy. Why didn't you give the diamond back to Ghentali? That's more damning than Max's claim you colluded with Bixhenta."

"I do not know it was a diamond!" Imogen shouted, jumping to her feet. Jeffrey gestured to her for silence, but she ignored him. "It was present from nice man and I think it is crystal and it would hurt his feelings to give it back! You—"

He clapped his hand over her mouth. "I'm supposed to be interrogating you," he hissed. "I don't want anyone coming down here—ow!"

He yanked his hand away and examined the place where Imogen had bitten him.

"You do not touch me," she snarled, and backed away to sit on the cot. "You say cruel things and you let them put me in this tiny room with walls that curve in and then you tell me it is all your plan. I hate your plan. I hate—" She buried her face in her hands and shook with the effort of suppressing her sobs.

Watching her struggle not to weep was too much for his aching heart to bear. In two quick strides he was beside the cot and sinking onto it beside her. It groaned under their combined weight, but held firm. Without a second thought, Jeffrey put his arms around Imogen, desperate to ease her pain even as his whole self cried out that it was a mistake, that she didn't want him and he had no right to behave as if she did.

"I'm sorry," he whispered. "It took all the discipline I had to watch those guards take you away and do nothing. I wanted to kill Max for forcing me to do that to you. He's going to suffer for this, I swear it."

She leaned into him, and for a moment they were just two people giving each other comfort. It felt so wonderful to hold her again. "I am sorry I bit you," she said.

Jeffrey smiled. She hadn't sounded entirely sincere, and the reaction was so perfectly like her it lightened his heart. "It was my own fault for underestimating you," he said, and lightly kissed the side of her face before he knew what he was doing.

Imogen drew in a sharp, startled breath. Jeffrey's heart plummeted again. What a fool he was. "I'm sorry," he began, and Imogen turned, put her arms around his neck, and kissed his lips.

Desire rushed through him, sweeping away conscious thought as he returned her kiss. Her lips on his were fierce and passionate, filled with a desperate longing that matched his. He tugged at her hair, pulling it loose from what was left of its arrangement until it fell across her back and he could tangle his fingers in its softness. He'd relived the memory of their first and only kisses so many times since that night, but this was so much better than memory—touching her and feeling her arms around him and kissing her until he almost forgot to breathe.

She pulled him closer, close enough that her body was pressed against his, and the sensation was so intense he groaned and slid his hands from her hair to her waist so he could pull her even closer. His awareness of where they were receded until all he knew was that he wanted to lie with her, there on the creaky cot—and with that thought, the cot groaned louder than he had, and the two of them froze, breathing heavily, until it subsided.

Imogen's eyes, enormous in the strange light shed by the fixture in the ceiling, focused on him. She said nothing. Jeffrey brushed a stray lock of hair from her face and said, "So much for impartiality."

Imogen let out a deep breath. "I was not impartial even when we do not court," she said. "I do not care about impartial anymore. I do not care about the other men. I care about you."

He felt as if he could run through the halls of the palace, singing and leaping like a moon-witted fool. A moon-witted fool in love. He smiled and ran his forefinger along the line of her cheekbone. "You gave a good impression of being interested in them."

Imogen's eyebrows went up. "I think—thought you do not care who I court with. You seem...indifferent, I think is the word."

"Hardly. I suffered the most agonizing jealousy whenever you accepted an invitation from one of those men who, I should point out, are not worthy of you."

"I liked some of them. Darin Weatherby was nice."

Jeffrey thought back to the reports Burgess had produced for him. "Darin Weatherby," he said, "told Max you knew Ghentali had given you a diamond and you refused to give it back even though you also knew it was an inappropriate gift."

Imogen's color rose, and her eyebrows furrowed almost to a point above her nose. "I think I must find him now and beat him until he bleeds."

Jeffrey laughed. "I probably shouldn't let you enact vigilante justice on people, but the idea has some appeal." He kissed her again, relishing how her lips curved to shape themselves to his. Staying here forever would be bliss. Unfortunately, he was still the King, and he still had a traitor to find. "I wish I could stay longer, but I think Max is starting to suspect I don't believe him, and I don't want him running."

"You cannot leave me here again," Imogen protested. "I cannot bear it."

"Imogen, it's just for a little—"

"No, you cannot, the room is getting smaller and I do not want to be crushed!" She tried to stand, but Jeffrey pulled her down and held her until her breathing returned to normal, ignoring the cot's protests.

"I'm sorry," he whispered, and kissed her forehead lightly. "I need you to endure this for just a few hours more. As soon as I find out what Max is planning, I'll send for you. I promise."

"You must do it soon," she whispered back, "because I think I cannot tell what is real anymore."

He turned her in his arms to face him, and kissed her again, his lips lingering on hers. "*That* is real," he said, "and I will think of you every moment until this is over, and then I will go on thinking of you because you make me happy."

She smiled at that, a wavery, uncertain smile that made him inwardly curse Burgess yet again. "I will remember that, and not how you looked when you say those things to me. It is better to remember, kissing is." She touched his cheek gently. "And you must shave before you kiss me again," she said, her smile becoming more genuine.

"I make no promises," Jeffrey said. "I don't know if I could help myself if you go on looking at me that way."

"What way is that?"

Words failed him. Her bright eyes, the smile on her lips, the way her hair fell over her forehead and cascaded down her back and over her shoulders—it was all too much. "As if those other men really do mean nothing to you," he managed, and stood, clasping her hand in both of his. "I'll send for you soon, all right? Just—be patient."

He pounded on the door and shouted, "I'm done here," all the while staring at her, wanting to memorize how she looked so he could carry the image with him until the moment she was by his side once more. When the guard unlocked the door, he walked away without looking back.

In his office, he straightened the stacks of papers and then dragged one of the chairs flanking the fireplace to a position directly in front of his desk. Then he summoned Arthur, who looked disgustingly alert and cheerful. Now that his time with Imogen was over, weariness had begun to descend upon Jeffrey, but he had no time to indulge in it.

"Ask Maxwell Burgess to join me," he said. "We need to have a talk."

JEFFREY: CHECKMATE

"Hold," Diana said. The men and women in Tremontanan Army uniforms lowered their weapons and made way for her. Jeffrey didn't relax. She walked past Fred Williams' body, collapsed on the map table, without even glancing at him, as if they hadn't been friends. Maybe that was true.

Diana stopped five feet from Jeffrey's remaining guards. "You don't have a chance, you know," she said. "I've already won." She was breathing heavily and her bloodstained coat, not military issue, was torn along one side.

"We've both lost," Jeffrey said. He stepped past the guards and paused within striking distance of her as she brought her sword to the ready. His guards twitched, but he ignored them, giving them the signal to stand down. If he couldn't convince her of Hrovald's threat, it wouldn't matter what she did to him. "Hrovald is marching on this city, thanks to..." He resisted the urge to scream at her for her stupidity and greed. "We have to join forces to hold him off until the main Army arrives."

Diana smiled. It was a coy, knowing expression completely inappropriate to the moment. "Desperate words from a desperate man about to die. Did you really think I'd believe you?"

He wanted to strangle her. How had he thought *they* had ever been friends? "I'm not lying, Diana. Lay down your weapons, and this can all be over."

"And I suppose you believe your Kirkellan allies will make the difference? Your foreign lover?" Diana's smile turned into a snarl. "She's dead, Jeffrey. I killed her, and I'm going to kill you, too."

Shock made him temporarily numb. "I didn't think you'd stoop to lying, however low you went," he managed.

Diana ran her finger down the flat of her bloody sword. "Lying isn't nearly so satisfying as the truth, not when it's a truth like this one," she said, displaying the blood on her finger. "Some warrior. She fell to my sword just like you will."

"Impossible." Imogen. She couldn't be dead. She was far more experienced a fighter than Diana. And yet Jeffrey knew that swooping, lilting sound to Diana's voice, the one that meant victory for her and a crushing defeat for her enemy. He pushed his anguish aside and focused on what mattered. There was no way he could convince Diana, but her officers had been his, once, and they were military. They would see sense.

He switched to addressing the man at Diana's left shoulder, who wasn't as impassive as the others. "You've seen Hrovald's army. You know what we're capable of if we—"

"Don't be a fool, Jeffrey," Diana said, "and don't try to sway my men. Even if you're right about Hrovald, you know what I've done is treason if I let you live. It's too late for any other solution."

He felt so weary. "Diana, we have a common enemy here. Don't *you* be a fool. Hrovald will destroy the city if we don't stop him, your forces and mine together."

"But with you still in command and your ass firmly placed upon the throne." Diana let out a short bark of a laugh. "You think I don't know what it means if I give in to you now?"

"You don't have to die. You can go into exile. I'll even pardon your officers. Just let this end." Once more he focused on the officers standing behind her. Two of them shifted uncomfortably. Impossible to tell what they were thinking, but he refused to give up hope. Imogen had taught him that.

Diana laughed, a horrible, cheerful sound. "You forget who has the upper hand here."

Jeffrey shrugged. "I'll admit you have me outnumbered. I'm counting on your officers—*my* officers—being unwilling to murder their King."

"My officers are loyal to me, not to you, Jeffrey. It's what happens when you fight together, day after day, for years on end." Diana's sword lowered, and she took a step forward, making Jeffrey's guards come alert. He signaled them again to stand down. If he was going to die here, he wouldn't let anyone else go with him.

Beyond Diana and her officers, the door swung open slightly. A figure appeared in the gap. Jeffrey's gaze flicked that way briefly before returning to focus on Diana. Then shock rooted him to the ground once more. "*Imogen*," he said.

Diana laughed. "The fat bitch is dead, Jeffrey. That's a pathetic ruse."

"The fat bitch is right here and thinks your aim is bad," Imogen said. For all her voice was faint, she sounded as confident as if she weren't clinging to the door frame to stay upright.

Diana's head turned. Faster than thought, Jeffrey thrust with his sword. The blade plunged into Diana's stomach, angling upward until it met the resistance of her ribcage. Diana's head came back around. The look of amazement on her face, pure stunned confusion, set his heart thudding. He had never taken a life before. Surely it ought to be more momentous than this. And yet he had never felt so certain of any action in his life.

Diana looked down at his hand on the hilt of the sword, spotted with her blood. Her own sword fell from her hand, its tip catching in the carpet and making it sway. Then she sagged at the knees. Jeffrey withdrew his sword and let her collapse atop her fallen weapon.

He aimed the bloody blade at the five Army officers, who looked as stunned as Diana had. "This ends now," he said in a voice that promised a short, painful future to everyone who failed to obey it.

"Drop your weapons and you won't hang for treason. One chance. *Now*."

Swords thumped to the floor, bouncing hollowly as they struck the soft carpet. "Good," said Jeffrey. "Go out there and tell your soldiers to stand down. They won't suffer for their leader's idiocy either, but if the killing doesn't stop *now*, they're going to suffer for their own. Go!" he shouted. They scrambled to flee.

One of them bumped into Imogen, who rocked unsteadily, then collapsed. Jeffrey dropped his sword and rushed to her side. She was covered in blood and her eyes were closed. "Imogen, Imogen, sweetheart, look at me," he said, putting his arms around her to lift her up. She opened her eyes and blinked at him. "She said you were dead. It's all right, it's not so bad, just—how stupid, I was going to say 'stay right there'—"

He set her down gently and raced across to the window, snatching up his sword as he went. With a slash, he tore away a swath of heavy silk and hurried back to her side, pressing the cloth into the deep wound. "Can you hold that?"

Imogen nodded heavily, her head flopping as if she could barely hold it up, and put her hand over the cloth. Jeffrey looked up at his guards. "You, yes, both of you, get her to the infirmary immediately. *Now!*"

The two men crouched to help Imogen to her feet—oh, good, she could walk, or at least stumble along. Jeffrey stood in the doorway and watched until she was out of sight. He felt too numb to fear for her. She was strong; she would survive this. And there was nothing more he could do to help her.

He turned and bent to pick up his sword, feeling like an old man with joints stiff and aching. His gaze fell on Diana's body, lying awkwardly where she had fallen. What an ending to their friendship, such as it had been.

Diana's arm twitched, sending a jolt of surprise through him. He crossed the room and crouched at her side. Diana's eyes were closed, but her mouth moved as if she were trying to speak. Impulsively, Jeffrey reached out to straighten her limbs, but let his hand fall before touching her. She was responsible for so many deaths, and she might be responsible for many more if they couldn't fight off Hrovald. She deserved no pity, even in such a small way as that.

"Jeffrey," Diana said. Her voice was barely more than a whisper.

"Diana," Jeffrey replied. He couldn't think of anything else to say.

Diana's mouth worked again as if she were chewing something hard and gristly. "I...was wrong," she said. Blood stained her lips. "You...king."

Jeffrey stood. He remembered striking Diana down, how he'd felt nothing but certainty even as he knew Diana had to die. How he'd stared down those officers, heard confidence ring through his words as he commanded them. He hadn't doubted himself and he hadn't thought about what his father would have done. "I am the King," he said. "And you should never have challenged me."

Diana let out a sigh. More blood trickled from her mouth. She didn't move again.

Jeffrey wiped his sword on the back of her coat and sheathed it. He cast another long look at Fred's body and cursed under his breath. Too many good men and women were dead, and there was no time to mourn them. Now Jeffrey had a kingdom to save.

JEFFREY: SAYING GOODBYE

The palace ballroom was as brightly lit as ever, but instead of the scent of perfumes and flowers, the air was filled with the smell of blood and antiseptic. Jeffrey stood at the top of the stairs and surveyed the many, many bodies lying on cots or pallets throughout the vast room. He tried to remember that this was good, that these people were going to survive, but with the sounds of moaning and quiet cries of pain echoing off the walls, it was hard not to see this for the disaster it was.

He descended the stairs and made his way around the suffering wounded to where the palace healer, Dr. Worthing, knelt beside someone who lay so still Jeffrey at first thought her dead. But the doctor clasped her hand, bowed his head, and the woman cried out through clenched teeth before controlling herself. Jeffrey knew almost nothing about magical healing except that it could hurt terribly, but he had faith in Dr. Worthing's abilities.

After about half a minute, the doctor's head came up, and he gently laid the woman's hand across her chest. "You should rest for another hour," he said, "while your body regains its strength."

"Thank you," the woman said, her voice still weak.

Dr. Worthing stood and gestured to Jeffrey to walk with him.

"That's the last of the critical cases," he said. "The other physicians are treating the wounded, and Dr. Gillan is resting."

"Are you...exhausted, then? Unable to heal more?" Jeffrey asked.

Dr. Worthing shook his head. "I'm not at the limits of my magic, but there are wounded still coming in, and I should conserve my strength, just in case."

Jeffrey reflexively looked at the ballroom entrance. It was empty. "Just in case," he agreed.

"I take it there's been no word of the ambassador," Dr. Worthing said.

The ache that had been Jeffrey's constant companion for the last twenty-four hours redoubled. "No," he said. "They're going to send out another search party shortly."

The doctor put a reassuring hand on Jeffrey's shoulder. "They'll find her. You should rest."

Jeffrey nodded absently. He wasn't going to rest until he knew what had happened to Imogen.

He wandered through the ballroom, greeting soldiers, doing his best to comfort them. Why the presence of their King should matter, he didn't know, but the wounded did seem heartened by a few words from him. He barely knew what he said. All his heart was focused on one horrible fact: Imogen was missing. They had found her saber stuck through Hrovald's heart, found Victory, who was badly wounded, standing nearby in the patient way of a good warhorse, but Imogen was nowhere to be seen.

She was almost certainly dead.

There was no way she could have survived without returning. Jeffrey knew this. But his stubborn heart refused to believe it. Until he saw her body, he would go on being certain she was alive somewhere, wounded but alive.

"Your Majesty."

Jeffrey looked up to see the *matrian* of the Kirkellan kneeling opposite the wounded soldier—no, it was a Kirkellan warrior he'd been speaking to. He hadn't realized. "*Matrian*," he said. "How are your people?"

"Our losses were not as heavy as yours, I think," Mairen said. She patted the warrior's hand and said a few words in Kirkellish before standing and indicating Jeffrey should walk with her. "Still, every loss is a tragedy."

"I can't express my gratitude for your assistance." Jeffrey stopped in a clear space away from the wounded. "I've spoken with Ingivar. He will make a much better neighbor than Hrovald."

"For now," Mairen said. "I don't know how long he'll maintain his power."

Jeffrey nodded. "I choose to be warily optimistic. There are too many chieftains interested in gaining power for Ingivar to sit easy on his throne."

"Very wise." Mairen looked out over the wounded as Jeffrey had done.

"I've assembled another search party," Jeffrey said.

"Thank you. It seems impossible that she—" Mairen's mouth closed sharply.

"We'll find her," Jeffrey said. "Don't worry."

Mairen looked at him. "You," she began, seemed to change her mind about her words, and went on, "She is your friend, I think."

The ache in his chest throbbed as if she'd stabbed him. "Of course," he said, trying to sound casual. "She fought and nearly died for Tremontane. It's more than anyone asked of her. I owe her a great debt."

"I see," Mairen said. Her tone of voice told him she wasn't fooled. Jeffrey was suddenly aware that this was the mother of the woman he loved, and he wasn't doing a very good job of acting as if Imogen meant nothing to him. But after the events of the last few days, the last thing he wanted was for Mairen to know about his hopeless feelings.

A commotion at the doors drew his attention. It was probably another wounded soldier, which was terrible, but he welcomed the distraction.

Two men appeared in the doorway, carrying a third between them and shouting for Dr. Worthing. The wounded soldier was female...she was Kirkellan...Jeffrey drew in a sharp breath and hurried toward them. It was Imogen. She wasn't moving, sweet heaven, she was dead after all, and Jeffrey thought his heart might crack in two with grief.

Dr. Worthing made it to Imogen's body first and snatched up her hand before the soldiers could lay her down. Jeffrey prayed as he never had before. *Just one more miracle, just one.*

"She's alive," Dr. Worthing said, "but only just. Set her down anywhere, but be quick about it. Your Majesty, please stand back."

Jeffrey realized he had reached Imogen's side and taken her other hand, squeezing it tightly in the hope she could feel it. He released her and stepped back. The soldiers set Imogen down practically at the foot of the stairs, and Dr. Worthing knelt beside her. Jeffrey waited for her to tense, or scream, or react in some other way to the pain of healing, but she lay unconscious, her mouth slack and her eyes closed.

He became aware of Mairen standing next to him, her whole body intent on the scene playing out before them. Something so momentous ought to be as dramatic as the fight that had wounded Imogen; she was bloody from half a dozen wounds, including the one Diana had given her that she'd sworn to Jeffrey she wouldn't tear open again. But no one moved, no one spoke. Jeffrey couldn't even hear breathing, not even his own.

Then Imogen's chest rose and fell once as if she'd sucked in a tremendous breath and expelled it. Dr. Worthing rocked back on his heels. "I can't get her to wake up," he said, "but that's not unusual. She'll sleep for a while as her body restores itself, creates new blood to make up for the quantities she lost. She should be removed to somewhere private."

"There is a suite in the east wing I'll have made up for her," Jeffrey said. "I don't think she should be moved to the embassy."

The look Mairen gave him convinced him that he'd given himself away. He returned her gaze coolly, daring her to make an issue of it. But she only said, "Thank you, your Majesty, that would be appreciated."

He spoke to the housekeeper himself, saw Imogen settled in a room not far from his own—a coincidence—and then extricated himself as quickly as was polite and hurried to his office, where he closed the door, sank to the floor in front of the empty fireplace, and wept tears of relief and sorrow. She was alive, but she was lost to him. It was almost worse than if she'd died.

IMOGEN DIDN'T WAKE UP FOR TWO DAYS. JEFFREY WENT ABOUT HIS business as if it didn't matter to him that his love was unconscious longer than Dr. Worthing had said was normal. He asked for regular updates on her condition, which seemed like a reasonable thing for the King to do.

At night he lay wakeful in his bed and tried to convince himself he'd made the right decision. Imogen had come to Aurilien as ambassador to learn the parts of her that weren't a warrior. And she'd done that. But in the battle for the palace, and the battle against Hrovald, she'd proved beyond question that however good she was as an ambassador, she was far, far better as a warrior. Leading charges, encouraging the troops—soldiers who weren't even Kirkellan!—killing Hrovald...it was clear Imogen belonged with the Kirkellan.

Which meant she didn't belong with him.

No matter how he tried, Jeffrey couldn't get away from that one fact. He wanted her to stay. He wanted her for his wife. But how under heaven could he ask her to give up her whole identity for his sake? It was ludicrous even to think the possibility. And it would be wrong for him to put that burden of choice on her. Which meant he had to let her go.

But...surely it wasn't fair for him to make the decision for both of them? That seemed wrong, too, as if he didn't believe her capable of choice. So maybe what he needed to do was tell her his conclusions and give her the opportunity to decide. Maybe he was wrong in thinking that was too much of a burden. And maybe—he made himself stop thinking along those lines. She wasn't going to choose him. He remembered their conversation the night they'd first kissed, how much she'd longed to hold on to her warrior self. She wasn't going to choose him, and he needed not to dwell on other hopes.

When he heard the news that Imogen was awake, it didn't do more than depress him further. He finished his daily tasks, ate a quick supper, and excused himself. Mother and Elspeth and Owen were attending a concert, Mairen had business with the Kirkellan, and Jeffrey could be alone with Imogen. He hoped she would be awake. Time to get this over with.

Unfortunately, she was asleep when he knocked softly on her door and let himself in. The last light of sunset showed her sleeping with her beautiful hair spread out over the pillow and trailing over her bare shoulders. He realized she was naked under the blankets, and his heart beat a little faster before he commanded it not to be stupid.

He thought about waking her, but the doctor had been clear that she needed as much rest as she could get. So instead he dragged a chair over to her bedside and settled in to wait. The sun set, and darkness fell, comforting him. He could pretend she wasn't there, that he was simply sitting in the dark the way he sometimes did when it had been a long day and his head ached.

After about an hour, Jeffrey felt like a fool for sitting there while she slept, like some kind of predator. He had nearly decided to return later when he heard the blankets rustle and the sound of Imogen rolling over. "Don't get up," he said, and felt for the Device light switch. The light came on, revealing Imogen half sitting up with the blankets pulled close around her chest, squinting.

"How long have you sat there?" she said.

"Longer than I'd like to admit," he said. "I apologize for the intrusion. Are you well?"

Imogen's dark eyes fixed on him. "I am hungry again."

"I can have someone bring you food." He made no move to pull the bell rope. "No pain? The healer said you should be perfectly recovered."

"I am not in pain. I do not feel tired now either. Just hunger."

Jeffrey rested his interlaced fingers on his knees and studied them. How much small talk did he have to endure before dealing with what would cut his heart out of his chest? "That's good. I—we were all very worried. Victory wounded, your saber left behind...it was as if you'd simply vanished."

Imogen scooted up, and the blanket shifted. Jeffrey kept his eyes fixed on her face. She leaned back against the headboard. "Thank you for tending to Victory. She is my dear friend."

More small talk, though at least Victory was someone who mattered. "Well, yes. I know how much she means to you, so I didn't think she should suffer."

Silence descended between them. "I am sorry," Imogen blurted. "I do—did not listen and you were right."

Startled, Jeffrey said, "Right about what?"

Imogen bowed her head and twisted the blanket around her fingers. "That I am too injured to fight. I killed Hrovald because I was lucky. He nearly killed me. I should listen to you. Please do not be angry."

"What? Imogen, I'm not angry with you." She sounded almost afraid. He couldn't understand why she would think he would ever be angry with her.

"Then what are you angry at?" Now she sounded confused.

He wished he dared reach out to her. "I'm not angry at all. It's just been a long couple of days, not knowing when you'd wake up. We've all been so worried."

"I am glad you care."

Her words were so civil, so *polite*, and so lacking in deeper feeling he wondered if he'd been wrong about everything, and she didn't actually care for him. Pain drove him to exclaim, "Of course I care! Imogen...." His words trailed off into silence.

A flash of misery crossed her features, so swiftly he wondered if he'd imagined it. "I think the Kirkellan will return to the Eidestal soon," she said. "I am looking forward to the hunts."

Jeffrey went still. "You're going back with them."

"I am a warrior of the Kirkellan. It is my home."

"I see." It was what he'd told himself to expect, what he knew would happen, and he felt nothing but a dull ache inside. "It's true, you're a natural commander. I've had the reports of Colonel Haverson and Major Randulf. People look to you for orders and they trust what you tell them to do. You're going to be the greatest Warleader the Kirkellan have ever had."

She looked sad again. "I think not. There is no more war for me to be Warleader."

Jeffrey shook his head. "The Ruskalder won't stay peaceful for long. Ingivar is strong, but there are others who see his progressive policies as a threat and will do whatever it takes to stop him. I give it another five, possibly seven years before Ruskald becomes a threat again. And your current Warleader—Kernan is a strong leader, but Mairen told me he's getting to an age where he's ready to lay down his saber. After what's happened in this war, no one's going to question your qualifications to take his place."

Imogen nodded. "I...think you are right."

She was so beautiful, and looked so miserable, that he understood finally that this conversation was as painful for her as it was for him. He cast about for some way to express his feelings. "Thank you for wielding your sword on my behalf. I would be dead now if not for you." That was wrong. It was too formal.

"It is what I want to do." Imogen sounded too formal, too. She met his eyes once again. "I do not belong here," she said.

Jeffrey nodded. "I know. I think I've always known." He stood. "I don't know if we'll have another chance to speak before your warriors leave—there's a lot to do still—but just in case, I want you to know I... feel honored by your presence here in Tremontane. Madam ambassador." That was better. It was the closest he dared come to *I love you*.

Imogen scooted back down to lie flat. "I think I must sleep again now."

"I thought you said you were hungry," Jeffrey said.

"I was wrong. I am just tired."

"All right. I'm glad you're well. Good night, Imogen."

"Good night."

He let himself out. The light vanished before the door shut behind him. The sitting room that lay beyond Imogen's bedroom was only dimly lit by a Device that burned on the mantel. Jeffrey leaned against the door and rubbed a hand across his face. It was over. They'd both said the right things. So why did it feel as if nothing would ever be right again?

JEFFREY: A FINAL DECISION

*W*aking before dawn had become a habit, these last three weeks. With the drapes pulled across the windows and no light burning by the bed or the door, Jeffrey's bedroom was as still and dark as if it had been sealed. No air moved except for his light breathing, and the darkness meant it didn't matter if his eyes were open or shut. That seemed like a metaphor for something, but he didn't want to pursue it in case the meaning was something dire.

He drew in a deeper breath and released it slowly, willing the knot in his stomach to untangle. That, too, was a habit—no, not a habit so much as an unwelcome guest. No matter what he dreamed or how soundly he slept, he always woke to the tense, burning feeling of his guts trying to twist their way out of his body. His mother, if she knew about it, would tell him to see the palace healer. He knew that was pointless. He knew what was causing it. And he knew no treatment would make it go away.

He wondered how far the Kirkellan had gotten in their travels the previous day. Not far, probably, since they were slowed by all those wagons full of still-healing warriors. That meant—

He swore and rolled onto his front, burying his head beneath his pillow. He had to stop thinking of Imogen. They'd both made the right choice, her in deciding to return to her people, him in not begging her to stay, so why did he keep torturing himself with the memory of her kisses? It didn't matter if she was five miles away or fifty; she was gone, and he needed to come to terms with that.

He made himself go over his plans for the day. Meeting with the Council. Meeting with the new Devisers' Guild leaders. Meeting... sweet heaven, were there nothing but endless meetings in his future? Imogen would tease him about never leaving time for himself... He groaned and squeezed his eyes shut as if that would block his memories. But, as always, he returned to thinking of her, helplessly, like a falling man grasping at a rope.

It still astonished Jeffrey that he had so many memories of her when they'd known each other barely more than two months. Imogen racing Victory, leaping hurdles and pounding along the straightaway. Imogen sitting next to him with strands of her hair blowing loose in the breeze. Imogen sitting hunched and defensive in the tiny cell. Imogen lying nearly unconscious, covered in blood. Imogen sitting up in her bed—he cut that memory off ruthlessly, not wanting to dwell on saying goodbye to her forever.

He was suddenly angry with himself. Why was he giving in to these sentimental, stupid emotions? Yes, he loved her, but who was to say she was the only woman he would ever love? He needed to throw his heart into finding a Consort here in Tremontane. Surely there were other women—

He sat up and flung the pillow away. Time to stop wallowing. Meetings, dear heaven, so many meetings, but then he would set about courting in earnest. And Imogen could remain a fond memory. He was the King of Tremontane; he owed it to his country to be strong. He'd proved that on Diana's body and he would prove it to his Council. He spoke, and they listened, even when he said things they didn't like. Someone had told him that—Mother? No, some other person.

Oh. It had been Imogen.

Unexpected longing struck him so hard he couldn't breathe. For once, he remembered not his physical desire for her, but the simple joy of being in her presence, of telling her things and knowing she understood him in ways no one ever had. She was clever, and wise, and a natural diplomat...*She's a warrior, it's what she's best at*, he told himself.

And in that moment, he knew he didn't give a damn what she was best at.

He was up and dressing before his brain could override his body. This was stupid. She'd only tell him what he already knew—that she wanted the Kirkellan more than she wanted him. But he'd never asked. He'd never actually come out and said *Imogen, I love you, I want you to marry me*. And if he never asked, how could he ever come to terms with her refusal?

He donned a plain shirt and comfortable trousers, pulled on riding boots, scribbled a note that he left on his sitting room table, and swiftly strode through the east wing, hoping his family would continue their habit of sleeping late because he didn't want to explain himself to any of them. At the door, he told the guards, "I'm going to the barracks for a workout before breakfast. Don't bother summoning my bodyguards," and hurried away before either of the men could comment on his inappropriate footwear.

Few people were about at this hour, and when he took the passage that led to the barracks, it was completely empty. Even so, he strolled casually around the turn before the barracks entrance, pretending it was normal for the King to go to the stables unescorted.

The stables, by contrast, were as busy and bustling as ever. The sky had begun to lighten, going from black to North blue in the east, and the warm murmuring of dozens of drowsing horses would have calmed Jeffrey's nerves on any other day. He walked to Harlequin's stall and waited for the black gelding to come forward, whickering a welcome.

"Saddle my horse," he told the young woman who approached him tentatively, as if she weren't entirely sure who had come into her domain that morning. "I'm going for a ride before breakfast."

"Yes, your Majesty." The woman hesitated again. "Shall I...arrange for horses for your guard?"

"They're waiting for me at the front door," Jeffrey said. His heart beat rapidly, and he sternly told it to calm down. He was the King; nobody was going to challenge his eccentricities. Certainly not this young woman. The stables were large enough she would assume some other ostler had provided horses to the nonexistent guards.

He waited, stilling his impatience, while the woman took her own sweet time about readying Harlequin. It was only his imagination that any minute now Micheline Branton and half of Internal Affairs would come pouring out of the palace, shouting at him to stop and return with them.

He accepted the reins, mounted as gracefully as he was able, and wheeled Harlequin around to walk at a sedate pace toward the stable yard exit. When he was out of sight of the woman, whom he could feel watching him as if her gaze were a burning brand, he urged Harlequin into a trot, kicking up gravel until they reached the paved courtyard. Then it was down the cobbled drive and into the streets of Aurilien.

Even at this hour, Aurilien was lively with men and women going to early-morning jobs or returning home from late-night ones. Produce wagons ambled through the streets to market, not making way for him. It cheered him to know he was anonymous for once. He refused to consider that this was stupid, traveling without his usual escort. It might be slightly dangerous—though if no one knew he was the King, who would be inclined to attack him?—but he had no desire to bring a retinue along to witness this meeting, especially since he had almost no hope she would accept him.

He reached the south gate just as the soldiers were opening it for the day and joined the small crowd of wagons and pedestrians waiting to leave the city. Screaming inside with impatience, he maneuvered his way through the crowd, politely avoiding his fellow travelers, until he'd passed all of them and could give the horse its head. He'd never ridden Harlequin faster than a canter, and the gelding's turn of speed surprised him. He crouched against the horse's neck and let him run.

Color seeped into the world around him, changing the trees from shades of charcoal to browns and greens. It felt as if the land itself were waking, and Jeffrey, too, felt like he was waking from a terrible nightmare. It didn't matter if Imogen rejected him—well, of course it *mattered*, but now that he was taking action, the dreadful burning pain in his stomach and the ache in his heart had vanished.

He calculated in his head how far the Kirkellan might have gotten the day before. Left Aurilien around noon, traveled no more than eight miles per hour, probably a lot less if those transport wagons were as ponderous as he imagined, so if Harlequin could keep up this speed for a while, if the Kirkellan didn't get an early start, he might reach them by noon. His stomach rumbled, reminding him he'd forgotten to eat. He didn't have much of an appetite.

Ahead, he saw a lone rider approaching, appearing at a break in the forest cover and then vanishing into the trees. He hadn't thought about other traffic on the road. With luck, he wouldn't get caught in someone's caravan. Every little delay would be torture.

The sound of Harlequin's hooves soon doubled as the other rider drew near enough to be heard. He was traveling almost as fast as Jeffrey. A post horse rider, maybe? Jeffrey twitched the reins to guide Harlequin to one side, not wanting to slow at all to dance around the other person.

Then the rider came into view around a corner. Jeffrey realized it was a Kirkellish horse just as the rider pulled up short several yards away.

It was Imogen.

Jeffrey jerked on the reins, confusing Harlequin for half a dozen steps until the horse finally came to a stop. "Why—Imogen, what are you doing here?" he said, too startled for politeness.

Imogen looked at him with her so-familiar steady gaze. "I am... coming to see you. To talk. Why are you here?"

She was coming to see him.

She wanted to talk.

He'd thought of what he might tell her, of the smooth words he might use to convince her to stay. Every one of them deserted him. He blurted out, "Don't leave. Stay with me. I love you, Imogen, and I don't want to lose you."

Her hands closed convulsively on Victory's reins. "You do—did not want me to stay."

How had he been such an idiot as to let her believe that? "No, I did. I desperately wanted you to stay. But you so clearly belonged with the Kirkellan I felt like a fool asking you to give all that up just to be my wife. Then I woke up before dawn today the way I have every morning for the last three weeks, trying to convince myself we'd done the right thing, and I knew I didn't give a damn what you were best at." He drew in a deep breath. "I know it's selfish and I have no right to ask it of you, but I want you to marry me and I don't want you to leave me ever again."

Imogen stared at him. Then she dismounted, letting Victory's reins fall, and took a few steps toward him. "I came to tell you I am not leaving," she said. "I do not give a damn either."

Jeffrey slid down off his horse, not very gracefully, and took a few tentative steps in her direction. Her words rang in his ears. *Not leaving.* It was so much what he'd wanted to hear he couldn't believe it was true. "Not leaving?"

Imogen shook her head. "I want to stay in Tremontane. To stay with you."

"Are you sure you want to give the Kirkellan up? It's your whole life, and I don't want you ending up resenting me for it." He didn't know why he was stupidly trying to talk her out of it, except that he knew deep down he couldn't gain his own happiness at the cost of hers.

She shook her head again, and her eyes grew distant, as if she were thinking hard about something. "It is...only part of my life," she said, "and this is another part, and I want to live in the part that has you in it, because you are my home."

He closed his eyes briefly and let out a long breath. "You are my home," he echoed. "You are. Oh, Imogen—"

She closed the distance between them and put her arms around him. "I love you," she said, "and—"

He smiled. "You've never said that to me before."

Imogen's brow furrowed. "I have not?"

"I promise I would have remembered." He was smiling like a fool and didn't care.

"Well, I will say it again if you want, because it is true."

"I hope so, if you're going to marry me," Jeffrey said, and leaned in to kiss her. It felt like the first time and it felt like nothing else in the world, and it felt like coming home. He didn't know what had changed her mind and he didn't care; it was a miracle, and in his experience, miracles weren't something you questioned.

How long they stood in the middle of the road, kissing and holding each other close, Jeffrey didn't know, but at some point he became aware of Harlequin snuffling at the grass that grew along the verge, and just then Imogen said, "We should not stand here. People will come."

"They can walk around us," Jeffrey said, but he let her go as far as holding her hand would allow. He couldn't stop looking at her. "I can't believe you came back. I thought I would have to chase you down and then beg you to love me in front of all your people, at which point you would tell me to leave and never return."

Imogen's eyebrows went up. "If you think it is hopeless, why do you try?"

When he heard his thoughts said out loud, Jeffrey couldn't imagine how he'd had the nerve to go after her. "Because I didn't want to spend my life wondering what might have been."

"Well, you do not need to beg me, because I loved you before." She released his hand and mounted Victory. "You just have the face that says you do not want to speak to me."

Jeffrey pulled himself into Harlequin's saddle. "That was actually the face that says I want you to have what's best for you even if it kills me, which it almost did."

Imogen scowled playfully at him. "You do not decide what is best for me, Jeffrey. But I chose to give up who I love, so we are both stupid together."

Jeffrey laughed. "Then let us return to Aurilien, where I will possibly be shouted at by Micheline—"

"Why will she shout?"

"I didn't take an armed escort when I came after you just now. I did leave a note. It wasn't a very informative note, but it was enough to make her have kittens knowing I was gallivanting around the countryside unescorted. Then we will have breakfast, and then you and I and Mother will plan the quickest royal wedding this country has ever seen."

Imogen brought Victory up beside him. "It must be quick?"

He thought back to sitting beside her as she slept, naked but for a few thin blankets, with her magnificent hair cascading over her bare shoulders, and his body stirred with the memory. "Very quick," he said.

Imogen's eyes lit with understanding, and she laughed.

They came around a curve in the road, and suddenly there was Aurilien before them, golden in the morning sunlight. Imogen drew in a startled breath. "Something wrong?" Jeffrey asked.

She shook her head. "Let us go home," she said.

Home. It thrilled him that she already thought of his home as hers —but what had she said? Home wasn't Aurilien. It was him. *And you are my home,* he thought. For the first time in his life, he had no doubts whatsoever.

EXILE OF THE CROWN PART THREE: AUTUMN, 945 Y.B.

*T*he loom was as old as Miss Merriwether had described, but in the patchwork way of something that had been repaired often over the years. The batten might be original, as worn as it was along the facing side; the heddles fairly shone with newness; the frame itself was seasoned with age except for one upright that was a different color from the rest. What had happened to require that single piece to be replaced? At any rate, it was a sturdy thing, and Zara didn't regret buying it.

She was less certain about the house, which was much, much older than the loom, and while someone had kept it clean, it had all sorts of little problems that said Miss Merriwether's illness had gone on longer than the woman had implied. But she'd bought the business, house, loom, and all, and now those problems were hers. Challenges, not problems, and Zara had never walked away from a challenge.

She left the large front room where the loom hulked in one corner, intimidating the spinning wheels, and went into the drawing room, which was a quarter the size and filled to overflowing with a couple of angular chairs upholstered in worn green twill and a narrow table holding an empty vase. Miss Merriwether sat in one of the chairs, placidly knitting despite the room's darkness; heavy curtains matching the chairs blocked most of the afternoon sunlight from reaching the room. Between the curtains and the chairs, Zara felt suffocated, as if the room were a tomb filled to bursting with funerary cloths.

She sat on the other chair, which dug into her spine, so she edged forward until she was perched on its edge and said, "Seems satisfactory."

Miss Merriwether nodded, her attention still on her complicated knitting. Maybe Zara could learn to knit; it seemed as soothing in its way as weaving. "Not regretting your purchase?" Miss Merriwether said.

"I don't think so. You didn't say how dilapidated the sheds were. I think the outhouse will have to come down." Zara had never owned an outhouse before, and the idea of using it made her cringe, but she'd put all her savings into purchasing Miss Merriwether's weaving business, and installing proper plumbing would have to wait.

"I'm sorry about that. I don't get outside much anymore."

"It's all right. Everything else is as you described."

"Good. Then I suppose it's time to tell you why you might want to change your mind."

Zara leaned back, startled, and regretted it instantly as the chair dug its knuckles into her spine. "Change my mind? Is there something you failed to tell me? If you've concealed material information, I'm within my rights to cancel the contract."

"It's something that came up after we came to an agreement. I thought you should see the possibilities before you made your decision." Miss Merriwether lowered her knitting to her lap. Her wrinkled face lacked its usual pleasant smile that Zara suspected concealed a world of pain. "Did you notice the large building in the town square? The one with no sign?"

"I did. What of it?"

"It's newly built. The owner, Quincy Pierpont, intends to set up a factory there. A weaving factory. He's been bringing in Devices for the last two weeks. It should open for business soon."

"A factory."

"He's already made overtures to many of the local weavers, offering them the...opportunity...to take advantage of the new Devices. Says it will save time and increase productivity. There's a lot of weavers in Longbourne, Mistress Weaver, and they're all in a tizzy wondering what to do."

Zara shook her head. "They have to realize this can't end well for them. It doesn't take skilled labor to run those Devices. All Mister Pierpont needs is to be able to pay more for wool than the rest of them do, and they're out of business."

"That's exactly true. So I'm offering you the chance to go back on our deal. It doesn't really matter to me; I'll be dead in a matter of weeks. But you came here expecting to make a life for yourself and happen it's not the life you might've wanted."

"I'm...not sure." This was bad. Factory goods wouldn't have the quality of home-crafted, but when it came to buying, most people wanted cheap more than they wanted good. "Does Mister Pierpont live here?"

"He's got a room at the hostel, next door to the tavern, but he works out of the tavern most days. You reckon on seeing him?"

"Might as well talk to him. Happen he's not intent on putting anyone out of business, and this factory will be good for Longbourne." This northeastern lilt, the odd vocabulary, was infectious.

Miss Merriwether put a withered hand over Zara's. It was hard to remember she was only a few years older than Zara; illness had not been kind to her. "I built this business from nothing," she said. "Built the customer base, refined my techniques, trained a dozen apprentices...and I'd hate to see it swallowed up by that man and his Devices. And I think you might be the woman to stop that happening."

"I'm not going to promise you anything, Miss Merriwether."

"Call me Sabrina. And I don't want promises."

Zara nodded and stood, grateful to relieve the pressure on her back. "I'll be back soon. Probably very soon."

She let herself out by the back door, which was strangely intimate, but Miss Merriwether—Sabrina—had insisted that real business in Longbourne was conducted via the back door. And if everything went well, it would be her back door. The small back yard was bare of grass, just hard-packed earth with some tall, autumn-dead weeds along the walls and around the two sheds, both of which were as weathered as the house. The narrow one, the outhouse, tilted a little, which made Zara nervous about using it; the larger one had once been painted a bright yellow that time had scoured into faded, peeling cream.

The main house, like most of what she'd seen in Longbourne, had a ground floor made of irregular stones pieced together and a smaller upper story of wood weathered silvery by hundreds of winter storms. She tried to imagine the wind blowing about the house, whether those storms really were as bad as Sabrina had said, but the day was warm, the wind merely a breeze, and winter seemed a thousand years away. Time enough to worry about it if she chose to stay.

She came around to the front of the house and set off down the street toward the distant plinking sound of the forge. Longbourne was bigger than most of the little towns she'd lived in over the last twenty-odd years, but still smaller than, say, Ravensholm or Ellismere, which was the last stop at the base of the mountains that marked the boundary of Barony Steepridge. The men and women she passed nodded and smiled politely, and she smiled back, but most of her attention was given to the large building ahead, facing the town square and the little white gazebo that sat at the center of it.

Unlike its neighbors, it was built entirely of wood, a deeply-grained oak stained dark brown that made it look heavyset and sullen. Windows lined both its stories, large-paned and dim in the light of the afternoon sun that backlit it. They'd let in plenty of light during the morning, maybe more than the workers would want, but they still didn't dispel the building's ominous air. Or maybe that was just Zara's knowledge of what it meant. She stopped in front of the building briefly and glared at it. It regarded her with indifference, which irritated her. Then she had to laugh at herself, privately. Irritated by a building. She must be getting old. Sixty-eight wasn't *that* old, was it?

The hostel was, unusually for Longbourne, three stories tall and shaped like a chimney. The tavern squatted next to it, friendly as a lapdog, with its door wide open and its many-paned windows shining with light even at three o'clock in the afternoon. The taproom was almost empty at this time of day, with one man seated at the bar eating a bowl of soup, a woman standing behind the bar setting bottles on the shelf there, and another man seated at a table near the window, a couple of bound notebooks in a pile beside him and a pen in hand. Zara crossed the room to stand in front of him. "Mister Pierpont?" she said.

The man looked up, scowling. Despite his expression, he was attractive, young—all right, mid-forties, but that was young to Zara—and dressed too well for Longbourne. His scowl vanished. "Can I help you, miss?" His smile was appreciative, and Zara felt irritated again. There was nothing wrong with being admired, granted, but the appraising way with which he looked at her said he wasn't going to take her seriously because she looked young and attractive.

"Agatha Weaver," she said, controlling her irritation and extending her hand. "I want to talk to you about your factory."

"Then you know who I am," Pierpont said, rising to take her hand and bowing over it the way a fashionable gentleman would. "Please, sit down. What's your interest in my factory?"

"I'm looking at buying a weaving business in Longbourne and I want to know how your plans are going to affect that."

Pierpont threw back his head and laughed, longer than he really had to. "A weaver named Weaver! You and the smith named Smith should become friends! That's hilarious."

"I really think it isn't," Zara said. "How disruptive do you plan to be?" After twenty years of aliases, she'd returned to Weaver as if coming back to her roots, and it angered her to hear him make light of that choice.

"Miss Weaver—it is 'miss,' isn't it?—Miss Weaver, I hope not to be disruptive at all. I intend to bring greater economic prosperity to

Longbourne and, by extension, the beautiful Barony Steepridge. Mass production is the way of the future. It's more efficient and faster and allows for better yields. I'm hoping to entice the weavers of Longbourne to take advantage of the Devices I offer, give them more leisure time and relieve them of some of the burdens of their work."

"And how will that happen? I don't know much about weaving Devices." A lie, to test him.

"Of course not." His condescending tone made her want to slap him. "Weaving Devices are made to set the warp of a loom faster than can be done by a single weaver—you must know how much of a difference that can make. And the shuttle is powered by a Device that regularizes its path, improving speed by up to forty percent. The operator—"

"The weaver."

"Of course. The operator monitors the heddles and makes sure there's no irregularities. You see weavers are still important to the process."

"I do. I assume you chose Steepridge because of the sheep."

"That's correct. The sheep of Barony Steepridge produce a quarter again what their lowland counterparts do, and it's the finest wool in Tremontane. Longbourne's wool fabric is renowned for its quality and softness—but you probably already know that."

"Yes." It was one of the reasons she'd leapt at Sabrina's offer; the reputation alone would be enough to make her wealthy, if she cared about wealth. "What about the demand for homespun?"

"I don't see why we, all of us working together, can't teach the world that Device-woven wool is just as good as homespun. After all, there's no reason it should be of lower quality, right?"

Zara watched him closely. He seemed sincere, but that was no guarantee of honesty. "You make good points," she said, and stood, prompting him to rise as well. "I'll consider them."

"Please do," he said, taking her hand even though she hadn't offered it. "I'd love to work with such a forthright and, dare I say, attractive young woman."

Zara smiled at him, though once again she itched to slap him. "We'll see."

She strode rapidly back to Sabrina's house and accidentally let the back door slam shut. Maybe it wasn't so accidental. The more she thought on the meeting, the angrier she became.

Sabrina was still sitting in the drawing room, though her knitting lay in a basket beside her. She looked as if she were in pain. "Do you need to lie down?" Zara asked, alarmed.

Sabrina shook her head. "It's worse when I lie down," she said. "Did you speak to him?"

Zara sat in the uncomfortable chair and leaned forward. "He's either stupid or a liar," she said. "There's no way a factory can do anything but put all the weavers of Longbourne out of business. He can't increase the wool production—I'm guessing as much land as possible is given over to raising sheep?"

"Yes."

"Then he'll have to take hold of the supply, which means reducing the supply available to the weavers and forcing them either to go out of business or work for him. Based on what he told me, he wants people to believe his machines are more efficient, which they aren't—"

"How do you know that?"

"I've seen them work before." They were a good idea for large cities, places where the supply of raw materials was elastic, but Longbourne couldn't afford to import wool, particularly wool of a lower quality than their own. "The only thing they are is faster, and he's right that they automate certain processes, but at a cost to the quality of the final product."

"But can he sell it cheaply?"

"Possibly." Zara tapped her finger on her lips. "How many weavers are there in Longbourne?"

"Thirty, maybe thirty-five. And then there are all those men and women living elsewhere in Barony Steepridge."

"How hard would it be to bring them all together for a meeting?"

Sabrina smiled. "Happen you're planning to stay?"

Zara smiled back. Hers was a good deal nastier than Sabrina's. "I've put everything I have into buying this business," she said, "and I'm not about to let it be taken away from me before I have the chance to see what I can make of it. And men like Pierpont remind me of... someone I used to know." She hadn't thought of Roger Lestrange in years, but he'd been just like Pierpont: smiling, self-righteous, convinced his way was best and condescending to anyone who disagreed with him. Crushing him had been one of the most satisfying things she'd done as Queen. She had no doubt she could crush Pierpont as readily.

"I can send messages. It sounds like they need to know what you've learned." Sabrina pushed herself out of her chair, shaking a little, but waved off Zara's offer of help. "I've taken a room at the hostel. I don't want to be in your way in your house."

"Actually, I...think you should stay here," Zara said. "I'm going to need your help convincing the weavers that they should listen to me." In truth, she felt guilty at turning the woman out of what was still, emotionally, her home—a sick, elderly woman who shouldn't be left alone in a rented room. *She'll die here,* she told herself, and to her surprise it didn't bother her.

"I don't want to interfere," Sabrina said.

"You won't. And I'm going to insist on it. You should know now that I always get my way."

Sabrina eyed her with a mischievous twinkle, a surprisingly youthful expression. "I hope for Longbourne's sake that's true," she said.

"So that's the truth," Zara said to the assembled men and women. "Pierpont's plan will either put you out of business or turn you into his employees. Is that what you want?"

"Devices make life easier," said one woman, a heavyset lady in her mid-twenties. "What's wrong with that?"

"It depends on what you're willing to give up for that life of ease,"

Zara said. "If you want to weave for someone else's gain—someone who's going to do nothing but rake in the profits—then happen you'll be satisfied with his plan. But I think you've all spent too many years mastering your craft to be swayed by that."

"But there's always been enough wool for all of us," a man said. His querulous voice put her already frayed nerves on edge. "Shouldn't there be enough for the factory as well?"

Zara swallowed her annoyance and the words *I've explained this twice already.* "Longbourne's wool production was optimized years ago," she said. "Its location in the mountains means its acreage is limited. The timber industry uses what the shepherds don't. There's no way to increase the amount of wool produced, and you weavers are already using all of it. The factory can only have raw materials if it takes them away from you. Less wool for you means less finished cloth and less profit. It's not a complicated equation."

She could see she was losing them with "equation." "Look, this is what it comes down to," she said, her exasperation building. "Pierpont is deceiving you. The factory will turn you into his employees. He'll pay you a wage, he'll take the rest of the profits, and you'll lose control of the industry you've spent your lives building. Stand up to him, refuse his offer, and Longbourne really will prosper."

The room was silent. Finally, the woman who'd spoken before said, "I don't like the idea of working for anyone but me. I don't want this factory here."

A murmur of agreement built through the crowd, and Zara relaxed. Finally, they'd seen sense. "One of you should tell Pierpont your decision," she said. "He won't be happy about it."

"Why not you?" said the querulous man.

Zara mentally kicked herself. "I'm just the newcomer," she began.

"And the one who understands it all. I'm still not sure I get why there's not enough wool to go around," he replied. "Besides, we're neighbors now, and happen we should trust each other."

She looked at him more closely. She'd seen him around town, true, and now that she thought about it she remembered him going into the house just south of Sabrina's—of hers, but she hadn't thought of that in terms of "neighbor." "I don't know your name," she said.

"Aubrey Martin," he said. "Welcome to Longbourne, Mistress Weaver."

Now the murmur was one of welcome, and the crowd was breaking up. The meeting was over. Dazed, Zara nodded her thanks and went to the bar. "What can I get you?" the woman behind it said. "Beer? Or happen you need something a mite stronger?"

"Whiskey," Zara said, and the little glass appeared as if by magic. She gulped it down, relishing the way it burned. "I think I need two."

The woman grinned. "Coming right up," she said. "Maida Handly. We're both newcomers to Longbourne."

"Are they all so...accepting?"

"They are. I had more friends by the end of the first week than I think I had in all of Ellismere, the whole time I lived there."

"I see." Zara had steered clear of making friends the last twenty-two years. It was so much easier not to put down roots when you knew you'd be moving on five or seven years down the road. "It's a little disconcerting."

"You'll get used to it." Miss Handly slid the glass across to Zara. "Welcome to Longbourne."

Zara sipped her whiskey and surveyed the room. She'd have to be careful not to rebuff anyone, but she truly wasn't interested in making friends. She could speak for them without making any commitments, certain sure, but she shouldn't make any lasting connections.

"Amelia Ponsonby," said the heavyset woman. "You make a lot of sense. You're buying Sabrina's place?"

"Looks like," Zara said.

"Well, you'll want to come to our knitting circle, belike. Everyone brings something and we gossip about our neighbors."

"Ah...I don't know how to knit and I'm a terrible cook."

"Not a knitter? Well, come anyway. It's a lot of fun." She patted Zara's shoulder and moved away into the crowd. Zara stared after her. What was that about?

"You spoke well," a man said, startling her. He was short but well-built, stocky, and his hazel eyes were amused. "I'm no weaver, but I live near that proposed factory and happen it's not the kind of neighbor I'd like." He stuck out his hand. "Robert Richardson, and I'd like to invite you over for supper sometime. My wife Eleanor is a good cook, and I just heard you say you weren't."

"I—" She felt as if the whiskey were having an effect on her despite all reason. "Maybe some time."

"We like to make newcomers feel welcome. Eleanor will call on you soon and talk you into it. Best of luck with that Pierpont fellow." Richardson clapped her on the shoulder and turned away. Zara set her unfinished glass down and made her escape.

The chilly wind had picked up, and she rubbed her arms to keep warm. She'd meant to buy winter clothes here rather than ship them up the mountain, but now she was a little afraid if she went to a clothier's she'd come out with an invitation to spend Wintersmeet with some well-meaning strangers. It was going to be very hard to stay aloof in the face of all this unrelenting friendliness. *You're only going to be here five years, maybe seven*, she told herself, *you're essentially passing through, and making friends only hurts in the long run.* But she remembered Miss Handly's kind words, and Mister Richardson's invitation, and a part of her that had lain dormant for years reached out for the light. She pushed it away. She wasn't going to be stupid. Never again.

THE WHIRRING OF THE SPINNING WHEELS, NOT QUITE IN RHYTHM WITH each other, made a nice background to the long, tedious task of dressing the giant loom for weaving. Zara pulled strand after strand of yarn through the heddles, counting silently. Her first weaving in her new home, and the fine yarn was a beautiful deep green that soothed her mind, which was eager to begin. Patience was not exactly one of her virtues.

Someone pounded on the front door. Zara dropped her hook and cursed. The spinning wheels came to a thrumming halt. "Answer that," she snapped at Mitchell, and the gawky young man stood, tripped on his stool, and almost fell into the door. Zara picked up the hook and went back to counting, trying to find her place. Whoever this was had better not be wasting her time.

"Agatha!" Amelia Ponsonby stood in the doorway, breathing heavily. "Agatha, he's stealing the wool!"

Zara threw her hook on the floor, where it bounced once with a dull *tink*. "Who's doing *what*?"

"Mister Pierpont," Amelia gasped. "He's buying up the wool. I went to Merden's today to pick up my purchase and he said Mister Pierpont had paid him a third again what I did. He said the other sheep farmers are getting the same offer. Agatha, what do we do?"

"That's idiotic," Zara said. "No, I don't mean you, Amelia. He can't afford to pay that much for wool without losing money." But even as she spoke, she saw Pierpont's strategy. He only had to cut off the weavers' supplies until they exhausted their funds and couldn't stay in business, then he could return to buying at the lower price. And since he'd be the only one buying, he could drop that price even more—and unless the sheep farmers could afford to send their wool down the mountain, at additional cost, they'd have to accept what he paid. "That *bastard*," she muttered. "Mitchell, Annetta, you're free for the day. Amelia, I need to speak to Mister Merden."

They crossed the valley in silence, wrapped tightly in their cloaks against the fine drizzle of misting rain. Zara berated herself the whole way. *Speaking to Pierpont was pointless. You should have known he wouldn't give up just because the weavers resisted him. You should have anticipated this.* She wished she knew the actual figures behind the economics. How much did it cost to ship raw wool as opposed to fabric? It had to be a substantial difference, or the sheep farmers would be doing it already. Pierpont was going to put *her* out of business; she barely had enough money to buy wool at current prices, let alone the inflated ones Amelia described.

Merden's farmstead was just outside the little village of Corraden, nestled into a fold in the mountains, from which his grazing pastures stretched out for miles. Zara didn't do business with him, since Andrew Hatten had been Sabrina's supplier for thirty years, but she knew him to be shrewd and successful—someone who was always looking to squeeze every ounce of profit out of a situation. If she could convince him of the facts, of Pierpont's true motives, Merden would be a valuable ally, because he wouldn't want to see his neighbors making more than he was.

They knocked on the front door of the sprawling farmhouse and waited. Amelia jigged from one foot to another. "Calm down," Zara said.

"I'm cold. And I'm not sure how you can stay so calm."

Forty years of practicing. "This is just a setback, and a small one. You'll see."

The door opened. "Agatha! And Amelia! What brings you here?" said Florence Merden.

"We'd like to speak to Mister Merden," Zara said.

"He's out the back, but happen he'd be glad for a rest in the warm," Florence said. "Come in and let me pour you a cup."

"It's not a social call, Florence."

Florence's face went still. "This is about Mister Pierpont, isn't it? He was here yesterday, but James didn't say anything about it, so I figured nothing had come of it."

So James Merden had been afraid to tell his wife what he'd agreed to. Good. That meant he felt guilty, and guilt was something Zara could play on. "I'm afraid Pierpont is attacking the weavers again."

Florence nodded. "I'll get him for you. Please, sit down. The kitchen's warm and you look like you could use it."

The plain pine table, scrubbed pale with years of use, felt smooth under Zara's hand. A memory of the Council chamber, with its centuries-old slab of oak worn smooth and shiny by countless hands, surfaced from deep within her mind. What did young Jeffrey think when he stood beside it, overseeing the Council? Did he remember her, or did he think of his father? Remembering Anthony's death still pained her, though it had been twenty years before, and mention of "King Jeffrey" always left her a little disoriented. She folded her hands in her lap and waited.

Before long, the back door swung open and admitted Merden, who was a big man with grizzled hair and a thick gray mustache. "What do you want?" he asked, keeping the table between them.

Zara smiled grimly. He thought belligerence would cow her? "To keep you from making a mistake," she said.

"I don't call increasing my profits a mistake," he said. He didn't sit down, so Zara rose to face him.

"I don't want to interfere in your business," she lied, "but I don't think you've thought this through."

"Haven't I?"

"What do you think is going to happen when the factory is the only one buying from you?"

His brow furrowed. "What?"

"If you don't have anywhere else to sell your product, the one controlling the price is your purchaser. How long do you think he'll be willing to buy from you at that price?"

Merden shrugged. "He's not the only one. The weavers are paying it too. I should have raised prices years ago."

That was a blow. "Not all of them can pay. You're going to put them out of business."

"Not my problem if they can't manage their affairs. Certain sure it's not."

Zara opened her mouth to say something she knew would be futile, and the door banged open again. "Aunt Florence, mama says I can visit with you, can we make pie?" said Annetta, Zara's younger apprentice.

"Oh, sweetling, happen now's not the best time," Florence said.

Zara looked at Annetta. Her resemblance to James Merden was probably too strong for anyone's comfort, and she wasn't going to grow up to be more than pleasant-looking, but she was a hard worker who already knew much of the weaver's trade. "Annetta's mother is your sister, isn't she, Mister Merden?" she said, an idea taking shape. "Rose Garrity."

"She is," Merden said, confused at the sudden change in topics.

"She's a tough lady, Rose is," Zara said cheerfully. "Very opinion-ated. Very strong-willed."

"Yes," said Merden.

"I know she doesn't shy from telling people what she thinks. And they tend to do as she says, if only because she argues them into it. But then, you'd know this well, being her brother."

Merden scowled at some private memory. "Certain sure she does."

"And all of you sheep farmers are determined on raising prices?"

Now he really looked confused. "What—why does that matter?"

"Well, here's an interesting fact, Mister Merden. I can't afford to pay those prices. So I'll probably lose my business. Which means Annetta here, as my apprentice, isn't going to have an apprenticeship anymore. Happen there's nobody else who'll be able to take her on, as I know all the other weavers already have apprentices. That would be a shame, wouldn't it? And what would be even more a shame, Mister Merden—" Zara leaned forward with her hands on the smooth wood of the table, her voice sharpened steel— "is if Rose Garrity were to learn who was responsible for her only daughter losing her apprenticeship. Especially with Annetta being so gifted. Because I think Rose would be interested in having a few words with that person. And I think those words would be the kind of words that make a man think twice about his future. Don't you agree, Mister Merden?"

Merden swallowed. "I...you're wrong."

"Am I? I don't think so. But if you persist in being a fool, I think we're both going to find out. Maybe you could pass your decision along to your fellows." Zara stood up, running her fingers just once against the table that felt so wonderfully familiar. "Good day, Mister Merden. See you at knitting circle, Florence."

Zara and Amelia walked back across the fields in silence. When they reached the outskirts of town, Amelia said, "You're terrifying."

"I am not," Zara said, welcoming the chill breeze against her suddenly warm cheeks.

"No, you are. I've never heard anyone speak the way you did. He's going to change his mind."

"I hope so."

"I don't think you've ever heard Rose tear into someone. She's almost as terrifying as you are. He's certain sure going to change his mind."

Zara didn't reply. She'd never thought of herself as terrifying. Forceful, yes; convincing, yes. But terrifying? She thought back over the conversation, if you could call it that, with Merden. She'd found his weakness and exploited it, just as she had a hundred times before, and she'd done it because others needed her to. Just as she had a hundred times before. "I'm not Rose," she said.

"You're not," Amelia said. She stopped on the path, making Zara stop as well. "Rose is...she's a good woman, mostly, but she takes pleasure in tearing people apart and she's not always careful as to whether or not they deserve it. You're more like...what's that knife Dr. Green uses?"

"A scalpel."

"That's it. You cut where it's needed and you strike clean. And everyone can hear the truth in what you say."

Now Zara's cheeks were flaming. "I don't know whether that's a compliment or not," she said.

Amelia shrugged, smiling. "I think it is. It just makes me wonder why you're a weaver and not...I don't know...ruling a County."

Zara realized she was holding her breath and let it out, slowly. "I think you have to be born to that."

"I don't know. Lord Harstow, Baron Steepridge I mean, he was appointed to the Barony only a few years ago. So King Jeffrey might ride into Longbourne one day and carry you off to join his Council!" Amelia laughed.

"I hope King Jeffrey doesn't think of that," Zara said.

CHICKEN SOUP WAS ABOUT THE ONLY FOOD ZARA KNEW HOW TO MAKE—

well, it was the only food she never ruined. It was fortunate Maida Handly served inexpensive meals at the tavern, because Zara would starve to death otherwise, metaphorically speaking. She fished out the chicken and shredded the meat from the bones, then stirred the meat back into the pot. It smelled heavenly. She hoped Sabrina could eat some of it. The woman looked like a bird herself, the bones of her face sharp and her arms and legs thin and brittle as a couple of matchsticks. Zara ladled the rich broth into a couple of bowls and carried them upstairs.

The upper story had three rooms laid out in a line, opening off a short hallway. Zara had firmly refused to take the largest room, the middle one that was Sabrina's, and probably wouldn't have even if Sabrina had been completely well and left Longbourne entirely. "Suppertime," she said as she entered the room. Sabrina was sitting up in a rocking chair padded with cushions and smiled at Zara.

"It smells delicious," she said.

"That's kind of you to say," Zara said. She knew full well that Sabrina's senses of taste and smell had vanished weeks before, but it didn't hurt anyone for her to keep up the pretense. "Let me set these down."

"You don't have to eat with me."

"I get bored all by myself." That was another lie, but a more plausible one. Zara hadn't minded being alone for many years now. "Besides, I wanted to tell you the knitting circle gossip."

"Does that mean you've learned to knit?"

"A little. I'm not good at patterns, but I can do a fine scarf. Besides, you know knitting circle is more about talk than knitting."

"So you've finally learned that, too."

"What do you mean?"

Sabrina laid her spoon down with a gentle *tink*. "I mean," she said, "you've finally let yourself make a place here."

Zara blinked. "But I—well, of course."

"Not 'of course.' You held yourself aloof for a long time. I think you're not used to having friends, which is a shame in someone as young as you are. What happened to you, that you're so bent on being alone?"

It was so unexpected it left Zara groping for something to say. Nothing came to mind but the truth. "I never stay long in one place. Leaving people behind...it's painful. Easier not to make friends at all."

Sabrina nodded. "I can see that. But happen you're not thinking about it straight."

"I've had a long time to think about it," Zara said.

"I know it seems that way to you. Young people always feel the weight of the years they don't have." Sabrina took Zara's hand. Her dry, loose skin felt like butterfly wings, soft and fragile. "Agatha, we all of us eventually leave folks behind, or they leave us. What kind of life would it be if we let that fact keep us from cherishing those relationships? We live, and we love, and we mourn, and we rejoice. Take comfort in those friendships, Agatha. Even if you plan on leaving Longbourne someday. Even if it's someday soon."

Zara clasped Sabrina's hand lightly. "I miss my husband," she said. "We didn't have long together, and when he died, I thought— what was the point of having him at all, if it was just going to end?"

"The point was having him at all," Sabrina said. "You willing to give up those memories just to give up the pain?"

Vividly she remembered the Wintersmeet morning when she'd kissed Hank for the first time, how wonderfully sweet it had been to feel his body against hers. "No," she said.

"Then that's that," Sabrina said. "It's why we make those relationships. We're not made to be alone, any of us, and I hope you remember that."

"I think I will." Zara set down her bowl of soup, which had grown cold. "Thank you."

"Thank *you* for caring for me. I meant to leave Longbourne, you know, but this has been my home for fifty years, and...it was selfish of me, letting you give me a home these last weeks."

"It's no trouble. You're no less my friend than they are."

"That's true." Sabrina handed her bowl to Zara. She'd barely touched her food, which made Zara's heart ache. "You know, you bear a remarkable resemblance to Zara North," she said.

Zara dropped the bowl. Soup and pottery shards flew everywhere. "Did I startle you?" Sabrina asked.

"I slipped," Zara said, and fled downstairs for a towel. She set the remaining bowl in the sink and sat at the table with her head in her hands. It had been so long that she'd stopped worrying about people recognizing her, for the most part, though she still wouldn't take the risk of living near Aurilien. And now this old woman had reached into the past and pulled out a memory that could mean disaster. Zara took a deep breath. No. Sabrina Merriwether was dying, and she didn't know the truth of her words, and she wasn't in a position to tell anyone even if she wanted to.

Zara came slowly up the stairs with the towel. "What a mess. Now your room's going to smell like chicken," she said.

"I don't mind." She'd scooted her chair a few inches from the puddle. Zara gingerly picked up the pieces of the bowl and stacked them together, then mopped up the spill. Sabrina shifted her weight, then said, "Zara?"

"What?" Zara said, then realized what she'd done. The shards of the bowl slipped from her nerveless hand once again. "I mean—"

"You *are* her," Sabrina said. "Zara North. I was at the Queen's coronation, and I've never forgotten her face. Your face. It's impossible, and yet you looked so guilty I knew it had to be true. Not dead, and looking little older than you did at your coronation.."

"You can't tell anyone," Zara said.

"Who would I tell?" Sabrina put her hand on Zara's head. "That would be quite a secret to keep, for all these years."

"It could mean the downfall of the royal family, if it were known."

"I see." Sabrina stroked Zara's hair. "Will you tell me? Tell me what happened to you?"

"To satisfy your curiosity?"

"To ease your burden. Am I right that you haven't told a soul the truth in...it must be nearly forty years now?"

Zara looked up at Sabrina. She hadn't lit the lamp, and the sunset glow had dwindled and turned pale blue as the moonlight took its place. "You're dying," she said.

"And therefore safe."

"Yes." She moved to sit on the bed. "It started," she said, "when I broke my leg."

The whole story took less time to tell than she'd imagined, even when she included Hank and being tracked down by Jeffrey and the years of moving from place to place to avoid discovery. "It was probably a bad idea to buy your business," she said, "if I intended to move again in a few years. That's not enough time to really build it up. I wonder if I didn't secretly want an excuse to settle down."

"Happen that's true," Sabrina said. "And Barony Steepridge *is* off the beaten path a bit."

"I just didn't count on making friends so easily. Or getting involved in local politics so quickly."

"Mister Pierpont hasn't left Longbourne yet."

"No, and it worries me. He's got some other plan and I wish I knew what it was."

"You'll find out. And then you'll destroy it."

"I hope that faith in me is warranted."

"In the woman who brought the Scholia to its knees? I think Mister Pierpont is going to regret coming to Longbourne with all his blackened heart."

Zara laughed. "You know what's true? It feels good. I've spent so much time hiding who I am that having an excuse to fight for something feels...wonderful. Natural."

"And Longbourne thanks you for it." Sabrina shook her head. "Will you help me into bed? I think I can sleep for a while."

"Of course." Zara saw her friend settled, then opened the window a crack; Sabrina loved the chilly night air. "Sleep well."

She went downstairs and tidied up the kitchen and the great room, thought about sitting in the drawing room and practicing her knitting, decided against it, and went to make herself some tea instead. If this were a play, Sabrina would die tonight, just in time to have received Zara's confidences, but she probably had another week or so. Zara prayed her passing would be peaceful. It did feel good, sharing that burden with someone else, but it would have to be the last time. Her secret could still bring down the North family, and she couldn't bear that.

She sat at the table and sipped her tea, looking through the kitchen window at the yard. She really ought to replace that outhouse. Maybe Ger Fuller, owner of the general store, would accept trade for lumber. She could get some of the husbands of the knitting circle women to do the labor. And they likely wouldn't want paying, because that's what neighbors were for. What friends did for each other. It was a warm feeling. Sabrina was right; however transitory friendships were, they were worth cherishing.

Hank, she thought, *I don't regret a moment of our life together, however much I still miss you.* And if she didn't regret him, there was no sense regretting the new friendships she was making.

She rinsed her empty cup, put it in the drying rack, and climbed the stairs to her room. Pierpont was definitely planning something, but she'd worry about that in the morning. Tonight, she'd sleep more peacefully than she had in years.

"I HOPE THIS MEANS YOU HOLD NO GRUDGE AGAINST ME," PIERPONT said, settling himself in the seat across from Zara. Outside the windows of the tavern, fat snowflakes fell. Eleanor Richardson had told her it was nothing, just a flurry, but it was hard not to picture snow filling the street and the fields and finally the pass to the lowlands. Zara settled herself more comfortably and smiled at Pierpont, a nice, friendly smile. Time enough for nasty smiles if this conversation went the way she thought it might.

"You're a businessman," she said. "Just like I am. We're both trying to make a living."

"Exactly," Pierpont said. "Tea?" He picked up the steaming pot that had been sitting on the table when she arrived, which annoyed her; how presumptuous of him to assume she was willing to share a companionable drink after how they'd clashed over the last few weeks. She shrugged and nodded, and he poured out a dark, rich stream into her cup.

"Thanks," she said, adding a bit of cream and stirring. "But you didn't ask me here just to show off your tea-pouring abilities."

"I asked you here to see if we could come to some sort of agreement," he said. "We shouldn't be at odds like this. I realize now that I didn't take into account how passionate your weavers are about their livelihoods. I apologize."

His expression was once again that of an indulgent parent, pretending to give in to a recalcitrant child, and she smiled sweetly back at him. "Why, that's nice of you to say," she said. "There's been misunderstandings all around, certain sure." She took a long drink of her tea, which was an unfamiliar blend and surprisingly good with a tang of unexpected sweetness.

"I'm glad you appreciate that. Now, if I may, I'd like to lay out the position we find ourselves in?"

"Go ahead, Mister Pierpont."

Pierpont set down his cup in its saucer with a *tink*. "Most of the weavers have made it clear they're not interested in working for me. And that's just fine. On the other hand, enough of the sheep farmers have agreed to sell to me that I have wool enough to be going on with, and some of your weavers—and I think you'll agree this is just the way business works—have found working for me to be in their best interests. My factory *will* start production, Mistress Weaver, that's just a fact. But I don't believe we have to be bad neighbors. I really do want what's best for Longbourne."

Zara raised one eyebrow, but decided against challenging him. Instead, she said, "And I suppose you have a plan for making that happen."

"I was thinking how much easier it would be for all of us if you weavers were to formalize your arrangement. Form a cooperative, so to speak. Then the cooperative and the factory could write up an agreement stating where the boundaries are, so there's no...poaching, you could say. You have boundaries, and I have boundaries, and we're each able to profit without hurting one another. What do you think?"

"I think the weavers of Longbourne are independent enough that they don't want to give over any control of their businesses to anyone, even someone with their best interests at heart." Zara took another drink, enjoying the aroma. "Getting them to agree to your proposal would be difficult."

Pierpont smiled, and this time it was genuine. "Oh, Mistress Weaver, you don't expect me to believe that *you* couldn't get them to see reason? You have a gift for showing people truth."

"I wish that were true." He had something else in mind, some other plan, but Zara couldn't for the life of her figure out what. Forcing the weavers into a cooperative—and since she didn't believe in it, it *would* require force—would weaken them by introducing the need for all of them to agree on its decisions, but Pierpont was right, it would give them a stronger position to defend themselves. "We'll consider it," she said, deciding to play for more time. "It's an interesting suggestion."

"Well, don't take too long, because once the snows set in and the pass closes, we'll all be stuck here in Longbourne all winter." Pierpont said.

"And that would be a shame," Zara said blandly, and pushed her chair back to go.

"You don't have to go," Pierpont said. "I was hoping you'd have dinner with me."

Zara suppressed a shudder. "No, thank you, Mister Pierpont," she said. "I appreciate the offer."

He stood and bowed politely as she left, pulling her cloak low over her face. The idea of having a civil meal with that weasel made her stomach churn. She blinked away a few snowflakes and trudged back along the street toward her home.

The factory loomed, dark and sinister, over the town square, its windows leaden sheets in the gray light. Zara walked up and peered inside. It was too dark for her to see much, but there was the impression of angular, bony arms with too many elbows, lined up in a row extending past the limits of her vision. She traced a circle in the patch of mist left by her breath, then scrubbed it out with a fold of her cloak and moved on. Her stomach rumbled painfully again. Dinner with Pierpont was a bad idea, but dinner by herself, or with Sabrina if she was awake, seemed an excellent one.

She held the back door carefully to keep it from slamming—she really needed to have that looked at—then called out, "Sabrina?" The house was silent long enough to frighten her, then she heard her name called, muffled and distant. Zara ascended the stairs and said, "I was going to heat something up for us, would you like—"

Stabbing pain tore at her stomach, making her gasp and drop to one knee. A second pain, worse than the first, made her vision go gray, and when it passed she discovered she was sprawled on the steps, her hand clinging to the stair rail. "Sabrina," she gasped, then groaned as a third pain struck. Stupid—Sabrina could barely help herself. Gritting her teeth against the agony in her stomach, she crawled up the stairs, then collapsed on the landing, curled in on herself. It felt like knives and hot pokers all at once. Something—

She once again saw Pierpont's hand on the teapot, smelled the unfamiliar aroma, and realized she hadn't seen the man take a single drink. *Poison.* Despite herself, she laughed, then gagged at how the laughter made the pain worse. He must be truly desperate to think killing her would solve his problem. Maybe it would.

She clenched her teeth on another cry and wept when the pain passed. His bad luck that there'd never been a poison that could do more than inconvenience her, though this one hurt so badly he'd certainly come close to finding one. Her heart pounded too fast, pain streaked from her stomach to her extremities, and she heard Sabrina ask a question that the walls made unintelligible. "Don't worry," she tried to say, and then her heart stopped beating.

She concentrated on breathing in and out, though that was pointless since her heart wasn't circulating blood, but it gave her something to think about that wasn't panic because her heart had stopped and she was still conscious and it hurt like hell, everywhere. Then, as if someone had grabbed hold of it and shaken it, her heart hiccupped back into life, irregular at first but then smoothly, *thumpTHUMP*, over and over again in a way she'd never fully appreciated before. The pains were subsiding, but she continued to lie on the floor for several minutes after she felt well again, just appreciating the blissful absence of pain. Then she got up and went into Sabrina's room.

"Pierpont just tried to poison me," she said.

Sabrina, who was sitting up in bed, gasped and covered her mouth in astonishment. Then she laughed. "He's going to be so surprised when you're not dead," she said.

"Oh, I think he'll be more than surprised," Zara said.

"I don't understand," Amelia said. "You want me to do what, exactly?"

"Just go to this meeting and pretend you haven't seen me. That you don't know where I am," Zara said. "I'm going to arrive late and I can't explain why. Can you do that?"

"I suppose," Amelia said, "but I don't know why you can't tell me."

Because you're a terrible liar, Zara thought. "I want it to be a surprise even for you," she said. "Trust me, you'll appreciate it."

Amelia still looked skeptical, but nodded. "Don't take too long, or you'll miss the meeting entirely."

Zara shut the door behind her friend and leaned against it. Pierpont was so obvious it was almost too easy. He'd asked the weavers to a meeting just hours after he'd poisoned her—well, he'd need to strike quickly, keep them off balance, wouldn't he? Without Zara, their resistance would fall apart. And if he waited until her body was found, "negotiations" would have to be postponed, possibly until it was too late for his plan. She checked the kitchen clock. Five minutes. She needed to strike as quickly as he did.

When the five minutes were up, Zara put on her cloak and walked over to the tavern. The door was open slightly, enough that she could hear the sound of voices from some distance away. They didn't sound happy. Occasional pauses in the rumblings told her Pierpont was talking, probably acting as if he were doing them all a favor. Or had he decided he didn't have to be polite now his nemesis was out of the way? She paused outside the door and listened more closely.

"—if Agatha Weaver were here. Where is she?" That was Aubrey Martin, querulous as always. A chorus of voices spilled over his, adding their agreement.

"I think you're all old enough to make up your own minds, don't you?" Pierpont said. "Or does Mistress Weaver control your decisions? I'd be embarrassed to admit to it, were I you."

There was another murmur, this one uglier. "Nobody tells us what to do," an unfamiliar woman's voice said.

"That's exactly right. You're reasonable, independent people. Now, I would never tell anyone what to do. I just lay out the facts and let you make the decision."

"Except when you're not giving us all the facts!" That was Amelia.

"You're not calling me a liar, are you?" Pierpont said. "I've never been anything but honest with you all."

"That's not entirely true, is it, Mister Pierpont," Zara called out. The whole room shifted as everyone turned to look at her. Zara walked forward, the crowd parting for her like waves before a warship's prow. "You've been much worse than dishonest. Care to explain how?"

"Impossible," Pierpont said. "I put enough—" He shut up fast. Well, she hadn't expected him to burst out with a confession. And this way was more fun.

"Happen you made a mistake," she continued. "More than one, really. What you did...not the most precise way to kill someone, is it?" Gasps, and muttered conversations, washed over her, but she had attention only for her prey.

"That's a serious accusation," Pierpont said. She was impressed at how well he'd regained his composure. "You've got no proof."

"You're right. I don't have proof. But Maida Handly does." She didn't dare look behind her to see Maida's expression, couldn't risk losing control. "You really should have washed the pot yourself. It's sitting in Maida's kitchen, waiting its turn to be washed—see, there's another thing you didn't know, that Maida's second barman always waits until he's got a full sink before he does a load of dishes. So that teapot is going to show the remains of whatever poison you put into it. The Baron has people who can test it for those substances. And then...then I have nothing *but* proof."

Pierpont was gripping the back of the chair next to him, his knuckles white. "No," he said.

"Yes, Mister Pierpont, very much yes." Zara took a few more steps toward him until she was within striking distance, though she'd never needed weapons other than words. "So here's what you're going to do. You're going to sell the factory building to the town of Longbourne at a price *we* decide. I should warn you it's not going to be a price you like. You're going to ship those looms back down the mountain—and you'd better do it soon, because I don't think you want to spend the winter up here. We'll let you return the wool you bought at full price—*we* aren't criminals. And you're going to leave here and never come back."

"I think you're bluffing," Pierpont said.

"*This is no game,*" Zara said, her voice low and intense. "I don't bluff with people's lives. Take my offer, Mister Pierpont, or take your chances with the authorities. And thank heaven I gave you an offer at all."

A muscle in Pierpont's jaw twitched. In his eyes Zara saw fear and anger warring with each other. She stared at him with the expression that had won her so many Council battles. *No fear, no mercy, strike cleanly and strike fast.* Then he blinked, and looked away. "I'll need a few days to put my affairs in order," he said.

"You get two," Zara said. "But I think you'll find us all extremely cooperative. We wish you a speedy journey, you know."

Pierpont shouldered past her without another word. Zara didn't move until she heard the tavern door shut. Then she leaned against the nearest table and took a deep breath as the shouting and arguing and even congratulations began.

"Did he *poison* you?" Amelia demanded. "Agatha, you could have died!"

Not really. "He tried. I suppose it wasn't enough."

"I think it would take more than a little poison to kill you!"

That is so true it's almost funny. "Well, I'm glad it didn't work. And now he's gone. Maida?"

"Agatha," Maida said, "I have to talk to you."

"I know. You already washed the teapot."

Maida's mouth dropped open. "How did—but you were bluffing! You said—"

"A white lie in the service of something vital. And I was only partly bluffing. Chauncey is the slowest, laziest barman I've ever met. For all I knew, the teapot wasn't going to be washed until the supper rush."

"Even so—"

"It's over, Maida. And it all worked out fine. Now...I think I'm going home for a while."

Amelia walked her home. "I'm still stunned," she said. "I hope Pierpont doesn't try anything else."

"He's lost. He knows it. We're all safe." Zara was familiar with the look Pierpont had worn as he left. She'd seen it dozens of times on the faces of her enemies. The look of utter defeat. Not for the first time, the memory made her uncomfortable. Was she destined to become a woman like Rose Garrity, who took pleasure in tearing people down? Was it enough that everything she did was in the service of someone or something else and not to the glory of Zara North? *It has to be*, she told herself, and refused to think on it further.

Amelia left her at her back door, saying, "Knitting circle tomorrow night—and just think of what we'll have to talk about!" Zara smiled, but when her friend was gone she sat at the kitchen table and removed her boots heavily, not wanting to track wet dirt through her house. It was barely mid-afternoon and she was exhausted, but not sleepy. Maybe it was time for some knitting; she didn't have the energy to work the loom today. She padded up the stairs in her stocking feet and knocked on Sabrina's door before opening it. "What a story I have for you," she said.

Sabrina was sitting in the padded chair, her head bowed and her hands relaxed on its arm. One of her feet was splayed outward at an uncomfortable angle—or one which would have been uncomfortable for a living person. "Oh," Zara said. She knelt by the chair and took one of those hands in hers. "I'm sorry I wasn't here," she said softly. "But I'm glad to have known you, Sabrina Merriwether."

She knelt like that for a few minutes, thinking of Hank and Sabrina and her brother Anthony and Anthony's daughter Elspeth, thinking how, from her perspective, everyone died too young. Then she patted Sabrina's hand and rose. Someone would know how to care for Sabrina's body before they could bury it, and she needed to make sure Pierpont left, and it was down to her to make a memorial.

Easier if you're not attached to anything, she thought, but it was a fleeting thought and she didn't try to make it stay around. Sabrina had been right: *We live, and we love, and we mourn, and we rejoice,* and none of that was possible without roots that ran deep. Longbourne was her home now, for however long she could stay, and she would defend it against whatever threat came next.

EXILE OF THE CROWN PART FOUR: SUMMER, 952 Y.B.

*O*n hot days, with the air still as a hunter waiting for prey and the sun hammering down on the gravel road outside, the loom felt like an extension of her. Its treadles pumped in rhythm with her blood, the shuttle flew back and forth in time with her breath, the heddles made her tingle with their thin, high rattling. Days like this, Zara fell into a near-trance, her mind roaming free of the great room and the two apprentices working the spinning wheels, returning only when her legs and arm ached enough she couldn't ignore them. Or when the back door slammed, as it was prone to do lately no matter how careful you were.

"Mistress Weaver! You got a telecode!" Sarah Anderson said, running into the great room. Sarah was twelve and at a stage where anything new was exciting. Zara let the loom come to rest and held out her hand.

"Back to work, girls," she said, more sternly than she'd intended. Sarah was a hard worker, and Alys...well, Alys was a little too preoccupied with her looks, but she was skilled enough. Zara tore open the end of the sealed envelope and shook the telecoder form into her hand, unfolded it, and read:

AM SENDING WOMAN TO STAY WITH YOU NEEDS INTRO-

DUCTION TO LONGBOURNE. ONE OF MY SPECIAL RETAIN-
ERS. YOU WILL BE HER AUNT. EXPECT ARRIVAL FIVE DAYS.
JEFFREY

Her mouth fell open. That boy had the *nerve*...! She stood, extricated herself from the stool that had become entangled with her
skirt, and tore open the front door, which stuck from disuse. If Jeffrey
thought he could demand this of her—what was he thinking!—he
was going to be sorely disappointed. She might not be his Queen, but
she sure as hell was his elder and he had damn well better show her
respect.

She stormed off down the street, kicking up gravel the whole way
and ignoring the greetings of the friends she passed, stormed
through the door to the tavern wishing it were closed so she could
have the pleasure of slamming it open. That would relieve her
mood...somewhat.

"Get up, Abel," she said, grabbing Abel Roberts' shoulder. "We're
off down the mountain. Now."

Abel blinked at her, then picked up his oversized mug. "Can't do
it," he said. "Too late. Happen we'd be stuck down mountain
overnight."

"Then we'll stay overnight. I'll pay for your room. But we are
leavin' *now*."

Abel shook his head. "No, not even if y'shout at me as I know you
will. It ain't safe."

"Safe? You drive that road drunk as a brace of skunks!"

"Not in the dark. I be drunk most days, but never stupid, certain
sure."

"Agatha, he means it," Maida said from behind the bar. "You'll
have to wait."

"This can't wait!" Zara sank onto a bar stool and glared at Abel.
"Fine. But happen you're takin' me down tomorrow, not day after."

"I won't—"

"You will, Abel Roberts, or I'll make your life a misery as only
Agatha Weaver can."

Abel looked at her sideways. "You're a harpy, certain sure."

"And a harpy what gets her way. At dawn, Abel." She slid off the stool, declined the offer of beer though she felt she sorely needed it, and walked home, this time kicking the gravel on purpose even though her irritation was draining away. Jeffrey could at least have given more details. "Special retainer"...that meant an agent of the Crown. Why an agent of the Crown in Longbourne? Why *her*? Surely an agent was accustomed to making a place for herself without the help of an outsider. Damn that whelp of a nephew of hers. Nearly thirty years of ruling Tremontane and he thought that gave him the right to make demands of people. Hah. It probably did. She just didn't think she ought to be one of them.

She was ready before dawn the next morning, ready before Abel, though to his credit (or possibly his fear of her) he showed up, sober for once, in the wagon yard behind the general store and hitched up the horses without complaint.

It was a pleasant ride down the mountain, cool and shady, though the ride back in the heat of the afternoon would no doubt be uncomfortable. Zara sat clutching the splintery seat and looked out over the pass, where dark green pines grew on the nearly vertical cliff faces and golden aspens, their leaves like bright coins, shivered in the slight breeze. Somewhere in the distance she could hear the river chattering its way down from Mount Ehuren, probably icy even at this time of year.

She rarely went down mountain, instead sending her wares for Josiah Stakely at the Hitching Station to handle, and every time was a new wonder. She patted her pocket, felt the paper crackle, and summoned up outrage again. However beautiful this ride was, it wouldn't make her forget what she was there for.

She barely stopped to say hello to Josiah and his wife Joanna before striding up the street toward the telecoder office, not even seeing the beauties of Ellismere she passed. At the telecoder office, she snatched up a pencil and telecoder form and scrawled out a message:

YOU HAVE SOME NERVE. SEND SPECIAL RETAINER ELSE-WHERE AM NOT INTERESTED IN PROVIDING INTRODUC-

TION OR BEING AUNT. DRAG ME INTO YOUR POLITICS WILL YOU. NOT MY JOB ANYMORE.

She handed over her form and some money and then, as an afterthought, said, "Waiting for a reply." Jeffrey almost certainly wasn't going to let her have the last word.

She was right. Thirty minutes later the telecoder operator gave her a sheet of paper. NO OTHER CHOICE SORRY BUT TIME IS CRITICAL. YOU REALLY ARE HER AUNT NOT A LIE. JUST GIVE HER A ROOM AND AN EXCUSE SHE HAS NO EXPERIENCE OUTSIDE THE CAPITAL.

She stood in a corner of the busy room and re-read the message. Really her aunt? She reviewed her family tree. Great-aunt, more like. It wouldn't be Crown Princess Julia, and Jeffrey's other daughter Caitlin was too young. Sylvester's daughters lived in Magrette, far east of Ellismere, and couldn't be said to have no experience outside the capital. That left Elspeth's daughter Telaine.

Zara closed her eyes and cursed. The frivolous Princess Telaine North Hunter, belle of a thousand balls and the center of fashionable society from here to Ravensholm, vain, giddy, and spoiled. Why Jeffrey thought she was a good choice to be an agent was a mystery of the ages.

She took up a fresh form and wrote: YOU ARE OUT OF YOUR MIND. SHE MIGHT FIGURE IT OUT.

The reply, a few minutes later: CHANCE WE BOTH HAVE TO TAKE. THIS IS IMPORTANT OR I WOULDNT ASK.

She snorted at that. DIDNT NOTICE YOU ASKING.

ASKING NOW. PLEASE.

She scowled at the paper. It must be urgent, if he could ask her to risk having her identity revealed. Well, she'd do it. But she didn't have to like it. She wrote: YOU OWE ME.

The answer came back: I KEPT YOUR SECRET. WE ARE EVEN.

He thought this made them even? This was closer to blackmail. She folded her many telecodes into her pocket and went to find Abel, who was asleep on the bar but woke into as much alertness as he ever displayed.

On the ride back, she was grateful for Abel's characteristic silence. So. It was possible she was wrong about the Princess, however unlikely that was; Telaine North Hunter was famous for her wild exploits, and even if she was an agent she was still an entitled, wealthy young woman who had no experience with the kind of life people lived in Longbourne. The outhouse alone would be a shock.

But what made Zara angry was the idea of an agent of the Crown rooting around in *her* home, pretending to be someone she wasn't and dragging the good people of Longbourne into whatever ruse she concocted. Well, she had to let the girl live with her, but she didn't have to make it easy on her.

The corners of her mouth turned up, ever so slightly, in a smile.

THE DANCE

(*Agent of the Crown,* Fall 952)

I have a very strong memory of writing the first three paragraphs of this story, but none of why I wanted to write it. Possibly it's that Ben went through a lot of changes over the twenty-plus years I carried the novel inside me, and I wanted to finally pin him down.

HE SCRUBBED HIS HANDS, TAKING HIS TIME THOUGH HE WAS PROBABLY already late. The pale suds turned black from the coal dust that filled the creases of his palms and was ingrained in his cuticles and under his nails. She wouldn't judge him for it, it wasn't in her nature, but he wanted tonight to be perfect. He couldn't do anything about the rough calluses on his hands, but he could make them clean enough not to feel embarrassed when he asked her to dance. Assuming he could summon the nerve.

He rinsed a final time and dried his hands, then went back into the bedroom to change. He wished he dared wear his best suit, but people would notice and wonder about it, maybe tease him for trying to outshine the groom, and anyway she was used to the men in the capital and his best probably looked dowdy by comparison. So he put on a clean shirt and trousers, slid his feet into shoes rather than his work boots, and combed his hair. He examined himself in the mirror, which took some doing because it was too small to show his whole body at once, slid his hand over his face to make sure he hadn't missed any spots shaving.

He paused with his hand still on his chin and looked into his own eyes. What did she think, when she looked at him? Did she guess how he felt about her? Probably not, because she treated him with casual friendliness, none of the flirtation she showed Jack and Liam and a handful of other men who all hovered around her like moths courting a lantern. Tonight he was going to change all that.

He was terrified.

He'd lost his heart to her the day she came to town. Standing there facing down Irv Tanner's gang with not a hint of fear, then turning to look at him with those hazel eyes that had such depth to them he'd felt for a moment that he was drowning. He'd barely been able to speak to her, even though all he said was directions to Mistress Weaver's home. Why he'd gone there that evening, he had no idea—or, rather, he knew exactly why he'd gone, he wanted to see her again; it was how he'd gotten up the nerve to do so that was a mystery.

Then he'd started watching for her, longing to see her coming down the road to pass the smithy with that confident stride as if she were setting out to conquer the world. He'd never known anyone so fearless, and it captivated him even as it worried him that she didn't take him seriously about the danger Archie Morgan was to her. If he had the right to protect her...but she wasn't the sort of woman who needed a lot of protecting, was she? Which made the idea all the more compelling. The thought of being the man someone like her might turn to in time of need—just thinking about it made his heart beat faster. *Tonight. Anything could happen.*

He turned away from the mirror, drew in a deep breath, and rubbed his palms on his trousers, though they weren't sweaty. The feel of the fine fabric against his hands calmed him. *You're the equal of any man in Longbourne*, he told himself, *and you just need to show her that*. Of course there was no guarantee she'd return his affection, but if he never said anything, he'd never know if she could. And that was the problem: he never knew what to say to her, didn't know how to court a woman with fancy words or a laughing smile. But tonight he finally had the chance to court her his way. Then it was up to her.

It looked like most of Longbourne was already down at the maypole; he'd taken far too long getting ready. But they weren't likely to start without him. He hurried through the woods anyway, arriving just as Trey and Blythe were approaching from a different direction.

"Ben," Blythe said, "do you think it's time?"

"Looks like near everyone's here," he said.

"Then will you start things off?" she said, grasping Trey's arm with her free hand. Trey looked down at her with such love in his eyes that Ben felt a little embarrassed at having seen it.

"Give me a minute," he said, and moved off into the crowd. Some of them had begun to turn and whisper that the bride and groom were there, but Ben took a little time to find what he judged was the center of the crowd. Then he tilted his head back and sent up a pure, high note that echoed through the woods before drifting away over the lake. Another voice joined his, then another, and soon the entire crowd had added their voices to the chord.

Ben shivered, though he didn't let it touch his voice and ruin the effect. He knew where he was when he was singing, even if it was just tuning like this. Years of training, of practicing—his mother had been furious when he'd made it clear he intended to be a blacksmith. She'd only agreed to apprentice him because his uncle had insisted he have a job that would support him if the singing didn't work out. She'd thought it was a betrayal of everything she'd sacrificed to get him the best instructors, especially when his voice changed and the sweet boy's soprano had turned into a magnificent tenor that could command an audience. Ben had never wanted to sing for anyone but himself—and now, for her.

He released the note—only fifteen seconds, he could sustain it for longer if he had to, but there was no call for opera here in the mountains—and listened with pleasure as the chord died away. He moved to the side with the rest of the witnesses and was barely able, from his position, to see Trey and Blythe walking down the aisle formed by the division of the crowd. He didn't really mind. It was her he wanted to see, but the crowd was packed tightly enough that he couldn't see more than a few paces away. He could hear Mister Bradford speaking the words of the marriage oath and wondered what she made of it all. Were marriage ceremonies the same in Aurilien? Did she feel like a stranger, here in Longbourne, despite the many friends she'd made?

His nervousness was returning. How would she react to his offering? Maybe he was being stupid. They were friends, after all; maybe he should leave it at that. Suppose she was embarrassed, or disdainful—no, that wasn't in her character either. But there were so many ways this could go wrong. *No,* he told himself, *you're not a coward, even if you can't bring yourself to talk to her, and this might be the only chance you get. And suppose she can someday feel for you what you feel for her? It's worth the risk.*

The crowd cheered, startling him; he'd been so preoccupied he hadn't heard the last words of the ceremony. People surged forward to congratulate the bride and groom, but Ben stayed put, looking around for a glimpse of her. She had to be here somewhere.

Then he saw her, and his breath caught. She stood in profile to him, unsmiling, her head tilted to listen to something Mistress Weaver was saying. Her hair, which she always wore braided, tonight fell in loose waves nearly to her waist, light against the dark green of her dress. *Lainie,* he thought—he dared call her that only in the privacy of his thoughts. She was so beautiful, moved with such grace, that he almost changed his mind right there. But he wasn't a coward, and tonight he'd tell her how he felt as only he could.

She vanished into the crowd, and he began moving forward, though he knew he likely wouldn't see her again until the crowd thinned out a bit. So he went to congratulate Trey and Blythe, who looked radiantly happy, then made his way to the review stand and sat down, waiting for the rest of his sextet to appear. They were good singers, maybe not his caliber, but able to blend well and all of them loving music as much as he did, which mattered more than skill to him.

"You sure you're up for this? That note sounded a little flat," Ed said, taking a seat next to Ben.

"You only think that because you're tone deaf," Ben retorted with a grin.

"Both of you wish you had my pipes," said Mickey. He had a deep bass voice that could rumble as low as Ben's could soar high. "Thin and pissy, that's how you sound."

"Sounds like a challenge," Ben said. "Who can drown out the other."

"Not now, boys," said Dave, the other baritone. "Time enough for that at Wintersmeet. Tonight's for the newlyweds."

And for me, Ben thought.

"Yes, ma," said Ed, mock-scowling.

Ben stood. "There's Lewis and Barnabas," he said. "Happen we should warm up a little." He was already warmed up, but nerves were making his voice shaky. He swallowed and scanned the crowd. There she was, sitting off to one side with Maida Handly and Jack Taylor. She looked lost. He caught her eye briefly and passed on. He'd have her attention soon enough, if he did this right.

"Ready," Dave said. "What'll it be, fellows?"

Ben swallowed again. "It's a wedding," he said casually. "Let's do 'Merry Be.'"

"Good enough for starters," Ed agreed.

The six men arranged themselves on the stand, Ben a step above the rest. This was it. He looked back at her, caught her eye. She smiled a little, and he felt his heart beat faster. He thought she looked sad—why sad at a wedding? *Let's see if we can change that.*

He lifted his head and let out the clear, pure note that the others harmonized around, his eyes never leaving hers. She sat up straighter, clearly surprised, and he smiled a little, opened his mouth wider, and let the words and the melody flow out of him in the effortless way that only came from hours of dedicated practice.

It was a song he knew well, so he barely had to pay attention to the words. *Hear me*, he thought, willing her to understand. *Hear what I'm saying. I want you, Lainie. I want your eyes to look at me with love. I want to take your hand in mine and walk with you. I want to put my arms around you and let your head rest on my shoulder. I want to kiss those lips that smile so easily. I love you. Hear me.*

He knew the moment she realized he was singing for her alone. Her mouth fell open a bit, her eyes went wide, and she glanced to either side as if wondering whether he really did mean her. Then her mouth closed, and she leaned forward to rest her arms on the table, as intent on him as he was on her. The stunned look never left her face. He poured his whole heart into his song, wondering briefly if anyone else realized what was happening, that he was courting her under everyone's eyes, and didn't care if they did.

The song came to an end. He held her eyes for a few seconds longer. *Hear me.* Then he turned away and said, "Wonder if we've made any more matches with that song."

The other men laughed. "Could give a man ideas, certain sure," Dave rumbled.

"Well, let's do 'Lightly Falls the Rain' next and let 'em cool down a bit," Ed said. "And I think Mary and Elana want a turn."

"Sounds good," Ben said, and shook his hands out. He hadn't realized he'd had them clenched the whole time. He didn't look at her again. He'd declared himself; now to give her time to think about it, decide what she'd do. And then he'd ask her to dance.

He sang a few more songs, then yielded the stand to the players and went to get something to eat. The chicken looked good but greasy; not a good choice for a man who intended to court a woman. He settled on ham and took his plate to the far side of the clearing from her. She was practicing a dance with Liam and doing it so awkwardly his heart nearly burst from his chest with love. *Next dance*, he promised himself, *or the next one. Soon.*

But dance after dance passed, and she never was without a partner, and the longer he waited the harder it was for him to rise from his seat and approach her. He started to feel anxious, then despairing. All that effort, and he couldn't bring himself to just talk to her.

They were friends, she wouldn't be cruel to him, there was no reason he shouldn't approach her. *Later, when she runs out of partners*, he told himself, but he knew his justifications were going to lose him what he wanted most.

Finally, he saw her laughingly turn down a partner and return to a seat set somewhat back from where the dancers spun and promenaded, and found himself on his feet and circling the clearing before his brain could stop him. As he neared her, he saw that she had her eyes closed and was rubbing one bare foot, her shoe kicked off on the ground in front of her. "Will you dance with me?" he said, and winced at how abrupt it sounded.

Her eyes flew open and she jumped a little. "The next dance hasn't started yet," she said. She didn't look embarrassed, or shy, and he realized he hadn't thought about what to say next.

"Well, seeing as how you were so popular," he said, "I thought I should ask before someone else swooped down on you."

She laughed, and it made his heart once again speed up. "It was a little like being dived on by predatory birds," she said, then looked away. "I didn't realize how many friends I had," she added, looking back at him, and there was something in her eyes he didn't know how to answer.

The music changed, and Ben said, "Do you know this dance?"

She shook her head, hesitated, then extended her hand to him. "Teach me?"

She had long, elegant fingers, a craftswoman's hands, and for half a second he considered not taking her hand in his rough one. Then his fingers closed around hers, and she smiled, and he nearly forgot why he was there, because he was holding her hand and she was smiling at him and he wanted that moment to go on forever.

He led her back a ways and arranged her arms, took her hands in his, and guided her through the steps. It was clear from the start that she was an experienced dancer, even if she'd never danced this one before; she picked up the steps immediately, and he led her to join the other dancers. She stumbled once or twice, and kept looking at her feet, and he couldn't understand why because she certainly knew what she was doing, and it wasn't until the dance was nearly over that she looked at him and he realized she was blushing. Blushing as if she were as sensitive to his nearness as he was to hers.

His hand tightened on hers as the music came to an end, and they stopped in the middle of the clearing, under the tent of lights she'd invented, and just gazed at each other. She took a step closer, her lips parting to say something, and Blythe Bradford called out, "Teach us one of your dances, Lainie!"

She blinked and stepped away from him, but didn't let go of his hand. "One of my dances?" she said.

"A dance from the city!" Blythe called out, laughing. "I want my wedding to be on the front edge of fashion!"

She looked at him as if undecided. Then she said, "Will you dance with me again?"

Ben nodded. He would dance with her forever if she'd let him.

She smiled, and ran off to talk to the players, then came back and said loudly, "It's a simple one-two-three beat. Men lead, ladies follow. Watch us." With no hesitation, she took Ben's hand in hers and with her other hand drew his free arm around her waist. She put her hand on his shoulder and raised their clasped hands high. "Just follow me for a bit, and you'll get it. It's not hard." The music began, and she drew him into the dance, just the two of them in the center of the clearing. Ben felt his face begin to flush. He was never comfortable being the center of attention, even when he was singing, and all of them watching him dance with her...

Then he registered how close she was, how her hair smelled clean and bright like fresh spring air, felt her hand on his shoulder and his arm around her waist, and he barely realized when she handed off the lead to him. She was looking at him, wordless, and he tightened his grip around her waist and felt her step closer to him. All around them, other couples joined in, but he was only aware of them dimly, as vague shapes in some distant dream realm. She was in his arms, she was looking at him as if she wanted to ask him something, and suddenly he was overwhelmed by it all, as if he'd been offered his heart's desire and was afraid to accept it. It seemed too good to be real.

The music stopped, and they just stood there together for a moment. Then she released his hand, and he stepped away from her. He'd gotten what he wanted and he didn't know what to do with it. He bobbed his head to her and walked away, through the crowd and into the woods, and when he was far enough away that the music and the laughter were too faint to be distinguishable as anything but a hum, he stopped and leaned against the nearest tree. He wanted to kick himself. Why had he just walked away from her? That look in her eyes...she knew how he felt, and it looked as if she was trying to decide how she felt about him. And he'd just walked away like a fool. Who knew what she thought now? That he was toying with her? That it was all a mistake?

He groaned and banged his head gently against the tree trunk, then walked the rest of the way to Longbourne. Safely in his house, he sat on the couch and cursed himself. He would never have another chance with her. He needed to go back and explain, not that he understood himself. He needed to just say it to her, to have the courage for once to speak to her instead of standing there like a moon-witted fool.

He got as far as the edge of the woods before his courage failed him. People were starting to leave the clearing, the music had stopped, and it was too late; the shivaree was over. Too late. He turned to walk away, once again cursing himself. But when he got to his back door, it occurred to him that she might still be there. She'd have to take down the tent of lights, and that would take a while. *No, you've lost your chance,* he told himself, *leave it alone.* He remembered how it had felt to dance with her, his arm around her waist and her hand in his, and shivered. It wasn't too late. He had one more chance.

He went quickly through the woods and found the clearing empty of tables and chairs and people. Empty of all but one person, that is. She was reaching up to tug at the strands of light and winding them onto a spool. She was so graceful, and so beautiful, and before he could stop himself he had crossed the clearing and was saying, "Happen you could use some help with that."

She squeaked and dropped the spool. "I didn't hear you coming," she said.

"Sorry."

She picked up the spool. "You can help by pulling those down."

He started tugging at the strands; they came down easily, and she wound them onto her spool until it looked like a flycatcher with a hundred fireflies stuck to it. "That's the last of it," he eventually said, handing her the loose end. "Let me carry that for you."

She looked down at it, then handed it over, and the two of them headed back toward town. Ben's heart was pounding again. "What happens to it now?" he said, trying to think of something more meaningful to say.

"I'll take out the motive forces and stow the whole thing in Aunt Weaver's store room," she said.

"Sounds like a lot of work." The back of her hand brushed against his, they were that close.

"Just tedious."

There it was again, that soft, almost imperceptible touch. "I'd help if I could," he said, and reached out to take her hand in his. For a moment, it hung there, unresisting, and he was sure he'd made a huge mistake. Then her fingers twined themselves with his, and she squeezed his hand just a little, and he thought he might fly away, carrying her with him.

They walked in silence, Ben afraid to break whatever it was between them by speaking, but when they reached the outskirts of Longbourne, she said, "I don't understand."

He smiled in the darkness. "Wasted a lot of effort tonight if that's so."

"I mean, I don't—I didn't even know you were interested in me."

"Never knew what to say." He gripped her hand a little tighter. "And you always had so many other men after you."

He heard her take a quick breath. "They weren't...it didn't mean anything, just...it was just being friendly. Having fun."

The happiness he was floating on burned a little brighter. She wasn't attached to any of them. "I couldn't compete with them on their ground," he said. "So I figured out a way to compete on mine."

He turned his head to look at her and found her smiling at him. "It worked," she said, and a smile spread across his lips, a real smile, not the fleeting half-smiles that were all he'd ever managed in her presence before.

They passed between Mistress Weaver's sheds and came to the back door of the house. She turned to face him and held out her hand for the spool. They would say goodnight, and maybe in the morning all this would be like a dream, and she wouldn't look at him this way ever again. The thought was unbearable. So he put the spool on the ground behind him, and said, "Just one thing, Miss Bricker. I'd like to kiss you, if you don't mind."

Her eyes were dark smudges in the light of the half-moon. She nodded, silently, and Ben stepped forward and brushed his lips against hers. It was extraordinary, sweet and tender and the most beautiful feeling he'd ever had, and he wished he dared kiss her again, but maybe this one kiss was all he needed.

He took a step back, and she made a noise that sounded like a protest, put her arms around his neck, and drew him close to kiss him again. It startled him so much that he froze, briefly, then he came to his senses and put his arms around her waist and kissed her as he'd never kissed anyone in his life. She was warm and alive in his arms, her body pressed against his, responding to his kiss with a passion that set him afire with longing. Everything else fell away, the moon and the sheds and the weeds dying at the edge of the yard; his whole world was narrowed down to this beautiful woman who was kissing him as if nothing else mattered.

Some unspoken signal made them separate, and she took half a step away from him, not breaking the circle of his arms, and looked at him with an expression unreadable in the low light. He raised his hand and caressed her cheek. "You are so beautiful," he whispered. "Miss Bricker—"

She smiled, and put her finger to his lips to stop his words. "After

351

that," she said in amusement, "I think you are allowed to call me Lainie."

It was so much what he'd always dreamed of that at first he couldn't speak, just smile at her like a lovesick fool. Which he was. "Lainie," he said, and her own smile broadened. "Lainie, will you walk out with me tomorrow?"

She nodded, still smiling, and she was so beautiful he had to kiss her just once more. Her lips tasted sweet, like apples. "Tomorrow, then," he said, stepping backward and nearly tripping over the forgotten spool. He picked it up and handed it to her, then walked away, quickly, afraid if he stayed any longer they'd spend the rest of the night kissing. Not that that would be a bad thing. He glanced back just once to see her still standing there, holding the firefly spool, and then he'd turned the corner and was walking away down the street, barely able to keep from skipping and jumping like an ecstatic child.

Safely in his home, he went into his bedroom without turning on the lamp and threw himself face-first onto the bed. Then he rolled onto his back and began to laugh. He'd kissed Lainie Bricker. She'd kissed him back. He felt her lips on his in memory and laughed again with joy. The love of his life was walking out with him tomorrow. And what a tomorrow it would be.

BEN: INTRODUCTION

(*Agent of the Crown*, Spring/Summer 953 Y.B.)

The following bonus scenes were written well after the first three *Crown of Tremontane* books were complete, but before Agent of the Crown *went through its fourth and final revision. The ending of the scene "The Truth," in which Ben and Telaine are reconciled, contains the original speechifying from version three that was revised out for the final version. I think it's a lot more awkward than what I eventually came up with, though some lines remain the same (and some have been in there since version one).*

BEN: REVELATION

*I*t couldn't be happening. He screamed again and strained against Liam's hands holding him back. One of the soldiers tied Lainie's hands behind her back and stuffed a handkerchief in her mouth. "No!" he shouted hoarsely, and felt tears spring to his eyes as the captain kicked her legs out from under her and dragged her to the gazebo.

"There's nothing you can do," Liam said in a low voice that was choked with anger. "He'll just kill you too."

Ben sucked in a harsh, sobbing breath. The Baron would murder her while he watched helplessly. There had to be something he could do. Lainie knelt up and glared at the Baron as he approached her. Of course she wasn't afraid. Not even facing death. The Baron lowered his pistol and pointed it at her head; she continued to stare him down. Ben sobbed, and closed his eyes. He couldn't watch her die.

There was the shot. He cried out again, felt Liam release him. "Ben!" he said, and Ben opened his eyes to see the Baron sprawled on the ground, Lainie wriggling near him, and Jack and Liam rushing to take the gun and subdue the Baron. Ben ran to her side, yanked the handkerchief from her mouth and untied her with shaking hands. She was alive, the shot had miraculously missed, and he pulled her into his arms and felt her cling to him, breathing heavily. He stroked her hair and tried to calm his own breathing.

"What is going on here?" a woman said, and Lainie turned in his arms to look behind them. He kept a grip on her shoulders loosely, reluctant to let her go, and saw a line of soldiers, far more professional-looking than the Thorsten men, riding up the street toward them. Their leader held a pistol as if she'd just shot into the air; her mouth was compressed and her brow furrowed.

The Baron shoved Liam away and took a few steps toward her. "Major, I am Baron Steepridge, and these people are rebelling against my rule. You can see my men and I are hopelessly outnumbered. These four—" he pointed at Jack and Liam, Lainie and Ben—"are the ringleaders. I demand that you take them into custody."

"He was going to murder an innocent person!" Liam exclaimed.

"Hardly innocent. A murderer," the Baron said, pointing at Morgan's body with the knife still sticking out of his eye socket.

"It was in self-defense!" Ben shouted, and the major looked briefly in his direction, then back at the Baron.

"I can see this is going to take a while to sort out," she said. "I'll have to ask everyone involved to come with me to the fort."

Lainie drew in a breath and moved a little under his hands, as if she wanted to say something. Then she gasped, and said, under her breath, "Jeffy."

"What?" Ben said.

From far down the line of horses, a soldier said, "Telaine? *Telaine!*" and leaped from his horse to run toward them.

"Your Highness! Lieutenant North! Return to your position!" the major demanded, but the young man ignored her. He shoved Ben so he fell to the ground.

"Get your hands off my cousin," he said angrily. "Telaine, what are you doing here? And dressed like a peasant?"

"Cousin? Telaine?" Ben said. He looked up at Lainie, who had her eyes on the lieutenant.

"What are you saying, lieutenant?" the major said, turning her horse and coming toward them.

"Major, I insist you take these four into custody," the Baron said.

"We thought you were recovering from lung fever," the lieutenant said. "Julia's been sick with worry, Telaine, how could you do this to her?"

Telaine. Julia. The names were familiar. Lainie still wasn't looking at him. "Lainie, what's he talking about?" he asked, hoping she would say something, anything that would cut through the confusion.

"Milord Baron, who killed this man?" the major said, looking down at the Baron where he stood, legs akimbo, coat open a little over his paunch and his elegant frock coat.

Lainie finally looked down at him, and the look of anguish on her face made his throat tighten. "I'm sorry," she said.

"That woman—" the Baron began.

Lainie took a few steps away from Ben, into an open space, and shouted, "Major!" The major and the Baron, who'd fallen silent, turned to look at her. "Major," Lainie went on, "my name is Telaine North Hunter...and I am an agent of the Crown."

It was like she'd started speaking Veriboldan. He didn't understand. Telaine North Hunter was a Princess of Tremontane and nobody who would be in Longbourne. *Telaine. Lainie. Telaine.* She was speaking again, but he couldn't hear her words because of the roaring in his ears. She looked exactly the same, but she was a stranger. A Princess. And an agent of the Crown. She'd lied to him from the moment they met.

He could hear her now, denouncing the Baron—a Ruskalder invasion? That's what she was here to discover? She'd had to— He swallowed hard against his throat tightening again. Of course. She couldn't say who she was because that would draw too much attention. She had to behave like an ordinary person. Cook her own food. Build Devices. Wear plain clothes. Use common language.

Find someone to fall in love with her.

He wanted to be sick. She'd used him to make the Baron trust her, keep him from noticing her. All those walks by the lake, evenings at the tavern, nights spent sitting close together in front of the fire—all ploys to make herself just another commoner. Every embrace, every kiss had been a lie. Had she known he loved her, all along, and pretended otherwise to draw him in? Those tears the night she'd claimed she loved him—manufactured to keep him from breaking free of her spell?

He pushed himself to his feet, feeling like an old man, and realized half the village was staring at him. He flushed. *That's right,* he thought, *I'm a fool. But you were fooled every bit as much as I was.* She was an agent; they were supposed to be good at making people see what they wanted them to see.

He reached into his pocket and fingered the smooth surface of the ring he'd made her. Her worst lie of all, letting him believe she wanted to make a life with him. Her uncle had to approve all the marriages—of course *that* was true, King Jeffrey couldn't let just anyone marry into the family. Not that she'd had any intention of marrying him; that was just another ploy to string him along. Couldn't have him realizing the truth and breaking it off.

"It's not enough," Lainie said, and suddenly their eyes met, and he went stiff with anger. A look of fear crossed her face. "Ben," she said.

"You showed us what you wanted us to see," he said. His voice sounded strange, empty and hollow like the gash in the oak tree he'd thought was their own special place. She must have laughed herself sick when he'd taken her there, the Princess who was used to ballrooms and theaters and glittering dresses.

She shook her head. "No, that wasn't—"

"You just said it," he said, cutting across her words. "You needed to make the Baron believe you were just an ordinary person, didn't you?"

"Yes, but—"

"You lied about who you were. You lied about why you were here."

"I never lied about—"

His voice grew hoarse. "Must've been your lucky day, finding a fool who believed you so completely that he'd love your false self. No better way to fit in than that."

She shook her head. Her face was as expressionless as his surely was. "That wasn't how it went."

His eyes ached with unshed tears. "That sounds like just another lie," he said. "We deserve everything you ever did to us for being such fools." He turned and walked away, pushing past that circle of villagers who were all looking at him with such pity he thought it might burn him down to the bone.

Once inside his house, he just stood there, unable to move, barely able to think. He looked over at the couch. She'd really had him that night, used her body to make sure he'd stay attached to her. He'd wanted her so desperately, her soft skin and her smile and those eyes —he turned away from the couch and yanked out the kitchen chair, sat down at the table, covered his face with his hands and wept. He'd fallen in love with a fantasy, a dream-woman manufactured for the sake of an agent's cover identity. He was the biggest fool in the history of Tremontane.

Finally, he wiped his eyes and took a deep breath. Enough self-pity. What had they said about a Ruskalder invasion? He'd barely heard Lainie—the Princess—say something about how the Ruskalder would reach the fort that night. The fort, and then Long-bourne. Well, he could do something about that.

He went into the forge and hefted his biggest sledgehammer. It wasn't anything he used in the forge and he couldn't remember what it was there for; it might well have been there before he came to Longbourne. It was as good a weapon as any, and it made him feel strong to have it in his hands, strong and capable and nobody's fool. He headed back toward the crowd, toward the major, and the villagers parted for him as if honoring his pain. It made him burn with humiliation. "Happen you could use a few more hands at the fort," he said to the major. "I'm with you."

"So am I," Liam said, then other voices joined in, and the major surveyed the crowd appraisingly.

"No," the Princess said, "no, you can't, you're not fighters, you'll just get yourselves killed."

He looked at her. She had the damned nerve to look as if she cared what happened to them. It made him furious, with her, with himself, with the Ruskalder. "Happen you don't get a say in this," he said, coldly, putting a deadly edge on his words. "Go back where you came from. You're not one of us."

She flinched as if he'd hit her. The pain in her eyes satisfied him with a wicked pleasure. It wasn't enough to make up for what she'd done to him, but it was something. He turned away from her and went to stand by Liam, who said, "Ben," then fell silent. Heaven bless him for knowing not to say anything.

BEN: THE TRUTH

*H*e hurt everywhere, sharp pain in his leg like a hot knife trying to cut it off, dull aches in his chest and arms as if he'd been working the bellows for twenty-four hours without a rest. He dragged his eyelids open and blinked at a ceiling far more distant than his own. The bed felt wrong, too, and the cold air smelled tart and bitter, the smell of an astringent liquid mixed with that of blood. He tried to sit up, and the pain in his leg spiked so hard it made his vision go black for a minute. He lay back, panting as if he'd run the length of Longbourne without stopping, and tried to remember what had brought him here. The wall, the siege towers, the—

Memory returned. The Ruskalder pouring over the walls, the screams, Lieutenant North laying about him with his sword and him smashing skulls and breaking bones with the hammer. How stupid he was to go to war forgetting that the point of it was to kill the other fellow before he killed you. He'd succeeded at that, anyway. He reached down to feel his leg, see if he could figure out why it hurt, and found a huge bandage wrapped around his thigh. *That* he didn't remember. Touching it made his leg twinge, so he stopped doing that and clasped his hands across his stomach. "Hello," he called out, "is anyone there? Anyone?"

Footsteps, crossing a wooden floor, then, "I was wondering when you'd wake up." Tabitha Green, Longbourne's physician. "How you feeling, Ben?"

"Like I went to war. What's wrong with my leg?"

"Nothing, 'cept you nearly lost it," Tabitha said. "Some Ruskalder bastard tried to take it off at the hip. Major Anselm's healer did what he could, but it's still going to take some weeks to heal fully. No need to worry."

"I wasn't," Ben lied. "Besides, you patched me up, so I'll do all right."

"Flatterer," the doctor said, and patted his cheek maternally. She treated everyone as if they were her children, her own brood having grown up and left Longbourne years ago.

"Where is this?" Ben said. He didn't try to sit up again.

"The old factory. We brought all the serious cases here. Easier for me to tend 'em than going around to houses."

"Were there a lot?"

The doctor's face went grim. "Twenty-five deaths. Maybe forty wounded as seriously as you. A handful of lesser injuries."

"Who died?"

"Ben, that's a long list, and—"

"Those are friends, Tabitha. Please."

The doctor sighed. "The Major wrote it all out to go to the capital, had 'em make us a copy. I'll bring it to you later." She patted his cheek again. "You're alive, and so are a lot of people. And we kept the Ruskalder from overrunning the fort, so we're all heroes. Much good that does the dead." She hesitated, then reached into her pocket, saying, "This was in your trousers when they cut them off you. Not sure you still want it, but I thought...I don't know what I thought. Here."

She held out something small. Lainie's ring.

Ben took it from her and gripped it tightly, unable to meet the doctor's eye. Tabitha withdrew without another word.

When she was gone, Ben stared at the ceiling and wondered whose names were on that list. Jack? Liam? Lainie—

He'd almost forgotten, in the noise and terror of battle, what fueled the rage that drove the sledgehammer. The Princess who'd used him and made a fool of him, gone back to the capital now. Maybe someday it wouldn't hurt so much. He clenched the delicate gold band in his fist. Why the hell he was still carrying it, he didn't know, but he'd put his whole heart into it and he couldn't bear to throw it away. He'd have to melt it down, turn it into something useful, like a thimble. Maybe Eleanor would want it.

"You're awake," Jack said. He dragged something across the floor, a chair or a box or something out of Ben's line of vision, and sat beside him. "I plan on calling you Gimpy from now on. Heard you were something to watch, up on that wall."

"I don't remember most of it."

"You must've killed eight or nine Ruskalder in that last push, before you were wounded. Saved that lieutenant's life, for one. Then he saved yours, stopped the bleeding long enough for the healer to get to you."

"I guess I'll have to thank him," Ben said, then remembered who they were talking about. Lieutenant North. Prince Jeffrey North. The Princess's cousin. He hoped he never saw the man again.

"Guess so," Jack said. He fell silent.

"What?" Ben said.

"They tell you...Ben, Liam's dead."

Ben's heart thumped once, hard, and he drew in a breath. "I didn't know," he said. "Who else?"

"You sure you're well enough for this?"

"Might drive me crazy wondering. Tell me."

Jack sighed. "Liam. Trey. Ed Decker, Merisa Stone, Gavin Treller, Annabella White. A lot of others."

The ache in his chest redoubled, and he felt tears come to his eyes. So many friends. "Tabitha said twenty-five. Jack, is Eleanor all right?"

"She collapsed when they told her the news. Blythe...she looks like she was shot and her body just hasn't gotten the message yet.

They're having to remind her she's got the baby to worry about, has to take care of herself."

"But Isabel's fine."

"Not even a scratch, but her best friend is dead and she's convinced it should've been her. I'll bring her to see you. She could stand to have another friend to talk to."

"What about Alys?"

Jack shrugged. "Fine, as far as I know. We're not courting anymore. I didn't realize how shallow she was until after the battle she started complaining about how the healer hadn't fixed her up, like she didn't even realize how many people were still dying. It felt like an insult to them." He grinned, regaining some of his good cheer. "Plenty of other girls in the world, right?"

"Guess so," Ben said. As if he wanted other girls. He wanted the woman he'd fallen in love with. The one who didn't exist.

Jack didn't notice Ben's sudden silence. "I promised Ma I'd be home by five," he said, pulling out his watch. "War's over, but she worries about me still." He checked the time, hesitated, then pushed the button at the bottom. And there was her voice, declaring *Jack Taylor is a handsome devil*. It felt like being knifed through the heart.

Jack looked down at him, flushed, and shoved the watch deep into his trouser pocket. "Sorry, Ben, I didn't think," he said. He stood up, shoving the chair or box or whatever away with a scraping sound, then said, "But..."

"What?" Ben said.

Jack shrugged and wouldn't meet his eyes. "Whatever else was true or false, she *was* a Deviser," he said. "You can't fake skills like that." His footsteps echoed off the high ceiling as he walked away.

Can't fake skills like that. Ben closed his eyes. Maybe that was true, but it didn't make her any less a liar. She'd still used him for the sake of her mission. He listened for the sounds of people breathing, wondering how many other seriously injured people there still were in the old factory. Nothing. Maybe they'd isolated him from the others out of pity; maybe they cared just enough not to want him to hear them laughing at the fool who thought he was getting married.

He shifted his weight a little and subsided when pain stabbed through his thigh. He wanted to be alone anyway. Easier than trying to make conversation about dead men and dead loves.

THE NEXT DAY TABITHA HELPED HIM SIT UP AND RELIEVE HIMSELF INTO an old chamber pot, then eat something soft and mushy. When he complained, Tabitha said, "Prove to me you can keep that down, and I'll make you a steak myself."

"Your cooking's terrible," Ben pointed out. "That's not a reward. That's a threat."

"Then I'll have someone else make you a steak. Just be patient. You'll be back to real food tomorrow."

Ben spooned up the gluey mess and made himself eat it. He was hungry enough it almost seemed appetizing. He finished most of it before his stomach told him it was full, then set the bowl on the floor awkwardly, trying not to overbalance and fall out of the bed.

"Garrett," someone said, and he wobbled and was saved from falling by a hand on his arm, pulling him up. "Sorry," the voice said, and Ben looked up to see Lieutenant North next to his bed. He jerked his arm away, not caring that it was rude, but the lieutenant didn't seem offended. His left arm was in a sling, and his uniform wasn't clean, but otherwise he looked completely healthy.

"I'm heading out," he said, "going back to Aurilien as part of the Baron's escort. I just wanted..."

Ben clenched his jaw and stared straight ahead. He didn't need this idiot lieutenant trying to...whatever it was he wanted from Ben.

"I wanted to thank you for saving my life," Lieutenant North said, and held out his right hand. Ben looked at it, then up at the lieutenant, and made no move to clasp it. The lieutenant withdrew his hand. Ben felt instantly guilty, but not enough to apologize.

"You saved my life, so I think we're even," he said instead. *Now go away and never come back.*

"Even so," Lieutenant North said. "Um."

Why was he still standing there? Ben went back to staring at the far wall. Maybe the man would go away if Ben refused to acknowledge him.

"I didn't know Telaine was a spy," Lieutenant North blurted out, and Ben wished he could leap from the bed and strangle him. As if he wanted to talk about her at all. "She's sort of frivolous, you know? Loves parties and dancing and she's always got a dozen men —anyway, I couldn't believe it when I saw her here, dressed like that—it's just not her. Or maybe it's just that I never knew her. But—"

"You going somewhere with this?" Ben said.

The lieutenant cleared his throat, and Ben realized he was talking to the man who was second in line for the Crown of Tremontane, and he had to stifle an urge to laugh at himself. He didn't feel awkward or self-conscious, talking to royalty, but then he'd gotten used to it all those weeks, hadn't he? Even if he hadn't known who she was.

"Lainie's a good person, Garrett," the lieutenant finally said, "even if she is a little giddy. I grew up with her, and I trust her, and I love her. I don't know what she did that's made you so angry, but I think you were friends, and I wish you could find a way to forgive her."

It was too much to bear. "Get out," Ben snarled. "She's not my friend. She played a part every minute she was here, lied to every one of us, and now she's gone and I want you gone too. There's nothing you can say to change what's happened."

Lieutenant North took half a step back as if Ben's words had physically pushed him away. "I'm sorry," he said. "Thanks again." Then he turned and left.

Ben leaned back and closed his eyes. He was royalty, but he was an idiot. As if he knew anything about it. As if he could make anything better by babbling about how the frivolous Princess wasn't so bad. No wonder she'd been so good at stringing him along. She probably had years of practice flirting with the nobles of Tremontane. One stupid commoner from the raw frontier must have seemed like nothing. A flirt in the city, a serious-minded Deviser in the country...how many roles had this agent played in her life? And who was she at heart? Furious with himself, he cast that question away. It didn't matter. Heaven willing, he'd never see her again.

"You're just being stubborn," John Anderson said to Mel Griffin. They were both sitting on beds across the room, though both of them were well enough to leave the temporary hospital; John was there visiting his wife, who'd been injured more badly than he. "I'm telling you she might've lied about her name, but nobody needs to hide their identity so bad they nearly get killed rescuing someone ain't even related to them."

"She pretended she cared about Longbourne because it got her into the Baron's home," Mel retorted. "That was just another way to make us believe her."

"Nearly got her killed, Mel," Susan Anderson said. "Wouldn't be much good as an agent if she was dead, would she?"

Ben turned on his side and put his pillow over his head. They'd been having variations on this argument for most of an hour, apparently not aware that he was in the room, or maybe not caring. Or maybe this was part of the Andersons' plan to get everyone believing that the Princess hadn't lied to them about anything that mattered. *She probably went after Sarah Anderson thinking she could walk out the door with her, then had to scramble to find a solution when that plan failed. Doesn't mean she didn't lie about everything else.* He refused to think of how she'd looked when she fell through Eleanor's doorway, her skin unnaturally pale and icy to the touch, her head lolling as if she didn't have the strength to hold it up, how terrified he'd been—that feeling was all for that imaginary woman.

Someone poked his shoulder. "I know you ain't sleeping," Mistress Weaver said, her voice a little muffled because of the pillow. He removed it from his head and found the argument had ceased, probably because of Mistress Weaver's entry. She looked calm enough, but her eyes had tense lines around them. Well, she'd come in for her share of criticism, once everyone learned she'd known her guest's identity all along. Strange to think of Mistress Weaver having any relation to the royal family, even if it was just by her brother's marriage. It had almost been worse when someone remembered Owen Hunter had been a Ruskalder warrior, and learning Mistress Weaver was only his half-sister hadn't made things much better. But there was something about the woman that made it hard to cross her, made people step quietly around her so as not to get on her bad side. Something in the eyes, maybe, or the tone of voice that could quiet a room in the space of two breaths.

"Leg doin' better?" she said.

Ben shrugged. "Still hurts some. But I've still got it."

"Good attitude." She continued to look down on him. "No other injuries?"

"I think the leg's enough."

She actually smiled a little. "How about the neck?"

Puzzled, he said, "What about it?"

She drew one finger across her neck in a throat-slitting gesture. "That knife looked plenty sharp. But I guess a little cut like that, it'd heal right away."

He had no idea what she was talking about. "I guess," he said.

She nodded at him. "Stay well, Mister Garrett." Then she was gone.

Ben went back to staring at the ceiling. What about his neck? He hadn't taken any injuries in the battle except the leg. He ran his fingers along his throat and felt nothing, not a scar, not a scab. She was mistaken.

Then he remembered. Archie Morgan's knife at his throat, his body arched painfully back, the thin sharp pain when the blade twisted just a little as Lainie's knife took Morgan in the eye. He'd been astonished that she managed to hit that tiny target. It was a one in a million shot for a beginner like her. She'd looked so horrified just before flinging the knife, horrified and afraid and anguished—

Her face rose up in memory, and he caught his breath. She'd been terrified for him. Terrified as if her own life were at risk. Then she'd swept that knife out of her boot and flung it in a perfect arc, and it found its target. She'd killed a man to save his life. And when she knew Morgan was dead, she didn't look elated or sick or guilty, she'd looked *relieved*. As if she'd averted the greatest disaster she could imagine.

She lied, he told himself, but was overridden by a louder voice that said maybe he hadn't seen anything straight. He'd already gone over every detail of her time in Longbourne, finding evidence that she was a liar who'd made a fool out of him and everyone else. Now memories started springing up from where he thought he'd salted the earth. If she'd needed to make herself become one of the villagers for her ruse to work, why had she put off making friends for weeks as if she were trying not to root herself too deeply? Why hadn't she accepted his proposal at Wintersmeet and ensured Ben would stay attached to her? And there had been that strange hesitation, that first time they'd walked by the lake, where he'd had a moment's fear she was going to tell him she wasn't interested in him after all; why hesitate to do what was part of the job?

He groaned, and buried his face in his pillow again. It was all starting to make sense, once he stopped thinking with his hurt feelings and used his head. She'd had to disguise her identity to come to Longbourne, not so the Princess could lie to everyone there for fun, but so the agent could conceal her identity as well. But all she'd needed to keep the Baron from being suspicious was to be a good Deviser, because he didn't care anything about her personal life and probably had no idea Ben even existed.

Ben was sure now she hadn't planned any of what had happened. Probably she'd intended her assignment to be over quickly, so it wouldn't matter what she did or said to the villagers. But it went on too long, and she had to pretend to be what she'd claimed to be, and then it wasn't pretense anymore. Telaine North Hunter had fallen in love with Longbourne and fallen in love with him. Him, the nobody blacksmith, when she could have anyone she wanted. She loved him, and he'd struck at her. Sent her away. He'd been a fool twice over.

He tried to stand, but fell shaking back onto the bed. He had to see her. Maybe it wasn't too late, and he could apologize and beg her to forgive him. Maybe she still loved him. He had to get out of this bed.

"Need something, Ben?" Tabitha said, coming to his side.

"Need to get up," he said, this time sitting up cautiously and swinging his legs over the side of the bed.

"Just wait," Tabitha said. "That leg won't support you. You need to give it a few more weeks."

"Don't have a few weeks. I have to go to Aurilien *now*."

"Figured it out, did you?" The doctor's smile was sympathetic. "Just lie back."

"Figured what out?"

"That Telaine North Hunter never lied about anything but her name and her reason for being here." The doctor pushed on Ben's chest to make him lie down. "Don't know as I can blame her, really. I think she never had a chance to be herself so long as she had to be the Princess. And we'd have been too awed by the title, if she'd come here as herself, to find out anything about who she really was. Unless you can make me believe Ben Garrett would have had the nerve to speak to a Princess of Tremontane when he could barely make himself talk to Lainie Bricker?"

Ben groaned. "She's never going to forgive me."

"I've seen the way she looks at you. I think you've got a better chance than you know."

"I said things—the way she looked, last I saw her—Tabitha, I have to leave *now*."

"You leave now, you won't make it past Ellismere, let alone to Aurilien." The doctor twitched aside the blanket and began unwrapping his leg. "Let's see how it looks."

It hurt a little, being prodded, but Ben was too caught up in his personal misery to care. Never mind the technicalities; they were betrothed, and he'd torn into her like she was his worst enemy, too caught up in his humiliation to listen to her. She was almost his *wife* and he'd done that to her. He groaned again, then shook his head at Tabitha when she asked if she'd hurt him. Finally, she put a clean dressing on the wound and wrapped it up again. "It's looking good," she said, "but you're not going anywhere for three weeks."

"Not going to last three weeks."

"We'll find you something to do. Eleanor can teach you to knit. Give you both something else to think about."

"Tabitha—"

"I can't make you heal any faster, Ben. Be patient."

He learned to knit. He learned to tat lace edging for Mistress Adderly's handkerchiefs. He learned to carve sculptures out of hard lye soap that Hope Richardson lined up in rows and knocked over with her wooden rabbit that ran by itself. Another way Lainie had left her mark on Longbourne.

"Do you suppose we call her Telaine now?" he asked Eleanor one afternoon as they were both sitting outside the laundry, knitting and enjoying the fresh air. Ben could just about hobble from his door to the chair and back, though standing for very long made him tremble and eventually fall over.

"That lieutenant, her cousin, he called her Lainie once or twice," Eleanor said. "I think it's actually her name, or one of them. Telaine, Lainie—you can hear how the one might've come from the other."

"I don't know what I'll say to her. Suppose she's changed her mind? Suppose she doesn't want this life anymore?"

"You won't know unless you ask." Eleanor looked so frail these days. Losing her sons, and then Blythe losing her baby, had hit her hard.

"She can't have changed her mind that much, right?" Ben said.

"Ben Garrett, Lainie might have concealed a few things about herself, but nothing about her heart or her mind or her spirit was false. She loves you and she loves this place. She'll forgive you."

"Wish I was down the mountain already."

"Ten more days, and you will be."

He went back and forth between despair and hope. At night, in the darkness of his bedroom—Tabitha had finally decided he was well enough to care for himself—he went over things he could say to her and found himself as tongue-tied as he'd been before the Bradfords' shivaree. If only it could be as simple as *Forgive me*, or *I love you*, or even *Come home*. He dreamed of her every night. They weren't happy dreams. He started to fear sleep, because he'd find her there, spurning his apology and telling him she didn't love him, she'd never loved him, and he really was a fool. It became increasingly hard to tell himself the dreams didn't mean anything.

To counter the dreams, he told everyone he was going to the city to bring his wife home and hoped that would make it come true. He practiced walking, building up the strength in his leg, telling himself when it hurt that the pain meant he was healing, and every step brought him closer to Lainie.

The morning Tabitha checked his wound and pronounced it healed enough for travel, Ben snatched up the bag he'd had packed for days and dragged Abel Roberts out of his bed—it wasn't his day to go down the mountain, but Ben wasn't going to wait any longer—and helped him harness the horses and did everything short of pushing the wagon himself to get them going. He limped through Ellismere to the ticketing office and paid for the journey all the way to Aurilien, a four-day trip, then had to wait an hour for the coach. Everyone was moving so *slowly* it was driving him mad, but finally the coach arrived and he took his seat across from an elderly woman and next to a boy barely an adult who carried his valise on his lap as though he were afraid someone would steal it. Ben got out his knitting and settled in for the ride. He was never going to be any good at anything complicated, but he could knit squares and secure them together to make a basic blanket.

"You going to Aurilien?" the old woman said. Her dark, weathered skin made her look as if she were carved out of teak. Ben nodded. "I'm going home to Daxtry. What about you?"

"I'm going to fetch my wife," Ben said. *Please let it come true.* "I mean, we're not married yet, we'll get married when I arrive."

"Long way to go for a wife," the woman said.

"She's worth it," Ben said.

They arrived in Aurilien four days later, very late. Ben limped his way off the coach, bag in hand, and looked around. The coaching stop was near a handful of inns; at a loss as to how to choose, Ben struck out randomly and paid some of his dwindling supply of coin for a small room in the smallest inn, down the hall from the toilet. It occurred to him, as he sat on the narrow bed, that if Lainie refused to see him, he might not have enough money to return to Longbourne. Assuming he wanted to, and face all those pitying faces. He fell asleep and into a dream in which Lainie, dressed in satin and feathers, laughed at his despair and let herself be kissed by a faceless stranger to taunt him.

In the morning, he dressed in his best clothes and set out for the palace. He decided to walk there and save his money, but it was a long way and his leg began to throb before he was halfway there. By mid-morning, he was exhausted and in pain and was having trouble remembering why this was so important. Lainie. Right.

He stopped for a cool drink at a public fountain where a dozen people stared at him, then continued on. Finally he reached the gates of the palace, where he'd expected to be challenged, but no one guarded them, so he continued up the drive until he reached the black granite steps leading to the front door. There were soldiers at the base of the stairs and more soldiers at the top, but none of them moved to stop him. Tentatively, he went up the stairs and through the front door.

The entry was a tall domed room paved in white marble, with stairs curving away from it whose delicate banisters looked woven of white lace. Several doorways led off the entry, some of them with closed doors, others open to hallways that went farther into the palace. Ben set his bag down and rubbed his thigh. He really wanted to sit down, but even though the chairs in this room looked comfortable, he was afraid if he did he wouldn't be able to stand again. And he had no idea where to go next.

A woman wearing blue and silver livery came through one of the doors. "What's your business here, sir?" she said, showing no surprise at his presence.

He'd practiced this, as simple as it was, because saying it made him nervous. "I'm here to see Telaine North Hunter," he said.

Now she looked surprised. "Is...is she expecting you?" she said.

"No."

"The Princess is very busy. You should really make an appointment."

He was shaking harder now and it took all his training not to let it touch his voice. "She'll want to see me. I'm a...a friend from Longbourne."

"Longbourne?" The woman clearly recognized the name, which made Ben feel a little more relaxed. "What is your name?"

"Ben Garrett."

She didn't recognize *his* name, but it didn't matter. "Have a seat," she said. "I'll have someone bring you to meet Princess Telaine soon."

Ben gratefully sank onto a very comfortable chair and stretched out his leg. He was still experimenting with positions that eased the strain on the healing wound, but the best one involved lying on his good side with the pillow between his legs, and it was unlikely he could do that here in the palace waiting room.

It was well-named. He waited for a long time, twenty minutes, thirty minutes, growing more nervous with every passing second. This was a mistake. She didn't want to see him. She didn't want to go back to Longbourne—and why would she, if she could live in luxury like this? Twice he began to get up and leave, twice his leg twinged just enough to remind him of how far he'd come, far enough that he wasn't going to waste the journey without even seeing her.

Finally, another woman came through one of the doors. This one was magnificently beautiful, with black hair gathered loosely on her head, cornflower blue eyes, and a perfect complexion. She was also probably six feet tall with a very generous figure that her white morning dress flattered. Ben gaped at her. She came to stand in front of him, unsmiling, and said, "So. *You're* Ben Garrett." She said it as if she knew who he was already and was totally unimpressed.

"I am," Ben said.

She surveyed him closely. "And you're here to see Telaine."

"Yes, ma'am." That just slipped out.

The intimidating woman smiled a little. "Come with me," she said, and Ben rose awkwardly and followed her through the palace, trying to keep up with her long stride. At one point, she glanced at him and said, "You were wounded, weren't you?"

"Yes, ma'am, at Thorsten Pass," Ben said.

"I remember. Jeffy told us. You saved his life." She slowed her pace somewhat.

"He saved mine too, ma'am."

"You don't have to call me ma'am, Mister Garrett. My name is Julia. But you should probably call me your Highness."

Julia. Julia North. *Crown Princess* Julia North. Ben wished he could run away. No wonder she was so cold to him. Lainie must have told her everything about how he'd treated her. It might not be too late to head back the other way, leave the palace and get on the first coach going east. But he was pretty sure he couldn't outrun her, and her Highness looked to have something on her mind.

They came to a long, wide corridor, at the end of which were heavy wooden doors flanked by two soldiers in North livery, fully armed and armored, who came to attention as they approached. "Thank you, lieutenant, corporal, he's with me," the Crown Princess said, and one of the women opened the door and bowed as they passed through.

The Crown Princess continued at speed down a couple of corridors, through a large, well-lit drawing room, and into a smaller room so packed with knick-knacks Ben felt claustrophobic. He sat on an uncomfortable, hard chair with rough upholstery and watched the Crown Princess settle herself onto the only slightly more comfortable-looking sofa opposite. Ben tried to sit back, but it felt as if sharp fingers were poking his spine, so he leaned forward a little and tried to figure out what to do with his hands.

His hostess watched him with narrowed eyes. "Comfortable?" she said.

"Not really," Ben said, figuring honesty couldn't hurt him at this point.

"Sorry." She didn't sound sorry. "So, you want to see Lainie. Why?"

"That's personal."

"You're good friends, aren't you?"

"I hope so."

"I didn't think she had any good friends left in Longbourne."

Despairing, Ben said, "I was hoping to change that."

The Crown Princess regarded him, chewing her lip thoughtfully. "I see," she said. "Excuse me a minute, Mister Garrett, while I ring for tea." She stood and left the room. Ben wanted to look around, but was afraid if he stood, he might fall over. It was dark despite the windows, and a little cold—the hearth was bare, the grate empty—and was the least welcoming place he'd ever seen. If the Crown Princess was trying to torture him for what he'd done to Lainie, it was working.

Eventually she came back carrying a tea tray which she set on the table between them. She served them both, then sat sipping her drink and staring at him while he looked everywhere but at her. If she ever became Queen, she might be able to rule the world. Funny how she resembled Mistress Weaver, when it was Telaine who was her niece.

"Tell me about Longbourne," the Crown Princess said abruptly. "What's it like?"

"Uh...it's a village, a big one," Ben stammered. "It has shops and there are a lot of crafters. About a third of the folks work in the sawmill or the quarries."

"What about the people?"

"They're...people, I guess. Same as anywhere. Friendly, mean, smart, stupid. Mostly friendly and smart, though."

"You don't seem very forthcoming."

"Not sure what you want to know."

"I want to know," said the Crown Princess, "what it's like to live there. Tell me about a typical day. What do you do?"

Ben told her. He talked about his life and his work. He told her about his friends, and Lainie's friends. He told her about shivarees and concerts and Wintersmeet. He talked himself nearly hoarse, with the Crown Princess listening attentively, all the while wondering why she cared.

He was flailing about for a new topic when the door was flung open, and both of them flinched. Standing in the doorway was Lainie Bricker.

He knew she was really Telaine North Hunter, a Princess of Tremontane, but she looked exactly as she had every day he'd known her: plain work shirt, slightly dirty trousers, scuffed boots, her hair dragged back into a braid that at the moment was messy and flaked with bits of white. He'd expected her to look different in the palace. He'd been prepared to see her dressed up, maybe wearing cosmetics, and he'd steeled himself against that because he wasn't sure he could talk to her if she looked that way. But she looked just the same as always, except she was glaring at him as if she wanted to put a dagger through his chest. The hope that had risen when he saw her started to fade. It wasn't a welcoming expression at all.

"Oh, Telaine, what have you—didn't anyone tell you we have *company*?" the Crown Princess said, sounding as if she didn't know whether to laugh or cry.

Lainie turned to look at her cousin. Ben felt as if he'd been under a giant thumb and then released. "No, I heard it from Jessamy," she said. "He just said you were looking for me."

"Trust Jess to leave out the most important part," the Crown Princess said. "Where have you been? Mister Garrett and I have been chatting for nearly an hour."

"Sorry, it's a secret. Can't tell anyone, even you."

"Well, sit down, Lainie, and have some tea. You look as if you could use it—oh, it's cold." The Crown Princess didn't sound sad about this. "Well, you did take an awfully long time."

Lainie took the offered cup. She was ignoring him. That was a relief. Then the Crown Princess stood and said, "Well, you both probably have lots to talk about, mutual acquaintances, et cetera, so I'll just leave you to it."

Lainie swiveled to follow her cousin as she passed toward the door. "Don't feel you have to go," she said.

"I do have other things to do, Telaine," the Crown Princess said. "Goodbye, Mister Garrett, and thank you for saving my brother's life."

Ben murmured something even he didn't understand. The door shut. And Lainie finally looked fully at him. He realized she didn't look exactly the same as before; her eyes, which had always been so brilliant and happy, looked dull, as if she'd seen things she couldn't forget. She was still so beautiful. He couldn't stop looking at her. *Say it, fool*, he told himself, but she was already speaking. "How's the leg?"

"All right. Still hurts some. But at least I still have it." He'd forgotten what he'd come here to say. She was so distant, so angry, and he couldn't think of a way to get around that.

She stood abruptly and moved to the fireplace, where she stood looking down at the empty hearth. "I heard about Trey and Liam," she said. "How's Eleanor? And Blythe?"

"Eleanor's recovering," he said. "Still a little frail, if you can believe it. And Blythe...Blythe lost her baby a week after Trey was killed."

Her shoulders shook briefly, and he thought he heard a quiet sob. "I'm sorry," she said.

Could he go to her? She clearly didn't want him here. What was he thinking? "They've had the whole village behind them," he said, awkwardly trying to offer her comfort, remind her that no one in Longbourne was ever alone. That she was still a part of that.

She thrust away from the fireplace and crossed the room rapidly to the door. "I can't stay in this room another minute," she exclaimed, and fear tore through him, fear that it was already too late. She caught his eye, and he saw something flash across her face too quickly for him to read. "If you have anything to say," she said in a calmer voice, "come with me. I just can't hear it in this room."

He limped along after her down the corridor a short distance, where she opened a door that looked identical to all the others. To his surprise, the room beyond was beautiful, warm and welcoming, filled with furniture of honey-colored wood and sapphire cushions. "I like it," he said. "It's much more comfortable than the other."

"Two weeks ago it was worse," Lainie said. "I've made a lot of changes."

He prodded a box of Device parts that protruded from under an end table. "I can tell it's yours."

She shrugged. "One of them. Go ahead and sit down. You probably shouldn't strain your leg. I have to change." She went through another door and closed it sharply behind her. Ben went to sit on the sofa, which was every bit as comfortable as it looked. He eased his leg around into a better position and looked around. They didn't have anything like this in Longbourne, all this beauty you didn't realize at first meant wealth because it was so simple and understated.

Despair crept back into his thoughts. She'd never want to leave this place for Longbourne, let alone his cramped little house where the kitchen and living room weren't even separate and the toilet had only just been added three years ago. He glanced at the door she'd gone through. And now she was going to put on a dress, and look as elegant and beautiful as the room, and he'd get his words tangled up and be completely unable to speak to her, and in a few minutes she'd show him the door, maybe walk with him to the front door of the palace, and then she'd walk away and he'd never see her again. He loved her past bearing and he would never see her again. He took a deep breath. He just couldn't let that happen.

The door opened again, and he looked up. To his surprise, she was still in shirt and trousers. She'd brushed the white bits out of her hair and braided it again, and her face was clean of smuts from whatever secret project she was working on, but she still looked like herself, and that gave him hope. "I thought you'd be putting on a dress. Like your cousin," he said.

"I'm going back to work later. No sense dressing up."

"Thought you'd look more like your cousin, here in the palace. Dressed up, I mean. I didn't think I could speak to you, but you came in looking..." He couldn't think of a way to end that sentence without babbling about how beautiful she was. "You look just the same," he said.

"I'm not the same person I was two months ago. Neither are you."

She came around to sit on a chair opposite him and rubbed her temples as if she had a headache. Then she said, "Ben, I've been trying to think of a way to ask you this without it sounding like an accusation, but—why are you here? Is your anger and embarrassment so great it can only be eased by you telling me again how well I pretended to be someone I'm not? I am *sorry* for what I did to you."

She paused, briefly, but Ben couldn't collect his thoughts fast enough to insert his words into the gap. She let out a laugh that sounded more like a sob. "I had a plan, you know? A plan for explaining it all to you in a way I hoped you'd understand. Several plans, actually, but they all began with me telling you I love you, because that's what got me into this whole mess."

I love you. Not *I used to love you.* His heart was beating so rapidly he could almost hear it. "Lainie—" he said, too quietly, because she kept on going.

"I never should have let you kiss me more than once. I never should have let myself believe I could make a home with you in Longbourne, because it was always going to end like this and if anyone's been made a fool of, it's me, and I did it to myself. So whatever it is you—"

"Lainie, stop," Ben said, a little desperately. "Stop. No. Lainie, I came here to ask you to forgive me. Please."

He'd made her stop speaking, at least, but the expression on her face wasn't very welcoming. It didn't matter. This was why he was here. "I've made the biggest mistake of my life," he said. "Didn't realize for so long how big a mistake it was. I don't feeling like a fool, and that day I stood there with everyone watching me and thinking, look at that fool who thought she loved him. And I had your ring in my pocket—I carried it everywhere, like a promise—felt like it was going to burn straight through into my flesh. So I took that feeling and I turned it into anger, and then I turned that anger on you. Then I turned it on the Ruskalder. Pretty sure for a while there I didn't care if I died."

He took a breath, and Lainie opened her mouth to say something. "Just—let me finish, please," he said. "I spent a deal of time flat on my back, healing, and the whole time all I heard about was you. John and Susan Anderson, talking about how nobody needed to hide their identity so much they'd rescue a girl not even related to them and nearly get killed doing it. And Jack, playing with his damned watch, saying you can't fake skills like that. Even your cousin, babbling about couldn't I forgive you, not that he knew anything about it. But then there was Mistress Weaver."

He swallowed, trying to moisten his dry mouth. "She asked me how my neck was, said a little scratch like that would've healed right away. And that made me remember how you looked when Morgan had hold of me with his knife to my throat, like it was your own life in danger. I remembered you'd killed him to save my life. And I knew...I knew no one was that good a liar."

"Ben—" Lainie said.

"Let me finish, just—give me that much. It took all the courage I had just to get on that coach to Aurilien, let alone to walk into the palace to see you, and if I don't say this now I'll never find the nerve again. Didn't expect your intimidating cousin." He smiled, thinking how overwhelmed she'd made him feel and how that was nothing compared to having to sit here and apologize, knowing his whole life depended on it. "She doesn't like me very much. Sitting there, talking to her...I'd almost rather face the Ruskalder. If you'd been five minutes longer, I'd have run out the door and gotten on the first coach back to Longbourne. Then you came in, looking like you wanted to burn a hole in my chest—"

"I didn't—"

"You didn't seem to want to talk to me. I—it was like I was meeting you all over again, tongue-tied and never knowing what to say. But I thought, I'll beg her forgiveness and go home." He took both her hands in his, daringly, and said, "Lainie, I'm sorry I didn't trust you. I'm sorry I said those things and that I said them in front of everyone. When I'm not having nightmares about killing Ruskalder, my nightmares are all about how devastated you looked last I saw you, knowing I made you look that way. I know you don't owe me anything, but if you can find it in you to forgive me, I wish you would."

She said nothing. Ben withdrew his hands from hers, but before he could move too far, she took his hands and gripped them. "I don't want your apology," she said.

He felt the blood drain from his face. He'd thought at least she might be able to forgive him, even if she didn't love him anymore. But then she smiled a little, and shook her head, and said, "You don't understand. Ben, I love you. There hasn't been a single day since I left that mountain that I haven't thought of you. All I wanted, through everything I've endured, even when I thought you hated me, was to have you beside me. So it's not an apology I want, but I'll take it if that's the price for me to hear you tell me you still love me."

He was so surprised it took him a moment to respond. Then he smiled, and said, "Recall telling you it's not something you turn on and off like a tap."

"I was hoping that was true," she whispered, and leaned forward to kiss him.

He put his arms around her and pulled her to him, settling her on his lap and holding her close. "Lainie, Lainie," he murmured, "I love you, I'm so sorry I left you."

"No more apologies," she said, and kissed him again, running those long fingers through his hair.

BEN: MEETING THE KING

*T*he drawing room was twice the size of his house and full of low-backed sofas upholstered in a soft, pale green fabric with a velvety nap. Ben brushed his fingers across it and shifted his leg into a better position. Four corridors led off the great room, making it impossible for him to sit anywhere without having his back to one of them. He relaxed his shoulders, which had hunched up, and clasped his hands in his lap to stop them fidgeting.

"You must be Mister Garrett," a man said, and Ben swiveled around to see a tall man with graying black hair and a short beard enter the room. "I'd like to say I've heard much about you, but I'm afraid Telaine wasn't very forthcoming about her time in Longbourne."

Ben swallowed, trying to force open a throat that had begun to close up. "Your Majesty," he began.

"I'm sure I won't get you to call me Jeffrey, but 'sir' will do," the King said with a slight smile. "Why don't you come with me."

He gestured in the direction of one of the passages, and Ben hauled himself up and limped in that direction. The King wanted to talk to him. He knew about Longbourne and he almost certainly knew what had passed between him and Telaine. He was going to kill Ben, and since he was the King he could probably get away with it.

They went through a dizzying number of passages, none of which were decorated the same, until they came to a short flight of steps that led to a hallway paneled in dark, heavy wood that loomed over Ben as if the walls bent inward. The King kept walking, immune to the spell the hall cast, and Ben had to follow or be lost.

They passed a marble-topped semicircular desk where a young man stood and bowed to them—well, probably not to Ben—and then the King opened a door and said, "My office. Come in."

It was a plain room by comparison to the opulence of the rest of the palace, with a giant desk whose legs were carved to look like lions' claws and a couple of chairs with tall backs drawn up before an empty fireplace. The King sat in one of them and gestured to Ben to take the other. Then he sat with his fingers steepled in front of his face, tapping his forefingers together and regarding Ben in a way that made him wish he could shrink into the depths of the chair. Finally, the King said, "Thank you for saving my son's life."

"We saved each other, sir—that is, I couldn't have let him die." The chair was more narrow than he'd thought, and it ground into his hip uncomfortably.

"Nevertheless." The King lowered his hands to his lap. "I owe you a great debt. What can I do for you?"

Ben's throat began to close up again. "Ah...there's nothing I need that you can give me, sir."

"I think that's untrue, but let's set that aside for now. I want you to tell me what Telaine did in Longbourne."

"Sir?" That was a question with too many answers.

"She never told anyone who she was?"

He remembered that cold morning, looking at Lainie who'd become a stranger in half a breath. "Never. We never guessed."

"So who did you think she was?"

Wonderful. Beloved. Extraordinary. "Just what she said. A Deviser from the city."

"But she was more to you than that."

Was he in trouble, or not? *My uncle has to approve all marriages,* she'd said, and it occurred to him that this man held his happiness in those two hands. Ben sat up straighter, ignoring the twinge in his leg, and said, "She was, sir. She means everything to me."

The King's lips quirked in a smile. "And you think you deserve to marry her?"

"Don't know about deserve, sir. I know I want to. I think she wants to marry me."

"Think?"

"When I asked her, she wouldn't make me any promises. Think she was being as honorable as she could. But she said she'd run away with me if you said no."

Laughter, deep and merry, rang out through the room. "I didn't know what to expect of you, Mister Garrett," the King said. "I should be furious with you for treating her so poorly, but the truth is I think your reaction, what I know of it from Julia, at least, was perfectly justified. Though—" He leaned forward, and there was no humor in his eyes. "Speak to her like that again, and I won't be so understanding."

"That's never going to happen. I haven't forgiven myself for that, sir."

"I imagine not. So, Mister Garrett, have you thought of anything I might do for you?"

Ben drew in a deep breath and let it out slowly. "Sir, I don't think Lainie ought to be some prize for whatever you think I deserve rewarding for."

"No? It hasn't occurred to you that you're effectively a fairy tale hero—save the kingdom, win the hand of the Princess? No, I can see you don't think that way. Good for you."

Ben shrugged. "I'm not much for speeches, sir. I just know that I love Lainie—Telaine—and I want more than anything to marry her. So I hope you'll give us permission."

"And it hasn't occurred to you that possibly a Princess ought to marry someone noble? Not an ordinary blacksmith from the frontier?"

"I...don't know." He hadn't considered that at all, after that first horrific day where all he could think was how no Princess could possibly be interested in a commoner like him. "Is that a rule?"

"It's tradition." The King smiled again. "But I've never thought tradition ought to overrule what's right. You intend to go back to Longbourne?"

Ben straightened. "With Lainie, sir, yes. Unless she wants to live here."

"What would you do in the capital?"

"They still need blacksmiths here, don't they, sir?" He didn't mention the singing. It was unlikely he'd be able to make a living at it after five years away from serious training.

"You think Princess Telaine North Hunter ought to have a husband who's an ordinary blacksmith? That she wouldn't be embarrassed by you at social functions?"

"I don't know about Princess Telaine North Hunter, *sir*," Ben said, "but I know Lainie, and she's not proud or disdainful, and I'll be whatever she needs me to be. But I think what she needs is who I am right now, or she wouldn't have fallen in love with me."

The King chuckled. "So, just to be clear," he said, rubbing his chin, "you think I should give permission for you to marry the daughter of my only sister and my best friend, on the grounds that she loves you and it's what you want."

"That's right."

"Well, I can hardly argue with that." The King extended his hand. "You have my blessing, Mister Garrett. To be honest, I can't imagine her ever being happy with the kind of men she used to socialize with. Did you know she lived in the woods like a wild creature when she was young? She's Owen Hunter's daughter, down to the bone, and he made my sister so happy...well. You're fortunate Owen's not still alive; he'd have set you some impossible task and glowered at you the whole time you were failing to accomplish it." He stood, prompting Ben to struggle out of the imprisoning chair. "Join us for dinner, will you? I'm sure the family will want to meet you."

"People keep warning me not to be overwhelmed by the North clan. I feel a little overwhelmed by that."

"Never fear. Telaine will keep them in line. None of them knew she was an agent either. It's been an interesting adjustment for her cousins, who were used to her talking about nothing but fashion at the dinner table. You can sometimes see their minds changing gears like Devices being repaired while they're still moving."

NIGHT BE MY GUARDIAN

I wrote this because I couldn't bear Alison not having her happy ending. I caught a lot of flak for the death of Anthony North, and I wrote this short story just for myself, right around the time I wrote "Long Live the Queen." I am so glad I decided to include it with Agent of the Crown.

Takes place in spring 963 Y.B.

THE CLEAR SPRING AIR CARRIED WITH IT A THOUSAND BEAUTIFUL smells, pine and flowers and the distant scent of a mountain river. Alison could hear it just at the edge of her perception, a murmur like that of a palace ball. She closed her eyes and pictured it, the Spring Gala with all those men in pale suits and cravats matching the pastel blues and pinks and yellows of the women's gowns. How fashion had changed in sixty years. Now they wore thin muslins and laces with puffy short sleeves and low necklines over silk or satin slips with narrow skirts. They'd put so many dances out of style, some of them her old favorites—but then it had been her doing that the corset had gone out of fashion, so she could hardly complain.

"You were always so beautiful, no matter what you wore,"

Anthony said. She could imagine his breath tickling her ear, hear his marvelous baritone smooth and warm like melted toffee.

"I still prefer trousers to gowns," she whispered back to him. No sense startling the driver, who probably needed all her attention to keep the carriage on the narrow mountain path.

"Even more beautiful with your dress off," he teased, and she smiled at the old joke and wished she could lay her head on his shoulder—but of course, he wasn't there, he was a memory, and a beloved one. She could hear his voice more clearly every day.

"I don't mean this as impatience, but do you know how much longer until we're there?" she asked the driver.

"I think it's another half-hour until the valley, milady Consort," the woman said, "and the man at the stables said it was another half-hour from there to Longbourne. Are you comfortable?"

"As comfortable as these old bones can be," Alison said. Her own voice was so creaky these days, like the rest of her. She'd turned eighty-three just six weeks before and considered herself fairly hale for such an old woman, even if her joints creaked as much as her voice did and her formerly smooth skin was dry and wrinkled as old paper. Jeffrey had been horrified when she proposed this trip, but he of all people knew why she had to make it. "I'm just surprised you didn't do this earlier," he'd said, "fifteen years ago."

"Fifteen years ago my granddaughter didn't give me an excellent excuse for the trip," she'd replied, "and I've kept this secret too long to risk revealing it, even now. The Norths are strong, but no sense stirring up scandal."

He'd shook his head, but hadn't argued further. Imogen had been more aghast even than her husband, and Alison wondered if she suspected there was more to this trip than the desire to see Telaine and her family in their own home. But she was still Alison North, with a will of iron and the determination to see things through, and now here she was bouncing up the pass toward Steepridge. It was actually a fairly comfortable ride, less jolting than the Device Jeffrey had imported from Eskandel that drove you around the city without horses. It was a novelty, a child's toy, but Alison had observed how easily it handled, how it didn't leave piles of dung wherever it passed, and predicted Tremontane was seeing the birth of a Devisery that would change it forever.

"We've seen so many changes," Anthony said. "I wonder what changes our children will see."

"What changes they'll make," she said quietly. "Telaine has already made a name for herself, even in her little village. When she gets her hands on that Devisery...imagine this trip made twice as fast. She already keeps the passes clear in winter."

"I've seen them all through your eyes. They're quite the legacy."

"Yours and mine."

She napped in the spring sunshine and woke when the carriage's pace changed, became less bumpy and a little faster, and sat up to look around her. Now she understood what Telaine had fallen in love with. If she'd come here fifteen years ago, she might have stayed here herself. Green grass stretched out in both directions, coming up against the darker green of evergreens in one direction and the silvery coins of aspens in the other. The sound of rushing water had faded somewhat, but in the far distance she could see a thread of white water spooling down the face of a mountain that still had snow on its peaks. Mount Ehuren was visible beyond that, its darker gray stark against the pale blue sky. The road wound on through the gentle rise of the valley, branching off toward unseen villages else-where in the barony. "Stop," she told the driver. "I want to stretch my legs a little, then ride on the seat with you."

"Are you sure you'll be comfortable enough, milady Consort?"

"If I'm not, it will pass, and I want to see Longbourne on my own terms."

She needed the driver's help to emerge from the carriage, tottered around until she felt she had full control of her body, then climbed up onto the seat and held on to its edge as the carriage continued along the road.

"You might take my arm instead of that splintery seat," Anthony said. She smiled, but didn't reply. Ahead, she could see the sun glinting off the blue-gray slates of roofs. Longbourne. It grew up around them, outlying farms becoming houses and then the two-story businesses that lined Longbourne's main street. The horses' hooves went from thudding on hard-packed earth to ringing out with the same sharp taps they did on the stone-paved streets of Aurilien. Telaine had written with great excitement about the paving of Long-bourne's streets four years ago, how it had replaced the gravel, and Alison had tried to imagine the life her oldest granddaughter lived now, she who'd been raised wild and then tamed into a society belle, or so they'd all thought. No wonder she'd thrived here.

The carriage came to a stop near the forge, where the sound of metal tapping metal and a hot crisp smell of glowing coal said Ben Garrett was at work. The forge was attached to a two-story house, which in turn was attached to a shorter building with large glass windows that would let in enough light for the most precise, finicky work. A couple of men standing at the forge rail turned to look at the newcomer, idly curious. Of course they'd have no idea who she was. The driver helped Alison down. "Where shall I take your bags, milady Consort?"

"Would you wait for just a few minutes?" Alison said. She approached the forge rail, where the two men's expressions had grown confused, as if they couldn't believe what they'd heard. She nodded politely to them, leaned on the forge rail, and said, "Might I have a moment of your time, master blacksmith?"

"Just a—" Ben said, then turned around fast, tongs in hand. "*Milady Alison!*"

"Hello, Ben," Alison said. It had taken most of a year to convince him to stop calling her *Milady Consort*, as if they weren't related at all. "Surprised?"

"Of course! *Lainie!*"

A small black-haired girl with extraordinary blue eyes that always made Alison catch her breath came running out of the house. "Ma's in the workshop," she said in that lilting northeastern accent that sounded like music. Her eyes went round. "*Grandmama!*" she shrieked, and threw herself at Alison's legs, making her totter just a bit.

"Zara, be careful," Ben said. "Go tell your ma who's here."

The little girl ran off. "She's grown," Alison said.

"Going to overtop me and Lainie both someday," Ben said, pushing back his light brown hair from his brow. "No question whose grand-niece she is, either."

"It breeds true, the North good looks," Anthony said. "I wonder if Telaine knew that when she named her."

"No question at all," Alison said.

The workshop door opened again, and Telaine Garrett came out at a run. "Grandmama," she said, hugging Alison. "You shouldn't have come all this way. Was it a comfortable trip? You should bring your things inside, we've got room—"

"Actually, I thought I'd stay with my old friend Agatha Weaver," Alison said. "She knows I'm coming."

Telaine's eyes went wide. "I can't believe she kept it a secret from me!" She laughed and shook her head. "All right, actually I can. Of course you would—" She stopped and glanced over her shoulder southward. "Happen you wouldn't want to come upon her unawares and expect her to just put you up. But I think she'd be happy to see you, awares or not."

"I hope so," Alison said. "But I'll have supper with you, if you don't mind."

"Not at all. Ben's cooking tonight, so it'll be edible. Do you want—"

"Yes, I'd like to see Agatha now. Will you show me where she lives?"

Telaine linked her arm with her grandmother's and led her down the street, the carriage following slowly behind them. Alison observed her covertly. She'd seen her and, later, her family once a year every year since her marriage, when they came to stay at the palace for a few weeks, but she'd always wondered if Telaine was different when she was at home. She sounded different, for one, dropped the cultured accents she always used, probably by habit, in the palace. She'd put on weight since she'd had her three children, which was as well because she'd always been too thin, just like her mother. Her walk was every bit as confident as it ever was, but there was something about it here in Longbourne that was different. It said this was *her* place, that she was a part of it as if she'd lived here her whole life. It warmed Alison's heart to see her so happy. If only Julia —but that was a worry for another time, and Alison was about to step into the past.

Telaine took her around the back of a long, low building that had an upper story half the size of the lower one, with three windows ranged across it. She pushed open the back door without knocking. It opened on a tidy kitchen with a pot of something that smelled delicious bubbling over the fire. In the distance Alison heard clattering and rattling and the faint whir of something spinning.

"Aunt Weaver, you have a guest," Telaine called out, and led Alison out of the kitchen and down a short hall into the great central room of the house. A young woman and a slightly younger man sat at spinning wheels; the young man turned to see who'd entered and let go the puffy wool in his hand, which the wheel, spinning on its own, swallowed up. An enormous loom filled the back of the room, clattering away, but its movement slowed and then came to a halt as the woman behind it let her hands and feet fall idle. Alison felt as if she'd sprouted roots that went through the floorboards into the earth and kept her from moving, kept her from falling, as the weaver left the loom and came to greet her.

Sweet heaven, she looked just the same. Older, maybe—she appeared to be in her mid-thirties—but the eyes, sharp as diamond, the black hair just like Anthony's, the firm chin and the look that said *You had better not be wasting my time*...how under heaven had she ever fooled *anyone* into believing she was an ordinary woman?

Mistress Weaver's expression was placid, but her voice was sharp as she said, "Maris, Jonathan, you're excused for the day. I ain't seen my friend for...a very long time, and happen we've a lot to talk about."

Maris and Jonathan wasted no time in tidying up their work places and running out the front door, shouting happily at their freedom. "Aunt Weaver," Telaine began, then looked from one face to the other, slipped her arm free of Alison's, and said, "I'll see you at supper. You're invited, Aunt Weaver, if you want." She left the room, and soon Alison heard the faint sound of the back door shutting.

Alison looked at Mistress Weaver. "It's been a long time," Anthony said.

"It's been a long time," Alison said.

"Sixty years," Mistress Weaver said. Her blue eyes glittered. "A lifetime."

She blurred in Alison's vision. *"Zara,"* Alison said, and went toward her sister, arms outstretched, as Zara did the same, and they clung to each other, weeping, though Alison didn't know if it was joy or sorrow at how fate had robbed them of those sixty years.

"You haven't changed," Zara said.

Alison laughed through her tears. "Because I've always been wrinkled and white-haired and limped a little from a broken hip that never healed right?"

"Your eyes are the same," Zara said, pulling away a little to look her into those eyes, "and you still walk like you own the world."

"Like you're about to take on the whole damn world at once," Anthony said in her ear.

"I never really believed in your inherent magic until now. It's just impossible to comprehend, when the last time I saw you you had most of your face blown away."

"By you. Thank you."

"I had nightmares about it for weeks. Thank heaven Anthony and I had each other. Was it worth it?"

Zara's eyes went distant. Alison wondered what she was seeing. "I imagine sometimes what would have happened if we hadn't killed me," she said. "I picture young Jeffrey wasting his life, waiting for me to die. All those children becoming nothing more than hangers-on at court. Telaine never becoming an agent, never finding her heart here. I won't say it wasn't hard. But I had love—I doubt I'd have found that if I'd stayed Queen—and I've made a life and I even got to see my descendants grow up. Though I thought about murdering Telaine when she gave that child my name. Said 'I thought she should have a little of my favorite relative's spunk' and I near burst into tears right there. Never tell her that."

"I wouldn't. And she does. Have spunk, I mean. She's the terror of the palace whenever she visits. The only time I see her quiet is when she's in the Long Gallery looking at her namesake's portrait. Who knows what she's thinking?"

"Probably that her Aunt Weaver looks uncommonly like Queen Zara North," Anthony said. "She knows it's time to move on and can't bear to. But I can hardly blame her for that."

"I wish I could have come sooner," Alison said. "But that was just one more sacrifice."

"It was," Zara said, "but I'm glad you've come now. Let's get your things inside. And then we can talk."

THERE WASN'T MUCH TIME BEFORE SUPPER TO TALK. ZARA SHOWED HER the room she'd be staying in. "Fitted it up with a better mattress," she said. "Used to be this old, thin thing with hardly any padding to it. Put Telaine on it her first night in Longbourne, see what she'd do. Not a word of complaint. I'd been expecting fancy manners and demands for special treatment."

"Even when she was pretending to be a brainless socialite, haughtiness wasn't part of her character," said Alison, lowering herself onto the bed. It was soft and welcoming and she thought about pleading tiredness and taking a real nap, but that wasn't what she was here for. "She's her father's daughter, down to the bone. There's very little of Elspeth in her."

"She says it skipped a generation and appeared in young Julia," Zara said, leaning against the bedroom wall next to the dressing table and idly running her finger over the mirror's rim. "The child does take after her great-grandmother, except for the eyes."

"Who knows how these things come out in the blood? Owen doesn't look like any of his maternal relations. Ben's never said the boy looks like anyone on his side of the family. Though he doesn't talk about them much."

"Doesn't talk about them at all. He's hiding something, but Telaine won't dig for it. Says it's his business and none of hers."

"She seems happy."

"She is." Zara stretched. "I'm going to pull supper off the fire and put it in the cold room. Won't hurt it to be heated again tomorrow. Then we can see what Ben's come up with tonight."

Alison had to work hard not to be appalled at Telaine's relatively primitive living conditions. How long had it taken her to adapt to this small house, with its plain furnishings and little rooms and the narrow staircase that led up to where the children slept?

"You're a little bit of a snob, love," Anthony said. "Would you have complained at all if I'd asked you to leave the palace and live in the forest with me?"

She shook her head, then smiled at Ben when he asked if anything was wrong. It was true, she was accustomed to luxury. She watched her granddaughter swipe a cloth across her three-year-old daughter's face, making the child laugh. *It's not about the furnishings,* she told herself, *it's about who shares them with you.*

After supper, she brought out presents: an old book of folk songs for Ben, a newly printed schematic for the Device that propelled Jeffrey's new toy for Telaine, picture books for Julia and little Zara, and a huge encyclopedia of Tremontanan animals for eight-year-old Owen, whose eyes gleamed when he saw it. "You remembered, Grandmama," he said.

"Your grandmama has never forgotten anything to do with books in her life," Telaine said.

"I'm afraid I'm a bit single-minded in my interests," Alison said, "but it's such a joy, matching people with books they didn't even know they needed."

"You don't mind if I spend all night in the workshop again, do you?" Telaine said, teasing Ben, who put his arm around her waist and pulled her close for a kiss. "Well, all right then," she said, a little breathlessly.

"Pa, sing for us," Julia said. She climbed onto her father's lap and turned the pages of his book.

"One of these?" Ben said. "I think I need some practice." But his hand stilled hers, and he ran his finger down the staves of music on one of the pages. "Or...happen not."

They settled in around the fireplace while Ben stood before them, moving his lips as he ran through the words of the song. "Good thing for me my voice has changed some since I was young," he said. "More a baritone than a tenor, these days."

"Still the most beautiful voice I've ever heard," Telaine said.

"Zara's going to follow his example, you know," Anthony said. "She's only five and you can hear it in her voice."

Alison said nothing, just watched Ben as his stance shifted and he began breathing rhythmically. Did Telaine know her husband was a classically trained opera singer? He'd never given any hint of being more than just a man with a gift for music and a love of folk songs, but Alison had attended many concerts in her day, most of them against her will, and in her boredom with the music had turned her attention to the singers, how they stood, how they moved, the way they held their chests and throats and lips. Ben Garrett might not have taken up the profession, but it wasn't for lack of either talent or training. Well, if Telaine wasn't interested in ferreting out her husband's secrets, it wasn't any business of Alison North's.

"I've heard this song before, but it never had words, not that I knew anyway. It's a very old lullaby that's supposed to come from the time of Haran, back when we still worshiped gods," Ben said. "The words are in—is this Kantnish?"

Alison took the book from him. "An old dialect of it. I can't read it."

"Well, whoever wrote it down translated it into something we can understand. Couldn't sing it else." He closed his eyes, took in a slow breath, then held the book where he could easily read from it, and sang.

Now the day is over,
The sun, it dips into the sea.

It burns a path along the waves
That brings you back to me.

THE STARS WILL BE YOUR BLANKET,
The moon will paint the grasses blue,
The night will be your guardian
'Til I come home to you.

THEN REST YOU ON YOUR PILLOW
Within your cradle, slumber deep.
I'll watch o'er you 'til morning comes
As peacefully you sleep.

THE LAST NOTES OF THE SONG FLOATED AWAY, LEAVING SILENCE BEHIND. Ben lowered the book. "I liked it," Julia said.

"That was beautiful. You can tell it's an old melody, can't you?" said Telaine.

"Don't know how good a translation it is, but it feels sad." Ben held the book so little Zara could look at it. "Thanks, Milady Alison."

"I knew you were the right one for it." She tried to hold back a yawn. "Excuse me. I'm more tired than I thought."

"You should sleep," Telaine said. "And tomorrow I want to show you everything. The lake is so beautiful this time of year."

"I'm looking forward to seeing it. Goodnight, children."

She hugged them all, then walked the short distance to Zara's house with her sister. Sunset came early in the mountains, and the snows on the top of Mount Ehuren were tinged faintly pink from the rays of a sun that had already dipped beyond the western peaks. To the east, stars glittered against the indigo sky, more than anyone could see in Aurilien, which glowed in the light of a million Devices every night. "How much longer will you stay here?" she asked.

Zara didn't respond. She stayed silent until they reached her back door and entered the kitchen, when she said, "Until the first snows fall. Can't afford to stay longer. Been here too long as it is."

"I can see why you wouldn't want to leave."

"Never hated this magic so much as I have these last two years. I almost wish she'd never come here. It hurts like hell, leaving 'em all behind, but...." She reached into a cupboard and took out a bottle of wine. "I say we get drunk and tell old stories. If my heart's goin' to break, I want it to break in company."

She lit a dozen candles and they sat at the kitchen table, talking and laughing and even crying a little, but just a little. "Doyle never gave away the secret," Alison said. "I miss him sometimes—he died about twenty-five years ago, probably from all the drinking. I thought he'd outlive me." She took a swallow of wine. "I thought a lot of people would outlive me."

"I wish I'd been there for you when Anthony died."

"It was horrible. Waking up to that, him lying there so...it's still hard to remember. It was a long time before I could think of him without crying."

"I never wanted to hurt you, love," Anthony said.

"I know," said Alison.

"Know what?" Zara said.

"It's nothing." Alison yawned again. "I think I'm ready for sleep now."

They climbed the stairs together, and at the top, Zara embraced her. "I'm glad you came," she said.

"So am I," Alison said. "Good night, Zara."

She sat on the bed in her nightgown, watching the stars. *The stars will be my blanket*, she thought. Would it be a warm blanket, or a cool one? How would it feel to be decked in those lights, wrapped in them so you took their brilliance with you wherever you went? She leaned out of the window and looked up the street to where lights still burned in the house by the forge. Did they still look up in wonder, or was all this beauty just a commonplace for them? The sky was growing darker; there was no moon to ruin the brilliance of all those twinkling diamonds. It felt as if heaven were drawing closer, though no one really knew what it looked like or where it was, just that it was bound to earth by the lines of power and populated by the dead. When she was a young child, she'd seen her grandfather's body before his burial, and for months afterward she'd pictured heaven as full of motionless gray people. Now the idea of heaven held no fear for her.

She lay back in the bed and closed her eyes. It was a good mattress, nearly as good as her bed at home, but she hadn't slept well for weeks. Possibly it was something that happened as you got old, needing less sleep. Some nights, she just sat up reading, or walked through the Library tidying up, but mostly she lay awake in her bed feeling guilty that she couldn't sleep like a normal person. The wine was relaxing her body but not her mind, which went around in fuzzy circles touching on half a dozen things she had to do when she returned. Possibly it was time for her to resign as Royal Librarian, spend more time with her family, but that would only give her fewer things to fill her nights with. And her body might have slowed down, but her mind was as sharp as ever, thank heaven.

Her circling brain began to slow as she drifted closer to sleep. The faint scent of pine tickled her nose. Maybe she should close the window, but it smelled so good, and the coolness of the air relaxed her further. *Finally*, she thought, and slept.

It felt as if she'd only slept for minutes when something woke her, a sound she couldn't remember upon waking. She knew immediately she wouldn't be sleeping again any time soon, cursed a little under her breath, and sat up. There was no point just lying there staring at the ceiling, so she got dressed and went carefully down the stairs, not wanting to light a lamp and possibly wake Zara, hoping she wouldn't trip and fall and break her damned hip again. Bright moonlight came through the kitchen window, enough to help her avoid the table and its single chair. *Oh, Zara. How lonely you must be.*

She stepped out into the back yard, which looked pale and barren despite the new growth of spring she'd seen sprouting around the edges of the sheds. The high creaking sound of she had no idea how many crickets filled the air, an invisible choir singing a series of notes all in the same key. A breeze brushed her face, bringing with it the now-familiar scent of pine and the unexpected smell of water. There was a lake, or a river, somewhere around here, and she wanted to see it.

It wasn't very hard to find the road that led westward out of Long-bourne toward the smell of water, but the road tapered off as it entered the forest of evergreens and then vanished, and Alison stood at its end and contemplated the woods. She ought to go back, but for what? More hours lying awake in Zara's spare room? And it wasn't as if she could get very lost out here. She left the road and continued walking, following her nose. A tune came to mind, and she hummed along, though she couldn't remember the words of the song. It was beautiful, and fitted the night perfectly.

It was much darker beneath the trees, dark enough that she had to feel her way between the trunks. It took only a few minutes for her to realize this had been a bad decision. She stopped with her hand on the rough bark of a pine tree whose branches brushed the top of her head and thought about turning around. *No, you'll just get confused and end up wandering these woods until morning. At least if you move forward you'll end up lost somewhere interesting.* That didn't make much sense, but the idea of finding the river, or the lake, had taken hold of her now, and she knew she was just looking for an excuse to keep going.

Feeling her way, conscious of the dangers of falling and injuring herself here in the dark, she kept moving. The cool, damp breeze came to her now and again, leading her in what she hoped was the right direction. With every step, that hope turned into something more certain, until she was walking more quickly, knowing her path as surely as if it were picked out by bright daylight. She breathed deeply and let the smell of clear water fill her lungs. She was nearly there, she could feel it.

She came out of the woods so abruptly she nearly fell over, having anticipated more trees where there were none. And there, spread out before her, was a vast black lake that glittered under the moonlight with hundreds, no, thousands of tiny waves stirred up by the breeze. Short grass covered the ground between her and the shoreline, which was shrouded in rushes that remained still despite the wind. The smell of water filled the air, but now it was mingled with the green scents of growing things that surrounded the lake, hidden by the rushes. The sound of crickets was quieter here, she didn't know why, and the low bass rumble of bullfrogs joined the choir. It was so beautiful it made her heart ache. She felt as if she could hear the tune now, as if it wound itself around the high thin creak of the crickets and the deep, echoing beat of the frogs. It was so familiar, and yet she still couldn't remember where she'd heard it.

Movement off to the right drew her eye. Someone stood about a hundred feet away, near the shore, someone who wasn't more than a black smudge in the moonlight. He, or she, stood almost motionless, and for a moment Alison thought it must be a stub of a tree trunk, burned and broken—but no, it was definitely a human figure, and although Alison couldn't make out a face, she felt certain the person wasn't looking at the lake, but at her. The whole scene seemed odd somehow—surely the moonlight should light up the person's features?—but then this whole episode had taken on a surreal quality. What had possessed her, and it did feel like possession, to leave her bed and go wandering in a strange land at what must be nearly midnight? She must be more drunk than she imagined.

She began walking toward the figure. Part of her considered that it might be dangerous, that whoever it was might not be friendly, but she was eighty-three years old and death no longer frightened her, if it ever had. And perhaps this person had been drawn to the lake the way she had, and maybe knew something about what that impulse was, and why it had taken hold of her.

The person didn't move as Alison approached, though she was still convinced that he—she was close enough now to see that it was male—was watching her closely. She was also, irrationally, convinced she should know him, though the only man she knew in Longbourne was Ben and he wouldn't just stand there silently waiting for her to reach him. And she couldn't understand why she couldn't see his face clearly. It was as if the moon was moving to put him in shadow, trying to deceive her. It made her a little angry, though she knew it was ridiculous to be angry with the moon. So she turned her anger outward, toward the silent man. "Who are you?" she said.

In response, he whistled a phrase of the tune. "Who do you think I am?" His voice was unfamiliar.

"I have no idea. Why did you come here?"

"Who do you think I am?"

Alison's temper flared. "I can't even see your face. If the moon—"

She stopped. There hadn't been a moon before, just the starry blanket over Longbourne. And this moon was too bright, too large, and it lit everything except the stranger's face. Alison looked back toward the woods. Nothing of Longbourne was visible, but she felt absolutely certain that if she were to retrace her steps, she'd never find Longbourne again. "Show me your face," she said.

The man turned, and in that moment she knew who he was, and before he could do more than say her name she flung herself at him, throwing her arms around his neck and sobbing, "Anthony, Anthony, I didn't know!"

She felt his arms, those familiar arms, go around her waist, and then his lips were on hers with a passion she had never forgotten, gentle and insistent and offering her his whole heart if she'd only do the same for him. She smelled again the spicy scent of his cologne and felt the faint roughness of his cheeks, and it felt as if her forty years of loneliness vanished, swallowed up by the lake. Anthony brushed tears from her eyes, kissed her forehead, then drew her into his embrace while she cried, not knowing whether she was happy or confused or grieving all over again. "It's forever now, love," he whispered to her. "Forever, and past forever."

"Were you speaking to me, these last weeks? Was that real?"

"No. But it is now."

"I woke up that morning, and you were just lying there—"

"I know. I'm sorry you had to endure that. It hurt so much knowing you were suffering and I couldn't comfort you."

"It doesn't matter now. You won't leave me again?"

"Never."

She heard the music again, and this time it made sense: the old lullaby Ben had sung, now filling her with joy instead of sadness. "Is this why I came to Longbourne? To make one last goodbye?"

"I don't know. There's a lot about this place no one understands. Like why earth is as invisible to us as heaven is to them. Or what we leave heaven for, when it's time. We only know there's no more pain, no more sorrow, just ourselves and our loved ones until we, too, pass on. Together this time."

She stepped away, just a little, and clasped Anthony's hand, and saw instead of the wrinkled, blue-veined, age-spotted claw she was used to, firm, smooth skin. He, too, looked young, as young as he'd been when they first met, and it pained her a little that he wasn't the forty-five-year-old man whose memory she'd carried all these years, but she'd have been just as happy if they'd both been eighty. "When does that happen?"

He shrugged. "When it's time. Whenever that is. When we decide." He tugged on her hand a little. "Come with me. There are so many people who want to see you."

"Just a minute." She turned to face where Longbourne would be, on earth, and took in a deep breath of green-scented air. "You won't hear this," she said quietly, "but it has to be said. You won't be lonely forever, Zara. And we'll wait for you. However long it takes."

Her words floated away into the distance, and the lullaby came back to her, so quiet it was impossible to tell who was singing it, or to whom. *Promise*, said the wind, and Alison held Anthony's hand more tightly and let it follow her all the way to the mountains and beyond.

RANSOM

(*Voyager of the Crown*, late fall 963 Y.B.)

I wrote this story as an indulgence. I liked Ransom from the beginning, his irascible nature and his secret soft side, his well-disguised chivalry and how he was attracted to Zara from the start. And that's really all there is to it. I can't remember at what point in the process I wrote this—it might even have been after the book was finished—but it was long after I knew who Ransom was, what he was like, so I think there wasn't anything more to it than wanting to see this meeting from the other side.

RANSOM POKED THE FIRE, SHIFTING THE BURNING LOGS UNTIL THE flames rose higher. It was too damned hot, even after sunset, to need it for heat, but roasted tubers and a hot drink refreshed him after walking through the jungle all day. He scooted his camp stool back from the blaze and stretched. Another day, maybe a day and a half, and he'd be at the village and sleeping in a real bed. A stuffed mattress high above the jungle floor, anyway. Not anything his mother would call a real bed.

Across the clearing, Nettles took a few hobbled steps and bit off a mouthful of leaves, masticating them into a drooling mess of green that stained his lips. The donkey was too smart to eat anything poisonous, or for that matter anything with medicinal value, but he was a messy eater and Ransom was just as happy not to watch him do it.

High above, a family of tamarins chittered at each other. Ransom looked up, but the firelight turned everything more than twenty feet away black and impenetrable. He couldn't even see the stars, thanks to the dense canopy. It was eerie, the way the jungle took in the light and gave nothing back, as though he was in a bubble of air at the bottom of the ocean where no light came.

He prodded the fire a bit more, then threw the stick atop the fire and rubbed dirt from his palms. He'd stowed all the plants he'd gathered that day, made sure Nettles had plenty of food, eaten his own dinner, and now he was tired but not sleepy.

Idly, he began composing a letter to his sister in his head—the sister he remembered, that is, not the woman obsessed with the Resurgence who resented him for not following her lead as he'd done all his life. *Sharon, tonight the tamarins slept in the trees above me. They're small monkeys, not much bigger than a large cat, and they're very intelligent. I wish I could show them to you. Some of them have never seen people before and come right up to be petted.*

He sighed and rubbed his eyes. Maybe he'd stay at the village for a week this time. It wasn't as if he needed human companionship; it was just that he was tired of not having anyone to talk to but Nettles, who wasn't a good conversationalist. And a week was about as long as he could bear the flirting of the young women, none of whom cared that he wasn't Karitian. So much better than the cities, with their laws restricting foreigners' movements and interactions with the natives. If he could go another year without having to enter a city, he'd be happy.

Something rustled across the clearing, and he heard a sound like a low-pitched gasp. Nettles grunted and took a few steps forward, behind a tree. "Who's there?" Ransom said in Karitian. No one replied, but Nettles took another step and a bush rustled again.

Ransom stood and walked toward the donkey. "Look," he said, "if you're hungry, I've got some food left, but it's ridiculous for you to go on pretending you're not there."

He was a few feet from the tree when the rustling started again, and a woman stepped out into the light. "I'm sorry to intrude," she said. "I wasn't trying to sneak up on you."

Ransom stopped with his hand outstretched to pet the donkey's neck. "Sweet heaven," he said. "I thought you were Karitian."

"You're Tremontanan," the woman said, apparently as startled as he was.

"I was," Ransom said. "No wonder you didn't respond when I told you to come out into the open. Where did you come from?"

The woman tilted her head to look at him. She was in her mid-thirties, with thick, messy black hair and eyes that were an extraordinary blue even in the yellow firelight. "That's a very long story. I'll be happy to tell you, but I'd feel more comfortable if I could see your face."

She sounded so confident, so unafraid, that Ransom's lips quirked in a smile. He backed toward the fire and sat on the stool, leaning forward slightly. She was beautiful in a sharp-boned way, and he couldn't help noticing the curves of her figure that the filthiness of her clothes couldn't obscure. She, in turn, examined him closely, and he thought *I wonder if she likes what she sees* and felt slightly embarrassed. He'd been alone for far too long. "Satisfied?" he said, resorting to sarcasm in his discomfort.

"I hardly think my satisfaction is what matters," she said, somewhat tartly. "My friends and I—"

"Friends?" He made a show of looking around the tiny clearing. "Do you keep them in your pockets?"

"We didn't know whose fire this was," she said, irritated. "Better to be safe than dead."

"You don't know I'm not dangerous. Or did you assume because we were born in the same place, we'd automatically be friends?"

"I assumed I'd have a better chance convincing someone who

speaks my language to help me than a Karitian who probably *would* kill me on sight."

"That's a typical Tremontanan attitude, that all Karitians are bloodthirsty bigots."

The woman took a deep breath, visibly controlling her temper. "I admit I don't know anything about Karitians except merchants' tales," she said, "so I'm sorry if I sound prejudiced. Are you going to let that stand in the way of helping us?"

"There's that 'us' again. Who are you?" He leaned forward with one elbow on his knee and propped his chin on his hand. He probably ought to offer her the stool—though were good upper-class Tremontanan manners worth anything here in the jungle?—but he was enjoying watching her, the way she stood as if preparing to conquer the world, or at least this part of it. He hadn't seen another Tremontanan in four years, but he was sure he'd never seen anyone like her before.

"My name is Rowena Farrell," she said, "and my friends and I were traveling by ship to Goudge's Folly when we were attacked by pirates and shipwrecked. We think we're the only survivors. We were going to Manachen to look for help, but we...accidentally went the wrong way and ended up on the banks of the Kulnius." A flash of irritation crossed her face again. "We're traveling upriver to where the Amgeli and Kulnius diverge, then we're going to follow the Amgeli north to Manachen. We were hoping you might be able to help us."

Ransom shook his head. "None of you have any more sense than babies. Do you have any idea how long it takes to get from here to the junction of the Amgeli and the Kulnius? Let alone down the river to Manachen?"

"Of course not," Miss Farrell said. *Miss, or Mistress?* "It's not as if we had much choice. Were you listening at all, or did you just miss the part where we were shipwrecked?"

"Even so, you ought to know traveling along the coast is safer."

"Well, we do now, and thank you so much for that 'help.'" She turned and stalked away across the clearing.

Even the way she walked appealed to him. "Wait," he said, and

Miss Farrell paused, though she didn't turn around. "The name's Ransom," he added. "You all might as well stay the night here. The jungle can be dangerous if you don't have a fire. Sometimes even if you do."

"Thank you," Miss Farrell said stiffly, but her stride relaxed. Ransom watched her go. That had been unexpected. Were her companions as unusual as she? Was that even possible? Ransom looked around the clearing. Well, they'd have to sleep on the ground, though he could offer Miss Farrell his tent, not that she was likely to take it.

Loud rustling in the undergrowth signaled Miss Farrell's return with her friends. There were five of them altogether, in varying states of exhaustion. A plump woman in her early forties looked the worst off; she showed signs of dehydration and her eyes were dilated as if she were in shock. A dark-skinned youth walked beside her, holding her elbow in support. Two tall Eskandelics brought up the rear, the man supporting the woman, who leaned heavily on him. Her forearm was bound up with two rough planks and she held it across her chest, protecting it.

"You didn't say anyone had been hurt," he said, rising.

"I didn't think you'd care," Miss Farrell said, disdainfully, and it made him smile. Lost in the jungle, filthy and exhausted and probably hungry, and she still had enough energy to snub him. He gave her an amused look and approached the Eskandelic woman. Her companion—looked like he might be her husband, or possibly her brother—immediately put himself between her and Ransom.

"You do not touch her," he said.

"I won't hurt her," Ransom said, "I'm a doctor. Or did you want her to go on suffering?"

The man glowered, but stepped back. Ransom freed the woman's arm from the makeshift splint and felt along it. He was gentle, but she hissed in pain anyway, and the man moved forward again. "It's broken," he said.

"We knew that," Miss Farrell said.

Ransom ignored her. "Sit down," he told the woman, and guided her to the stool. "You'll want to hold her for this," he told the man, who knelt behind her and took her in his arms. Husband, then. Ransom knelt in front of her and took hold of her broken arm with both hands, spaced evenly on either side of the break.

It was impossible to explain to a non-healer what he did, so in general, he lied about it. No, he didn't so much lie as weave a story that would make sense to the person being healed. He might say that he was teaching skin and bone to become one, or that he was destroying the germs that caused infection, but the truth was he spoke to the body, and the body responded. It was nothing so simple as sight or sound or touch that let him perceive the body at its deepest levels; he just knew where the damage lay and could encourage the body to repair itself, faster and more surely than if left to heal on its own. The young woman's bone was cracked; he held it in place, then let his magic wash over them both.

The young woman shrieked in pain, then sagged, unconscious. Her husband shouted and let go of her with one hand, reaching for Ransom's throat with the other. "Don't be a fool," Ransom said, not raising his head from where it was bowed over his work. "I'm healing her arm. It accelerates the natural healing process, and it hurts like hell, but it shouldn't take long. You're Eskandelic, you should be more sensible about this."

"You should to warn," the man said.

"Sorry, I thought I did," Ransom said. Hadn't he? *You were too preoccupied with looking good in front of Rowena Farrell.* Another rush of embarrassment startled him. She was a good six or seven years older than he, they were in the middle of the jungle, she no doubt disliked him, and all he could think about was impressing her.

When he felt the bone was sound, he released the woman's arm and pressed the tip of his forefinger to the center of her forehead. *Wake,* he thought, and her eyes fluttered open. She flexed her arm in wonder. "Thank you," she said.

"You're welcome," said Ransom. "Now, will you make introductions, Miss Farrell?"

"We won't be here long enough for that to matter," she said.

"Nevertheless, it's polite, don't you think? You can call me Ransom," he added, addressing the group at large.

Miss Farrell scowled. "Belinda Stouffer," she said, indicating the plump woman. "Theodore Jenkins. Zakhari Cantara and her husband Arjan."

"Welcome to my camp," Ransom said with a bow. "Now, why don't you all find spots around the fire. Nettles will give warning if anything large comes calling, but there's no point not using every advantage." He ducked into his tent before Miss Farrell could respond with something scathing. Just as well she was moving on tomorrow; she might be attractive, but they were too alike to be comfortable companions for long. And he didn't have time to take them all back downriver to the coast.

He rearranged some things to make the little tent more roomy, then went to where Miss Farrell and Miss Stouffer lay. Miss Farrell had used some fallen branches, whip-thin and loaded with soft leaves, to make bedding for both of them, but Miss Stouffer still looked uncomfortable. She must be at the end of her reserves. "Miss Stouffer," he said, squatting next to her, "I think you should take my tent. You're suffering from dehydration and what looks like the delayed effects of shock. You need more rest than a bed on the ground can provide."

"But—"

"Go on, Belinda," Miss Farrell said. "No one's going to begrudge you."

Miss Stouffer sat up. "Well...all right. Thank you, Dr. Ransom."

"It's just Ransom," Ransom said, and helped her rise. He escorted her to the tent and took a minute to assess her physical condition, then gave her a salt tablet and a drink from one of his waterskins. Rest would take care of everything else.

He stood outside the tent, scanning the clearing. The Zakharis were cuddled up together near the tent, and it looked like Mistress Zakhari was asleep already. Young Mister Jenkins lay a few feet away on a bed of leaves similar to Miss Farrell's. They might be completely unsuited to surviving in the wild, but they weren't stupid. A twinge of guilt struck him. *You don't have time, and following the river will be easy for them. Stop feeling guilty over something that's not your fault. It's not as if you made them be shipwrecked.*

Miss Farrell lay on her back on the far side of the clearing from Nettles. He'd have imagined her afraid of the donkey if he weren't totally certain she wasn't afraid of anything. On a whim, he crossed the clearing and settled down to lie beside her. "She'll be all right in the morning," he said. "Just needed some salt. Lack of that can kill a person here in the jungle."

"Thank you," Miss Farrell said stiffly. She refused to look at him, but under her irritation he could hear embarrassment. Well, it wasn't as if she should be expected to know how to survive in the jungle.

He chuckled. "I've got some in my supplies you can have," he said. "I'm not completely heartless."

Miss Farrell snorted. "Heartless enough to abandon us."

"It's hardly abandonment if we weren't traveling together in the first place."

"Whatever you want to call it. You pointed out we're not prepared to survive in the jungle, but you're not willing to help us even though you are?"

She knew how to strike with words, and the twinge of guilt pinched him harder. "I'm not going to drop my responsibilities just to play nursemaid to a bunch of strays."

"Yes, you certainly look like a responsible man, you and your donkey in the middle of nowhere."

"You're awfully quick to judge, aren't you?"

"As quick as you are to criticize."

Ransom rolled onto his side to face her. "It's hardly criticism to point out the blindingly obvious."

"Well, it's not as if we chose this, so you're not criticizing so much as taunting us. If you were—"

"If I were what?"

"Nothing. There's no point us arguing. Thank you for giving us protection tonight."

Ransom went silent. It wasn't the kind of gratitude he felt

comfortable accepting, as grudgingly as he'd given them the protection of the camp. After a few moments, he said, "If you keep an eye on the monkeys, you can avoid the caimans. They won't drink where the monsters are."

"Thank you. I'd noticed that." It didn't sound the least bit sarcastic.

"What have you been eating?" *Stop being drawn into this!*

"Papayas."

"I'll show you a few other trees with edible fruit in the morning."

"Thank you."

They both fell silent again. Eventually, Ransom said, "You'll want to avoid the low-hanging vines. Some of them are snakes."

"How can you tell?"

"It's hard. Sometimes you just have to watch for the movement. Just avoid them altogether."

Miss Farrell rolled onto her side to face him. "Too bad we don't have someone to show us the difference."

"If you'd—" Ransom rolled onto his back and flung one arm over his eyes. Then he swore, eloquently, in Karitian. One beautiful, sharp-tongued, powerful woman showed up at his camp and his good judgment flew south for the winter. "I'm doing this against my will," he said finally. "You're all nothing but a burden. I have work to do and I don't have time to be your nanny. You had all better do everything I say, without question, or I really will leave you behind."

"Don't do us any favors."

"Oh, I'm not. I'm just softheaded enough not to want your deaths on my conscience. Go to sleep, Miss Farrell, and no more insults or I might change my mind."

Miss Farrell made a noise of disdain and turned her back on him. Ransom lay looking up at the blackness for a while before sleep claimed him.

THIS NIGHT OF ALL NIGHTS

(Voyager of the Crown, Wintersmeet 963 Y.B.)

This short story had to be cut from Voyager of the Crown *because it overburdened the ending. Since that book already has two endings, one more was just awkward. I'm sad it had to work out that way, because in* Voyager *I jumped from Zara and Ransom leaving Dineh-Karit together to Zara and Ransom contemplating marriage, and readers didn't get to see the middle bit—until now.*

THE ROUGH CANVAS COVER OF THE LONGBOAT, DAMP WITH SEA SPRAY, had lost its earlier warmth. Zara ran her fingers idly along the ridge where it stretched over the boat's edge and shifted her weight to a more comfortable spot. It was almost midnight, and she should probably be in her berth, but on this night of all nights she couldn't bear to be indoors. There was no moon, and the ship's lights weren't bright enough to draw the eye from the million glittering stars that wheeled above. The night was as cool as most nights were at this latitude, which wasn't very, and she felt relaxed and comfortable despite having soaked up all the residual sunlight from the longboat's cover.

She closed her eyes, breathed in the wonderful salt air, and waited for midnight.

The boat rocked, and she threw out both hands for balance. "Sorry," Ransom said. "I didn't think it was quite so mobile."

"You startled me." Zara scooted over so he could lie beside her. "Didn't you go to bed two hours ago?"

"I did. Couldn't sleep. And I realized I didn't want to spend Wintersmeet Eve alone." Ransom settled himself and put one arm behind his head for a pillow. "I guessed you might be here, when you weren't in your berth."

"I was restless too. And..."

"And what?"

"It just feels wrong to experience the solstice in the belly of a cargo ship."

"I hadn't thought about it. But you're right. And this is a beautiful sight."

He fell silent then, and Zara tried to go back to contemplating the stars, but she couldn't stop thinking about how close he was, how easy it would be to move toward him, let him take her in his arms and kiss her so neither of them knew when the solstice happened. They'd been on this ship for nearly two weeks, and they'd spent nearly every minute of that time together.

And she'd never been bored.

She'd never been sick of his presence, never found excuses to get away from him. It wasn't just the kissing—there hadn't been much of that, really, what with limited privacy and her feeling that they shouldn't be alone together in her berth. It was the joy of talking to him, of telling him things she'd never told another soul and letting him do the same for her. It was finding out all the things they had in common and arguing over the things they didn't. And now she couldn't imagine being without him. It had happened so quickly—and yet she'd always known her own mind, prided herself on being decisive, and this was just another example of that.

"Is Wintersmeet a happy time for you?" she asked.

"Because my family is selfish and single-minded, you mean? It's not so bad. Better, actually, when I'm not in Aurilien. My family has a Wintersmeet Ball every year, and every year since I became an adult my mother has played matchmaker with me and every eligible young woman in Tremontane, most of whom are only interested in my fortune."

"I didn't know you were personally wealthy. I thought that was the De Witt fortune."

"I have money settled on me by my parents. Or did. I have no idea what happened to it when I left. I might be penniless. You don't mind that, do you?"

"You have good earning potential. I think that's more important."

He laughed and took her hand. "So practical."

"Well, you'll need to make a living in Veribold."

"I'm worried about not speaking the language. How successful can I actually be there, given how insular Veriboldans tend to be?"

"Veriboldans need healers and doctors as much as anyone. And I'd be happy to translate for you. I could be your assistant."

"If you're sure you don't have anything better to do."

"I don't really have a plan, other than exploring Haizea. I haven't been there in...forty years. Right after Hank died."

"Long time," Ransom said. His voice sounded strange, distant, and she wasn't sure whether he was reacting to her allusion to her dead husband or her abnormally long life. She drew breath to ask him about it, then felt the unmistakable tingle as the lines of power shifted their alignment—and there they all were, Jeffrey and his wife and children and grandchildren, feeling as close as if they were standing next to her and as distant as if they burned among the stars overhead.

She let out that breath in a long, warm stream, imagining she could see it trailing away from her, coiling through the breezes that brushed her cheeks. Then the feeling was gone, and she wiped away a few tears with her free hand. It would have been nice to sense Telaine's family, but Telaine had adopted out of the North family years before, and Zara would have to return to Longbourne to see her again, which she wasn't going to do. She wiped away a few more tears and scowled. She never cried and she wasn't about to do so now.

"It must be hard, not being able to go home," Ransom said quietly.

"I might say the same to you."

"I can go home. I just don't want to. It's different."

"I'm used to it."

"Still…"

"What?"

"Nothing. It's none of my business." He fell silent again, the touch of his hand their only connection.

For the first time since they'd left Goudge's Folly, Zara felt uncomfortable around him. She'd wanted…what? To tell him her feelings for him had gone from mere attraction to something more profound? He'd sounded so distant. This was the wrong time. Maybe there wouldn't be a right time. His displays of affection were always casual, teasing, the kind someone who wasn't serious about her might give, and how awkward for her to admit to love when they were both on this ship, unable to avoid each other. She wished she knew what he was thinking.

"You aren't regretting this, are you?" she blurted out, then closed her eyes against how stupid that had sounded.

"Why would I regret this?" He squeezed her hand gently.

"I…don't know. Forget I said anything."

"Rowena, this has been the most exhilarating two weeks of my life. I have no regrets. Besides, this is much nicer than the jungle, which is full of insects and things that want to eat your arm whole."

"I'm glad. I…"

"You're behaving strangely. Are you sure there's nothing wrong?"

"Nothing. I'm just feeling my age tonight, I suppose."

"Hmm." Ransom shifted toward her. "Come over here." He slid one arm under her shoulders and put the other across her stomach to encircle her in his arms. "I guarantee I'm not feeling your age at all."

Despite her melancholy, she had to laugh. If only they could go on like this forever, though not with the sailors moving around nearby. "Thank you," she said. "I...I'm glad you came along. I'd be so bored otherwise."

"Is that what I am? Your cure for boredom?" The sardonic tone was back in his voice. He hadn't sounded like that for weeks. She felt him begin to withdraw his arm, and clutched at it, suddenly afraid of what might happen if he let go.

"No," she said. "That's not what you are. You're caring, and funny, and clever, and you always know exactly what to say to me. If you hadn't come with me I'd be miserable right now because I'd have left my heart back in Dineh-Karit with you."

Ransom went still. She could feel his breath across her forehead, warm and smelling of mint. She didn't know where he'd found it, but it smelled nice, and she closed her eyes and wished she hadn't just said that. It was too soon, she was going to ruin everything—

He shifted again, drawing her closer. "I know," he said. "I love you, too."

She realized how tightly she was gripping his arm and released him. "But it's only been—"

"Three weeks, I know. But I've never been happier than I have that whole time. Now I can't imagine not spending every day with you."

"It wasn't the whole time. You and I fought quite a bit the first few days."

"You tell it your way, I'll tell it mine. I was attracted to you from the moment I saw you, tangled hair and all. I just didn't know I was going to fall in love with you."

"I thought you were stubborn and arrogant. And handsome."

"And then you came to appreciate those qualities."

"Once you started taking me seriously. And you weren't as stubborn and arrogant as you wanted me to think."

Ransom chuckled. "Now I know you must love me, if you're willing to admit that." He kissed her temple. "And I hope you know how much I love you."

She rolled over to face him. "Show me," she said, and he kissed her, his lips soft on hers. She put her arms around him as they kissed, slowly, enjoying the feel of his smooth skin against her face and the smell of him, mint and cedar. He slid his hand up to stroke her hair and she kissed him harder, savoring the light touch of his hand contrasting with the intensity of his kisses. Kissing her love under the stars on the first day of the year—she remembered Hank briefly, how they'd begun their life together on a Wintersmeet Day fifty-five years before, and hoped he was happy, wherever he was in heaven now. As happy as she was.

A long, appreciative whistle broke out somewhere above their heads, and Zara saw a sailor high above, gripping the rigging and waving at them. She reddened and covered her face with her hands while Ransom roared with laughter and waved back. "We should away to our beds," he said. "I'm not interested in giving the sailors a show."

"Beds," Zara said. "I think we're still not ready for anything else."

"I agree. Love or no, it has only been three weeks." Ransom helped her out of the longboat, then kept hold of her hand as they walked together to the companionway. "And these beds are too narrow to be comfortable."

"I'm satisfied just spending every day with you." Zara stopped outside her berth and put her arms around his neck. "And kissing you. And holding you. And feeling your breath on my cheek."

"Definitely all that," he said, putting his arms around her in turn. He glanced up and down the narrow hall, leaned close to her ear, and said, "I love you, Zara, for everything you are and all the things you can't tell anyone else. I love you."

She shivered all over with delight. "I love you, Ransom, and to prove it I won't use *your* other name to tell you so."

He laughed and kissed her. "Here's to the morning, then."

"Until morning."

She undressed in the quiet dark and lay on her bed, unable to stop smiling. She remembered Hank again, and this time let the memory play out, his rugged face and the smile that said he loved her, body and soul. "I hope you don't mind that I'm finding happiness again," she whispered into the darkness. "I'll always love you, but this is a different love, and it makes me happy in a different way. Someday I'll see you again, in the far future, and I hope you and Ransom will like each other."

Falling in love again was something that had never occurred to her, yet here she was, loving and beloved. *This time next year, we'll be married,* she thought as she fell asleep, and carried the thought with her into her dreams.

APPENDIX: THE TREMONTANE
ENCYCLOPEDIA

I. Geography and Other Nations

Tremontane is a kingdom defined by three large peaks, Gandner Peak, Mount Tendennon, and Mount Ehuren, in a range of mountains called the Rockwild Range, the Spine of the World, or just the Spine. The ridge runs roughly east-west with a curve southward on the eastern side. Tremontane's borders are the Rockwild Range to the north; Mount Tendennon, the Snow River, and Veribold on the west; the ocean and a ridge of foothills to the east (east of which is unclaimed territory and wastelands); and Eskandel to the south.

Tremontane has several immediate neighbors with which its relations range from cordial to hostile.

Eskandel: Tremontane's southern neighbor, Eskandel is known for its devotion to the arts and sciences, as well as for being the place where Devices were invented. It is nominally ruled by a Conclave of princes, but the real power in Eskandel is held by those princes' harems. These groups of four to six women make the real decisions and then tell their husbands how to vote in Conclave. Eskandel prides itself on its cordial relations with all its neighbors and occasionally acts as intermediary in international disputes. Tremontane and Eskandel have been friendly almost since the founding of Tremontane.

Veribold: Tremontane's western neighbor. The oldest country in the region, Veribold was once a vibrant, outward-looking culture that in the past century or so has grown decadent and obsessed with former glories.

Veriboldans put great stock in ritual and ceremony, and although they do not have the literal family bonds Tremontanans do, they consider family connections very important and most can recite their lineage seven or more generations back. Even the lowest-class Veriboldan considers himself superior to anyone of any other country, and upper-class Veriboldans may refuse to be "tainted" by speaking directly to someone not Veriboldan (though this does not stop them learning other languages). This belief notwithstanding, Veriboldans carry on strong trade relations with their neighbors and are known for the high quality of their exports (mainly luxury goods like tea and silk).

Veribold is ruled by a limited-term King or Queen chosen by an intricate set of challenges incomprehensible to most outsiders; rulers serve for seven years and may not serve subsequent terms. Veribold and Tremontane have a very formal, somewhat chilly relationship in recent years due to the presence of hostile Veriboldan outlaws along the Tremontanan border whom the Veriboldan government has been unable, or unwilling, to rein in.

Ruskald: Separated from Tremontane by the Rockwild Range, Ruskald has had an uneasy relationship with its southern neighbor for many years. Source is particularly scanty there, and skirmishes and the occasional war result from Ruskald's interest in controlling Tremontane's magical riches.

The Ruskalder tend to be very direct in their dealings with others and are not afraid of conflict, friendly or otherwise. They put a great emphasis on family (though, again, they do not have the Tremontanan family bonds) and large families are the norm. Ruskald is the only country in the region that still worships gods rather than **ungoverned heaven** (see **Religion** below for more on this). Ruskald is ruled by a King who is first among the Ruskalder chieftains, all of whom have a say in the government (to a degree).

The Kirkellan: This large "kinship" of nomads lives in the region called the Eidestal, which in Kirkellish means "land of the winds." The Eidestal is located west of Ruskald, is part steppe, part northern forest, and the Kirkellan travel throughout the year to take advantage of what the changing seasons bring. They are famed as horse breeders and consider their horses a part of their spiritual family; the horses themselves are large but agile, trained for speed and jumping.

The Kirkellan have no surnames, as they consider themselves all part of a single family, but can immediately tell outsiders what their blood relation to another Kirkellan is. They frequently clash with the Ruskalder over territory, as Ruskald would like to annex the Eidestal to gain better hunting grounds, and most Kirkellan spend at least part of their lives as members of a *tiermatha*, or warband/kinship group. They are matrilineal, with their ruler being called the *matrian*, though in centuries past both men and women were allowed to lead the Kirkellan. Until recently, Tremontane has had little contact with them.

II. Magic Through the Centuries

The world in which Tremontane exists is crisscrossed by ley lines, what they call lines of power, that are the connection between the physical world and the spiritual (either the realm of the gods or ungoverned heaven, depending on one's religious beliefs). The places where they cross form a "bump" of magical energy called source that can be sensed and tapped into by people with the right inborn talent. These lines are not distributed evenly throughout the world, and Tremontane has more of them than the neighboring countries, with a correspondingly high number of sources and accessible magical energy. This high level of background magic allows for the Tremontanan family and marriage bonds (see below), which are a literal and sometimes tangible connection between individuals.

Tremontanans have been aware of the existence of the lines of power since Kraathen of Ehuren founded the country in what was later called Year 1 of the Binding, using the lines of power to create those family and marriage bonds. However, it was not until many centuries later that people discovered the sources created by the lines of power and learned to tap into them using one of two kinds of innate abilities.

The first kind, known originally as **dowsing**, allows someone to perceive source and draw on it, though dowsers lack the ability to do anything with the magic thus tapped into. The second kind, referred to as **inherent magic,** lets its possessors passively absorb magical energy from source and use it to alter the environment, manipulate objects, and so forth, effectively becoming their own sources.

Inherent magic always manifests during adolescence as a single talent—examples include seeing through solid matter, telekinesis, or the ability to heal others—but with training it may be used in other, more powerful ways. Inherent magic is stronger the closer it is to a source, but as it does not include the ability to directly sense and manipulate source, dowsers ended up trading their talent to those with inherent magic, mapping out regions where they would be most powerful. Only in rare cases is a person born with both types of magic.

The inherently magical exist everywhere in the region, in numbers proportional to the amount of source present in the area. Tremontane, with its rich background magic and many lines of power, produced a correspondingly great number of people who could use that magic. Over the years, as those with inherent magic grew in power and influence, a new social class arose. Calling themselves **Ascendants**, they shaped Tremontanan society to their desires.

Initially these men and women believed their role to be to better their country, but as time passed, and more of them gained positions of power, most Ascendants could not resist using their magical abilities to benefit themselves. They grew to perceive themselves as superior to non-magical people and behaved accordingly, occasionally using their magic to manipulate and control others. Children who manifested talents were taken, usually with their parents' good will, to schools where they were taught to use magic as well as indoctrinated in the tenets of the Ascendants.

Ordinary citizens were caught between hoping their children might ascend to this better life, because the families of such children gained a measure of the child's new social standing, and resenting their underclass status and the high-handedness of Ascendants. Even so, because most Ascendants continued to use their abilities to defend and support Tremontane, the balance of power remained secure and the average citizen was disinclined to revolt.

This situation changed during the Valant dynasty, when the structure of Tremontane's government was altered to give Ascendants more political power. Under the Valants, no Ascendant was allowed to become King or Queen; instead, the monarch was supported by a Ascendant relative with the title **Eminence** who acted almost as a co-ruler, the King handling the mundane aspects of government and the Eminence responsible for managing all things magical in the kingdom. The Eminences learned to expand their field of responsibility over the years, as well as frequently manipulating weak Kings or Queens, and eventually Ascendants held most of the public offices and exercised great influence on policy and law.

By the reign of Edmund Valant, beginning in Year 691 of the Binding, civil unrest and resentment of Ascendants were growing, and fear and distrust of them had spread enough to spark violence against those suspected of developing inherent magic. This caused a backlash by the Ascendants, increasing the tension within the country.

As this situation was developing, other countries were trying to overcome the limitations of their relative scarcity of lines of power and resulting lack of magic. Most of these countries had few or no Ascendants, as the presence of magical energy was necessary for them to manifest, but as the dowser population was not dependent on the amount of source, there were many people who could experiment with manipulating source. They discovered that a dowser could imbue certain metals with source, allowing those metals to transfer their magical energy to objects that could perform the same magical talents as an Ascendant, but without the necessity of being surrounded by lines of power. A trade in manufacturing these

Devices, as they were called, sprang up in Eskandel; dowsers, now called **Devisers**, gained influence and notoriety as people realized that magic could be accessible to all.

This new trade began spilling over into Tremontane's southern regions (bordering on Eskandel) and influenced more rebellion against the Valants, who again responded by cracking down on the rebellious. Ultimately the Valants were overthrown by Willow North, who spent her reign destroying the power of the Ascendants while trying to curb the public's desire to see all such men and women dead. Inherent magic became a byword for evil and those who demonstrated such talents might be killed by mobs, despite laws passed to protect them (which were often not enforced at local levels).

Those with inherent magic hid their talents if they were able, and as the centuries passed, and the memory of the Valants and the Ascendants faded, people became less fearful of the possibilities of inherent magic. Those who had the power to heal others helped in lessening this prejudice. By Zara North's time, a little over two centuries after Willow's rule, inherent magic appears so rarely (that is, is hidden so completely; genetics is still what it is) that most people think of it as nothing more than a story to frighten children—though when it does appear, people are still quick to panic and attack.

III. Family and marriage bonds

Kraathen of Ehuren, founder of Tremontane, discovered a way to connect every person in the kingdom to the lines of power, allowing them to create tangible bonds between themselves. This was eventually codified in the family bond, which links parents to children, children to siblings, and so forth, and in the marriage bond, which more closely connects two individuals and can provide for the creation of a new family bond.

Most marriages in Tremontane are performed first with the **adoption** of one party into the family of the other, then joining the two with the marriage bond. Same-sex marriages are given equal standing with traditional marriages.

The family bond provides for strong connections between people, to the point that lengthy sexual relationships with someone with whom you do not share a family or marriage bond become physically and mentally painful. It is not uncommon for Tremontanans to wait to consummate a relationship until their wedding night, especially among the titled families.

Despite (or possibly because of) the unusual structure of Tremontanan families, incest is not only practically unheard of, but abominated, even though technically two siblings could have a long-term consensual relationship with no adverse physical effects.

IV. Adoption and Inheritance

A family bond is essential for a Tremontanan's well-being, as well as being the instrument through which inheritance passes. Failing to provide a child with a family bond, as in cases of extramarital affairs, is a crime, as are falsely accusing someone of failing to provide a bond and knowingly claiming false parentage of a child for the purpose of receiving an **entailed adoption**.

There are four types of adoption in Tremontane:

Direct adoption: The most common form. A person is bound to his or her partner's family and is then considered a son or daughter of that line. The adoptee gives up his or her birth family name and all inheritance rights depending on that name, i.e. a woman of the Smith family who adopts into the Jones family would not be automatically entitled to a share in her parents' fortune, but might have money settled on her in her new name. An adoptee may inherit anything but a title through his or her spouse; a man who marries a Countess is not a Count, but her consort. Men are equally likely to take their wife's name as the other way around, and the decision as to who will adopt into whose family upon marrying is based on considerations such as whether one partner is an only child, or what kind of inheritances are involved. Children born to such a union inherit the family bond at birth.

Indirect adoption: two people marry, but retain their status in their birth family as well as their own family name. The marriage bond is the only one that joins them. This is usually done when both spouses are the sole inheritors of their birth families (meaning that one adopting into the other would be the end of a family line) and

431

noble titles are involved. Their children inherit from both parents and take a doubled last name created from both their parents' birth names, arranged in order of highest social standing.

EXAMPLE: Elizabeth, daughter of Amanda Smith and Christopher Jones who are joined by indirect adoption, would be Elizabeth Smith Jones. If she married, and her husband adopted into her family, his surname would become Smith Jones as well. With an indirect adoption that would result in a child having more than two last names, the lowest social status name is dropped.

Children born to this kind of union must undergo a ceremony joining them to one of their parents' families to receive a family bond, usually that of the higher social status parent.

Combined adoption: two people marry and both add each other's name to theirs, forming a new family bond unconnected to their birth families (i.e. Amanda Smith Jones and Christopher Smith Jones). They combine their personal property, but no longer inherit through their birth families. Children born to this union inherit the new family bond at birth. Very rare.

Entailed adoption: Used when two people who either cannot marry or have no intent to marry have a child. This allows the child to benefit from having a bond to both parents even when one of those parents is unsuitable or unwilling to raise a child. The child is legally bound to the family of one parent, but is entitled to support from the estate of the other parent. An entailed adoption requires a special ceremony to create the family bond, usually performed by the patriarch or matriarch of the family the child is adopting into. Due to Tremontanan celibacy customs and the availability of reliable contraception, this is also fairly rare.

A similar ceremony to that of the entailed adoption is performed when a couple wishes to adopt an unbonded orphan, or transfer a child's family bond from one couple to another (for example, if a child's parents are killed and his mother's sister wants to raise him).

V. Religion

Ungoverned Heaven: The religion of the region to which Tremontane belonged, for centuries before the time of Kraathen of

Ehuren, reflected a belief in the strength of threes, specifically body, mind, and spirit. After Kraathen unified the three tribes of ancient Tremontane, the Tremontanese came to believe in a unified god embodying all three of these characteristics, a god whose name was known only to the high priesthood. But a century after Kraathen's rule, a minor priestess named Haran, while meditating before a daily ritual, received a vision of the empty, treeless Eidestal. For ten days after this, every meditation produced the same image. Finally, counseled by the high priestess of her community, Haran traveled to the Eidestal to learn what her vision meant.

Throughout her journey, she fasted and meditated and was drawn toward a particular spot in the Eidestal, a hill on which grew a single pine tree. She made camp there and continued to fast and pray, and then her vision changed: she saw the same spot where she now camped, but populated by the spirits of the dead. She recognized some of her own deceased family and other people who were identified to her by her family. They spoke to her of heaven, of being reunited with loved ones, but said nothing of being judged either by one of the old gods or the new god she served.

Over the course of ten more days of meditation, fasting and prayer, she continued to speak with the dead, and eventually realized that there were no gods in heaven. Instead, heaven was a holy place shaped by invisible lines of power which bound it to earth and allowed it to judge the souls of the dead by weighing them against their sins, counterbalanced by their virtues.

Haran returned from the Eidestal and began preaching what she had learned. She sought out men and women whose dead relatives had given her messages for them; these people, convinced of Haran's word, became her first disciples. Haran, who had previously been a rather quiet, timid priestess, was transformed by her experience into a daring, eloquent speaker. Her first convert was the high priestess who had encouraged her on her quest. As her message spread, more people of Tremontane, and then further abroad, came to believe what she preached.

Then the wars began. Those who believe in god, or gods, attacked

Haran's followers, demanding that they recant. However, most of them were so convinced in the power of ungoverned heaven to welcome them home that they refused to fight. This, in turn, caused some of those who attacked them to be moved by their devotion and convert as well. Others of Haran's followers took up arms in defense of their brothers and sisters and fought so ferociously that they became known as the Lions of Heaven.

For a century, these wars raged, until over time the unified Tremontanan tribes came together in a shared religious belief that boosted its spread throughout the region. Eventually, the wars ceased, and the religion of ungoverned heaven was adopted everywhere except Ruskald, where the lines of power are scant and therefore give them no evidence that Haran's assertions are true.

Heaven accepts almost every soul. However, those who believe in ungoverned heaven also believe that evil people are drawn into hell, of which little is known in heaven's theology. Most Tremontanese are pragmatic about this, saying that heaven judges as it will and there's nothing they can do except live as good a life as they can. According to some philosophers (ungoverned heaven requires no clergy, and there are no theologians in Tremontane), there are a few souls rejected by both realms, and they are fated to roam the world until the end of days. Most people consider this wild speculation and it doesn't affect their lives, though a few people like to make guesses about who will end up where.

The Lost Gods/Ruskalder Gods

Because the worship of the Three is maintained only in Ruskald, the three gods, who were known by different names among the different countries, are now referred to solely by their Ruskalder names.

Siger—Manifesting as male (Sigerd) or female (Sigerda) depending on the situation, Siger represents the power of mind to control the body and the spirit. As a result, Siger "rules" the Three, though it would be more accurate to say that he/she brings balance when one of the other two dominates. He/she is the patron of rationality, reason, and memory and is invoked by those practicing the creative arts.

Siger is worshiped solely by the priesthood, though this "worship" is very different from the rituals and sacrifices ordinary Ruskalder make to the other two gods and is kept secret from those not of the clergy. Older stories recorded in the Eskandelic traditions say that Siger is the youngest god and rose out of the conflict between the other two. The Ruskalder don't believe this. Siger's symbol is an S-curve bisected by a diagonal line, like an elongated yin-yang symbol.

Balderan: God of strength, physicality, and often masculinity. He is an unsophisticated god, dealing with humans at the most basic level of primal urges. Although he is usually worshiped by men, he welcomes the worship of women, particularly those who celebrate their physical strength and endurance. Ruskalder towns have annual celebrations of Balderan in which feats of physical prowess are performed. The Ruskalder Samnal grew out of this tradition, though it's no longer a religious ceremony. His symbol is a U balanced on a horizontal line—horns, representing maleness, but in reference to Balderan's own sex and not that of his worshipers.

Hevda: Goddess of spirit and will, Hevda is extremely powerful and a little frightening. She is not considered evil, but invoking her is dangerous in the sense of biting off more than you can chew; she responds to her worshipers' requests, but often in unexpected ways, and sometimes in ways the supplicant doesn't like. As a result, people who call on her are generally desperate, and despite her superficial appearance of indifference, Hevda is generous with her aid and known to help the weak and downtrodden.

Hevda accepts as sacrifices acts of self-deprivation that require willpower to maintain, such as fasting or breaking a habit. Her symbol is the Eye—two arcs with a pinpoint pupil in the center— which is often carved or painted on things people want Hevda's attention to pass over, the idea being that if she sees the symbol, she will believe she's already watching over it.

The worship of each god has gone in and out of vogue during the centuries, reflecting to a degree the Ruskald national character of the time. At present (the fifty-year span between *Servant of the Crown* and *Agent of the Crown*) there is a strong divide between male and female roles, with men worshiping Balderan and women worshiping Sigerda.

VI. Holidays

The solstices and equinoxes are particularly important to Tremontanans due to how the lines of power are affected by them. They are at their strongest at the solstices (the Tremontanan holidays of Midsummer and Wintersmeet) and at their weakest at the equinoxes (Harvest and Springtide).

<u>Wintersmeet</u>: the biggest festival of the year. Though customs vary throughout the country, it is a time of gift-giving and celebration, with lots of parties and dances. It is considered good luck to get betrothed on Wintersmeet Day.

<u>Springtide</u>: A time of new beginnings. One universally celebrated tradition is a thorough housecleaning, which usually leads to Spring Fairs in which people sell things they've made over the winter or things they no longer need. Marriages are never performed at Springtide because of how weak the lines of power are, despite the symbolism of the new beginnings.

<u>Midsummer</u>: A more religious holiday than Wintersmeet. Tremontane does not have an official clergy or church, as there is no one in ungoverned heaven to receive their devotions, but Midsummer is a time for people to consider their lives, make new goals, reconcile with others, and commit to changing bad behaviors. It is considered lucky to get married on Midsummer Day.

<u>Harvest</u>: Though this holiday always occurs on the autumn equinox, its celebration varies widely from year to year and in towns and cities across Tremontane because it is intended to reflect a community's needs and wishes. Most often it is simply a celebration of the harvest, with feasts and community gatherings. In places less dependent on the harvest, it's a symbolic, sometimes perfunctory observation. Some towns don't celebrate it at all.

ABOUT THE AUTHOR

Melissa McShane is the author of many fantasy novels, including the Crown of Tremontane series, beginning with SERVANT OF THE CROWN; The Extraordinaries series, beginning with BURNING BRIGHT; the Company of Strangers series; and THE BOOK OF SECRETS, first in the Last Oracle series.

After a childhood spent roaming the United States, she settled in Utah with her husband, four children and a niece, four very needy cats, and a library that has finally overflowed its shelves. She wrote reviews and critical essays for many years before turning to fiction, which is much more fun than anyone ought to be allowed to have.

You can visit her at her website www.melissamcshanewrites.com for more information on other books.

For information on new releases, fun extras, and more, sign up for Melissa's newsletter: http://eepurl.com/brannP

ALSO BY MELISSA MCSHANE

THE CROWN OF TREMONTANE

Servant of the Crown

Exile of the Crown

Rider of the Crown

Agent of the Crown

Voyager of the Crown

THE SAGA OF WILLOW NORTH

Pretender to the Crown

Guardian of the Crown

Champion of the Crown

THE HEIRS OF WILLOW NORTH

Ally of the Crown (forthcoming)

Stranger to the Crown (forthcoming)

THE EXTRAORDINARIES

Burning Bright

Wondering Sight

Abounding Might

THE LAST ORACLE

The Book of Secrets

The Book of Peril

The Book of Mayhem

The Book of Lies

www.ingramcontent.com/pod-product-compliance
Lightning Source LLC
Chambersburg PA
CBHW071635260626
47170CB00001B/113

* 9 7 8 1 9 4 9 6 6 3 3 8 9 *